Tuesday

In September 2004 *Richard & Judy*'s Executive Producer, Amanda Ross, approached Pan Macmillan: her production company, Cactus TV, wanted to launch a major writing competition, 'How to Get Published', on the Channel 4 show. Unpublished authors would be invited to send in the first chapter and a synopsis of their novel and would have the chance of winning a publishing contract.

Five months, 46,000 entries and a lot of reading later, the five shortlisted authors appeared live on the show and the winner was announced. But there was a surprise in store for the other four finalists.

On air Richard Madeley said, 'The standard of the finalists is staggeringly high. All are more than worthy of a publishing contract.' Pan Macmillan agreed and published all five.

The winning books are *The Olive Readers* by Christine Aziz, *Tuesday's War* by David Fiddimore, *Journeys in the Dead Season* by Spencer Jordan, *Housewife Down* by Alison Penton Harper, and *Gem Squash Tokoloshe* by Rachel Zadok.

Leeds Metropolitan University

17 0400878 5

Tuesday's War

DAVID FIDDIMORE was born in 1944 in Yorkshire and is married with two children. He worked for five years at the Royal Veterinary College before joining HM Customs and Excise, where his work included postings to the investigation and intelligence divisions. *Tuesday's War* is the first in a proposed trilogy featuring Charlie Bassett.

DAVID FIDDIMORE

Tuesday's War

PAN BOOKS

LEEDS METROPOLITAN
UNIVERSITY LIBRARY

1704008785

192.08   Don

4FF-B FE

HC - 93545

F FID

First published 2005 by Pan Books
an imprint of Pan Macmillan Ltd
Pan Macmillan, 20 New Wharf Road, London N1 9RR
Basingstoke and Oxford
Associated companies throughout the world
www.panmacmillan.com

ISBN 0 330 44121 3

Copyright © David Fiddimore 2005

The right of David Fiddimore to be identified as the
author of this work has been asserted by him in accordance
with the Copyright, Designs and Patents Act 1988.

All rights reserved. No part of this publication may be
reproduced, stored in or introduced into a retrieval system, or
transmitted, in any form, or by any means (electronic, mechanical,
photocopying, recording or otherwise) without the prior written
permission of the publisher. Any person who does any unauthorized
act in relation to this publication may be liable to criminal
prosecution and civil claims for damages.

5 7 9 8 6

A CIP catalogue record for this book is available from
the British Library.

Typeset by SetSystems Ltd, Saffron Walden, Essex
Printed and bound in Great Britain by
Mackays of Chatham plc, Chatham, Kent

This book is sold subject to the condition that it shall not,
by way of trade or otherwise, be lent, re-sold, hired out,
or otherwise circulated without the publisher's prior consent
in any form of binding or cover other than that in which
it is published and without a similar condition including this
condition being imposed on the subsequent purchaser.

for

EMILY HARPER REA

25 October 1911–14 April 1945

an American heroine

PART ONE

Tuesday's Child

Krefeld

We called Piotr Paluchowski the Pink Pole.

That's because he wasn't quite a Red, if you see what I mean. Not that there was anything wrong with being a Red. In 1944 the Red was our ally in the Roman sense: our enemy's enemy. Anyway, to get back to the Pink Pole: the night this began, he nearly killed the lot of us, and then he saved our lives. That must have been about late August 1944 – I'll check the date for you in my logbook later, if you like – and we were into the seventh trip of our tour, flying in a lovely used-up old lady of a Lancaster bomber.

We had come through the first few trips, which was when most crews got the chop, and were well into the next danger area. That was the cocky *we know the bloody lot* stage. That's when most of the rest copped it. If you could keep going, get through ten or twelve trips, your chances of surviving another twenty before they screened you out of operations for a rest increased spectacularly, although it never felt like that at the time. We were too cocky by half the night the Pole almost killed us. It was on a trip to Krefeld – you never forget Krefeld.

We had overlooked two vital factors. First was that we hadn't yet met a single Jerry night fighter, and second was that Paluchowski, like most of the Poles and Czechs, had joined up to kill Germans. Personal longevity wasn't in his business plan. Looking back, Krefeld cured us of this curious oversight: we had to watch him after that.

We had this simple drill: everyone in the aircraft not actively involved in flying the damned thing, or dropping bombs on the gut volk in Germany, was supposed to spend every spare moment trying to *spot* them: gazing into the night sky looking for Mr Kraut and his radar-directed night fighter, as well as our brother aircraft: flying into another Lanc, or worse still a Hallibag or Stirling (both were hefty, strong brutes), could kill you just as efficiently as the Kraut could, believe me. If you caught a glimpse of anything out there that was darker or lighter than the rest of the night sky, you shouted out. No time for thinking; you just hollered. If you stopped to think it was already too late. You hollered 'Corkscrew port!' or 'Corkscrew starboard!' and the Old Man threw the bus into a violent corkscrew flight pattern towards the shape you thought you had seen. In fact some crews even used *corkscrew left* or *right* as the commands. You could say that just a fraction of a second quicker. No one complained about false alarms – they were just too relieved to blame you. Having screamed out the command, a gunner, if it was a gunner that had seen whatever it was, was free to open fire. Pete the Pole was our rear gunner: he was more interested in killing Krauts than getting us out of the way, which is something we should have anticipated. You following me so far? We were coned by searchlights on the run in – the bomb run – over Krefeld, and the Old Man, Grease – our Canadian pilot – flung our thirty tons of fully laden bomber around the sky like a sports plane, to throw off those lights – and then, because we were cocky and immortal, told us we were going to circle around, gain height, and do it all over again to put the eggs we were carrying into the right basket (ten trips later we would have dumped them in the nearest bloody field and bolted for home). It was during the dive away from that second stupid run across the target that the fighter ran in behind us, and the Pole, instead of shouting out, let him in close enough to get a good shot. Looking back, I think the three things happened simultaneously: Paluchowski started firing at the Kraut, shouted 'Corkscrew port!' and the Kraut pilot let us have it at close range. Our bus physically staggered, like someone who has been unexpectedly slapped several times around the face. There was a lot of noise, both inside and outside the aircraft – bits were coming off, after all – and behind us in the sky was a light like those thousand suns you've read about, because the Kraut, flying down the Pole's bullet stream, simply blew up: two Krauts in an Me 110 most like, doing the Valhalla Quickstep wondering what the hell had happened to them when the music stopped.

Grease recovered the old lady at about 7,000 feet – which meant that we'd lost 10 in less than a minute – and it was immediately obvious that all was not quite as it should have been: she'd lost her knickers. At least, that's what it felt like. It was bloody draughty, for a start. There were big holes all over the shop, letting in the freezing cold air at 150 miles per hour. You get the picture. There were several small fires, which I helped the Toff, our mid-upper gunner, extinguish, then we had a call through on the intercom, and found that we were all still there and alive. Almost immediately the radio gave out a spitting stream of blue sparks, and lapsed into sullen static. Toff had taken a shell splinter through his right ankle. He didn't notice until after we had finished with the fires.

Something was very wrong with the way our old girl was flying – turning stubbornly to starboard all the time: Grease was having to fight her into a straight line. It was the port outer of our four engines: we could see that it had taken a slap, because the cowling was missing. Every now and again a small flame would shoot out behind it, and then *bang*, like a car's backfire. It was racing way beyond its maximum rev rating, and we couldn't kill the damned thing: Fergal – our engineer from Belfast – couldn't cut off the fuel flow to it or fully feather its propeller, which was racing faster than the other three, pushing us to starboard around the axis of the wings. You still following this? You need a quick course in bomber design? All you need to know is that, unlike its frightened crew, the old cow wanted to fly in a circle. The port aileron had also copped it and was flapping around like a Wren's drawers, both elevators had stiffened up, and there were pieces missing from one of the rudders. Both main wheels had dropped, and one of the bomb-bay doors had badly distorted, letting in even more cold night air: don't get me wrong, she *could* fly like that, but had definitely seen better days.

That wasn't the last time we left pieces of aeroplane all over Germany, but you remember your first time. It's just like your first kiss.

Conroy, the navigator, unflappable as usual, passed Grease the first direction for an unorthodox course for England, Home and True Glory. I should have had a lot to do – but there was a hole in my radio I could pass my arm through: cold air was rushing in. I tried stuffing that with Conroy's spare maps but after a few minutes they started to smoulder – so the cold proved to be the lesser of the two evils. I made myself useful binding up the Toff's foot and giving him a shot of morphine. What might surprise you is that there was no talk of putting it down in Krautland and surrendering, or using our chutes. You might call that British pluck. I'd call it something to do with rumours we'd heard about angry Kraut civilians killing bomber crews with spades and forks. They are an agricultural race at heart, your Germans.

It was Conroy who passed me a shakily written note from Grease: Fergal must have written it down, because Grease's hands were full at the time. It read: *Charlie – fix the fucking radio. NOW.*

I got frostbite that night, with my fingers inside my smashed-up RT and WT equipment, and got an honourable mention in the squadron operational daybook as a reward. I always wanted one of those.

As luck would have it I brought the internal communications back very quickly. A piece of shrapnel had laid open an insulated wire, and bridged it to the cage, creating a mark one short. As I pulled the shrapnel clear with my fingers I didn't feel the jolt from the electrical short until it reached my wrist – I was already that cold. You can't work inside radios with gloves, you see. At least we could talk to each other then: other than that it was mostly a dead loss. After an hour's work all feeling in my hands had gone and my upper arms were hurting so bad with the cold that I was crying. I was able to hear other bombers exchanging with base and station controllers, but the signals drifted in and out randomly, like spirit voices at a seance in Surbiton – I had no control of them. On a couple of occasions I was able to speak to one of the aircraft myself, but never to England. Grease thought that they were physically very close to us – once I got an acknowledgement just as we wallowed in the airstream of a Lanc overtaking us in the race for home. I remember feeling very lonely at that moment, even in the knowledge that my pals were in the aircraft all about me.

One of Fergal's jobs was keeping a record of the fuel consumption, and reminding the skipper of what we had left: arguably a futile activity when one engine's racing away consuming fuel twice as fast as you normally allow for. It was glowing red hot, with less time between the misfires, and at least one of the wing tanks had been holed and was squirting out fuel into the air.

Martin Weir, Marty, the bomb aimer, had just called back: 'Dutch coast; Channel ahead – no flak,' when Fergal said, 'Skipper?'

'Yes, Fergal?'

'You know I said that we had fuck-all fuel left, back there?'

'Yeah, so what?'

'Well now we've got *fuck* fuck all left. If we clear the Channel put her down on the first bit of flat you see.'

Conroy broke in. 'Don't worry, Skip. Keep this heading. Manston's coming up in about . . . seventeen minutes – they've got a nice long new runway there.' Conroy was lying about the elapsed time, but we all felt better for it.

Grease said, 'Thank God for that. Charlie, where the hell is that radio?'

'Most of the best bits are still in Germany, Skip.'

'Keep trying for us, Charlie. Keep trying until we're on the deck.'

'OK, Skip.'

I privately agreed with Conners: sometimes you have to lie to the bosses to keep their spirits up, you know – otherwise they're likely to give up on you and go to pieces. What I was actually doing was sitting on my hands to get the feeling back, rigid with fear, and chilled in the airstream of my exploded radio. I tried again.

More than seventeen minutes later – it seemed hours – Marty shouted, 'Runway lights,' from up front in his glass blister, and then, 'Aw Christ!'

Grease said, 'I see it. Heads down everyone,' to which he added, 'Sorry, Charlie, not you – keep trying to raise them: we'll do one quick low circuit, then barrel straight in – I might just beat the fog.'

'What fog?' I asked Marty.

'The fucking great bank of it rolling down from the north, it's—'

'Shut up,' said Grease, 'I'm thinking.'

The truth was, he was *straining*. It had taken all his strength to fight the line against our runaway engine, even though Fergus had looped a belt around the spade grip of the control column and was taking a share of the pull. I was shamed into doing my bit, spinning the dial and broadcasting to anyone — *anyone* — with the wit to be listening out for it. Grease was taking us on a great leftward sweep low around the airfield, at one point flying parallel to the great malignant wall of fog. The runway lights kept on flashing on and off. That must have been a nervous duty flying control officer in the cabin down there, scared of intruder night fighters stooging around, waiting for busted birds like us. I got a weak response from someone, but lost it immediately.

Grease said, 'Don't mind,' then, 'OK we're going in — lining her up *now.*' He had this flair for the dramatic you see.

Don't believe all the guff they tell you about spatial disorientation. When you fly a lot as a passenger you get instinctive messages from your body which tell you about the attitude of the aircraft: most of them are right. You don't always have to see an outside world to work out where you are in relation to it. I knew that Grease had levelled her out, straightened her up and was putting her down — without flaps to slow us through the air, without brakes to slow us on the ground, and an undercarriage which would collapse if it hadn't already locked down.

Again Marty shouted, 'Aw Christ!' and before I could assume that the fog had beaten us to the runway, added 'There's another Lanc in front! Less than fifty yards . . .'

The new guy must have gone straight in like us, trying to beat the fog.

I want you to understand this problem. The new guy was making a slower, routine approach, and had brakes to slow himself on the ground. We could land behind him no worries, but once on the deck we would collect him as soon as he slowed down. And we would be travelling too fast to turn aside, even if the undercart held up – a turn at a hundred miles per hour would rip it off, and we would cartwheel. Up his arse most likely.

Grease didn't have to shout 'Charlie' the way he did, I was already spinning the clock and screaming at the radio, begging the newcomer to get off our road. Toff told me later that I was screaming so loud he reckoned they could have heard me in the other kite even without the radio.

Afterwards Marty always used to say that what happened next was the most beautiful thing he ever saw. He couldn't take his eyes off the Lanc in front of us. When he tells it he says, 'That Lanc was *death* in front of me, and it hypnotized me; I didn't move to a safer place or anything, because there wasn't one. I knew that we were going to fly into it, and that stuck out there in front I was going to get it first. And I didn't care. I don't think I ever really cared again.' Just as the new Lanc touched just as its wheels kissed the runway in a very sweet three-point landing – the pilot turned the taps on again, raised his main wheels and flaps, and climbed away into the fog. One moment he was there, and the next he was gone.

Grease had his hands and feet too full of Lancaster to think about it. He produced an unusually acceptable landing, and then proceeded to weave the great wounded beast gently from side to side to get the speed off. The engines died on us just as Fergal moved the throttle controls down their box – he had been right about the rate we had been using fuel. Instead of running off the end of the runway, as we anticipated, the old bus slowed quite quickly, but started to pull perversely in the other direction, to port. As I recall, Grease swore quite imaginatively about this last trick she played on us. When we were down to walking pace, he let her pull off the runway to the left and park herself on the grass. Then the fog swallowed us.

It turned out that the port main wheel was punctured and three-quarters deflated. It had acted like one of the brakes we no longer had before the tyre ripped itself to shreds at the last knockings.

One of the things I can confirm is that when you've landed a kite that's full of holes and unfriendly pieces of German ammunition, you don't hang about in it. I can't remember getting out, sliding over the main spar, stomping down to the little square door near the tail; what I *do* remember is how quiet it was out there in the fog. We stood in a group. The Pink Pole looked unconcerned, and as usual was the first to light up. The Toff was hobbling about, trying to find out why his ankle wasn't working, and Grease stood awkwardly, his right arm clenched hard into his body – like a response to a stomach pain. I wondered if he had been hit and had kept quiet about it, so I faced off with him and tried to straighten his arm. I couldn't.

'It's locked. Can't move it,' he said.

In finding the strength to hold the Lanc against its natural inclination to fly in tight circles, he had locked and cramped the muscle in his arm. It unlocked about an hour later.

It was one of those wet, noise-distorting fogs, but we could hear a vehicle crawling around the perimeter track at the edge of the airfield, hopefully looking for us. You could see that Grease was listening hard, but it wasn't for that. It was for the Lanc who'd made way for us. You could hear its four Packard Merlin engines moaning as it circled low looking for a hole in the fog, or for the airfield's FIDO fog lights to be switched on. We all knew the score; if it was still stooging around instead of sloping off to an airfield which wasn't fogged-in yet, then it hadn't enough fuel to do so. Sooner or later it would have to have a shot at landing or excavate an unfriendly hillside.

The vehicle found us first, a small Bedford five-cwt. lorry with a tilt, and benches in the back. An old crew bus, most likely. Surprisingly the driver was a sparks – a radio operator – like me, and his passenger up front a full wing commander. The Wingco was a tall, lanky type; tired looking with a bit of a cadaverous face, and deep sunk dark eyes.

He offered cigarettes, and when he spoke it was with a languid almost drawling accent. 'Nice landing, Skipper.' He held out his hand to shake Grease's, but Grease could only offer his left. They looked odd for a moment, two men holding hands like girls. 'I saw you touch down just before this lot rolled in – no brakes left?'

'Not much of anything left, sir.'

He laughed with us. Not a bad type. It was good seeing Grease standing there swapping jokes with a wingco as if there wasn't a half mile of rank between them. It was often like that – out there on the runways and the field you all could be just fliers – the rank nonsense didn't kick in until you were standing inside RAF bricks and mortar.

'Care for a lift?' he said.

'Thanks, but we've got to wait for . . .' Grease raised his left thumb towards the sound of the circling Lancaster.

'Of course. I'll just wait in the bus then.'

'Thank you, sir.'

'Pleasure, old boy.'

He angled off towards where the lorry was parked with a stiff, deliberate gait, like a heron stalking minnows in the shallows. I heard the door click shut, and then the engine die. I was left alongside the sparks who had been driving him. He was a ranker too – a full flight lieutenant – but you could tell he had been a sergeant; he had the look.

'Your fingers don't look too clever,' he said.

'That's the trouble with Lancs; they either burn you to death or freeze you.'

We both grinned: we were alive, after all.

'Any other damage?'

'Toff – mid upper – he's got a cut foot, and it's a funny shape. I haven't told him that yet.'

'I suppose you all want to wait for the other guy to get down. From your mob, is he?' We ducked instinctively as the lost bird thundered low overhead again, looking for a way down, poor sod. The fog eddied in its wake, then stilled again.

'Haven't a clue, but . . . yeah, we'll wait, if you don't mind.'

There was one of those moments when everything seems momentarily *crisper*, as if life comes into sharp focus, and every detail is etched on to your brain like a photograph. As if you are an actor in a film.

What do the Japs call it? *Kamikaze* — divine wind? Well, it might as well have been. First I felt a tug of breeze. It seemed to blow the droplets of moisture in the air against my cheek as if I was crying again, but I wasn't. Then it came on again, but stronger. Not for long, but long enough. You often get these eddies on the edge of a fog bank, but rarely just when you need them — like this one. It must have cut a swathe through the fog a hundred yards deep, across the runway. Control used his noddle and flipped on the lights, and our late saviour saw his one chance and went straight for the gap. Gear down, flaps down, engines cut as the wheels touched. If Grease's landing had been unusually neat then this one was poetry. The pilot ran on, on his main wheels this time, American style, holding the tail wheel clear of the runway until the speed was off her; then he dropped her tail and pulled her off the concrete to port, and parked not thirty yards from the heap of junk we'd just brought back from Germany.

Up close the new Lanc had no markings — it could have been a special squadron. It was brand new, I'll tell you that. Maybe we could make some sort of a trade for it. Pete was good at deals.

However, we came to the conclusion that the Lanc which had saved our collective bacon was a new replacement kite being delivered by one of those civilian pilots. They were definitely second division jobs. That might seem a bit bloody silly — but like all first-time crews at the start of their tour of ops, we were a bit like that: God's gift to the RAF. The position of operational aircrew was one we thought the civilian bus drivers couldn't attain. And now we owed one a favour, and had the sneaking suspicion that this guy — whoever he was — was probably a better pilot than Grease. Somebody was throwing away my team's carefully constructed social status rule book. You can see that it was an interesting little problem: but not half as interesting as when we actually faced the bastard.

He didn't bother with the short ladder that drops beneath the fuselage door in the Lanc. This small pilot, with the face of a fourteen-year-old boy, just swung his feet over the ledge, dropped the four feet to the grass and strolled over. Then he pulled off the old leather flying helmet he wore (over an equally old Sidcot suit — probably from the twenties) and black curls tumbled to her shoulders. Yeah, you heard me: *her*. Some girl. Some girl who had just given us the rest of our lives back, after the RAF had nearly thrown them away.

Grease always held that the first thirty seconds you spent with a woman dictated whether you were going to make it or not. He believed that a man needed to be noticed. It made him unpredictable around females. This time it made him throw himself lengthwise on the grass and kiss her flying boots. My first glance at her face told me it didn't usually come to rest in humour lines, because she grimaced. As she pulled her helmet clear of her hair she looked serious, even a little cross, like a schoolteacher — but then Grease on the ground in front of her earned a smile, and a little gurgling laugh.

'Is he always like this?' she said.

I stepped forward and held out my hand. 'He loves flying, and he loves girls and he loves still being alive. So you've brought out the worst in him,' I said.

She couldn't move because Grease had wrapped his arm around her ankles, but she asked me, 'And you are?'

'Don't laugh at my name — I'm Charlie Bassett, the sparks,' — that smile again — 'and the man at your feet is Grease McKenzie, sergeant pilot and our skipper. He's Canadian.'

The other five came forward to introduce themselves and give thanks for deliverance. The Pink Pole, who was short (a lot of the good rear gunners were), stood on the small of Grease's back to make up for it, and raised her hand to his lips. When Grease stood up there was grass and mud on his clothes, and the stupidest damned smile on his face that I've ever seen a man wear.

She said, 'I'm Grace . . .'

Grace said her family name was Baker, although it turned out to be Ralph-Baker (she said 'Rafe'), and she held back the double clanger until she knew us better. Later in the tour, after we had met a few, we came to realize that many of these civilian delivery pilots were ex-airline pilots or racing types, who had all-round flying skills we could only wonder at.

She dealt with this very directly whilst we were crammed into the back of the truck, and driven around to the admin block. Grease said, 'That was a great touchdown,' but you could tell from his voice that, as tired and in pain as he was, he was brooding over it.

'How many hours have you got?' Grace asked him.

'On Lancasters?'

'On anything.'

He looked relieved, and waved his good arm expansively. He said, '250; a few more. What about you?'

'Thousands,' she said, and blew out a long stream of cigarette smoke. Turkish: Passing Clouds. I guess that we all looked away for a moment.

I cut into the silence, and asked her, 'Did you overshoot and go round again because you heard me on the radio, screaming for you to get out of the way?'

'No, Charlie. I heard you, but not in the way you think. There was nothing on the radio except the duty controller giving me my approach, and asking me to get a move on. My coccyx heard you.'

Marty snorted, and Conners Conroy grinned. I could see him in the gloom.

'I don't understand,' I said.

'It's the small bone at the bottom of your spine,' offered Toff. Then he said, 'Ouch!' because he was beginning to feel his ankle.

'I *know* what it is, dummy. That still doesn't help.'

Grace said, 'When something important is going to happen – when I have to do something, and do it *now*, my coccyx vibrates: tingles, if you like. It's a danger signal. As soon as my coccyx spoke I put the throttles through the gate, switched the mixture, lifted the wheels and the flaps, and went round again. It never fails.'

I wasn't sure if she was serious. 'It could have killed you this time, if you hadn't got down through the fog,' I said.

She said to me very gently, as if I was a child, 'If you had landed on top of me, I would have been killed for certain, wouldn't I?'

By the time we had crawled up to the red brick admin buildings the fog had seeped into the truck, and into our bones. A door opened letting out a faint light. The man who came through it was big, portly and wore an RAF greatcoat over flannel pyjamas and carpet slippers.

'Are you the intelligence officer, sir?' I asked him.

'No sonny, the *medical* officer. What's the use of you being debriefed by an IO who doesn't know where you've been, what you were supposed to be doing there, or whether you're shooting a line? Do that on your own station when you get back. Hop out now, chop chop. Who needs the medicine man?' He spoke with a rich, plummy Welsh accent.

Grease took charge again. 'You'd better see to Charlie's fingers: they got too cold, and Toff's got a flakky foot and I suppose you'd better have a look at my arm. The kite was pulling to starboard all the way back, and I had to pull it the other way: now my arm's locked up.'

Whilst he was saying this Toff hopped out on to the road, and fell down because his ankle had finally stopped working. The fog now felt horribly refreshing, but I suddenly wanted desperately to lie down and go to sleep: the voices around me faded in and out like radio signals caught in the Heavyside Layer. I heard the sparks who drove us saying something like, 'You keep these three Doc; we'll shoogle up the mess boys and find some breakfast.'

Shoogle, I thought — he must be a Scot: Glaswegian most likely.

My memory stops there for some hours. They must have done whatever they needed to my fingers, and bandaged them up. I was always awake early in the morning — a habit I never managed to break — and found myself cleaned up, wearing service flannel pyjamas, on a ward in the station medical unit. I felt good. Toff was in the bed opposite, snoring as loudly as the flak which had almost killed him, and they can't have had a busy week on the Kent airfield because we had the ward to ourselves. Grease, Marty and the rest of the crew were competing in the snore competition, lying sprawled fully clothed on top of other beds. Marty was cuddling an empty beer bottle. He liked cuddling things. Grease was cuddling the girl from the new Lanc — they were curled up, her back to his front, like a couple of commas: his huge arm was around her. I remember thinking, *So that's how it is*, then someone farted, someone else began to stir, and I noticed that my fingers hurt.

For a fighter station the whole place was astonishingly well organized. All of my gear was hanging in a long open locker by my bed, my uniform had been brushed down, and even my flying boots had had a once over. Nothing had been stolen: if they treated their sergeants like this I was in the wrong command. As the others came round it was obvious that they had been on a bender, and probably felt worse than the Toff and me. They were horribly hungover — but they got both of us out of our pits, washed, shaved and approximately dressed us, and found a stout walking stick for Toff.

The MO caught up with us having an illegal private breakfast at a table in a corner of the officers' mess. It was quiet as a church. Didn't anybody from here fight before noon?

'You all right, Sergeant?' he barked at me.

'Somebody's put bandages all over the ends of my hands; I'm not sure that there are fingers in there any more,' I said.

'Nor am I. Get a pal to cut up your food for you for a couple of days, and see your own MO when you get back. Now; what about *you*?' he said to Toff.

The Toff sniffed and said. 'My foot's flopping about a bit. Doesn't go where I tell it. I borrowed this stick.' He waved it.

'I know: it's mine. Get someone to do your walking for you for a couple of days, and see your own MO when you get back.' Then he pulled the chair back with a scrape, sat down with a beaming smile, and added, 'You'd have to pay for that in Civvy Street!'

The tea kept on coming forever, and it remains one of the happiest breakfasts I remember.

We hadn't expected an engineering officer who spent his days polishing Spitfires to come up with anything original to do to a fucked-up Lancaster, and we weren't disappointed. He was a lieutenant in a set of snow-white overalls – the cleanest engineering officer I had ever seen. He came marching starchily up to us after the table had been cleared by the mess servants, glared at us distastefully, and waited for our response. Grease leapt up, overzealously stamped to attention and saluted, his eyes fixed about three feet over the EO's head. There was a problem with his salute. It was a right hand fingernail inspection: Nazi-style. Every time he was close to promotion he fucked it up with a stunt like that. We all followed suit, but with proper salutes. Except for Toff, who tried and fell over. The fat MO grinned, and Grace giggled.

'Sergeants in the officers' mess. Irregular. Don't like it,' said the EO.

'Station commander's order, sir. We slept in the hospital,' said Grease.

'That's all right then.'

'Yes, sir.'

'Your kite's a bloody mess. What's more we've got nothing heavy enough to pull it out of the way.'

'Sorry about that, sir.'

'Not your fault, Sergeant. Just bloody inconvenient.'

'Yes, sir.'

'Anyway. Came to tell you that she's not going anywhere under her own steam again. I've spoken with the salvage and reclamation johnnies, and they've put things in train. Which is what you've to do, by the way — spoken to your squadron leader. You're to proceed to your home station by rail as soon as you can — they miss you apparently. Spoken to the watch officer — there will be rail passes at the gatehouse. Bus in about an hour's time.'

'Sorry I won't be flying her home, sir.'

For the first time in this exchange Grease wasn't taking the piss. There was a change in his voice and in the EO's attitude. He sighed and said, 'Yes, I know, Sergeant,' and there was a short embarrassed silence, which he broke with, 'It's very irregular, but seeing as you're here now, I suppose I better get these bastards to open the bar and buy you all a drink.'

The MO closed it down with, 'Well said, Willy,' and the rest of us added noises, the sum of which meant that although we would be embarrassed to be seen drinking with fighter johnnies, we could swallow our pride if someone else was buying.

Grace wasn't buying. The EO was trying to become the living embodiment of his Christian name and do a job on Grace, but she wasn't buying. Secretly, I think that he, too, was fascinated by the thought that someone so small could fly something so big, which she capped by explaining that the first multi-engined aircraft she had delivered had been Sunderland Flying Boats – each about as big as Blenheim Palace: they even have beds for half the crew and a fully equipped kitchen. Eventually he asked her when she was taking the new Lancaster away, and to where.

'The controller wants me away between 1415 and 1430. I've got to drop it off at an airfield near Cambridge – Bawne. But I probably shouldn't be telling you that. Then I get a long weekend off. My family live close by,' she said.

The EO initially thought that we were laughing at him, and looked miffed – he was buying, after all; then Grace twigged that we were laughing at *her*, and popped her mouth into the upside-down smile – there was something going on here which she didn't understand, and she didn't like that. So we rearranged ourselves in a line facing her, performed a crew-left-turn, and held out our right fists to her, thumbs up. Miss Baker was filing a flight plan for the field from which we had set out twenty hours previously.

'In that case,' said the MO, 'you boys have got time, guests or not, to buy me another couple of pints before you leave.' It would have to be on a slate. We flew without English money.

Flying Down to Rio – you'll have seen that film, of course, fleet-foot Fred and gorgeous Ginger – anyway, flying home took less time than it takes to see the film. The new Lanc smelled of paint and hot, new wiring, not of piss and fear: she was fast, responsive and skittish: a pleasure to fly in. Bloody thorough-bred. We all huddled south of the main spar, but Grease flew the dickey alongside the pilot, where the engineer usually parked. Fergal didn't complain: he went to sleep. Marty produced the stub of his lucky pencil, and we all wrote our names on the aircraft's inside skin. It was obvious to us that we wouldn't be flying our dear old girl again, and this new one would suit. There was a sort of unwritten – forgive what turns into a pun – squadron rule, that if a team signed an aircraft it was more or less theirs. It was a bit cheeky for a crew of rookies like us to sign a brand new kite, but seriously, you don't look at life straight on when you measure it in days rather than years. The point is that no one liked flying a kite which had been signed by another crew; although you had to, from time to time. So we were making a pre-emptive strike to put off the opposition, because there was always a scrap for a new aircraft.

Grace flew with old pre-war goggles on her forehead, and a map strapped to her left leg like a single-seat pilot. When Conroy told her later that he was impressed by her navigation she gave him a *just how dumb are you?* stare, and said that she flew along the railway lines. We learned that she had bucket-loads of stares where that came from. Her dad would have said that it was breeding; mine would have called her a stuck-up cow. Sure enough, when she turned the folded map over there was a creased and tattered *Railways of Great Britain* map underneath. She made a bloody good landing too and, directed by Grease, parked it on the hardstanding we'd vacated with our old lady just the evening before.

Three khaki vehicles set out in leisurely fashion from alongside the watch office caravan as soon as the props stopped spinning. There was the CO's nasty little Hillman, another Bedford crew lorry and the meat wagon. Our CO was Squadron Leader Delve. We called him Bushes on account of his huge moustache. It took me weeks to get used to the fact that his principal method of communication was by shouting at the lower ranks. It would be nice to write that we would have flown through the gates of Hades for him: I should cocoa. Although many did, of course.

He leapt out of his car, ran towards us and shouted, 'And where the fuck do you think *you've* been? Bloody AWOL? . . . and where's your bloody aeroplane? Throw the Toff in the ambulance, you lot take the bus down to debrief – the IO has been waiting all bloody morning for you – and where's the tart? She's with me.'

'The tart's here,' answered Grace, stepping from behind Grease, pulling off her flying helmet and ruffling her hair, 'and she's got a bloody name, if you'd care to use it. Unless you want to start collecting your own bloody Lancasters.'

One of those frozen moments. No one speaks to Bushes that way. Grace is smiling icily, and the rest of us are pretending not to have heard. Then Bushes – bright red in the face, rather than just the nose, for once – snorts some sort of a laugh, claps a hand over his mouth and says, 'Oops! Sorry, Miss,' for us all to hear.

Then embarrassment number three that day. Bushes grabs Grease's hand as if to shake it, but doesn't – they just hold. He doesn't have to say, *I'm so pleased you all made it*, because it's all there in the gesture, and written all over his ugly mug. Fergal had a big happy grin, and Conroy turned away with watery eyes. We'd all joined the Silly Buggers Club, I think. The Pink Pole looked bemused and fumbled for cigarettes because he'd left most of the feelings he'd started life with in Warsaw.

We weren't as gentle with the Toff as we should have been. The wince-and-moan show he put on for the MO would have been worth at least a ten-day leave ticket on any other station. As we climbed over the tailgate of the Bedford, Grease asked Bushes, 'Are we on for tonight?'

Bushes shook his head. 'Naw. You've no kite, have you?'

Grease glanced at the new one.

Bushes followed his glance, and shook his head. 'I know what you're thinking, but you've no bleeding chance. I'll give it to someone who'll look after it. You're only good for cast-offs at the moment. Anyway, it will take three or four days just to get her ready. They need work before they're ready to go – or didn't anyone tell you that? A complete set of radios and a bombsight would come in bloody handy for a start.'

'So what do we do, whitewash the coal until you find us some bucket to fly in?' Then he added 'sir,' after just the right length of pause. The bastard Canadians are real aces at insolence when they want to be. Anywhere else, and with anyone else, that would have earned him five days cooling his heels.

'What's today? 'asked Bushes.

Conroy supplied. 'Friday. Pay day, sir.'

'Well then, you're stood down until, say, Tuesday. Crash leave. Fuck off to London and get drunk, Just keep out of my way.'

Just as the WAAF driver was about to start away with us Bushes stepped back again to the tailgate of the truck. His question didn't seem to be addressed to any specific one of us. Grace had just spoken to him, but we hadn't heard what was said. Something was happening and I had missed it. Bushes indicated the new Lanc and asked, 'You've flown in her: what's her name then?'

Grease started to say. 'Gr—' but he was stopped by the Pink Pole, who surprised us by saying, 'Tuesday's Child. We called her Tuesday's Child.'

Bushes just shrugged and walked away to his car, where Grace was standing by the passenger door, smiling prettily.

Marty offered, 'D'ye think we'll get crash leave for every one of your landings we walk away from Skip? They're bad enough, most of the time.'

Grease hit him. We scrummed around enough for the truck to swerve in response. Marty asked, 'Do you think that Grace's a bit of all right?'

'Pretty,' Pete said. 'Pretty well used. Pretty clever. Maybe pretty damned dangerous.' Pete was good at women. He asked, 'What does Charlie think?'

'She'd never look at me,' I told them. I probably looked away.

*

There was one thing to remember about the debriefing with the intelligence officer, apart from the fact we each insisted on our post-raid rum from the padre, even though we'd been back thirteen hours already. We heard the Pink Pole saying, '. . . so I let the bastard get in very, very close, so I knew that I could hit him, and then I pissed all over him with my .303s. Then *pouff*, he blows up, just like a firework!' Then he shut up, because he could see that we were all staring at him.

The IO looked unimpressed. 'Any witnesses?' he asked.

'I saw the glow. There was the rear turret firing away, then a goddamned big explosion behind us,' said Conroy.

'It flung us forward about thirty feet, then down about 10,000,' Grease added.

'The Toff saw the whole thing. He'll confirm it. The Pole got his Kraut all right,' I said.

'OK,' said the IO, 'I'll put him up for it.'

And Grease again. 'And put Charlie up for being a gallant gentleman. He almost froze his bloody fingers off keeping the radio open.' He glared at the Pink Pole, who looked away. I tried to hide my bandages, but the IO took them in with a glance, and nodded.

Outside the IO's office the station seemed dead. No people; no vehicles. No sense of urgency. No ops tonight. Grease said, 'You got your Kraut then?' to our rear gunner.

Piotr nodded – guardedly, because he could sense something odd was coming.

Grease said, 'But he could have got *us*. All of us. You realize that?'

'Killing Krauts is all that matters to me Grease, you know

that. Poles killing Krauts is all that matters. Sure, he could have got me first. So what? A few Poles more or less do not matter.'

'Canadians *do*,' said Grease. We were just rounding the corner of the parachute shed, and he hit Pete so hard in the body that he lifted his feet clear off the ground. The only other person I had seen do that was my old man, ten years before. The little Pole seemed to crumple while he was still in the air, and fell to the ground like a half-filled sack of something. Grease didn't even break stride. Neither did we. Piotr had to see the way things stood. Firstly, Grease was the leader, and what he said *went*, and secondly we didn't appreciate near-death experiences. This meant that the Pole had to co-operate in order to prevent them happening to us. No grudges. Finis. That was the end of it. Piotr caught up with us as we reached our Nissen hut, and the conversations jerked back and forth as if nothing had happened.

I should say something about the hut. One of the advantages of having an all-sergeant crew was that we all lived in the same place. At Bawne we were lucky enough to get one of those small, eight-bed Nissens – which meant that the crew did literally *everything* together. Going out to fight together, coming back to a hut which had become like a home to us, to weep together – yeah, we did that a couple of times – eating together, drinking ourselves stupid together. It formed the sort of blood connection that those mixed-rank crews of ponces (officers) and NCOs could only dream about. Even if they try to tell you otherwise.

The lads were better than brothers to me.

*

If you think that having a mad Pole in the rear turret was a bit of a downer, I have to tell you that it had its upsides as well. He was an ace finder. He found things before their previous owners knew they'd lost them. And we didn't complain about the things he found, because they included coal for the stove when the rest of the station had run out, and only the officers' mess was supposed to have any. He could also find fresh eggs, and potatoes we could roast. He found petrol for Grease's Red Indian motorcycle, and extra blankets when the Cambridgeshire winter was trying to freeze our balls off. And he always had a stock of fags and whisky, and nylon stockings to bribe girls with – when only the Yanks had them. What I liked best about him was that he was free with the things he found. We didn't ask, but he always hinted that he had political sources. Although he spent some time each leave with us, he always went up to London or Edinburgh for the rest of it. Sometimes one or two of us went up with him to London, but never saw much of him because he was with other Poles most of the time – he had contacts in the embassy: a 'Government in Exile', Mr Churchill used to call it.

He always went away with a couple of empty kit bags, and always brought them back full. It was a bit like sharing a hut with Father Christmas – something for everyone. Maybe it was black market. Maybe it was Polish government largesse – you know, keeping the gallant allies happy. Maybe it was a bit of cloak and dagger. Or maybe it was just a bit of blagging. Who knew or cared? Not me; not till later. We didn't complain when he appeared with a huge French box radio in the back of a small Tilley pickup. I had to retune it, but it had great range, and we could get all of the English stations, some Yank ones, and even the illegal Kraut propaganda broadcasts. They were good for the news our people were too scared to broadcast. It was the only news service that gave a halfway decent count on the aircraft we were leaving in Germany each night. Mostly it was tuned to music, though. The Savoyans, and the dance jazz the Americans played. I asked him once where he'd got it from. He said from an English infantryman who brought it back from Dunkirk. There were a lot of French souvenirs knocking around soon after Dunkirk, but nobody talked about that.

Later the afternoon that Grease had hit him, Piotr wandered over to my bed and sat on the edge. Big Hearted Arthur was belting out 'Get in Your Shelter' and 'Kiss Me Goodnight, Sergeant Major' on the radio. How could the Kraut hope to beat people who thought that the war could be funny? I was stretched out reading a Zane Grey, and shoved over to make room for him.

'Hello, squirt. Wanna smoke?' he said.

'You call me squirt because I'm small, or because I'm younger than the rest of you?'

'I call you squirt because I don't have a younger brother any more.' That was a new one. Something was eating him, because he launched straight into, 'You know that I like you all, Charlie? You *do* know that?' He offered me a Players Airman cigarette from a new packet. I took one.

'Of course we do, Pete. You're the best tail gunner there is. We wouldn't change you for anyone.'

'I should hate it if anything happened to any of us.'

'I know, Pete. You just forgot that up there for a sec. I don't suppose it will happen again.'

Everyone else was earwigging us, of course — as they were supposed to — this was Piotr saying *sorry*, and me saving face for him. I expected him to get up and amble away, but he sat quiet for a while and then he said, 'I don't think Krefeld likes me, Charlie. I was *scared* up there last night.'

Looking back, I should have paid attention to what he was saying. But I didn't. I said, 'Don't worry about it, Pete. When Kraut bastards are trying to kill us all night long *scared* is probably a very sensible thing to be. Situation normal.'

I started to turn back to my book. He gave a sad little smile and stood up. Grease was waving our dog-eared pack of playing cards at him from the far end of the hut. Pax. He left the cigarettes on my bed. He always made sure that we never ran out.

So why, you ask, hadn't we packed our kit and shot off for four days' leave already? It was because of the dame, of course.

Take-off was delayed by unspoken consensus, which is one of those things that happens when seven people live together. Someone must have said, *I think I'll go up tomorrow*, and that made up everyone else's minds for them. That night we smartened ourselves up, which meant a shave and borrowing one of Grease's clean shirts — he always had bloody dozens of them — and fetched up in the sergeants' mess just after seven, refreshed by a sleep sponsored by knowing that you were going to stay alive for another few nights at least. Pete had clipped his moustache back to a thin line; I thought that he looked just the thing.

Grace had a good sense of timing: we weren't through the first pint before she walked in to the bar looking for us. She was wearing a plain uniform with an ATA flash, similar to a navy blue Senior Service uniform, except the skirt was cut shorter – to just below the knees – which showed off her shapely short legs, and hinted at the fine black stockings which covered them. Her dark curls bobbed as she walked. She looked wonderful, and when she gave her tight little smile across the room and marched directly to us, I was proud enough to die.

'You still here?' she said. 'Gin and tonic, please.'

The mess boy, who had immediately started to hover, would have normally laughed that one off, but he blushed, turned his back, and produced one from nowhere. Yeah; it was going to be an all-right night. She didn't leave our table, which made all of the other types jealous. Bonza. I remember Conroy, who was usually the soberest of the lot of us, being six months older than me, sort of giving her a quizzical look across the table and asking, 'We got it then? *Tuesday's Child?*'

'Yes, of course you did,' Grace said. 'What do you take me for? This Tuesday's child has a rich daddy who never says no. Few men do!'

Grease asked, 'What d'ye have to give for it?' He wasn't being moody. He was just finding his way with a new woman. It was his way, and he wasn't being facetious, either.

'Well; let's say that it might have been not so much a case of

Tuesday's child being full of grace, as much as Grace being full of something else. He's an energetic old sod, by the way.'

She said this in a conversational tone that said *situation normal*. Grease looked away: maybe not as concerned as he thought he'd be. She could have been shooting a line, of course.

'Dirty sod!' Marty said.

Grace gave him a cheeky grin and said, 'Don't worry. Wait around and maybe you'll get your turn. I can be choosy, without being fussy.'

No. She wasn't shooting a line. Grease had got his girl. He'd been making a pitch for her since he had first seen her – and she had accepted his offer, but it wasn't a one-to-one. It's just the way she was. I'm not sure that I believed it at the time; I remember worrying about what it could do to us. Then I got a hard-on, and in a man's game that's the trump card, isn't it? I can recall several conversations from the evening before we started to fall down all over the place – except the Toff, who, drunk out of his skull, started to walk straight for the first time in twenty-four hours.

That night she slept with Grease in berth eight. The one that belonged to no one. Being a crew of seven we only needed seven beds – and in our eight-bed hut, the eighth had become the guest quarters. It was a slightly larger bed than the others, and we had hidden it behind green curtain partitions liberated from the medical section. Fergal was a passionate water colourist on the quiet and had painted the insides with fantastic flowers and creatures like unicorns and centaurs. There was a utility bedside cabinet with a vase for flowers (and when appropriate, a drawer for rubber accessories), and a battered armchair that the officers' mess had discarded. It was the berth on the left as you came in, nearest the door — the furthest part of the hut from our pathetic stove, and the coldest, but the way we saw it was that when we slept there we weren't likely to be bothered by the cold. You see, it was where you took your girl if she didn't have a room and you couldn't afford one of the local hotels. I hadn't used it much. I didn't have a regular girl, and it's not much fun sleeping alone in a whorehouse bed. To be honest it was Pete the Pole who used it most frequently, then I suppose it was Grease, because he always worked so much harder at it than the rest of us. Anyway; that was something like privacy in a country which no longer had any to spare.

I told you before that I have early habits. Just as the Toff was the last sleeper, who invariably topped up the stove at night, so it was me who stoked it in the morning; not a job I relished. Marty once pointed out that I was the baby of the outfit, and that kids were always up early. He got that wrong: I just never saw the point of lying awake in bed on your own. After rattling up the stove until it roared, and putting the two kettles on to boil, I did what I always do with my headaches: went outside and stuck my head into the fire bucket until the cold water crushed my brain. You know the old joke — it's not much of a cure, but you feel much better when you stop. Mind you, I sniffed it first. It wouldn't have been the first time that someone had pissed in it. It takes several days to get the smell of urine out of your hair.

Grease stepped outside in his singlet, shorts and running

shoes. 'Some night,' he said, shook his head from side to side, and performed his warm-up routine.

He had been a professional hockey player in some dick Canadian town before the war, and had an obsession about physical fitness. He was more serious about it than about the war effort. He was always at his peak, and did what was needed to retain it. That meant punishing his body most mornings. He was going back to the game after all this was over. Ergo, he was not only fast, but also as strong as an ox – which suited us, because you sometimes needed a brute to wrestle a bent Lanc back from Krautsville.

I guess I nodded some sort of reply. He ran and jumped up and down on the spot until he was wreathed in steam, and the sun climbed above the horizon into a yellow and grey sky.

Then I remembered something. 'How's Grace?'

He gave me the *Grease done it* toothy grin, which made me want to throw up, and said, 'I guess I'll run the full five miles this morning Sparky. Should take about, say, thirty-five minutes or so. You may find that our Grace needs her radio tuning while I'm away.' I'd never been invited to help myself to a woman before. Then he ran out on me. Literally.

As I turned back I experienced a real man's reaction to an unexpectedly available female: I was scared. Inside the hut, the stove was glowing pink with the heat, and wispy steam was just beginning to show near the kettles. And near Grace. She was standing close to it, wrapped in one of Grease's shirts. She faced the stove, her back to the door, and me and as far as I could make out she was holding the front of the shirt open, gathering in the heat the stove pumped out. From five beds came snores and sleep noises at an acceptable level: Marty was asleep fully clothed *under* his, his body convulsing periodically with erotic shudders. My opening the door let in frozen air, and Grace turned.

Photoflash.

This image lasted maybe a millisecond, and burned itself on to my memory forever: a pretty girl with a snub nose, not tall, my height, say, which is five two; dark hair rested on her shoulders; small breasts with big, uneven nipples and some freckles. She had freckles on her belly too, and her patch of pubic hair was dark, dense and very small. She even had a scattering of freckles on her thighs. And she smiled a lopsided cheeky girl grin that stopped your breath. It was like standing in front of a magnet. Is that what they mean by beauty? Was it anything to do with the fact that Grace was the first naked woman I'd ever met in daylight?

Her voice was a hoarse stage whisper. 'What are you like in the mornings?'

Hey; I can come on with the smart phrases too. I mouthed, rather than said, 'I'm a bit of a morning person,' and tried to return her crooked smile with one of my own, attempting to sound as nonchalant as Charles Boyer, but it didn't work. I must have looked like a schoolboy with the twitch.

Grace was fast asleep in the crook of my arm by the time the others began to stir. I was warm and comfortable, and didn't welcome the morning chorus of farts and curses which signalled waking airmen getting *chocks away* before levering themselves upright. Someone had put the radio on: Fred Astaire sang that 'it was a lovely day to get caught in the rain'.

Fergal thrust his face through the partition curtains and said, 'Christ, Skipper, she's worn *you* down, you're no bigger than the Sparks!' Then he asked, 'What's the met, Charlie?'

'Fine and clear outside, and bloody freezing. It'll be a good weekend.'

'Where's the Skip?'

'On finals. Bloody running. Don't wake Grace.'

He nodded at her, and asked, 'Will Grease be all right about this?'

'Yes he will,' replied Grace, without opening her eyes.

'What about me then?' from Fergal again, whose grin was wasted on Grace, because she wasn't looking.

'Wait your bloody turn,' she said, and pulled the blankets over her head.

Grease's Red Indian motorbike had had a sidecar for the last fortnight. Piotr had found it; we didn't ask him where. After Pete had washed, shaved and carefully combed his hair, he set off on it to the kitchens, with a carton of American cigarettes tucked into the open top of his battledress jacket. He returned with the makings of eight breakfasts which we cooked on two shallow baking tins balanced on the stove, and a squadron-sized urn of tea which we waxed with Polish vodka. In fact the sidecar was so full of food that we had to store some. Grease returned, stripped off outside, and emptied the ice-cold contents of the fire bucket over himself. He steamed in the cold sun momentarily, before rubbing himself down.

Grace glanced at his cold shrivelled prick and snorted, 'If I had known that's what it looked like last night, I wouldn't have bothered!'

Grease replied, 'Maybe it needs warming up.'

'Then stick it on the stove with the other sausages.'

Between Bawne and St Neots, there's a fair-sized village named Crifton. Grace told us that her father and stepmother owned most of it, and Crifton Park, the estate around it, and most of the farms between Crifton and the next airfield at Gransden. She asked us to stay for the weekend. Seven unplanned-for semi-domesticated guests wouldn't be a problem, apparently. Somehow it was decided that only Grease, Marty and the Toff would go with her: Fergal, Conroy, me and the Pink Pole would head for the Smoke. Fergal volunteered to fiddle travel warrants for us, and Piotr surprised us by tossing a set of keys to Grease and saying, 'You take the car.'

Grease asked, 'What car?' Not an unreasonable question.

'Ours. It was Abbot's. He missed the bus yesterday. I will take the money to his widow.'

'I didn't know that he was married,' Conroy said.

'No. Neither did the RAF. No permission. It is better I give the money to his widow. Less embarrassment.'

It was a small, four-seat open Singer: at a push you could get a full crew of seven into it. I know that because that was what Abbot and his people used to do. They would drive up to their aircraft dispersal, and leave it there until they got back from the trip. I recalled, then, that I had noticed it standing forlorn in an empty revetment as *Tuesday's Child* had taxied in. I suppose that no one had since wanted to move it, just in case. That was just the sort of thing that wouldn't worry the Pole.

Before we split, Grace found she had something to say. She had her smart little uniform on again – without the jacket yet – and had her smart little bum facing the stove, one high altar of our little hut warming another. She cleared her throat as if she was embarrassed, which embarrassed us, so we stopped stuffing bags with shirts, shaving kit and condoms and listened.

'We have seven or eight Lancs to deliver here, all from Ringway. That's usually about one a week. I can probably get them all. They offer you most of the flights anywhere near your home. It's the way we do things in the ATA – there aren't many other perks. That way you get to see your family, if you want to. I wondered if I could count on your spare berth now and again for the duration . . . although I'll always go on to Crifton if I'm in the way, and you can come on with me if you like.' She sounded oddly uncertain; as if she was unused to asking for favours. That was disconcerting.

The Toff jumped in before the rest of us, and killed the gentle smile on her face stone dead. 'We don't have a spare berth,' he said.

Grace said, 'Oh,' and her mouth went round, then turned down at the edges. Put down. Her cheeks coloured.

Then Toff said, 'We just have a spare bed called *Grace's Place*. You can have that if you want.'

Grace blushed: the one and only time. Grace kissed everyone in turn, starting with the Toff. I thought that the kisses she gave to Grease and me were not as sexy as those she stuck on the others. Always you learn. Looking back forty years it's hard to tell if we ever fell in love with her: if we did it must have started about then.

By late afternoon on Saturday we were at the bar of the Trocadero, and halfway to drunk. On the tiny dance floor I had a couple of dances with some American Red Cross girls, who were pretty and able, but definitely not willing. It made you understand why the Yanks went mad for British women; their own are born with their knees tied together. So we stayed in the bar after that. We had taken a taxi from the station to Green's, where we always tried to stay: it was a bomber hotel. Then we dumped our kit and made straight for the Troc, because we'd scored there before. We couldn't get tickets for a show, and didn't fancy queuing in the cold for returns, so it was supper somewhere, and then clubs or pubs. Maybe a dance; if they'd let us in.

Somewhere along the evening we lost our tail gunner, and merged with an American crew from the 306th at Thurleigh. That was near Bawne. Neighbours. They were taking a bit of a beating, but you didn't talk shop to strangers when you were on leave. In the bar of the Bag O'Nails club, after we tossed a couple of stroppy fighter types on to the pavement, we ploughed across the furrows of the same American Red Cross girls from the Troc. The Yanks gave them the treatment. We remembered the score, and didn't come on to them. So they came on to us, and I woke up with a plump little redhead.

After I had washed and shaved and dressed in clean clothes, and breakfasted alone because the others didn't show, I felt kind of flat. Fergal and Conroy surfaced for beer at lunchtime, and after that it was pretty certain to be pubs and bars all the way to Monday night.

Conroy voiced what I had been thinking. He looked up from the book he was reading – he always read and got drunk at the same time: this time it was Juvenal, I remember – and observed, 'If there's an afternoon train we could be back in the pub in Eltisley by tonight, and drop down a surprise visit on the bike to this Crifton place on Monday. What was it they were doing then?'

'Impromptu shoot,' said Fergal. 'Apparently her old man likes shooting things.'

'Like the Pole,' I said. 'Where is he by the way?'

'Sloped off from the Troc early. Said he was going to pay Abbot's widow. He'll find his own way back.'

'Always does,' Conroy said.

In the train that afternoon I thought that Grace had stepped out of an aircraft, and changed everything. That's what I thought. Conners asked me what she was like. I told him, 'I don't know. You turn your back, and when you look again she's become someone else.'

'I know what you mean, but I'm not going to complain.'

'Neither am I,' Fergal said. 'Gift horse.' There was something about the way he said it that made me wonder if he was even less experienced with women than I was.

I said, 'Maybe she's her own woman.'

Conners winced, and looked at me as if I had gone mad, then turned away and lit up without offering them round.

I know a little about architecture because the art teacher at my grammar school in Surrey found a few lessons spare at the end of my last term, and gave us a quick gallop through the history of architecture. It meant that I could name shapes, and Crifton Park House is Palladian. The drive to it started in the village. As you burst out of the trees and into the light you found the house in front and slightly below you, doglegged about another half mile further on. It was a two-storeyed mansion as big as an aircraft carrier. I could have fitted my parent's old three-bedroomed semi into the portico alone. Fergal steered for that: Conroy was on the pillion, and I occupied the sidecar. Fergal wasn't terribly good at motorbikes, but he was better than either of us.

When he pulled up, with a slither that took a stripe a foot deep out of their gravel, he spoke for us all. 'Strewth. Fuckingham Palace! Are we at the right place?'

A gravel path as wide as a runway, which appeared to surround the house, was dotted with elephant-sized grey urns sitting on plinths. They hosted great trailing falls of geraniums, splashed red. Red is a colour I had come to dislike since joining up.

There was a gardener working at one of them, at the top of a wooden set of steps. I crunched up to him. He looked down and gave me an uncertain smile. He wasn't badly dressed for a working gardener, partly hidden by a huge leather apron. It was huge, because it fitted him, and *he* was. He must have had four inches on Grease, which would have made him six five at least, and he was heavy with it. His face was a hunting and shooting brown, and topped with a fringe of white hair, through which his pate climbed. That was brown as well. He carefully wiped his hands against the apron and stepped down. He held one hand out to shake – mine, thinly bandaged fingers and all, disappeared inside it. He bent slightly to meet me. He said, 'Fuckingham Palace. Very original. I must take that man's name. He could write some of my speeches for me.' He scrutinized my battledress trade flash and said, 'You're the sparks.'

He didn't sound like a gardener to me, so I responded with, 'Yes, sir.'

'I'm Peter Baker. My people make some of the bullets your people fire at Germans. Have you got time to look at my radio? I salvaged it from a B17 that made a mess of my long ride, and I'm trying to get it going again.'

'I'll have a look at it, but won't make any promises. I don't build the things, I just twiddle the knobs, talk into them and rattle away with the Morse key. America is another country as far as radios go; a lot of things in their sets work back to front.'

'Come to see my Grace?'

'That was the idea, sir.'

'She's off shooting with your skipper and your gunner. The one with the limp.'

'We call him the Toff.'

'See why. He speaks the language better than most. Anyway – you've time to give my wireless the once over before lunch?'

'Absolutely, sir,' and I waved the other two over. Safe landing. Good touchdown.

He walked fast. In a bloody great house like that you'd have to or starve to death between meals. He dropped Fergal and Conroy in a library the size of a railway station chapel, with bottles of beer at their elbows, and then led me north, west and up to a small room in a corner of the building.

'Servant's room,' he observed. 'Used to have dozens in the 1800s I'd say. Room enough for a battalion of them. I get by with six – all too old for the services or war work.'

'What about the estate? The land?'

'I unretired the last estate manager, and gave him a dozen land girls. He thinks he's died and gone to heaven. Treats them like a ruddy harem, and works to the government's plans, not mine – but we get enough off the top to feed the place without straining the local black market.'

There was a bed with a striped mattress as old as the house, two hard chairs, a shelf with several books – some about radio telegraphy, and one on astronomy – and a table bearing a standard US bomber radio with a battered case. There were WD charts pinned to the walls: the Western Approaches and the whole of Europe.

'What do you think?' he asked.

'Most of the bits are here. Where's the aerial off to?' The thick lead climbed up through a skylight window.

'One of the chimneys. All right?'

'Should be.' I went through three induction circuits. On. On. On. Valves lit, and I began to smell that warm, friendly electrical scent of an excited radio. Then static. Well; so what? After Krefeld I spoke static fairly fluently.

'This might take me some time.'

'No problem, Sparks.' Then he said, 'Look; I can't keep calling you Sparks. You have a name?'

'Charlie Bassett.'

'Charlie then?'

'That's fine.'

'I'm Peter.'

'That's fine too. Our tail gunner, the Pink Pole, is a Peter too; only it's "Piotr" – the Polish way of saying it.'

'I'll leave you to it then. Lunch at one, OK? Can you find your own way down?'

'I'll follow the smell of food until I get there.'

'If you get thirsty try the bag at your feet. Bye for now: I appreciate this,' he said, and moved out. Quiet and quick on his feet for a big man. The bag I hadn't noticed was an old doctor's case. It contained a bottle of bourbon, and a thick glass tumbler.

I worked for an hour, but got further down the bottle than the radio. I'd come back in a week, if he still wanted me to. I found Fergal in the library with paper spread around a writing desk, and three empty bottles of Angers beer. He waved me away, and said, 'He has to give a speech at the Manchester Trades next week, and wants *me* to liven up what he's written. Conroy's helping him in the garden. They were talking poetry.' As I left him he added, 'Grease is around somewhere. He stinks of gunpowder and dead things.'

Grease was cleaning a shotgun in a spare kitchen. He was

surrounded by heaps of dead birds. You could see the feather dust dancing in the rays of light admitted by high windows. I asked what the birds had been. He said, 'Those are snipe, and those are woodcock. That heap are grouse, and those are pheasant. The big thing is a swan that the Toff took against. Great isn't it?'

'I'm not sure. What happens to them now?'

'Folk eat them. The Boss will have woodcock or snipe tonight.'

'The Boss?'

'Grace's dad. Met him yet?' I nodded. Seeing Grease reduced to man-the-mighty-hunter, and surrounded by bird corpses had temporarily robbed me of sensible speech . . . but silence didn't worry him. Grease asked, 'You want the good news or the bad news?'

'Good news.'

'Grace is one of the best bloody deflection shots you've ever seen in your life. She tumbled most of these birds.' What was good about that?

'Tumbled. She didn't *tumble* these birds, she bloody massacred them. This was Custer's Last Stand for birds.'

'You must have pulled a girl in town,' Grease said quickly, 'because you've come back picky. You're always picky when you've scored.'

'What's the bad news?'

'The Toff's off sulking somewhere. Won't talk to anyone. Grace is a bloody sight better shot half pissed than he'll ever be sober. He can't stand the competition.'

We ate lunch in a huge kitchen: eight at the table – Marty

mooched in from the fields; he'd met a land army girl who was teaching him to plough. He smelled strongly of warm horse, or *eau de land girl*. It wasn't always easy to tell the difference. The Toff looked quite low. Grace sat at one end of the table – furthest from me – and her father at the other. Kitchen or no, the lunch was still served to us, although the staff looked so far gone I thought that I should be waiting on *them*.

The Boss read my mind. He said, 'Don't say it, lad. You get shot at most nights, so let them do their bit – there'd be a revolt if I tried to retire them now.'

'Have they been with you long?'

'Since '36. That's when I arrived. They were already here. They've more right to be here than we have.'

Lancashire hotpot. A real one. Huge hunks of fleshy mutton under carrots and onions, and crisp slices of potato over a thin layer of mash. At some point between that, and the bread pudding with custard which chased it, Grease blinked owlishly several times and said, 'I think our Charlie became an *ace* last night. I think he dipped his wick in the wicked city. He's come back early, and very picky.'

'What makes one an ace?' the Boss asked.

'Two shags with two different girls on two consecutive days.' That's the Toff, coming out of it at last.

No one asked me who the first of the two had been, but Grace was suddenly looking at me.

'What was she like?' she asked.

I think I probably looked at my plate as I said, 'An American girl, from Bedford. She was . . . an enthusiast, I suppose.'

Grace sniffed and looked away. 'Oh,' she said, 'one of *those*.'

After lunch broke up I took an enormous mug of tea to the front of the house, and sat under one of the windows in the sun on a stone bench made for giants. The sun on my face felt precious. Grace's father, who everybody else seemed to be calling the Boss now, strolled up. He had a black curved briar pipe dwarfed by his hand. At first he sat without speaking – the tobacco he smoked smelled sweet and rich. Then he asked, 'What are you doing?'

'Making memories. Things to think about when you're scared.'

'Good idea. I wished I'd made more when I was your age. We were a nice little middle-class group then. Me and my partner. Comfortably off and respectable.'

'How did that lead to this?' I waved at the house stretching away on each side of us.

'Bullets breed bullets. The Germans may have stopped fighting in 1918, but nobody else did. Nice little wars absolutely ruddy everywhere, all needing bullets. That kept us ticking over. I took over from dad in 1926, just after his first stroke. I took a pal in with me. He had contacts, and was good at numbers, but it didn't work out in the long run. Soon after that there was all the fuss about Afghanistan and the RAF, and they needed millions of .303s for that one . . . and then someone began to agitate about rearming. Probably Winston, he was always keen on wars. Baker and Baker couldn't lose, could it? There was no point in not moving with the times – so I expanded into gun barrels and liners as well. If you buy my gun barrels, then you're going to buy my bullets to go with them, aren't you?'

His pipe had gone out. He made a production of relighting it, and added, 'More than 3,000 employees now, and two great factories just outside Durham to keep them in. Wealthier than ever, and never stop bloody working.'

'What happened to your partner?'

'Died. Sad. I never wanted that to happen.'

'You moved here in '36, sir?'

'Had to do something with all the bloody money we were making, didn't I?'

It was a very good moment, sitting with the old man like that. Then Conroy ambled along, and changed things. He could be a cuss when he wanted to be. As soon as he opened his mouth I knew that he had something he was going to pursue. He asked Baker, 'Can I ask you about Grace, sir?'

'You'd be better off asking *her* wouldn't you?'

'She may not know the answers.'

We could see Grace and the Toff in the half distance, on the margins of the slope the Boss called his Long Ride. I saw her catch his hand in hers, and they veered off to one side and tree cover. They were probably going to discuss deflection shooting. Baker puffed at the small fire he had created in his pipe, and didn't give Conroy another chance. He said, 'Don't ask me about Grace's relationships with men. All you need to know is that she is as straight about them as she is about everything, except the big lie.'

'What's the big lie?' I asked.

'Ask Grace.' Then he turned back to Conners with, 'Don't try to complicate her; nor yourself, come to that. Right?'

'Yes, sir. I was thinking about the crew. Worried, if you like . . .'

'Bollocks. You were just clearing your decks.'

Conroy smiled. I've seen him use his smile before. He defuses difficult situations with it. 'Maybe that as well.' He stood up, threw us a sloppy salute and wandered off.

I sat in silence with the old man for a few minutes, and then he said, 'That boy thinks too much.'

Then we talked radios until the sun began to dip.

Grease and I didn't stay to supper, but we stayed for a drink before they ate. Grace's stepmother still hadn't appeared. Grace had a couple of small leaves in her hair. The Toff was talking animatedly again, although it was about gunnery, and Conroy had books in his hands. Fergal had to be dragged down from the library: he had completely rewritten the Free Trades speech and wanted us to test it for him. Under his guidance it seemed to be recommending the union of the two Irelands as an independent country. I'm sure that it hadn't started out that way.

Our Eltisley pub was crammed that night. No flying, although it had been a good weekend for it. Dasher – he was another Canadian pilot who had been on the same conversion course as Grease – told us that no one had flown since we left. A *big* stand down. He called it a 'jumbo scrub', and gave me a cynical glance when I asked him why.

'Not enough crew or kites, are there? Too many new faces at the bar, and the aircraft we have left are being overflown just to keep bombs in the air: they're falling to bits on us. They say that Butch gave the CO six days off to effectively put a new squadron together. On my last trip I was the fourth consecutive pilot to sign for the bastard aeroplane.'

Butch, or the Butcher was the name we gave our chief of staff, Air Chief Marshal Sir Arthur Harris. That's what the press thought, anyway. After the war they called him Bomber Harris didn't they? In 1944 I heard him called other things.

'Which was that?'

'*Queenie*. Won't do it again – we burned the old bitch on Coldharbour Farm on the way back in I'm afraid.'

'Oh.'

'No worries, as our Australian brethren say; we all got out. What about you?'

'Grease left pieces of our old *Yorker* all over Germany. We left the bits we brought back at Manston.'

'Wizard new runway at Manston I hear.'

'Yeah, wizard. Even Grease can get down in one piece on it.'

Grease got Mrs Harrison, the landlady, to open up the small bar for us: he wanted to talk, and we couldn't hear each other over the aircrew and WAAFs around us. The small bar was just that. It was about six feet square and contained a round table carved with hundreds of names and initials, and polished by a thousand elbows in service cloth. Later we would have to make way for an airman and his girl – it was always in demand late evening. Two uncomfortable upright chairs left just enough room for two people and their drinks. I once spent an hour reading the table. A WAAF named Helen seemed to figure on it too frequently for chance. If she was that unlucky with her choice of partner she was a lady to avoid.

Grease started by saying, 'That's a pity.'

'What is?'

'Squadron stand down. I thought that old Bushes was being kind to us, giving us an extra few days' leave. Looks like the whole of the flying side got them. It'll mean that our six weeks start here, before we get any more.'

We were given six days' leave at the end of every six weeks' flying. Some squadrons were awarded nine every six weeks – it was the luck of the draw I suppose. We had already done three weeks, so Grease had been hoping we'd just picked up a buckshee five days, and would have only flown another three weeks before another six.

I said, 'I'll do the sums, but I think that we're still ahead. We got leave early, that was all, and if we get the chop in the next three weeks we wouldn't have had any at all.'

'I'll think of that as we're spinning in with flames shooting out of our arses.'

'What did you want to talk about anyway?'

'Grace.'

'Not you too! Conroy was on about her to the old boy this afternoon. What a tit!'

'What did the old man say?'

'Something like, "Shag her as much as you want to, but don't come crying to me about it if it all goes wrong." I don't think that he gives a damn. With a bit of luck Conners and Fergal will satisfy their curiosity by tomorrow morning, and that will leave

Pete. Then maybe we can get back to thinking about flying, and staying alive for our thirty trips.'

Grease pulled at his top lip. 'I don't think it's going to be quite as simple as that, Charlie,' he said.

'Aren't you satisfied with getting a new kite, a free shag, and a weekend's accommodation out of it – what more do you want?'

'Don't get me wrong. I haven't gone soft on her or anything, any more than you have, I just like her around. I think that I just *like* her around more than anyone else I've met.'

'And she's a good shag.'

'Yes . . . that too; she's a very good shag, isn't she? It seems like too much of a good thing. Do you think that we were chopped over Krefeld, and have gone to bomber heaven?'

'There are no Lancasters in heaven. Not even *Yorker*.'

'Anyway, we'll see what happens when she flies the next one down from Ringway. I've just had a very depressing thought.'

'What's that, old son?'

'There's a joint services parachute training school at Ringway. I bet she's good at that too.'

'Do you mind?'

'Do I mind what?'

'That Grace spreads it about a bit. That she's not always with you?' I was asking him about myself, as much as about him.

He pulled at his lip again. 'No. I know that's a bit odd; but no, I don't.'

'Nor do I.'

'You're too young to know better. I should.'

He grinned, and swilled his pint down. I copied him. We

talked until an American airman and a very pretty WAAF put their heads around the door, then stood up and made way for them. Normally that would have irritated me momentarily – seeing a happy guy with a nice girl, when I hadn't one of my own. That didn't matter any more, and just like Grace's earlier flash of jealousy, that was quite interesting.

Bushes' hairy and unexpected face beamed at us across the crowded main bar. He belched and said, 'See you tomorrow lads.'

He did, too. Grease and I took the bike out to dispersal to see *Tuesday's Child* – she must have been diverted from a Canadian order, because she had that satin finish paint which the Canadian squadrons favoured, and gleamed under a weak sun. One of the ground crew had painted TUESDAY'S CHILD in neat small yellow capitals under the small window just aft of the bomb-aimer's bubble, and GREASE just under the sliding window to the pilot's left shoulder. She had been given the squadron code, and her individual code letter Y. I have to admit it; she looked a good one. Bushes was bawling out the ground crew chief, who bore the rasping sentences like a stoic. One of the armourers was working at the machine guns in the front turret, above the bubble. He grinned when he saw us, and moved his left fist up and down in the international call sign. When Bushes noticed us he shouted, 'Look at the bloody paint. It's as shiny as a pimp's Lagonda!'

'That's not the Chief's fault,' from Grease, 'it came like that.'

'They've had four bloody days to paint it with our flat paint!'

'Not if you want its acceptance checks completed, the compasses serviced, and guns in it. What are they like by the way, Chiefy?'

'Great Mr McKenzie. Baker barrels: beautifully machined – they'll never let you down.'

Grease said to me, 'Now why doesn't that surprise me?'

'What does that mean?' Bushes asked.

'The ATA who flew it in, sir. She's Baker's daughter. That's Bullets Baker the bullet maker – he's diversified into gun barrels apparently.'

Hurt always showed on Bushes' face immediately – it was as if it turned itself inside out momentarily. He did that now. 'And how'd the hell you know that, when *I* didn't?'

'We just spent the weekend at his place, sir.'

'Fucking hooray.' Bushes glared at Grease and Chiefy in turn. Then he said to me, 'I spoke to the squadron radio officer about your call sign. Can't be *Yorker*. *Yorker* has gone to the knackers. She survives as bits in the spares boxes of thieves like the Chief here. I thought Y-*Yoke* would do. OK?'

'Yes, sir.'

'That's all right then.' Then he turned on Grease again. 'You'd better air test it as soon as the remains of your crew crawl back from the brothels they lost themselves in. Tell the watch office I said so.'

'Yes, sir,' said Grease, who threw him a peculiar slow salute, but a salute even so. It was a polite way of telling him to sod off, to let us get on with the work. Bushes could take a hint. Some sentient officers could. We were standing close to the port main undercarriage wheel – which was as big as us, if you must know – and Grease asked, 'What do you think of her.'

Chiefy said, 'Absolute fucking corker, Grease – just make sure your people look after her. It almost seems a shame to take her to Germany.'

'Maybe they'll let me fly a war bonds tour around the Dominions instead.'

'Fat chance of that lad; we've got to be up to operational strength by Thursday or Friday. Mr and Mrs Fritz must be missing your visits.'

Grease wanted some wakey-wakey pills from the MO, and I wanted my fingers signed off, so the medical unit was the next stop, and there was no problem. In the roadway outside there was. We were suddenly confronted by two flight lieutenants and a sergeant – I recognized them as all being from the same crew. The sergeant was a sunny Yorkshireman – a rear gunner, like the Pole, but the smaller of the FLs was a pugnacious sod of a pilot: one of those universally loathed VCs-in-waiting, provided he lived that long. Gerry Brookman. Everything about him spoke confrontation – especially the way he stood in front of us now, legs apart, fists on hips, cap pushed back. If I had still been in the school playground I would have been running in circles by now, yelling *Fight! Fight!*

As it was he spat, 'Look here, Mr McKenzie. How come you get the brand new kite, whilst the squadron officers are soldiering on with the old tat we started with? I don't know what stroke you pulled, but whatever it was, you'd better watch your step.' His voice rose an octave with each syllable, it seemed, until he sounded as if his voice hadn't yet broken: it spoiled the effect.

'*Mortified* FL,' said Grease, 'I'm sure,' and stood there towering above him like Mount McKinley. FL was service slang for French letters or rubber johnnies: maybe I already told you that. It really pissed the officers off if we abbreviated their rank and title.

Brookman went red in the face: a vein throbbed at his temple. 'See here—'

'No Brookie. *You* see here. Butt out of our business, and we'll keep out of yours. Get your own new kite. You do that by bringing your own one back with wounded on board, and so many bits missing that it's flying on farts and last night's funk.' Grease poked Brookman in the chest with a broad forefinger, which pushed him back a yard, '. . . and if you care to take this any further, the next time I see your kite over the other side I'll order my gunners to shoot you down. Unlike the shite that flies with *you*, they'll do it.'

As we walked away I said, 'You really *haven't* any idea of squadron or wing, or bloody RAF, or discipline, come to that, have you Grease? As far as you're concerned it's just the crew; there's no one else.'

'That's right boy, seven of us against the rest of the world. Eight, if you count Grace.'

I wished he hadn't said that.

Duisburg

On Thursday evening we were walking from the crew wagon –
next stop Duisburg. Grease lit a fag, took one lungful of smoke,
and then ground it out under his boot. That was his ritual. He
wouldn't smoke again until we were back. Or he wouldn't
smoke again; it was as simple as that.

Conroy said, 'An arch of spears through which a defeated
enemy of Rome had to walk as a gesture of submission. That'll
do for me: very appropriate.'

Marty stretched – one arm after the other – that was *his*
ritual before he counted his bombs, and asked, 'What the hell
are you blathering about, Conners?'

'Our call sign: *Yoke*. It's a very old word. All to do with
defeating your enemies.'

'That'll do for me as well,' I said, and followed Grease, and
Fergal, Conroy and Marty through the small door and up into
Tuesday's Child. Bloody Duisburg.

We had a milk run. Grease was just beginning to show some
canny signs. We had to fly circles over Cambridgeshire and
Lincolnshire, to reach our operating height and form up with

the others. I think that Grease's circles were larger than anyone else's, and as a consequence we didn't bump into anybody, and saw few other Lancasters until we set course for the fleshpots of Greater Germany. Grease actually called Conroy and me forward to see a remarkable sight. I usually tried to keep close to my work table, and pretend I didn't know that there was a war going on outside . . . unless Grease ordered my head up in the astrodome looking for fighters. The astrodome was a bubble of perspex, big enough for your head, behind the office – that's what we called the cockpit. There was a good moon: not full, but getting on that way, and at 18,000 feet we were about 600 above a shallow, dense, cold cloud layer that stretched all the way to Germany – allegedly it would thin about thirty miles from target. In light almost as clear as day we could see aircraft all around us – maybe 250 of them in front, and 600 following. On the Home Service they spoke of 'aerial armadas' going to Germany night after night.

For the first time I wondered about the poor old Kraut underneath. The black bombers seemed to swim forward slowly, gently moving up and down in the airstream as if they were puppet aeroplanes on invisible strings; it was awesome. Before Grease ordered me back down, I saw one brief bright yellow and crimson flash maybe a mile or so ahead, followed by green lights slowly tumbling from the sky. They were target indicator flares – TIs: that was a Pathfinder dying.

Grease clicked the RT and said, 'Night fighters, chaps: that's one of the Pathfinder's gone. Nav, please note that.'

'Roger, Skipper.'

From Marty up front there was, 'He had six green TIs. They burned on the way down.'

Conroy said, 'OK. I logged it.'

Grease again: 'OK, everyone. Pete, watch for them coming up out of that cloud.'

'Roger, Skipper.'

'Charlie, listen out for the fighter controllers. And yell out if you get the bad feeling.'

'Roger, Skipper.'

Situation normal. You didn't like to say that you were scared shitless, just in case anyone agreed with you. The 'bad feeling' was something funny that happened to W/Ops from time to time: you could hear the German night fighter controllers on the ground vectoring a fighter on to some poor sod, and even if it was in German, and in codes which changed weekly, you sometimes *knew* that the poor sod in question was you. It's not something I can explain. It happened. They even warned you about it in training. It had happened twice in seven trips so far. Conroy noted seven other Lancs going down that night, and Marty remarked later that there had been something peculiarly awful about seeing it in such a plain light.

As I said, it was a milk run for us. The target area was clearly marked and glowing red with a hundred fires by the time we drove serenely over it. Marty did a neat, sharp job – minimum time over target – and got the photographs to prove it. Grease put the nose down and dived for the suburbs along the same vector, took the course home from Conroy, and lifted us into and through that deadly cloud layer again. We saw a lot less aircraft on the way back. It was always the same: you got into a fight, or some bastard above you dropped his bombs on you – you know the sort of thing. So the stream was always spread out and at different heights on the way home.

About five minutes from the Dutch border Peter the Pole yelled out, 'Corkscrew port, fighter,' followed immediately by, 'No, it's a Lanc.'

I suppose we lost, then gained, about a hundred feet in a great lurch.

Grease asked, 'OK, Pete?'

The Pole replied, 'Yeah. OK. It's a Lanc. It came up out of the cloud in the fighter position.' Then he added, 'It's taken a hell of a bloody thump, though!'

Although I was standing with my head in the astrodome I still couldn't see the newcomer because it was below and behind us. I felt Grease weave us gently to starboard, to get out of its way, but even so it took its time. It was struggling to reach our height, barely skimming the cloud cover before pulling another few feet. Grease let down alongside it; maybe forty feet out. It had our squadron codes and a big red 'P' on its side.

Fergal said, 'P-*Peter*. It's a bit of a mess. Isn't that Gerry Brookman?'

I offered, 'He never took your advice, Skip.'

Grease snapped, 'Shut up. Not amused.'

Fergal eased our throttles back to match our speed with Brookman's kite. That was when we got a proper look at it. Grease sounded characteristically in touch with events – as he invariably was when he had his hands and feet on an aircraft. He said, 'Rear gunner, keep sweeping for fighters. You too, Toff. And Marty.' They all rogered in sequence. Then he told me, 'Sparks – see if you can speak to them. They may not know all of the damage.'

I ran one long ranging glance along *Peter* before I dropped out of the astrodome to my radios. There were great chunks out of the tail turret, and the barrels of its four .303 machine guns slopped drunkenly downwards, bouncing slightly with the aircraft. The holes in the starboard side of the fuselage seemed like exit holes to me. No port rudder. Their astrodome had been shot away, and there were bits of the canopy flapping – it must have been desperately cold in there. The starboard outer engine, nearest to us, was shut down and the propeller was windmilling, but quite slowly – I couldn't make out if it had been fully feathered – and there were burn stains around it which suggested that a fierce fire had been successfully extinguished. Brookman looked across at me and waved a hand slowly, as if it had suddenly become too heavy; he might even have been trying a tired, tight smile. Where was his engineer?

'P-*Peter*, P-*Peter* . . . this is *Yoke*.'

Their W/Op's flat south country vowels came calmly back at me. Sometimes you can be quite proud of your fellow in trade.

'Hello, Charlie. We got roasted back there.'

'Hello, Paul. The pilot wants to know if you want us to spot your damage for you.'

'Wait one, *Yoke*. I'll ask my skipper. He's got his hands full at present.' There was no air of urgency. But his signal was weak. When he came back, it was with a very snappy, 'Y-*Yoke*, Y-*Yoke*, P-*Peter*.'

'Yes, Paul?'

'The skipper says, yes please. Don't worry about the holes and the cockpit, we can see them ourselves, and we know there's no left rudder: but we haven't heard from the tail since the attack, and can't get it moved or opened; and also – what does the starboard outer look like on your side? There's also a personal message for your skipper.'

'Send.'

'Gerry says, don't waste your bullets – he says your boss will understand.'

I closed down, went forward again, and shouted the gen close to Grease's right ear. He nodded, then pointed to me. He had that determined glint in his eyes that always worried me. On the intercom he said, 'Gunners. We're dropping behind P-*Peter* to examine her damage. Keep watching for those fighters.'

Conroy's voice cut in: 'Just crossed Dutch border, Skip. Change of course fifteen minutes.'

'Thanks, Nav. Hold on everyone.'

I don't know what he did, but *Tuesday's Child* seemed to stop in mid-air, and at the same time drop about fifty feet, whilst the ponderous P-*Peter* drew ahead, taking my stomach with him. Then Grease pulled us slowly up to within about twenty feet of his tail. The port side of the rear turret – the side which had been away from us – was badly shattered. There was an infrequent blue spark from an electrical short inside it. The gunner was slumped against the perspex with his face towards us.

As we got in close Marty said, 'I can see him: I can see his face, he's . . .' Then there was a long pause before he finished flatly, 'Tell them he's exceptionally dead. I can see his eyes.'

Fergal wrote on his pad, so that I could see it, a capital 'P', which he circled, followed by *No fire. Slow oil leak. No visible damage to wing. No aileron damage. Fuselage damage? Hydraulics?* I held my thumb up to show I understood, and turned to leave him. Grease grabbed my arm, touched his mask mike and said, 'Tell Gerry to try to gain another couple of hundred feet. We'll fly astern and below him, in his blind spot, and watch out for him. Radio him our course changes as they come up.'

I did the thumbs up thing again. As I squeezed back past Conroy to my radios he handed me a scrap of paper with the imminent course change and time on it. I passed P-*Peter*'s radio op the information we had. His response, apart from a terse 'Thanks,' was, 'The heading's particularly useful; we've only one nav between the two of us.'

There are some things you don't want to think about. Among them are what the inside of an aircraft looks like after Stripping the Willow with a Jerry night fighter. After we made the turn, and were doing a slow waltz, to extend the metaphor, across Holland towards home, Conroy came on and said, 'Excuse me for mentioning it, Skip, but is this a *good* idea? We're making twice the radar target than we would on our own, and flying at *their* pace, not ours. If the nasty Hun comes out of the cloud, we will be between it and Brookman: he'll see *us* first.'

Grease had that icily reasonable edge to his voice that was always there when he was going to be stupid: 'That's the idea, Conners. Gives Pete the chance of his second kill.' Then he added, 'Their rear gunner's dead, and if their hydraulics and electrics are shot, then they've no mid-upper or front guns to speak of, either. We stay: Brookman would do the same for us.'

Conroy said, 'Brookman's a cunt. He hates you.'

Grease said, quietly, but we all heard him, 'Brookman's wounded.'

'How do you figure that, Skip?' from the Toff, who had been uncharacteristically quiet on this trip.

'Dunno. But he is. Now shut up everyone. Dutch coast ahead, Nav?'

'Six minutes, Skip.'

We gave Manston plenty of warning this time, and Brookman made a very low, very straight approach. We watched his wheels lock down. Grease flew a parallel as we watched *Peter*'s touchdown. And then flew a slow, low circuit of the airfield to see him stopped. It was a grade-B landing, but everything held together. As *Peter* pulled away on to the peri-track Paul Nash called, 'Thanks,' and, 'see you later.'

At Bawne we were the last one down, not counting Brookman, and the last crew interrogated by intelligence – a new, pretty WAAF officer. Bushes had got back first, but he was still there, alongside her. We had to tell him twice that Brookman's kite had made it. Bushes was becoming detached, I thought. Not quite with us. He stumped moodily to the hut door, but when Grease asked him, 'How many'd we lose tonight, sir?' He swung back on us and glowered, because it was one of those questions an Englishman doesn't ask.

Then he beamed, and barked, 'None. None at all. Bloody hallelujah.'

Bushes paraded the crew the next morning. *Another fucking bawling out* was what was going through my mind as we squeezed into his overheated office. I was sure that he was going to tell us that Brookman was going to get *Tuesday's Child* away from us. He looked tired; Bushes always looked tired these days. When had he stopped looking angry and started to look tired? I wondered how many trips he'd done this time round. What he said was, 'Gerry Brookman won't be flying for a while. There's a bit of his leg missing.'

'I figured that,' said Grease. 'He was flying very carefully. Very neat. Usually he's a bit flash; almost sloppy.'

Bushes shook his head and glanced out of the window, cross-hatched with a cream-coloured tape which was peeling, then back at us, before responding.

'There you go again, goon. I try to do it by the book, and tell you what a fine job you all did last night, and you spoil it before I start. *Don't* insult your senior rank: not in front of me, anyway.'

'OK, sir. You got me there.'

'Doesn't alter it, does it? You did a good thing last night. A good thing, a brave thing . . .'

'Probably a stupid thing . . . sir,' said Conroy and looked pointedly at Grease. We all saw that, but Bushes ignored him.

'. . . and Brookman and his crew – they all made it except Tallow, the rear gunner, by the way – anyway they're all asking for you to be put up for it. They want gongs all round for a shower like you lot!'

'They're just glad to be alive,' said Grease. 'They'll soon get over it.' Then he remembered and added, 'Sir.'

'*I* won't, and I just wanted you to know that, even if you *can* whistle for your medals. I wanted to say thank you, that's all. Old-fashioned sort of phrase, isn't it?'

'But rarely misplaced I think,' said our Pole. He gave Bushes an oddly Germanic little bow which seemed to start chest high, and added, 'And we thank you for it, sir.'

Conroy, who had a professional interest, asked him what had happened to the nav.

'Cannon shell exploded in the cabin. Blinded him – temporarily the doc thinks – burned all his exposed flesh.'

'His hands,' murmured Conners, 'and his face. I wondered why he couldn't plot.'

'Now you know, son. Keep your gloves on out there in the wild night sky.'

'Yes, Boss,' said Conroy. The exchange had put it back into a formal mode, which made us more comfortable.

'Anyway,' said Bushes, 'it's written into your service records. Bloody good show. Now, carry on.' And when we hadn't moved for surprise, 'Yes; that's it. Bugger off.'

Outside I asked Piotr if he had known Tallow, the gunner. The Pole spread the fingers of his left hand then moved it this way and that – not so well, I guessed.

I explained. 'He was the only happy Yorkshireman I've ever met. Could sink a few when he had a mind to.'

Paluchowski said, 'He was too big. For the turret — it meant that his head moved too slow.'

'Not any more.'

'I see the welfare committee. Maybe he had some good things. We can buy them.'

Sometimes the little sod took his cold-bloodedness too far.

Berlin

We didn't fly the next night; just mooched around. The night after we went to Berlin, and the night after we went there again. That made ten, and three in one week was the most we'd flown up until then. The first trip was OK, as Berlin trips go. Near Terschelling on the return trip the Toff saw a night fighter flying about 500 yards from us, parallel and above. It was an Me 410 Toff says. As all our guns swung towards it Grease clicked, and forbad them to fire. We must have flown in company like that for miles, moving out over the North Sea, when suddenly the Kraut did a half-roll away from us, and dropped into a vertical dive. Marty watched him all the way down. There were no parachutes.

There was a click, and Marty came on. 'What the fuck happened to him?'

'Dunno,' responded Grease, 'and I don't much care. Keep your eyes skinned for the next one.' But there weren't any, and for once we were the first home to Bawne.

We talked about the Jerry night fighter while we kicked around waiting for the crew bus to pick us up from the dispersal. Grease said, as if we were still in the middle of a conversation, 'Yeah. That was funny, that.'

The Toff grinned and asked us, 'I saw him before he saw us. Do you think that I can claim a kill?'

'I think that they simply went to sleep. Maybe they were dead already.'

'I think I *looked* him to death. Let's tell intelligence that.'

So we did. We had the pick of the room, so we chose the new WAAF intelligence officer. She wrote down that we had looked the Kraut to death. Marty tried to date her, and she turned him down. Piotr tried to date her, and she said *yes*. We didn't push off immediately, but hung around waiting for some of the others to come in.

You don't want to hear about the second away game to Berlin. We didn't get into trouble, but loads of others did, and we had to watch. The returning stream was unusually compact that night – like sheep bunching up in fear of wolves. We flew down the stream overtaking ruined aeroplane after ruined aeroplane, knowing that many of them couldn't possibly make it back. The Toff kept on coming in over the intercom whistling 'Let's Face the Music and Dance', until Grease told him to belt up. But the tune got inside my head and stayed there.

At the debriefing Conroy refused to read the notes in his log. He sat alongside the little WAAF, and turned the pages as she read for herself. After the first half page her pretty mouth was pursed up tight. When she had finished she left out all of the really dumb questions she was supposed to ask, and let us go quickly. I saw Bushes and his crew at another table; a nerve under his left eye was twitching uncontrollably, but I don't think that he even noticed it.

In the hut I threw myself fully clothed on to my bed. I was too tired to undress, and no one was saying anything at all. Except Grease:

'That wasn't war; that was just bloody slaughter,' he said. And he had said it for all of us.

I awoke with a real start the next morning, having dreamed I was still in *Yoke Tuesday* suspended over that roiling red mess we had made of central Berlin. I knew that I was in her because I could smell her all around me, and smell burning Berlin, which had got inside the aircraft. I spotted my mistake as I opened my eyes. It was my clothes which had the smell of her, of course, and my face was buried in my tunic sleeve as my arm cradled my head in sleep. I had been breathing her in all night — what was left of it, anyway. It was a mistake I tried never to make again: no matter how tired. I went outside and gave my head the cold water treatment. Grease appeared about five minutes later, and commenced stretches and press-ups in the homely drizzle which was a feature of our Bawne life.

'What's up with you?' he asked.

'Didn't sleep well. Dreams.'

'Do I want to hear about them?'

'I shouldn't think so.'

'That's all right then.'

But it wasn't, because the morning proved that several of them had made similar nocturnal excursions, and eventually told Grease. His reaction, ever unpredictable, was to hop on the Indian and disappear for ten minutes. When he came back he had three crates of Muggles bottled beer in the sidecar, and announced, 'No ops tonight. Blowing a sodding gale right across Europe for a change. Apparently we could get there in less than half the usual time, because the wind speeds are as high as we can fly flat out.'

Conroy yawned – he was stretched on his pallet – 'That means we fly off Tuesday, and arrive in Krautland before we set out.'

'Bollocks,' from Grease, 'it means that no matter how far we get, we couldn't get back. We'd keep being driven east; might end up in some godforsaken Arab country.'

'Wherever,' said Marty, finally starting to pay some attention to what was going on, 'it's got to be better than here.'

'In Mesopotamia they cut your bollocks off for just *looking* at their women,' the Toff contributed.

Marty said, 'In that case I withdraw my last comment. Mesopotamia's worse than here.'

'Worse than Berlin probably.' That was Fergal. Pete was quiet. He was often quiet, but you could see his dark, smiling polecat eyes glancing from face to face as we spoke. Lying in the billet in comparative safety, swigging beer from cold, old bottles, and no flying tonight – I can remember that as one of the good feelings. Isn't that crazy? Now I know that it was better than sex. In 1944 I would have argued with you over that.

After two bottles Grease said, 'From now on flying clothes get dumped in the porch. There's a hook for each of us and one over. We might as well start using them.'

73

I suppose that we were fortunate. Each of the accommodation huts for NCOs at Bawne had been built to a different pattern. It was a design evaluation exercise carried out early in the war. Some, for instance, had room for fourteen or twenty-one beds – and eventually became the standard pattern. Ours, as I told you, had eight, and had a narrow porch tacked on to the front door, which faced out towards the runways, and a washroom with two latrines at the stern. It was an experiment to see if you could keep a Nissen hut warmer if you had a double door to keep in what the stove generated. It would have worked if the wind and the winter air against the single-skin corrugated-iron walls of our gin palace hadn't sucked the heat straight out through the metal and the ill-fitting window frames.

'Anyway,' said Grease, 'I'm glad I don't have to get back into *Tuesday* with you lot tonight. You look fucked. Especially you, Charlie. As it is, we've got beer – and . . .'

'Brandy,' said the Pink Pole, 'four bottles of Polish brandy.'

'Polish brandy. Which several of you are going to drink to death before you sleep the afternoon away, to catch up.'

Fergal observed, 'Grease, you may be the skipper up there, but down here the Royal Democratic Air Force likes to think of us as simple sergeants: equals.'

'The RAF got it wrong,' muttered the Canadian. 'If God approved of democracies he would have made everyone the same size. He didn't, and I'm bigger than you lot. Do as you're bloody well told.'

I think that my pillow hit him fractionally before the Toff's. The rest followed.

Lunch that day had been RAF dog-meat stew and dumplings,

followed by a 1941 vintage jam pudding, paddling in make-believe custard. I suppose that they did their best. The fat flight lieutenant who ran the joint bawled, and chased the mess staff around. We were in what was now our usual corner of the dump, at our usual table, which was being cleared by a girl who looked about fourteen years old. She had a livid fresh bruise on her right cheekbone. I asked her how she had collected that, but she lied to me, looking over my head and saying, 'Fell off me bike, Sergeant.' She giggled. Her mouth was smiling but her eyes weren't.

After she left Grease leaned over the table and gave me a friendly poke in the chest with one of his big fingers. He always did that if he wanted you to remember something.

'Remind me,' he said, 'to do something about that.'

We all sat longer over mugs of tea than we intended, and Marty observed, 'Look, Skip, leaving anything I fly in outside the hut might be a small problem. I haven't got much else. I've got nothing more than my first issue, and that was incomplete and some of it's well shagged.'

'Is OK,' from Piotr. 'We all need more uniform. Isn't it so?'

We couldn't disagree with him. Group stores officers were so notoriously parsimonious with uniform issue that Butch had dubbed one squadron the 'Flying Scarecrows' after inspecting a neighbouring bomber station.

Fergal must have read my mind. He said, 'We could always send a signal to Butch: I don't think he ever takes a day off.'

'I'll fix it,' the Pink Pole said. 'You give me your sizes . . . you say "sizes"?'

'We say sizes,' Marty confirmed.

'Give me your sizes tonight. I'll fix it. I have contacts.'

I didn't doubt it. We'd all end up with Polish admirals' dress whites. Conroy blew on his tea and asked, 'Leaving all that gear in the outside porch, or whatever you call it . . . What happens if some bugger nicks it all?'

'From *my* hut?' said Grease.

I didn't doubt him either. I took a sleep that Monday afternoon. No dreams.

An LAC cycled over from ops just as we were all waking up and thinking about the evening. I had a sinking feeling about the note he carried. Perhaps we were to fly after all, but no, ops had taken a signal from Grace's ATA mob in the place that new Lancasters come from. She was bringing a second new Lanc in on Thursday. Their operations room respectfully requested that Sergeant McKenzie make the same arrangements as before for the accommodation of their pilot. Grease read the note, and nodded slowly. Twice. He told the LAC to signal back that base accommodation had been booked.

Neumunster

On Tuesday we went to Neumunster and made such a hash of it that we knew in our hearts that we'd have to come back again, even as Grease dived away from our *bombs gone*.

He dived to starboard this time. Two leading Pathfinders had been shot down close to each other in fields maybe five miles from the city – and most of the sheep in front of us bombed on their burning target indicators and corpses. They were probably the best bombed corpses in Germany that night. Conners was adamant that they were in the wrong place, and put us over the centre of the darkened city, where Marty thought he acquired the target and toggled our bombs – which were the curate's egg: a 4,000 pound cookie for main course, with a speckling of 500s for afters. The black city seemed to swallow our bombs, belch, and forget them. Marty reported no fires on the ground. We saw one or two bombers over the target – but they were Halifaxes: from 4 Group most like, and the Toff called out for a fighter, and pulled his triggers, as we left the Fatherland between Husum and Heide. We had been warned of Ju 88 night fighters haunting this stretch of coast.

Over the North Sea, as the sweat was beginning to cool in our suits, Grease clicked and said, 'There weren't many of us over your target, Conners.'

Marty chipped in. 'Don't worry, Skip: Conners got it right. That *was* the target – or near enough anyway. Those other two or three hundred were bombing shit out of some pig farm in the Kraut wilderness.'

'Rear gunner to pilot.'

'Yes, Pete?'

'You'll soon know about it in the morning, Skip; if we got it wrong the Boss will put you on the carpet first thing. I bet you.'

'Thanks for that.'

Half an hour later as we were letting down over the Wash he did it again.

'Rear gunner to pilot.'

'What is it, Pete?'

'A Mosquito has been trailing us for half a minute. I'm sure he's friendly: I saw him before he saw us.'

'Where is he now?'

'400 yards behind us and level. He's playing silly buggers. Probably calibrating his radar.'

'Fire off the colours of the day please, Sparks, just in case.'

That was for me. It was one of the jobs I hated. You could identify yourself to friends by banging off a couple of agreed coloured flares down the flare chute. The colour combinations varied at the whim of some cog in the high command's squeaking wheel. I hated the feeling of exposure I experienced as I left those glowing colours hanging in the air. But Piotr saved me that time. He called Grease.

'*I* give them the colours, Skip!' and must have pressed his tits immediately. His four .303 machine guns rattled for a good two seconds before Grease screamed him down.

Even the Toff grumbled. 'For *Christ's sake*, Pete!'

'He's gone,' said our Pole, and, 'Chicken!'

That was a word he must have picked up from the Americans. The first controller I picked up was 1 Group, as we approached the coast close to Mabelthorpe. It was the temporary station, and was using the call sign *Hardbottle*. He sounded like a laid-back recycled RFC type, gave us the friendly 'Heighho' then said, 'Some night fighter training squadron's complaining about one of theirs being fired on by one of ours. Specifically a big black job like you. Wouldn't *be* you by any chance, old boy?'

'Negative, *Hardbottle*. We saw off an 88 over the Wash. Nothing friendly has shown us the COD.'

'Roger, *Yoke*. I'm sure I understand that. Your people have been informed.'

'Informed of what?' muttered Grease over the intercom, 'That we're on our way back, or that we tried to shoot down one of our neighbours?' then he went all skipperish on us again, and said, 'Keep your eyes peeled lads, the Kraut's still out there, even if we're nearly home.' He was right of course. Through the astrodome I scanned the yellow streaks in the early morning sky. Unless you were looking for where death was hiding, it could be beautiful, but death was almost always there, inside your head. Grease had used a word that I liked, though: he had said 'home'.

Late morning, when we were showing again, the ground crew chief passed word for Grease. Fergal and I went with him out of curiosity. When we climbed out of the little Singer, which we parked out of the standard Bawne drizzle under *Tuesday*'s great port wing, Chiefy said, 'Where the fuck *were* you last night?'

'Place called Neumunster we think, why?' That was Fergal. No point in Grease taking all the flak.

'You seen the belly, and the bomb doors?'

We hadn't, but we did now. From just under the pilot's office, to six feet short of the tail, it was pitted with flak, and paint scrapes. What was remarkable, then, and forever after, was that not one of the seven of us could remember it happening, even though it had probably made a hell of a bloody noise at the time. Oddly, although the skin surface was bent and scarred, there were no perforations – the flak must have exploded at just beyond its effective range.

Grease did the tugging at his upper lip thing again; perhaps it was the beginning of a twitch. He said, 'Mother Germany reached up last night, and gave us a kiss. God bless Mother Germany. When's she going to be ready again, Chiefy?'

'Tomorrow. We'll press the dents out from the inside, and give her a lick of paint.'

Just then Pete roared up on the Red Indian. 'I told you,' he said to Grease, 'the CO wants you for a bollocking. I'll give you a ride over there.'

*

Grease tells it like this.

After the argument Bushes asks him, 'Where the fuck were *you* last night?'

His desk is covered in large target photographs, and he doesn't look a happy man. Situation normal, but the twitch is back.

Grease says, 'Dropping high explosives all over the good folk of Neumunster, previous to our visit a jewel in the crown of the Reich, now a little bit second hand . . . sir.'

'And the silly bloody thing about it is that you *were*, too.' He waves our bombing pattern photograph at Grease. 'Only a dozen aircraft even found the right city last night; and you and your team of morons were in one of them. What the hell am I going to do with you?'

'Gongs and caviar all round, sir?'

'That's the problem, you dumb Canuk: if you reward twelve crews for finding a target the size of Leicester, then you might as well phone up the *Mirror* and confess that the other 300 didn't! That would be bloody wonderful for civvy morale, wouldn't it?'

'No gongs and presentation leave yet then, sir?'

'Sod off, McKenzie, and stop spoiling my days.'

Grease said that the odd thing was by the end of the conversation he was getting quite fond of the old stick. The argument which preceded that had been about Sergeant Quelch's failure to get airborne for the same operation.

The Quelch crew were a set of beginners. Neumunster was to be their second or third op together. At the last minute they couldn't get their bomb doors shut, and cancelled their booking.

Bushes had been calling off Quelch for a coward before Grease arrived, and threatened him and his crew with a grade-A posting to latrine duties. Looking more depressed by Bushes than the enemy, Quelch had slunk out as Grease arrived. Grease said that the poor little sod looked like a fourteen-year-old caught playing truant.

Grease thought this unreasonable, and told Bushes this as soon as he was stood easy. He said that he wouldn't have flown all the way to Germany and back with the bomb doors open either.

Neumunster

On Thursday we went back to Neumunster and shat liberally all over it. We had been given the signal honour of leading the squadron's bold boyos into action that night. Bushes had grabbed Grease's arm as we left the main briefing and snarled.

'You do realize that it's because you're the only sod who appears to know the sodding way, don't you?'

The flak was worse this time: our previous visit must have annoyed them.

Throughout the bomb run a Lancaster formatted on us at the same height, and about thirty yards behind. It attracted all the predicted flak we were too early for, and flew straight through it. Piotr told us he had a view of it all the way, and it was the coolest, bravest flying he had ever seen. Gong material. The pilot must have told his bomb aimer to let go when we did, which must have given someone down there a bad surprise. The Lanc stayed with us as Grease dived away – straight ahead this time – to turn back across Germany to the North Sea. It landed the same distance behind us. The Pole said it was a great landing.

Grease's landfall wasn't so good – more like a controlled crash, which must have popped out a few of *Tuesday*'s rivets. When we finally strolled to a standstill at our dispersal the Toff called out, 'Why don't you get Chiefy to take all the wheels off, Skipper, and replace them with springs? Then you could bounce her down the runway on purpose.'

When we were out on the concrete I noticed that Grease was holding his arm oddly again; the cramp must have returned. I asked him, 'Do you think that Grace is in yet?' and got a tired smile.

The crew bus picked us up, and then went on for the bods who had followed us across Neumunster and back like a faithful dog on a short lead; it had been Quelch, of course.

At the debrief Grease eschewed the pretty WAAF IO's table for the one alongside Bushes' crew.

It must have been an odd moment for Grace. The stove was still on. It was usually dead by the time we got in after a trip; she must have kept it alive for us. I was first in through the door, dressed in grubby white silk long johns, a silk vest decorated with sweat stains and a couple of ragged holes, and thin black woollen socks. We were leaving our outer clobber outside, remember? The six piling through the door behind me were similarly unattired. I stopped dead when I saw Grace (*Take heart of Grace, thy steps retrace, poor wandering one* – that's W. S. Gilbert), and the others slammed into me, then fanned out. I had already forgotten that she would be there. She had pulled one of our old upright wooden chairs as close to the stove as she could, and was turned away from it, towards us, as we blundered in. She was wearing white: what we called in those days silk French knickers – kind of high-waisted with wide loose legs – and a short white silk wrap, which she hadn't bothered to button or tie, and paint on her toenails. In fact that's what she was doing as we came in. She had one ankle up on a knee, and was painting them.

She gave us one of the up and down looks that Lauren Bacall became famous for later, and murmured, 'Now now, boys. Not all at once.'

From the fear, to the let-down of the intelligence debriefing, to a pretty girl with a few clothes on who could crack good jokes. The laughter was very good for us. It did the trick.

Later I told her, 'Grease's arm's not too good again.'

'I think I know what to do about that,' she said, and linked her arm in his and almost *marched* him the length of the hut, to good old number eight. They looked like a bride and groom from an American movie about Camelot: her in her shimmering white silk, and him in his white and tarnished armour. Well; almost. They pulled the partition curtains around the bed, and we didn't see them again until daylight. Situation normal, I was beginning to think.

I met Grease outside again at about 0800. I was first to the fire bucket, and his arm seemed to be working again. He was doing arm swings to warm himself up before his run. I asked him if the other bits were working as well. He gave me the pained look he was so bad at – the one that says *would you tell me, if I asked you that?* He was right: probably I wouldn't.

I did a few stretches, just to see what it felt like. Bloody awful. Grease laughed. When I went back into Casa Nostra the stove was pulling again, the kettles were beginning to heat, and Grace was no longer alone. I don't want you to get the impression that she lay down with all of us each time she got back for a few days: she didn't – and if you'd known her then, you'd realize that that would have been perverse. She just did *most* of us, *some* of the time because that was . . . what she did. She was Grace. That was it. Finito. And if you got left out, you didn't feel too bad about it, because she was always better to you in other ways. Friendlier. And more flirtatious. In some ways the ones who didn't get the shag were the ones who had the best of her. It did occur to me, however, to wonder if, on those cold lonely flights from Manchester, she was looking forward to us, or just to Grease, because he had been the first?

The fat lieutenant's people in the mess cooked up the best fried bread in the world. They saved up the week's stale bread until Friday mornings, then served it fried in golden one-inch squares after the regular breakfast was a memory. They put one enormous soup tureen full of them on each table, with a small bowl of precious, coarse white sugar to dip it in. That taste combination of dripping, fried bread and sugar has meant utter luxury to me ever since.

The young girl's bruise was fading, but now she seemed to have a cut lip. Grease leaned towards me and the poke in my chest from his finger was more like a jab. He told me, 'I thought I asked you to remind me to do something about the fat bastard that runs this shop.'

'I'm reminding you now, Skip.'

'Well. Seeing as you've asked, I'll have to do something about it, won't I?'

We were accosted by the pretty WAAF intelligence officer outside. She slithered her bicycle to a halt in the middle of us in a flurry of flapping skirts, flashes of stocking tops, whistles and quick feels. It took Grease minutes to sort us out, and if the girl was left blushing, that's officers for you. She said, 'I've been looking for you lot since yesterday. Something terrible's happened.'

Piotr said, 'You just discovered that an officer like you can't date an NCO like me? We knew that. You should have known that when you said *yes*.'

'Don't be daft. It's not that. Of course I'll come out with you.'

Piotr's face assumed the expression of one of life's innocents – he replied gravely. 'Do not worry on my behalf, lady. I *always* come.'

We had heard Piotr in action before, so Grease did the *I-am-the-skipper* sorting out thing again before the conversation took the wholly pornographic direction that he was flying in. He asked her.

'What's so terrible Ma'am?'

'When you came back from Berlin. You were all amazing and so relaxed. I couldn't believe it: like boys out on a spree. That was one of my first . . . well, whatever I expected, it wasn't that. You were joking about a German night fighter that you'd seen crash. You wanted me to put in my report that Sergeant Mansell—'

'You mean the Toff.'

'Whatever you like . . . anyway you wanted me to report that he'd looked the fighter pilot to death. It sounded like fun, and there's precious little of that in my job here so far. So I did.'

'Sodding hell,' said Marty. 'I bet *that* went down well at group.'

'It would have done. I didn't believe that anyone actually read the debriefs I write. No one noticed. Not at first. Then some busybody picked it up, assumed I'd mistyped it, and amended it to read "shot the pilot to death". Now I've been sent a confidential memo asking me to confirm I've no objection to the amendment. I wanted to ask you first. What do you want me to tell them?'

'Sod them,' said Marty. 'Let them believe whatever they want.'

'And the Toff gets his first kill credit for killing nobody?' asked Grease ponderously. I wanted to shake him, but he would have probably shaken me back, and my teeth would have fallen out.

'Yes, I suppose so. If that's all right with you, and no one else finds out.'

Grease was great when he was decisive. He laid his big arm around the girl's shoulders and addressed the Pole. 'Pete, this lady is officially one of us. Take her to lunch on Sunday – we're paying – and give her a good time afterwards: if that's what she wants. Gentlemen all, take note that we now have a friend in intelligence.'

The WAAF blushed again and began to remount her bicycle. Piotr didn't blush. He helped her into the saddle, turned his Count of Monte Cristo smile on her, and asked, 'What *is* your name, my dear?' He made you want to vomit sometimes, but they invariably fell for it.

'Harriet,' the girl replied.

Walking away from her we agreed that it was a name we all liked. Nobody said that she had a nice bum; after all she was Pete's date. I wondered if we were going to tell Grace that there was another girl on the team, and what she'd feel about it if we did.

I suppose that I had better tell you some more about those bloody bomb doors.

Connors had got hold of some RN rolling tobacco, so four of us and Grace sat around the hut stove having a cigarette-rolling competition. Mine came out the size of matchsticks. Grace's could have passed for fags from a packet. The other three played cards on Pete's bed.

Grease was a great delegater. And if he delegated a job to someone who made an arse of it, he just delegated it again to someone else – until he ran out of bods; in which case he would do it himself – and usually make an arse of it too.

He said to me, 'Charlie, there's something the matter with the bloody bomb doors. That's why Quelch squelched the other night.'

'I thought you sent Fergal to find out. Didn't he ask Chiefy Bryan?'

'I did, and he did. Several times if I know Fergal. He's a persistent little bugger when he chooses to be. But the Chief's saying nothing. Fergal says he won't even *discuss* bomb doors. There are no longer such things as bomb bay doors apparently.'

'So what do you want me to do?'

'Find out what he knows, Charlie. He knows *something*. Buy it from him.'

'Just like that? What do I buy it with?'

'Whatever it takes. Ask Pete what we've got. There's bound to be something. Just *find out*. It's giving me the twitch.'

Marty met my eye and nodded. We didn't want Brother Grease with the twitch. Not over fucking Berlin or somewhere.

Grace said, 'Wait a mo; I'm coming too. I fancy some fresh air, but wait until I'm togged up for it.'

Grace could exhibit a curious, inconsistent coyness. She changed behind the curtains of berth eight, and when she came out she was wearing her shapeless old Sidcot flying suit, over small laced-up brown boots. By then I had crossed to the Pole. He was playing rummy with Fergal and the Toff, and had heard every word of the exchange without taking his eyes from his cards. We had three liberated lockers by his bed, all with small padlocks; we called them the loot boxes: Piotr reached inside his tunic and fished out three keys on a piece of string from around his neck. He said, 'Help yourself. Whatever it takes.'

I shoved a small kitbag full of goodies up into the nose of the sidecar: Grace got in on top of it as I was kicking the Indian into life. The late afternoon sun was making a rare autumn appearance, and the bitter little wind that seemed to curse bomber airfields throughout the war had dropped. Even swaddled into her ten times too large all-in-one, with its matted fur collar turned up to conceal her hair, I thought that Grace looked quite the thing; exotic.

' . . . an inward and a spiritual *grace*,' I said.

'Ah, Charlie. You betray your learning. You've read books.'

'Church; when I was small. It's from the catechism.'

'It's the "inward" bit I'm interested in these days!'

Her directness could be disconcerting, but I had to come back at her. 'I know that Grace, but let it keep until after we've snared the Chiefy and solved the mystery of the bomb bay doors – sounds like an Edgar Wallace.'

'You'll write better than that one day.'

First things first. *Tuesday's Child* wasn't where we had last left her on her dispersal pan. That's the sort of discovery which gives you an immediate bad feeling. The ground crew had made themselves a neat little hut alongside the dispersal, from a small covered goods railway wagon which had lost its wheels it had been a chicken coop in Bawne's peaceful farming days. Sited on the grass alongside *Tuesday*'s round concrete parking space, it was usually crouched under one of her huge wings, but that afternoon it was alone, and ruling the roost. They had kitted it out well with a cooking brazier, bench seats and cupboards, but had never quite rid it of the heady aroma of hen pen, with which it glowed in summer.

Only two of the working airmen, or Erks, were there. The elder, Wally, came from Bawne village and had once been a farm labourer on the very ground they planted our airfield into. He had a wife and child less than two miles away. He described the difference between his pre-war and wartime work as, 'more bosses, more pay, less hours, no horses' – unless you counted the hundreds sitting in the engines along *Tuesday*'s wings of course. I brought the Indian combination to a reasonably decorous halt by the open sliding side door of the hut. I noticed that they had recently camouflaged it with green and black paint: touching. We smelled bacon, ground crews for the cooking of.

Wally stuck his head out of the ex-coop and asked, 'Want a sarnie, ducks?' I assumed he was asking Grace. Either that or I was in trouble. She half laughed, half giggled, and shook her head.

'Where's the kite? Where are the rest of our people?' I asked him.

'Down at the T2. Chiefy had something he wanted done inside. He wanted it finished today. Nothing to do with me, Sergeant. I'm only a fitter.'

'Bomb doors, is it?'

''Ow do you know about them now?'

'You know, Wally. Word gets about.'

'So don't go telling him I told you.'

'Course not,' I said, and kicked the bus into life again.

The T2-type hangar the Erk had spoken of was one of our two big hangars – each about 200 feet wide and 350 feet long. They were made completely from sheets of corrugated steel, prefabricated in factories in the Midlands, and erected on site. In high winds they shook, creaked and whistled like a sailing ship in a storm. Looking back they were constructions so much ahead of their time – form dictated by function. I wonder why more of them weren't listed for preservation. I suppose that after the war we just couldn't wait to pull down anything that reminded us of it. We only had the two T2s. And four smaller blister hangars which also could take a Lanc apiece if need be – they were also corrugated steel, but shaped like great flat arches: no straight walls. They still build hardened hangars that shape today. The truth is that Lancs were designed to be worked on mainly in the open air, which is what the poor sods of ground crews did most of the time. If they dragged one into a hangar it was either for a big job, or because they didn't want anyone else to see what they were doing to it.

Our nearest T2 was three-quarters of a mile along a perimeter track as straight as a Roman road, and as wide as the Railway Straight at Brooklands. I got the Indian's speed indicator jammed against the stop at eighty miles per hour before we were halfway along it. Grace let out a wild long shriek of excitement and pleasure, and her hair, flipped out of the fur collar of her suit by the speed, stood up as if she had been electrocuted. Slowing down wasn't as easy: there was a complicated brake on the motorbike's sidecar which was out of sync with the bike; it threatened to take us ploughing the infield. I caught the slide we went into as we hit the square of roughened concrete in front of the T2. I aimed at the open doors – not easy to miss because of the gap they left – but stopped the beast before it slid across the portal and into the gloomy hangar. A crowd of ground crew Erks waiting around the doors had to scatter out of the way – like peewits sometimes scattered in front of our aircraft in spring – and when I turned to Grace I saw that her face had turned quite white.

Chiefy Bryan was under *Tuesday*. Her bomb doors were open, and he had set up a small trestle workbench on the hangar floor, underneath and virtually inside her. The scattered Erks regathered outside in the fading light and lurked – the Chief would either need some light from somewhere soon, or would have to stop working. He appeared to be dismounting the individual bomb shackles, and everything he could reach in the bomb bay, washing and scrubbing them in petrol, greasing them and bolting them back into place. Routine maintenance, except that *Tuesday* was only about three weeks old. Because we were hidden by the bomb bay doors the Erks in the doorway couldn't see what gave – which was just as well. They could probably see our legs from the knees down.

I offered, 'Forgive me for asking, Chiefy, but seeing as *you're* the ranker here, how is it that you're in here doing all the work, whilst those shiftless sods of Erks of yours outside are hanging about watching you?'

'Nice of you to come straight to the point, Charlie, so I'll do the same. It's that Bawne Billy again.'

'Sounds disgusting. Is that a disease or a goat?'

Whilst we spoke Grace began to unpack the goodie bag, piling two bottles, chocolate, a slab of butter, nylon stockings and a round tin of fifty cigarettes on to his small workbench. He transferred his attention to them from the bits of bomb bay disassembled around us, stopped working and wiped his hands on what was obviously a petrol-soaked rag.

He said, 'A bit of both. And neither. Bawne Bill's a ghost: a dead person. An aviator from the *last* flap come back to visit. Not that I *believe* in ghosts, you understand? He haunts this

94

hangar, usually at around dusk, so after 1500 I can't get any of those yellow bleeders in here.'

'Don't take the piss, Chiefy. This is a new airfield. It wasn't *here* during the Great War, and it definitely hasn't been here long enough to pick up some old ghost. Threaten them. Put them up on charges.'

'Doesn't do any good. They'd rather do jankers than be in here at nightfall. I put the whole damn crew in front of Mr Delve last week, and he let them off. Said it wouldn't do for morale to force the point.'

'He's fucking obsessed with morale! Where did the ghost story come from?'

'Dunno.' He held a bottle of Scotch up so that what light there was caught its label. He mouthed the words on it as he read them. Then he said, 'It's supposed to be the ghost of a First World War airman who shot down a Zeppelin near here, but crashed himself, and was killed, so he never reported it, and never got the credit. I think that the anti-aircraft batteries in Cambridge got the shiny medals for that one; someone always does. A few weeks later some other flying corps type shoots down another Zep somewhere down south, Hornchurch way I think. Only he lives to tell the tale, gets the VC, and the undying fame of being the first man to bring one down. Bawne Billy is still supposed to be peeved about being overlooked, and is still hanging around here for his medal.'

'Why here?'

'Why not? They say he fell in the fields about here: certainly a Zep fell the other side of Bawne in 1917. Our Wally's got some of its girders holding up his greenhouse back home.'

'That's all crap, Chiefy. Now tell us what's the matter with the bomb doors.'

'Nothing as far as I knows.'

'So why have you got the bomb bay in pieces?'

'Routine maintenance.' His tone was light. The light was worse. He was squinting at the whisky bottle label now.

'On a new Lanc? That's crap too, Chiefy.'

Grace was impatient. She was at one end of his small workbench, and I was at the other. Chief Bryan stood in the middle, facing us. He was examining our offerings, but wouldn't look at us. He looked distinctly uncomfortable. Twice he wiped his hands against his overalls – and it wasn't to get them clean; I think that it was to dry off the sweat. He was a regular: lying to flying crew did not come naturally.

I said, 'Chief, I've got to *fly* this thing. I'm one of the guys you expect to bring her home each morning. If there's something the matter with her you've got to tell me.'

Grace made a disrespectful snorting noise. At my lack of progress, I think. Maybe she was just that much more direct than the rest of us. It's what her father had hinted at.

She moved very close to the old man. He probably wasn't old, but, what the hell, I was twenty. What was he? In his forties? Grace had got about halfway down her buttons when she leaned against him, looped an arm around his neck and kissed him. She had to stand on tiptoe. She had backed him away from the bench until his back was against one of the open bomb bay doors. Nowhere left to go, Chiefy. It creaked as his weight went against it. No problem. Situation normal.

When she let him up for air he said, 'No, Miss. You don't—'

'No one can see us. No one except Charlie here . . .' and lunged at him again.

I suppose that was enough, because the Chief broke away quite violently: I could see that his hands were shaking, and he didn't know where to look. I was placing the goodies back in the goodie bag, on the work top, but leaving it open, so that everything was visible. Chiefy looked as frozen as a rabbit in a headlight's beam. I lost patience.

'What the fuck's the matter with the bomb bays?' I asked him.

He took too long in replying, and lost his denial. He snarled, 'You're a *bastard* Charlie Bassett,' and reached for the bag. Then he seemed to notice Grace again. He sort of sniffed, and said, 'You can do yourself up again Miss,' and sounded pre-war pompous, until he added, 'You never had to do that to me.'

That sounded sad. Lost empires, Chiefy: lost worlds.

At least Grease and the boys were pleased with us. Marty paid particular attention – I think that it probably made sense to him. Chiefy Bryan told us a bad tale in simple words: the grease that they had been applying to kill the friction between adjacent moving parts in the really sexy part of our aeroplanes – where the chicken keeps her eggs, if you follow me – was contaminated with steel shavings, some of them small, some of them large. All of them sharp, and all of them harder than the parts they were supposed to lubricate. Result? Grade A fucking catastrophe. Hard steel cuts soft steel and aluminium to bits. Doors jammed open. Doors jammed shut. Bombs failing to release, and then falling off anywhere between the target and home. F-U-C-K-ing catastrophe. Delivering squadrons grease tins contaminated with steel shavings was either the good old British worker at his best, or sabotage. And Supplies Branch didn't have to fly, so why would they care? Whatever the reason, *nobody must know*, least of all the poor sods who fly the damned things. Just as we thought: situation normal. It was Bushes who got on to it of course. He was sneaky enough to get the squadron's senior engineering officer to take Quelch's bloody bomb bay doors off. Eureka. Now he had ordered the entire bloody squadron's strength into maintenance – but secretly. No point in making the natives restless.

Once Chief Bryan had both hands on the bag he wasn't going back. He was the sort who stuck to bargains. He didn't ask us not to repeat what he had told us: that wasn't possible. He just expected *Tuesday*'s crew to cover for him when word got about. That was unspoken. Implicit. Then he told us the tale I later related to Grease and the chaps. I didn't disbelieve him, but there must have been an element of doubt in my expression, because at one point he left Grace and the goodies under the Lanc, to walk me out of the hangar, and round the corner to the three-tonner they used. His people parted to let us through, although I noticed an Erk named Dobson – they called him Dobbo – was absent. He was sitting in the cab of the truck.

Chiefy growled. 'Put up your mitts, Dobbo. Show the man.'

Dobson winced, and held up two fully bandaged hands. I didn't think that frostbite was catching.

'Dobson is ever mindful of the need to conserve our valuable resources; he's our ferret – like your Pole: so instead of throwing out *all* of the quart tins of grease the way I told him, he opened them up and put his hands into each one, to sort out the good 'uns, from the bad.'

'What happened?'

'Cut me bleedin' fingers to bits, didn't I, Sergeant Bassett.'

Bryan said that Dobbo was lucky not to be up on a charge of self-inflicted, but there was a kind of pride in the way he said it. He filled out the story in terse little sentences on the way back into *Tuesday*, gathered up the bribe bag, and his tools, and beat the retreat, but not before saying, 'She'll be ready for you tomorrow night, son. Don't fret.' He looked for a moment as if he was going to give Grace the soldier's warning, but must have thought better of it. He gave her an affectionate little salute, and said, 'Ma'am,' before turning away. Just before he reached the hangar door he called back. 'And shut the bloody doors after the pair of you.'

We heard the voices, animated now, glad to be going back to the world of fags, and mugs of char, and wads. We heard the bellowing roar of the three-tonner fade and die. Then nothing.

Grace gave me an impish grin. I said, 'I thought maybe I'd disqualified myself after I missed my slot this morning.'

'Naw. I don't keep accounts.'

'You could get all of my accounts on the fingers of two hands.'

'Don't worry, Charlie – you'll soon run out of fingers!'

There was nowhere to lie down. We could have gone into *Tuesday* of course. But that didn't seem right, so I didn't suggest it, and neither did she. It might have changed our luck. Halfway down the hangar there were some small workshops and offices against the wall. They were all locked, so we settled for the vertical, against a rather flimsy wooden office door. The light hadn't died completely, and I stood about four feet off Grace as she leaned back against the door, and slowly unbuttoned her canvas bag from shoulder across her body almost to her knee – underneath she was as naked as I had expected, and the waning light through the internal supports of the hangar threw zigzag patterns on her: the bagginess of the garment gave her all the room for movement an experienced girl and an inexperienced boy could need, without her having to take it off. Something told me that she had done this before.

Fitting myself slowly into her was the most exciting sexual moment I had known, although what followed almost pushed it from my memory for ever. Not far into the ferocious routine of her silent fucking she shivered, and whispered, 'Christ, Charlie; I'm cold. We'll have to finish quickly.' Then she giggled and bit my ear.

Then it was a whisper again. A calm and basically informative whisper: 'Don't look now, Charlie, but someone's watching us.'

I glanced over my shoulder at the man to whom Grace was giving a smile. I wish she hadn't done that.

He was standing no more than thirty paces away from us. His clothes were as old-fashioned as Grace's – a closely fitting leather flying helmet without spaces for earphones, a tan leather double-breasted, knee-length flying coat, which he wore open (you could see the khaki tunic jacket underneath, and a medal ribbon), trousers cut like riding breeches and calf-length riding boots. He had a pencil-thin moustache, and I could smell the

Turkish cigarette he smoked in a stubby black holder. I'm not sure how much he saw of Grace, or *if* he saw her. I know that he made eye contact with me, and that I knew immediately that he was as dead as a fucking dodo, and that I was so scared that I wanted to piss myself.

He turned his head maybe an inch to the right, as if a sound had captured his attention, but he never took his eyes from mine. Then he smiled. And then he wasn't there any longer. Grace buttoned up. So did I. Watching each other's faces, not saying a word. Grace's face looked white again, but she didn't look as scared as I felt, and we walked hand in hand towards the doors. I deliberately walked over the piece of concrete I had seen Bawne Billy standing on. It was one of the braver things I have done in my life.

I mounted the Indian, and Grace climbed the pillion behind me, instead of tucking into the sidecar. Her arms around my chest comforted me.

'You know what they say, don't you?' she said.

'No. Not until you tell me.' It *had* been cold in there. My nose was dripping. I sniffed.

'You learn something new every day.'

'Not sure that I want to.'

I switched the petrol on, retarded the ignition, closed the air slide and it fired on the first kick. It was just light enough to get back without the headlamp.

Grace slept alone.

I didn't say that the Chief had hinted we were on for tomorrow, but I elected for an early night, and the others, except for Pete who was still out in the Singer, took the hint.

Pete drove out through a hole we'd picked in the perimeter fence behind our billet. He hid the hole behind a bottle of gin every Monday night. The cops always found the gin but not the hole. It was big enough to get the Singer through now. The first I was aware of his return was him shaking me gently awake, and beckoning me to get clobbered up and follow him to the door.

It turned out that he needed a lift into the billet with five exceptionally large and heavy cardboard boxes. I don't know where he had been, or how he'd got them all into the Singer in the first place. We stacked them between his bed and the loot boxes, doing what we could not to wake anyone else, and covered them with spare sheets.

What was it this time, I wondered as I tried to get back to sleep, *the contents of the V&A's jewel room?* Then I remembered that it couldn't be, because they were safely stowed down some mineshafts in Wales. Then I slept. He was secretive about it in the morning, insisting that he wasn't going to open them until after our next trip. He was right of course: it was to be number thirteen.

Krefeld

As soon as they drew the blind back from the map at briefing I glanced at Pete.

'I don't want to go to Krefeld again. They want to kill me in Krefeld, Charlie,' he whispered.

'They want to kill us everywhere, Pete. The Krefeld Kraut is just a bit pushy about it.'

Bushes couldn't have heard our conversation from up front, but he must have heard the murmur, because he turned, glared and barked, 'Pipe down there. Just bloody listen for once.'

There was a squadron tradition of booing the met officer as he left the podium: this was the first time I'd heard him slow handclapped. Not a scrap of thick all the way to the target and back. The fighters would see for miles. All the way to bloody Krefeld and back with a rear gunner with the twitch, and no chance of friendly covering cloud to dive into. Not that we were leading the squadron; Bushes was doing that. We were about third in line — which Grease pointed out was as far to the front as a sensible man wanted to get. Take-off at 2020 and breakfast about seven hours later. Don't say *With a bit of luck,*

Charlie; luck didn't come into it. It was science, numbers, and something else; anything but luck.

Something had happened to the non-flying wallah who came round the locker room to get your locker keys, so the padre was there doing it. Pete turned him down outright. He said, 'I will keep it. I'll not give my keys to a focking thief.'

'Come on Pete. I'm not a Catholic, but I'm still your padre. Your stuff's safe with me.' He smiled that chaplain's smile, glanced at Grease for support, and got none: Grease shrugged.

Pete said, 'You stole the grace of God: *nothing*'s safe with you.' That seemed to be it.

As we filed out to the big crew bus we sometimes had to share with Quelch's mob, we found ourselves alongside Bushes' crew, and their bus.

Grease asked Bushes, 'What about the fucking bomb doors?'

Bushes didn't reply immediately. He blinked twice. Rapidly. The tic on his cheek danced. He said, 'Heard your gunners got their second Jerry the other night. Why didn't you tell me? Damned fine show.'

Grease looked at him hard and said, 'Bally good for morale, what?'

Then they boarded their separate trucks. Bushes leaned out the back of his, and shouted across, '*Sir*. You're supposed to bloody well say *sir* when you're talking to me. You fucking animal.' Then he bewildered us all by laughing, as if something was genuinely funny. It wasn't genuinely funny; we were off to bomb Germany again and not many of us wanted to go.

Grease leaned across to me and gave me the chest prod. 'Remind me to find out how many trips that mad sod has done.'

Tuesday looked big and black and reassuring lurking in the drizzle. Maybe I didn't tell you that it was raining. Didn't you bloody guess? Before signing for them, Marty lovingly touched each of the bombs in turn like a man touching a girl's tits for the first time. Grease went for a pre-flight natter with Chief Bryan. He frowned when he found me behind him. His voice was tight; tense. He sounded as if he had a sore throat.

'Did you get the work done?'

The Chief looked away. 'She'll do.'

'Don't fuck us around Chiefy. Yes or no?'

'No. Not all of it. I'll finish tomorrow.'

'Do I have anything to worry about?'

'She'll get you there, and bring you back. What more do you want?'

'More than that.'

'I'll fly with you if you like. Will that satisfy you?' and I suddenly noticed a spare parachute at his feet. He was ready to do it.

Grease briefly squeezed his shoulder. 'Naw, Chief. Just the offer will do.'

They shook hands. Livingstone and Stanley.

'If we get chopped tonight I'm bloody well coming *back* for you. You remember that!' Grease said.

We clambered into *Tuesday* after the others. Grease asked me, 'How do you think he looked when I didn't call his bluff?'

'Relieved. Wouldn't you be?'

*

Krefeld was hot, and Pete was terrified. He sang sad hymns in Polish all through the ten-mile approach to the bomb run, until Grease told him to shut the fuck up.

It was the first time I had heard the words used in that order. The stream had been spread out fairly widely, but about twenty minutes into Germany a Lancaster came galloping up behind us from way back in the pack, and then settled down at the same height and about thirty yards behind. Pete reported it.

'Lanc, Skipper. Thirty yards dead astern. He's not gaining.'

'Thanks, Pete. Keep an eye open for the Krauts beneath him. Charlie, give him a twinkle.'

'Aye, Skipper.'

'Twinkle' was Grease's word for signalling between aircraft in Morse, by Aldis lamp. He throttled back enough to bring the visitor up alongside. We twinkled, then we pulled ahead back to our station.

'It's the Quelch gang again,' I told them.

'Bollocks,' said Grease. 'This is getting tedious. Remind me to do something about them.'

I guess that inside our masks we were all grinning. Once the bomb run commenced it turned into one of our most interesting. What we were used to by now – which doesn't mean to say that we liked it – was a command sequence between Marty, who aimed and dropped the bombs, and Grease, who repeated Marty's words aloud. It would go something like this:

'Bomb doors open.'

'Bomb doors open.'

'Master switch on.'

'Master switch on.'

'Bombs fused and selected.'

'Bombs fused and selected.'

Then there would be Marty's flying instructions to Grease: *Left, right* or *steady*. Then his words of power, *Bombs gone*, which we knew about anyway, because *Tuesday* would leap as if she'd been kicked in the arse, then Marty would gibber something like 'Bomb doors closed: photo OK, Skip – now get the hell out of here.'

That gave Grease all the excuse he needed to fly her the way he'd always wanted to, and I would start to feel airsick. That all happened within about two and a half minutes, although it seemed a lot longer.

Now *this* is why the bomb run of our second Krefeld trip was interesting:

Marty said, 'Bomb doors open.'

Grease: 'Bomb doors open.'

Grease again: 'Bomb doors gone.'

Marty: 'What?'

Grease: 'You heard me: I think the fucking doors fell off. She shook herself and now she's crabbing. Just get rid of the bloody things.'

Tuesday leapt. Grease pulled her gently round to port without losing height, and called out for a reciprocal to get us home. Quelch's Quommandos followed us every yard of the flat turn, with flak bursting all around them. The Pink Pole cursed them from his turret, and waved them away, but they weren't having any of it. I heard Grease muttering, 'Get out of it, you mad sods, go home.'

Not a bloody chance. They were flying where they wanted

to be, and it obviously rattled Grease a bit. We left Krefeld a bit redder than we found it, but God knows where our bombs went.

Over the North Sea Piotr reported, 'He's pulling out to your port, Skipper, and there's an unknown pulling up to your starboard, prepare to corkscrew,' then, '. . . wait one. It's another Lanc. We've got a focking display formation up here!'

I said, 'Don't shoot at them, Pete. Too many witnesses.'

'You think I'm stupid?'

'Shut up.' That was Grease. 'Just do your jobs.'

Grease pulled me up to the astrodome a few minutes later because Quelch had come surging up alongside again. We exchanged twinkles. I told Grease, 'Quelch says, *Why did you drop your bomb doors on them as well? Can I do that next time?*'

'Ha bloody ha!'

Then the other aircraft surged up on the other side, so that we were flying three abreast about a hundred feet above the North Sea. The newcomer twinkled too; it said: *Tell Sergeant McKenzie to go back to Germany and get the rest of his bloody aeroplane.*

Grease said, 'Bollocks. I think that's the Old Man.'

The only problem we had to cope with after that was cold, although it wasn't my problem because the heater was working well enough, and its port was alongside me. The others complained because as quick as the heat was pumped into the aircraft, it was sucked out again through the open bomb bay. I gave my spare pair of gloves to the Toff. Pete pulled out the spare parachute and wrapped it around himself. For some reason we had difficulty in raising Bawne at first, but then I got call sign Rutley, which was the Yanks at Duxford and suddenly we were receiving our own runway caravan, and getting lights. We twinkled at each other in the circuit – there was only one other down before us, and that had been an early return after a night-fighter attack. Bushes twinkled *Follow me*. Grease had me twinkle *After you, son* to Quelch, who came right back with *Thank you,* Tuesday, *age before beauty*. Without the bomb bay doors it was a very loud landing.

Bushes must have made a nifty exit, because he got around to our dispersal in his horrid little car before we unwrapped Piotr from the parachute which had kept him from freezing to death, and climbed wearily back to earth. The Toff solemnly gave me back my spare gloves, and then kissed me on each cheek. Bushes leapt out of his car and galloped up to Grease. 'Get the Chief to get her into the T2 before dawn; and not a bloody word to bloody *anyone!*'

His moustache seemed to bristle with aggression. Then, suddenly, he and Grease began to laugh uproariously, and actually hugged each other. Bloody flying types.

The interrogation didn't take too long because Bushes had forbidden us from saying that the plane began to fall to pieces on its own over Krefeld. Piotr fixed his first date with Harriet for the next day. Then there was a surprise waiting for us in the Nissen hut. On each of the small lockers alongside our beds Grace had placed a lighted candle in a jam jar, and on the small table near the stove was a bottle of whisky – which had probably come from her father's pre-war stock, because it wasn't one of Pete's – and eight glasses. She had tried to stay awake for us, but was sleeping in one of the utility armchairs, snoring. Piotr gently tucked a blanket around her before we began to drink. It was an oddly calm and satisfying drinking session – maybe because it was unplanned. We didn't actually say much; just chatted about this and that. I think I probably smiled a lot; I know that the others did. Later, as I lay in bed and drifted into sleep I watched the dancing lights of the candles against the curved roof. It was good to be reminded that fire was not always an enemy. Thirteen down.

We slept late; most of us in our silks, just as we were. When I awoke Grace was no longer asleep in her chair, and Fergal's bed was empty: the dirty dog. I fired up the stove and Grease staggered out of his pit groaning – he always had trouble with whisky. Part of my admiration and affection for him came from the number of mornings I had seen him in that state, crawl into his running gear, and set off doggedly along the peri-track regardless of the weather. When he came back he was invariably Grease again. I shaved, pulled on my number ones, left the airfield by our private gate and cycled down to the church at Bawne – not for the religious comfort of the service, but for another comfort deriving from its ceremony and its history. It gave freely. It was one of those flint and rubble churches which speckle the south Midlands – long dark naves, and a bell tower which always drew your eye on finals. Then I cycled back.

Grace was up, and in country civvies of shirt, pullover and baggy tweed trousers with turn-ups, which would have looked ridiculous on any other woman. Her hair was damp. She was delicately nibbling toast, and I could smell freshly brewed coffee. Where the hell had that come from? She gave me a mugful; it was as delicious as it smelled, and she said, 'Don't ask.' Then, 'Where did you get to?' When I told her she pouted, and said, 'I would have gone with you. I want to see the church – I haven't been there since before the war: one of Daddy's pals was buried there.'

'What do you want to see?'

'Musty old graves in a musty old churchyard. Will you take me?'

'How about me driving you down there at opening time? It's not that far from the Wellington. I can sip a few pints and wait for you.'

'You won't be flying tonight, then?' One of the things I liked about Grace was that she could say that without sounding relieved.

I said, 'No. Not unless Bushes puts us into another kite. *Tuesday* needs some loving.'

'Oh! Was it so bad a do last night?'

'No. Some non-essential bits fell off.'

'Bomb doors?'

'Can't say. Unlike the big black rectangular things that used to hang on the bottom of our aircraft, my lips are sealed. I shall think about Mrs Tocsin's cider that I shall be drinking in the Wellington in about an hour.'

Grace smiled. She said, 'Pints of cider are like tits you know.'

'How d'ye make that out?'

'One isn't enough, and three are definitely too many.'

My turn to smile. 'Where'd you learn that?'

Without intending it, I had suddenly said the wrong thing. Grace looked down at her shoes and turned away.

'The Americans say that about their Martinis,' was all she'd say.

We took the combo. Piotr was away with his intelligence officer in the Singer, and nobody apart from Grease was up yet. Even he'd wandered off whilst I was at the church. I suspected that he was up at the T2 consoling *Tuesday* for her lost virginity. There was a group of Yank flyers outside the Wellington trying to make sense of English licensing hours. It was with real pleasure that I recognized among them a few of the crew we had met in London. They whistled at Grace as she made a leg for them getting out of the sidecar. One of them shouted, 'Hi, Grace.'

She made no move to join them, but just pushed me towards them with a 'See you later,' and made for the churchyard.

Her awareness of focused male attention put at least five degrees of yaw on her swinging bottom as she walked off. The child I remembered as the pilot from our London encounter pushed his way through; I remembered his battered soft cap, and stained flying jacket. He was a full captain.

'Ya made it, huh?' he said.

'Yes, how about your team. They all OK?' I said.

'Yeah, what d'ya expect with me flying them? Safe as babies.'

At least two of the guys with him winced as he said that, but we'd confirmed that we'd all come through the last two weeks without making a dance about it. That was good.

'I don't remember your name, and I guess you don't remember ours,' he said.

'I'm Charlie Bassett. Sparks. Radio op.'

'I'm Peter Wynn.'

That's how I became reacquainted with Pete Wynn, Sandy Lyon, Walt Graham-Smith and David Kovaks – who everyone called 'the Jew'. Kovaks wasn't in fact Jewish, but a Polish American Calvinist just making a point. He thought of war as an art form, and himself an existentialist. He was going to be a great artist after this shit was over.

Pete Wynn had the face of a twenty-year-old wearing sixty-year-old eyes – it was an Eighth Army Air Force look. He asked me, 'This call for a pint or two of your dreadful English beer?'

'I should say.'

'I should say,' he mimicked to his guys, who laughed. Then, 'When's this shop opening?'

'Just about now, I should say.'

When our first pints were in our hands, and we were in the middle of telling each other what shit-bags of aircraft we were being forced to fly this war in, the Jew touched my arm to get my attention, and said, 'That Grace with you: she was dating one of our guys a while back. Haven't seen her for a couple of months.'

It wasn't a warning: it was something else, but I couldn't make out what.

I left them after three pints of cider, and a promise to set up a drinking and darts (Marty always used to call them 'arrers') match between the crews before it was too late. Grace hadn't reappeared, which was a little strange because I had expected her to seek me out after seeing whatever she wanted to in the churchyard. Which is where she wasn't – I had a fair scout around before I went into the church for the second time in a day. Grace was sitting in a pew right at the front, and before you get the idea of piety, she was smoking a cigarette.

'OK?' I said.

'Fine. This is a good old church, isn't it?'

'Is it Norman?'

'I doubt it. Medieval probably, but the Victorians really messed it up. Have you seen its little bit of pagan idolatry?'

'Don't be daft.'

'Come here, and look.' She had stood up to greet me, and now walked down to the west end of the church, under its bell tower. She stopped by the font. So did I. She said, 'Look down. There,' and pulled a square rug to one side.

The tiles of the floor made a red and black pattern.

'What is it?'

'It's a maze. The only one inside a church in England. There's another one in a cathedral in France. A pre-Christian ritual site inside a Christian place of worship: revamped by those same bloody Victorians of course; I'd love to know if there was one older still, underneath.' She gave me the crooked Grace smile, and then said, 'Come on: something else to show you. What I really came here for.'

Outside, in the churchyard, she walked me to a corner which was catching the sun, and four neat tombstones, similar in size and standing together. Part of my mind was saying that what war really meant was graveyards getting used too often, although these graves didn't look new. She squatted by one at the end of the row, and ran her fingers over the engraved words as she read them aloud. ' "William Hanley Hamilton, Royal Flying Corps. Born 1889, Killed in action 14 July 1916." '

'Did you know of him Grace? Was this your father's pal?'

'No, nothing like that.'

'What, then?'

'He's someone you met.'

I didn't get this. I laughed, and then stopped because she wasn't smiling.

'Don't be idiotic, Grace. I wasn't born in 1916.'

'Meet Bawne Billy,' she said.

My advice is that when it happens, own up right away: to being made speechless. There was a new small bunch of flowers on the grave: late violets; I didn't think that they were Grace's – somehow that wouldn't have been her style.

As I started to open up the bike on the way back Grace tugged my sleeve and shouted for me to pull up. We were at the end of an unmade, rutted road which led between Bawne, Caxton and Haldicot – the next villages west. The locals called it the Drift, or Haldicot Drift. We parked the combo off the road, and Grace linked her arm in mine as we walked the Drift's ruts. She had said, 'Don't get your hopes up, Charlie; I just want to walk a bit.'

'I've got to tell you that I'm not really one for the ghosties,' I told her.

She stopped. I stopped with her. She said, 'Neither am I.'

'So I won't be telling anyone about it.'

'Neither will I.'

'Good. That's settled.'

We still hadn't moved on. She said, 'This place is magic, isn't it?'

Grace kissed me.

Hamburg

I remember the next few hours as being a time of greater
mental confusion or fear than on any other trip, previous or
subsequent. Damn it. When we returned to the hut everyone
was there except the Pole, and you could cut the tension with
a knife. Grease stood by the stove, and even though his hands
were in his trouser pockets you could see that he was bunching
them into fists, as if ready for a punch-up.

'At least we've got a bloody radio operator,' he said, then
very bitterly, 'We're up for tonight; briefing is in an hour.'
And, 'Do you know where Piotr went?'

'Up to London, I expect. You gave him the day off with
what's-her-name.'

'Harriet.'

'Yes, that's right.'

'Fuck it.'

'Indubitably.'

'I'm warning you just the once, Charlie. Try to be funny
today, and I'll punch your lights out. This is bloody serious.'

I probably haven't told you before that Conroy was prone to

bouts of sudden gloom and introspection. He offered, 'Either we fly a trip without our tail gunner, or we fly with someone else's and Pete ends up doing jankers, or we scrub the trip. We'll all get CB, or something, for collusion, and Grease'll get the book thrown at him.'

'Thanks Conners. I wouldn't have worked all that out for myself,' I said.

'I won't warn you again, Charlie.' That was Grease.

'Oh, shut up the lot of you,' Grace suddenly shouted, 'stop bickering, and use your fucking heads.'

It was the unusual sound of her swearing at us that brought us round immediately. I said instinctively, 'Sorry, Grace.'

That was for all of us. Grease gave us his shamefaced grin, and our brains kicked in again.

Grace was relieved, and shakily asked, '"Indubitably". Where did you learn that, Charlie?'

'Jennings books. The black fellah was always saying it, I think.'

Marty told us, 'My mother always made tea when things went wrong. Tea cures everything. Let's have a cup of char, and make up our minds what to do, *quickly*: I don't want the death of a thousand cuts.'

He was right, and that's what we set to, but in our hearts we knew that we had committed ourselves to a trip without a gunner. I'd heard of other crews doing that − or flying a trip with a crew member too drunk, or sick with fear, to contribute: but I'd never heard what their survival rate was.

'Must have been a quick turn-round job Bryan's people did on *Tuesday*?' I asked Grease.

'That's part of the problem. *Tuesday*'s not ready. We've got that shit-heap we helped Brookman get back to Manston. They actually put the bastard thing back together again!'

'I suppose there's no hint of the target?'

Grease said, 'They're just briefing three of us. That means we're going gardening for certain.' 'Gardening' was the word we used for dropping anti-shipping mines in enemy seaways — and it was a damned sight more awkward than anyone credited.

'Where?'

'How the fuck should I know? Heligoland or some other godforsaken patch of water the Kraut's keen on!'

After the outburst he suddenly went quite calm, as if his anger had been replaced with solid purpose. Like a fighter before a fight, I suppose.

Then Grace said, '*I'll* do it,' and we all turned and looked at her.

I know that this has been a longish preamble, but *that*, really, was the start of it.

PART TWO

The Rear Gunner

Almost immediately we heard a car drawing up outside, and you could have collected our relief and spread it on bread with jam. Not that it lasted. It wasn't Piotr, but the bloody Boss. He actually knocked on the door before he came in – he must have gone to one of those schools.

He sniffed, and said, 'Always wanted to see how you'd done this place up. Heard things about it of course – the adjutant says it's a proper tart's paradise, but what would he know anyway?'

'Come in, sir.' That was Grease. He already *was* in of course, and he beckoned Grease over to have one of those one-to-one conversations between the prefects that everyone else is supposed to hear. The Boss had got Grease's attention for once, and Grease asked, 'So what's going on, sir?'

'Make no mistake Mac,' – *Mac?* – 'you lot weren't first choice for this, not even second; after all you've never bombed the sea before, have you? The first crew on the board have all found reasons not to be up for it. Bad planes, bad guts, bad eyes . . . bad fingers they can't get out of their bad arses.'

'Bad nerves; they're windy,' said Grease quietly. 'They don't like gardening.' I'd never heard him put down another crew before. Finding reasons not to fly was too much like common sense. Grease was usually in the corner of the Common Man against the Boss Class.

'That too. So I thought we'd show them how,' Bushes said.

'*We*, sir?'

'You, me and Quelch, and the mindless bunch of bastards you fly with. Only I wanted to tell you to your face. Before the briefing.'

Grease said, 'OK,' as if he'd agreed to come to a dinner party.

Bushes looked around for the first time. 'Where's your mad Pole?' he asked us.

'He'll be there,' said Grease icily.

'You sure?'

'I'm sure, sir.'

Then Bushes noticed Grace, and looked horrified. On his face his brain was asking *what have I said*? He choked and spat out, 'Good God! What are *you* doing here?'

'She brought a new kite in yesterday.' Grease returned the serve for her.

'Did she, by *Timothy*!' Bushes squinted at her, then barked, 'Suppose you heard all that guff?'

'Not a word of it, sir,' Grace said. Then she smiled and looked down, as bashful as a fourteen-year-old.

At the briefing Bushes was rare: relaxed and joking. I reckoned he really had the wind up, although for once the met prediction was spiffing and gave us a chance. That didn't alter the fact that we were going to mine the sea as close to the approaches to Hamburg as we could. Bastard place.

The Boss summarized, close to the end of the brief. 'Let's just get this straight. I hate gardening trips for the Blue Jobs just as much as you do, especially rush jobs like this: it ain't our proper business – but if command tells them we're going to do it, then we will. Just follow me in a close, flat vic at 150 feet, and don't fuck around. I'm going straight in, turning ninety degrees to port, parallel with the coast and directly on to the run. I'll be making another ninety-degree port again at the end of it, showing them my arse, and getting back across the North Sea as fast as I can: just like the tip and run raids the Kraut does on the south coast, except with Lancasters. OK?'

His navigator said, 'Plot if you like, but you should be flying close enough to follow me. If *we* go in, McKenzie's to lead. If we get separated, just bugger off home however you like. Just make sure you make it.'

His sparks said, 'No radio traffic on the way out please, chaps. Use the Aldis lamps. I'll give you two longs as each turn comes up. You give me one short in reply. That means the radio operator will have to be up in the office, behind the pilot's seat.'

His rear gunner said, 'If his night fighters come out to play they'll have to jump us from above. Watch the cloud. They should be silhouetted against it for once. You might get a half-decent shot at them.'

His bomb aimer said, 'Just like laying eggs really. We'll have eight each. Lollipops with braking parachutes. Select a thirty-second delay between them, and drop as soon as you see mine go. Don't get too low; you won't want the entry splash to fill your kite up with water. It'll tear your bomb doors off.'

'You listening Mac?' Bushes said.

We actually grinned back at the mad bastard.

'Don't think me excessively pessimistic, sir, but where do we put the mines if you buy it before we reach the target?' Quelch asked.

'Wherever Sergeant McKenzie wants you to. Bloody Pompey if you like. *I* won't be too worried about it by then.'

'And Mr McKenzie knows what our aiming point is, sir?'

'No, but then, neither do I. I said we'd put them in the Hamburg channel. That will satisfy the Blue Jobs, apparently, and get the bastards off our backs. Any more questions?'

At the end of it Bushes stood with his feet apart, fists on his hips and glared at us. The station commander had not attended, so Bushes was the ranker, and could say what he liked. What he said was, 'Gardening trips usually credit a half sortie only, thanks to some fool in the War House who thinks that they're less dangerous just because the sea doesn't shoot back: not this time – get back, and you chalk another whole trip off. Savvy? And McKenzie?'

'Yes, sir?'

'Where's your fucking rear gunner?'

'Getting changed, sir. He was late back. We'll pick him up in the wagon on the way to the kite.'

'Make sure you bloody do. Good luck, everyone, and stay close. See you back in the bar.'

We were going to fly at 150 feet over the approaches to Hamburg, and drop mines into the seaway. Every German flak-gunner in the world would be able to see us coming. All we needed were a few Kraut dams within easy flying distance, and Guy Gibson himself could come charging out of the woodwork. This sort of trip would have been just his style, wouldn't it?

We took the small Bedford QL with Fiver, our usual WAAF driver – one of the few who didn't roost in the Waafery in Bawne village, because she was married-with-permission; which meant that she lived with her civvy husband off the station. He was a humourless roads and buildings contractor with a Hitler moustache, whose small crew did some of the maintenance work on the station. Grease had asked her to drive to our hut en route to the dispersal, to pick up our tardy gunner, then he told Conroy to distract her from what we were doing. Conroy rode up front – he said it was nav's prerogative – he was supposed to be able to find his way about in the dark, after all, and he often used to joke with her about needing to keep his hands warm if his navigation was going to be up to scratch.

There's a story told about how Fiver had a fit when she learned that Fiver was her nickname. Some cow of a parachute packer told her that it labelled her as a pro – you know: 'King's Cross, and anything you want for a fiver.' It was probably Conners who gave her an alternative version and set her right, which is why she had a soft spot for him. She was a small, well-fed lady, as I remember her at that time, with a round little face, small mouth and short thick hair a few shades fairer than Grace's. Bloody ace driver.

The story was that she wasn't too good at picking her husband out in the dark, if you take my meaning, but I didn't know her well enough to know if it was true. The other guys said she had two identifying characteristics. One was that she had obtained a smart pair of black leather women's driving gloves. The other was that she always wore small black leather lace-up shoes, whether they were topped off with uniform trousers or a skirt. There was a third thing, and that was whenever she did it with someone who wasn't her husband she always kept her gloves and shoes on, as if she was holding something back. You might be able to work out why someone referred to her as the five of spades one night, and that got shortened to Fiver.

Connors kept her occupied as we scrambled Grace over the tailgate dressed in the Pole's dirty yellow gunner's coverall, over her own baggy Sidcot suit, two layers of silks, and padded out with a deflated Mae West. I was scared. Grease looked it too. Grace was as excited as a schoolgirl on her first pony. When we reached *Peter*'s hardstanding on an unfamiliar part of the airfield, you could see that the kite had more patches than a chorus line of Long John Silvers. Grease moved out immediately to distract *Peter*'s crew chief, who was waiting for us; Marty got inside the bomb bay and started to lay hands upon his first mines, as if it was a religious rite; he wouldn't sign for, or drop, a bomb he hadn't first touched; sometimes he even kissed them before boarding the aircraft – that was truly disgusting. The rest of us gathered around Grace, and sort of huddled her into the kite out of sight of the prying eyes of the Erks who had gathered to look at the crew they were trusting with their precious Lancaster.

Before take-off the Toff told Grace, 'I'm going to tell you

how to traverse the turret, depress and elevate the guns, and fire the buggers. Then I'll tell you the same things over again – it's all we have time for. After that it's all yours: nothing complicated. Basically it's what you kick, what you pull and what you push. Just like shagging. Don't worry about it and it'll come naturally.'

Grease mounted up last for a change. 'Brookman's chief says she's a bad old cuss, but if we treat her kindly she'll bring us back,' he told me.

'Bloody better, Skip. She owes us one.'

The Toff clambered up to his top spot from the rear turret where he'd given Grace her five-minute air-gunner course.

Conners stuck his head through the black curtain he sometimes pulled closed behind him. 'I hope you showed her how to open the back, and clip her 'chute on.'

'No. I clipped one of the small chest 'chutes on her already. Pete's spare. She's sitting on the other to give herself enough height for the sight.'

I remembered then, that that was one of Piotr's foibles. A rear gunner usually kept his parachute pack in a small rack in the fuselage next to his turret exit. Our Pole didn't wholly trust that arrangement – it meant he had to get away from his guns and back into the aircraft in order to get to his 'chute. So he carried a smaller one in the turret with him – like an insurance policy. It must have been crowded in there, but he had never complained.

Grease and Fergal talked through the start-up sequence over this conversation, then Grease said, 'Shut up everyone. We're off to bomb the sea.'

I did the intercom call-through then. Grace came on without a pause when it was her turn; she said, 'Rear gunner OK, Skip,' as I felt our waddling beast turning on to the big runway.

Fergal said, 'That's a green,' as the flare arced into the sky from the watch office caravan; the Boss must have been rolling already, because we began to motor immediately, and somewhere behind us so did Squelchy Quelchy. Grease must have been showing off because he pulled her off the ground quicker and smoother than he had ever done before.

Marty, up front, said, 'Well *done*, Skipper!' and spoiled it for him.

I smiled at that; I'm sure the others did too. We only made 1,000 feet this time, in a slow climbing circle that put us to starboard of Bushes, and slightly behind. Quelch matched us to port and, being a bit flash, tucked in even closer. I went up to Grease's office and stood behind him, steadying myself with a hand on his armour-plated seat back. From the clear astrodome behind the cockpit of Bushes' Lanc an Aldis winked twice – *Change of course coming up; follow me.*

'Change of course, Skip,' I said.

'Saw it,' Grease said.

We followed Bushes' Lanc, diving gently towards the coast and a hundred feet, and went gardening.

Just before the change of course, as we climbed away from Bawne, I fancied I heard a voice in my earphones. It said '*Now* we've bloody done it!' It might have been me.

Compared with a large-scale raid I could reduce the debriefing for the gardening sortie to three words – *little to report.* Sure, things happened, but nobody who shot at us got anywhere near, and we didn't tempt the Kraut night fighters up. The Boss showed us what a skilful pilot he was, and scared me shitless in the process, by forcing us closer and closer to the waves on the way out. He may have said 150 feet at the briefing, but what he did was nothing like that – the sea was battered flat by our prop wash as we passed over it, and when he approached the start of the bombing run he had to put us into a climbing turn to reach the 150 feet he wanted. I hung on to the top of Grease's seat and shut my eyes in the turn: I was convinced that we were about to dig a wing tip into the briny, and become a submarine.

Marty had his eyes glued to Bushes' aircraft – which was only yards in front of him anyway – and shouted, 'Bomb doors open,' as he saw the leading aeroplane opening up.

After that it was routine. 150 feet was just about right, because braking parachutes on the mines just had time to open. The columns of water reached up for us as each mine plunged in. As we turned off track behind the Boss, Grease muttered, 'Every one's a coconut.' He had this thing about coconuts; I forgot to tell you that.

Here's hoping, I thought.

Closer to England we had this conversation. You tried not to relax *too* much because that could kill you, but it was difficult not to begin to unwind.

It was either Conners or the Toff who said, 'Hey, Skip. Were you asking about the squadron leader's numbers a couple of day's ago?'

Grease said, 'Yes. He's getting barmier by the day. Bomb happy. I wondered how many more trips he had left in him.'

'He could pack it in now if he wanted. They'll tell him soon, if he doesn't do it himself. This is number thirty-two on this tour.'

'What about earlier?'

'Two tours. One as a Piss Off I'm Stupid, and one as a French Letter. Twenty-eight trips on the first one and thirty on the second. His radio op reckons he's looking for a round hundred.'

'Piss Off I'm Stupid' was a pilot officer, and I've told you about 'French Letters' already; they were flight lieutenants.

'He'll kill us all before then,' I said.

Grease said, 'Naw,' in that big Canadian way of his, 'he'll be looked after. God flies beside him. I seen him.'

I was doing sums in my head. If we flew the same missions as the Boss until he reached his hundred, we'd be on our twenty-fourth when he finished. Nearly home. Everyone needs something to look forward to.

We had the problem of getting Grace away again without being spotted. Grease had bet on the Pole returning before we did, and had left a note on his bed. Somewhere between the kite and the interrogation table we had to switch one for the other. At some point in the trip we forgot that Grace was there anyway – that's the simplest and most truthful way to put it. We knew that the turret was traversing and her four heavy machine guns were moving, because as they did they fractionally changed the trim of the aircraft. When she spoke on the intercom she was terse and factual – as if there was another Grace inside her who came out to play in an aeroplane. She wasn't Grace any more, she was the gunner, and I felt as safe as I did when the Pole was there. She moved back into my consciousness as Grace as we did the last call through coming over the coast near Skegness. I suddenly thought *Jesus Christ, that's* Grace!'

The Hamburg trip changed me: threw a switch. As I've indicated, I was usually happier out of the war, head down in the radio compartment – put it down to an hereditary lack of courage if you like. This trip was different. I asked Grease if I could stay up in the office for the landing – some WOPs did that every trip – and he nodded. As we went into the circuit he suddenly pulled one of the throttles all the way back, then banged it forward again. Which is what the port inner did; banged, then spat out a trail of sparks and smoke, before settling down again. He muttered 'Sorry,' which was to the aeroplane, I think.

Then he switched over to talk to the caravan down below us in the dark.

'P-*Peter*. I've an intermittent problem on the port inner.'

Bushes was ever the gentleman. Like I said, he had been to that sort of school. He broke in before the watch office caravan, which controlled the runways, could answer. He said, 'OK, *Peter*. In you go please.'

'Thank you Leader.' Grease sounded comfortable with the formalized language that they were using. Thinking about it, he was beginning to sound like a bloody officer.

Then he said, 'We'll set up the pints.'

A load of cock, of course. We didn't drink beer after a trip, we slept. It was all about getting down on the deck first, and leaving Bushes out there until last so we could lose Grace before he got to us. Grease was still showing off to Grace because for once he put a Lancaster down as softly as in a morning sunrise. Which is a song, if you didn't already know.

Grease had worked out an absurdly simple plan. Grace would stay in the plane. He told us that as I was worming over the main spar to disembark. 'Absurd' was a good technical description for it. It could never bloody work. The Toff told him that it wouldn't work before I could open my mouth. For me a thought came unbidden for the second time in minutes: Grease was beginning to sound like a bloody officer – only an officer could think something as stupid as that.

Toff whispered back to him. 'And what about the Erks then? What are *they* going to do when they find her in here? Start to believe in Santa Claus? I can hear the bastards *clucking* out there already – they've formed a welcome home party.'

The Toff had stopped moving. I sensed Grease shrug behind me. He asked, 'What's *your* idea then?' Silence. *Peter* creaked, and her engines clicked as they cooled. Marty's voice seemed to wriggle at us from a long way forward. It probably was. He dropped 'h's inconsistently when he whispered, and sounded like this.

'Give 'er your helmet Toff, and get her to 'old it over most of her face. We'll huddle her on to the bus somehow. If anyone asks, say Pete banged his head. Now get a fucking move on.'

No one bid that up, so we did. The one Erk who got in too close was 'accidentally' bowled over by Grease. By the time he stooped to lift him up, we were all in the Tilly that Fiver had brought out to meet us. Grease even had time to shake Chiefy's hand before he boarded, and tell him that *Peter* was as sweet as a cherry, and good-mannered with it — although he'd had a backfire from the port inner as he lined up.

The Chief returned a big grave nod with his big grave head. 'It's always done that. I should ha' warned you. No harm done then.'

'No, Chiefy. It's OK. I promise you.'

The Chiefy sniffed with what could have been disapproval or congratulations, I thought. He said, 'First time in weeks someone's not brought her back full of holes. I should be grateful I suppose.' Bloody Eeyore.

Grace peeled out of Pete's faded yellow oversuit as we fired around the peri-track to the debrief. Somehow she managed to kiss everyone in the back with her. Fiver, with Conner's hand over hers on the wheel, brought the small truck to bay in deep shadow between the brick interrogation section and the parachute store: she didn't ask him why. As I told you: she had a soft spot for him already. He described it more exactly; he said it was a soft and slightly sticky spot. Navigators are prone to shooting a line, have you noticed? Anyway Conners kept Fiver occupied for a vital few minutes. We made a noisy business of climbing down out of the cramped little wagon. Groaning. Laughing. Looking for fags. Lighting them. Our lost Pole stepped out of a recessed side door in the parachute shed, where Grease had written him to be, and into the group, as we pushed Grace back into its cloaking dark. He was in his flying clobber, and unshaven. When we draped the yellow survival suit over his arm he looked just the thing.

The only evidence of Grace passing chez nous was warmth, a

cherry-red stove, the curtains around berth eight pulled close, and a lingering smell of the bacon sarnies she had breakfasted on – which smelled a damned sight better than what had been thrust at us in the new dawn. We had stripped off our flyers in the lobby, of course, and traipsed in in our silks, Grease leading. As he passed old number eight Grace's hand snaked out from the partition curtain, and touched his arm. Then she gently pushed him away again, and moved him forward. He looked back over his shoulder, shrugged and grinned. The Toff was next. Grace felt his arm, like a blind person feeling a face, and again moved him on. Then Fergal. Then it was me. I am sure that she couldn't see us. That she was doing it with her finger-tips. She touched my upper arm, and then fastened her hand on to it, grasping the bicep. I stopped, and she pulled me through the curtains. None of the others seemed to mind. I heard Piotr yawn, and say something like, 'These gardening trips: very tiring. I think I'll turn in now.'

There was a sound which may have been a pillow being thrown at him, but I can't remember the boys saying much – they were tired, and anyway, I was in Happy Valley by then.

Because Grace had given the stove a late boost the temperature in the shed wasn't glacial when I slipped away from her in the morning. I stacked it up, being as quiet as I could, and then went out to the fire bucket. Grease was out and warming up with stretches soon after. That didn't surprise me – he was the lightest of sleepers – and I always woke him up no matter how quietly I moved. What did surprise me was that Grace joined us, wearing long-sleeved one-piece silk underwear (flying for the purpose of) which clung to her like a second skin. She didn't dunk — but quickly washed her hands and face. She gasped and said, 'Now I know why you do it. Wonderful!'

I told her, 'No you don't. I do it because I did it the morning before my first trip. I'd a skinful the night before and needed to get my head clear. I was certain that I was going to make a mess of it and let everyone down. So it might have something to do with it.'

'To do with what?'

'Surviving.'

I never expected Grease to bat for me. He had no superstitions of his own, apart from the one-drag cigarette. He said, 'If you're going to laugh at Charlie for thinking like that, you're going to have to laugh at us all, chicken — we each have something like that: some keepsake, or something we do for good luck.'

Grace said, 'Don't worry: I won't laugh at you. Especially if I'm sitting at the back.' She ran her damp hands through her hair, and told us, 'Do you know? Last night. I can't believe I did that.'

'Neither can we.' That was me.

'It was all right, though, wasn't it?' That was Grease.

Grace said, 'Smashing. I always felt that I was copping off; doing the easy part; delivering aircraft for men to go out and fight in, but never risking that much myself. Now I know what it's like. It will be different from now on.'

'They have squadrons of female fighter pilots in Russia,' I told her, 'I expect the men just sit around on the ground and give the orders.'

'I could go with that,' Grease said.

Grace looked away from us, and out to the airfield. You could just see *Tuesday*'s dispersal this side of the slight hump in the ground, and *Tuesday* sitting on it again glistening with melted early frost. 'No you couldn't,' she said sadly. 'Really, you couldn't.'

Grace and I shook everyone awake and up, except Marty, who seemed comatose. We once worried if he was diabetic, or had beriberi, but he was just an incredibly deep sleeper inclined to idleness. Waking him was like encouraging a submarine up from the depths. Grease reappeared, grinning, sweating and damp in an unsavoury way. Grace waved him off when he tried to hug her, and most of us made it to the red brick for the last breakfasts.

Grace took a piece of bacon gristle from her mouth, and put it on the side of her plate. Then she asked Fergus, 'How does it go? How does your day work? When do you know if you're flying tonight?'

'First,' he said, 'is the airfield closed: shut down? If it is, then *some* bugger is flying, whether it's you or not. There are two squadrons here – it's not necessarily our gang that's going out.'

'Then you look at the board,' said Conroy, 'that's posted up by lunchtime. If your crew's up there then you're going. Unless you can think of a Bushes-proof excuse, but that won't do any good in the long run. He always gets his own back, and schedules you for a real pisser next time.'

Grease told her, 'That gives you a chance in the afternoon to make certain that the kite has been properly checked and repaired from the last time she was flown, and air test her if

someone's got to tell you that our gunner's mad: totally doolally: what the Scots call "away with the fairies". So don't fly close to us, because he *will* do it. He'll fire on you.'

'Then I'll report the little bastard.'

'No you won't, Skip, you'll still be in Germany. He's not only a mad little bastard but a bad, accurate little bastard as well. I don't want you hurt.'

'You're kidding me,' he said.

I shook my head.

He said, 'You're kidding me,' again, but the edge of certainty had gone from his voice.

He was shaking his head as he cycled off, as if he'd just realized that the world had gone crazy. It was 1944, for Christ's sake: where had he been for the last five years? Grace had stood with me, her arm linked loosely through mine.

'See,' she said. 'I said that he wouldn't hit you if I was here.'

'"My Grace is sufficient for thee, for my strength is made perfect in weakness,"' I said.

'Is that John Donne?'

'Who's he? No, that was by Lord God Almighty. The Bible. It's another one I remember from Sunday School.'

'I didn't go to Sunday School.'

'Ours was like a Nissen hut alongside the parish church. Painted white inside. Sunday School was at 1030. Mum and Dad used to send us there and then go back to bed to rest. I was in the RAF before I realized what for.' I laughed. It was a good memory. 'Apart from the hymns, and a few quotations from the Bible, all I can remember is the curate telling us stories about Africa and the Caribbean, where the happy little niggers scamper up coconut trees, like Little Black Sambo, and throw down coconuts to the benevolent white Sons of the Empire. At least we'll get rid of all that tosh when this lot is over.

I had revealed something of myself to her, and was suddenly embarrassed. I think that she was too. She was doing the *looking away into the distance, I didn't really hear what you were saying* thing that girls do, then asked, 'Is the airfield closed today?'

I looked about. No one seemed to have that air of purpose which presaged a raid. 'Doesn't look like it.'

'Does that mean we could go out? We could visit Daddy again, and be back for supper.'

'Let's ask the others,' I said, although I meant *Let's ask Grease.* You've always got to give the Devil his due.

Astride the Red Indian: retard the ignition, close the air slide, kick it. Wait until it fires then tickle the carburettor as you accelerate – which was the process of progressively opening up the air slide and advancing the ignition. I was getting rather good at this. Maybe I'd make Pete an offer for her now that he had the Singer as well.

The flight to Grace's Pa's pile – because that's what it felt like – took twenty minutes. Grace hugged my back and crooned 'Coming In On A Wing And A Prayer' in my right ear, whilst I could hear Marty relentlessly chanting Spike Jones's 'Der Fuehrer's Face' from the other side. Somehow they managed to harmonize with each other. Now that I had a memory of the road from the village to the house I was able to throw the bike along it flat out, bursting from the dark tunnel of the woods into the bright sunshine. Sliding it around the dog-leg corners and on to the gravel was splendid. I locked up the brakes and slalomed us into the shadow under the giant portico. Grace squealed. She hopped off the bike and said one word, which was, 'Home.'

Then she gave each of us a hug. Marty hung on for another. I didn't mind. Her father was in London, his butler informed us gravely. He spoke like a Co-op undertaker. Where do they learn to speak like that? Grace was disappointed, and I liked her for that. She told us that she was going to run an illegally deep and scalding bath, and soak in it for at least an hour, and added, 'and if either of you disturb me you shall never pass my lips again.'

Mrs Bassett's son could always take a hint. Marty was nippy to get off anyway; he'd been using long vision to try to locate Anna, his land girl, ever since we had emerged from the trees, and although he had tried to disguise his keenness he hadn't fooled me. I'm not sure about Grace. I told him, 'Do you mind if *I* desert you for a couple of hours too, old man. I promised Grace's father that I'd try to get his radio going again. It's one of those Yankee jobs from a Fortress that crashed near here.'

I got the impression from him, although he didn't say anything, that I'd dropped one. Grace was doing her *I didn't hear that* bit again, and staring vacantly at the butler – his name was Mr Barnes. That's another thing about butlers and table servants – have you noticed that their parents forget to provide them with first names? Poor Mr Barnes: I think that Grace's catatonic stare quite unnerved him. He started to tremble anyhow, and we became aware again, suddenly, of the age of the house staff.

Grace grabbed his arm and said, 'Come on Barnsey. Show me a bathroom I can use, as far from Mummy as possible.'

'She's driven up to town as well, Miss Grace. We're not expecting her tonight.'

'With Daddy?'

'Good Lord, no, Miss Grace.'

'Good,' said Grace. There was a story there, and I would get it one day. 'Show me to my bath then. You can stay and scrub my back if you want.'

They were already moving away from me, and Marty was moving even faster in the opposite direction, out to the meadows. I heard Barnes say, 'Mrs Barnes wouldn't like that Miss,' with reproof in his voice, and a peal of laughter from Grace. It was good that he placed Mrs Barnes's opinion above those of Grace or her father, wasn't it?

As I remembered it the radio room was somewhere high up on the west face, and under an overhang. I could find it again without ropes. Sure. Nice of somebody to ask.

The radio was sort of OK after a couple of hours of work. I rewound a coil and jury-rigged the connections: all the lights were there, but the tuner was fucked, and I would have liked to have replaced three of those odd little valves the Americans employ. I sat back and savoured Mr Baker's new very old whisky from the bag under the workbench (the last bottle had been replaced) and wondered how to get Yankee doodle radio parts – nothing from our stores would fit it. Half the label on the whisky bottle had been torn off – it was 'Red' something or other – and what was left had recent water stains.

While I was sitting there, swirling the smoky liquid around in my mouth and diluting it with saliva before swallowing it, a face swam up from my memory, and a name to go with it: the American, Peter Wynn. If he was alive he would have a radio op – just like me – and the radio op would have access to spares. I leaned the chair back on two legs and whistled a tune: it was that Spike Jones thing again, I'm afraid. There was only one telephone in the house, and that was in the main hallway. Grace had told me that the Palladian mansion had been built around an older, smaller Jacobean one, only the entrance hall retaining its original form. It was all still there if you bothered to observe what was in front of you: its flagged floors were of huge, rough, dark grey slates and the room was panelled in a dark wood – maybe chestnut – and had small leaded windows. I took this all in again when I lifted the telephone.

The village switchboard lady at the post office kept me waiting, but she was pleasant for all that. A picture came into my head: she was youngish, married and maybe lonely. She had the inclination to prolong the conversation, so I said I'd call in to buy my stamps next time around. She didn't believe me. I liked her laugh. Before long she had let me know that her name was Susan, and had wormed Charlie out of me. She connected me, after some odd pops and bangs on the line, to the American airfield at Thurleigh, and the telephone was answered by a polite but firm top sergeant who followed his rank with the surname Earl.

I said, 'Hi,' which was how you should always greet Yanks. Connors had told me that.

'Hi, yersel,' Earl said, and asked me what I wanted. I was in no doubt that I was talking to some kind of a policeman.

'I'm Sergeant Charlie Bassett. I'm a radio op with a Lancaster squadron of the RAF at Bawne, not far from you.'

'Good for you, bud; I know the place. Wet and windy.'

'Would it be possible to speak with a pilot: Captain Peter Wynn?'

'No, sir, it would not.'

'Is he still OK?'

'I couldn't say that, sir.'

'How about if I phoned later on, say after 2000 hours?'

'You might be able to speak to Major Wynn then sir.' Good: alive then.

'Major?'

'Yes sir; Captain Wynn got the jump last week. You missed his big party.'

'I'll make the next one. Can you tell him I called?'

'I certainly will sir; Sergeant Bassett you said? You can depend on that.'

What he'd told me without telling me was that Wynn's wing was somewhere over Germany or the Low Countries in the bloody thick of it. I hoped that I hadn't left it too late. I put the telephone down as Grace walked in. She was barefoot, had changed into a gingham summer dress, and was rubbing her hair dry as she walked. I loved her smile: the memory of it still draws a smile from me in return.

'Who were you talking to?' she asked.

'A top sergeant at the American base at Thurleigh. That's—
'

'I know where it is, thank you.'

'I was just trying to contact a pilot I know. I need some pieces for your old man's radio.'

'Don't invite them here. I don't want that.'

'I didn't plan to. I just want some bits.'

'Good. I'm glad we understand that.'

'We do. Indubitably.'

'Stop taking the mickey, Charlie. I'm serious.'

'I know.'

She gave me her other smile: the contrived, coquettish one. I remember that too, but not with any pleasure. I got the idea that I had performed her a favour, and yet I knew not what.

'Do you play tennis, dear?'

Dear?

'Yes, I do as a matter of fact.'

'Play a couple of sets with me, then, before we go in to tea?'

I phoned Thurleigh Field, as the Yanks liked to call it, after 2000 that evening. The American soldier who manned their switchboard was not the same man I had spoken to earlier. This one was more guarded, but he had expected my call, which impressed me. He asked me if they could call me back – Major Wynn had returned, but was not 'currently adjacent to a telephone, sir'. He would send a runner, he said. I smiled in spite of myself; it was the sort of phrase used by my father, who'd soldiered through the First lot. Before he hung up he told me that I might find the Major 'kinda tired' – it had been a long trip, he said. Read *bad trip*, I thought. Grace had made herself conspicuously absent from the vicinity of the telephone when she saw me heading for the hall. I just hung around waiting for it to ring.

They didn't keep me waiting long. Peter Wynn said, 'Hiya, Charlie, how's it going?' He sounded a million years old.

'You're a Major. I don't know that I'm allowed to speak to you any more. Congratulations by the way.'

'Thanks. Is this about that darts match?'

'That too, but I wondered if you'd let me talk with your sparks — your radio operator — I'm trying to repair a bashed up B-17 radio which has come my way, but there's a spares problem.'

'There usually is, buddy.' He let the conversation die.

'I'm not sure that what I'm doing is strictly legal,' I said into the gap.

He laughed a short, bitter laugh. 'That's all right then. It's just the sparks who's the problem. Mine is . . . kinda tied up at the moment. I'll find you one though. Can he call you at Bawne?'

'Yeah. Or here. Now, what do you have on for next weekend? If we're OK do you fancy that match?'

'I like the idea, I really do, but it's too far from the weekend for me to know. I'll catch you later. That OK?'

'That's fine, Major.'

'Don't give me that Major crap.'

'OK, Captain.'

'Not that either; I'm a Major now.'

'Yeah; pretty shitty, isn't it? I'll see you later.'

We were both laughing a bit. Which is always a good way to leave these things. What had happened with his radio operator over Germany that afternoon? Just bad luck. People don't ever get the chop or get sliced up – they just have a bunch of bad luck. I told you: I don't go for that. *Tuesday*'s people didn't go for luck. I told you that, too. A shadow moved in one of the six doorways which opened into the old hall.

'It's OK, Grace. They're not coming here,' I said.

The shadow didn't say anything. It moved back out of sight. I guess that she had to be sure.

I left Grace, Marty and the Indian outside the pub at Caxton that night, and walked back along the Drift in the dark. Grease and the others were already inside. He told me later that there were a lot of people from the airfield at Gransden there – they had far more WAAFs than us, and their company was always welcomed – with Grease, Fergal, Conners and the Toff. It looked as if some kind of a party had reached take-off speed. These days pilots call that V1. In the forties V1s were nasty little rocket-propelled bombs that the Nazis flung at you whenever they lost their sense of humour. Plus ça change. I remember that pub at Caxton, it was called Malachie's in my time. There must have been a reason for it; probably years ago. Where the Caxton Road crossed the west/east Bedford to Cambridge road, to the north of Caxton and Longstowe, there was one of the original gibbets which sat on the county line in medieval times.

Anyway, that night was one for being alone. Grace had appeared possessed of a wild and wayward gaiety when I found her in the Crifton billiard room after my call to Thurleigh, but there was a desperate fragility behind that which made me uncomfortable. She was suddenly someone I needed a rest from. Neither she nor Marty sang on the bike this time, and when we made it she hopped off the pillion, gave me a quick peck on the cheek, and moved determinedly for the bar door. Marty unwrapped himself from the sidecar – I swear I heard his joints uncracking – and gave me a good-humoured punch on the arm before strolling after her.

'Charlie,' he said, 'sometimes you can be a proper tit.'

'I know; only this time I don't know what I've done,' I said.

'Tell you later.'

I left him and the boys the Indian. As I walked, the ghosts of 4,000 years strode beside me on the Drift. I didn't see a single one of them.

The Drift had a surprise in store for me, though. It was when the tree spoke to me. This was an old, old oak tree that had been cut back by lightning years ago, and flew left wing low as a result. It was closer to Bawne than Caxton. It said, 'Hello, Charlie,' and, 'where are you coming from?'

I'd made a fair dent in old man Baker's bottle of whisky that afternoon, but I wasn't that pissed. So after the first shock I guessed that it wasn't the tree which had addressed me thus because it had the same voice as Quelch, which wasn't too bad.

Quelch had an East End accent with a touch more to it than that, and he was perched in the lower boughs of the tree, like an owl. He obviously had better night vision than me – but that's pilots all over for you. I saw he was holding a lighted cigarette cupped in one hand, but the other was out of sight behind his back.

'What the fuck are you doing up there?' I said.

'Roosting.'

Quelch sniffed, and hopped down to the ground. Three dead chickens preceded him. Sometimes asking the obvious is the thing to do. So I asked, 'What are you going to do with these?'

His hand moved to one of the breast pockets of his uniform. 'Sell them probably. Want a fag?'

'Thanks.'

He lit it for me with an American lighter. They were all the rage if you could get them because you could run them on aviation fuel.

'Want a hen?'

'No thanks.'

It was a great clear night, which meant that it would be raining by morning in this sodding part of the world. We leaned on a gate overlooking a newly ploughed field. Quelch picked out the stars and constellations. There was always something not quite right about Quelch that you couldn't put your finger on. Something about the way he treated all officers except Bushes with even more contempt than Grease did. Something about, now I came to consider it, his uniform. He was too old for his sergeant's colours to be so new, and he never seemed comfortable in them: always tugging down the bum freezer tunic jackets they gave us for ordinary wear. A picture formed.

'You were an officer once, weren't you?' I said.

He was small. Smaller than me, with crinkly black hair and a crinkly genuine smile which went with it.

'Yeah. They scraped my brain out, and grafted on an officer bit, like they do with roses; but it didn't take.'

'How did *that* happen?'

151

'It was working all right; although I was flying Beaus, and I didn't like them. Then I stole a car. It was the CO's from the other squadron – a smashing little Clyno.'

'What did you do that for?'

'To sell the bloody thing of course. Haven't you heard? It's what I *do*. I steal things. It's a good trade; car thieving will be very big one day: give it twenty years.'

'Doesn't your family mind?'

'Charlie, stealing is what my family *does*. Stealing things for money. My old man's well off, and he's not a tailor or a diamond smuggler. We're bloody good thieves, and not too violent with it; three generations of East End Jews and not a Rabbi among us.'

'I thought they slung you in the glass house for something like that.'

'They did. Very unpleasant, but at least no one's shooting at you several times a week.'

'Quelch isn't a Jewish name.'

'No. It's not mine either. I started out as Lipstein, but the RAF decided to rename me in case I was captured. The Kraut wouldn't be too tasty about an RAF pilot named Lipstein. I was asked what name I wanted, and all that came into my mind was Billy Bunter stories.'

'What happened next?'

'Some blighter worked out that I was likely to live longer in prison than out here flying. That offended their sense of natural justice so they told me to go back to flying, only as a sergeant. Butch must have had a particularly bloody week, and been getting short of pilots again. I suppose a thieving sergeant pilot is better than no pilot at all.'

'Why are you telling me all this?'

We were standing close together at the gate. He said casually, as if he was asking me the time, 'I don't suppose you'd care to give me a kiss?'

I put a yard between us before saying, 'Don't be bloody daft!'

'No harm done though?'

'No,' I said, 'course not. I can see why you think the Kraut wouldn't be too keen on you though. Don't get caught, will you?'

He sounded pensive for the first time. 'Would that be don't get caught for being a Jew, or for being a queer or for being a thief?'

I laughed because I didn't know what else to say. 'It couldn't be much worse for you, could it?'

'Oh, it could. I might have been a Catholic.'

Time to head for home, little Charlie.

In the billet Pete was lying on his bunk with only the light near the stove on. He was looking at the ceiling and smoking. It was smooch time on the radio: that show with Anne Shelton and Jo Stafford. Occasionally they'd take a break, and play Dinah Shore. Pete was very fond of that show, and would try to get alongside a radio each week for it. There was a new uniform draped decorously over the end of my bed. There was one at the end of each bed.

Pete waved at me with his cigarette, and between songs said, 'You said you needed a new issue. They cost me nothing.' As if that was that.

I knew that it would be a perfect fit. I had wondered what was in the boxes he'd stacked up a couple of days earlier.

'Where were you?' he said later, when he decided he wanted to talk.

'I left them in that pub at Caxton. I didn't fancy it. I walked back along the Drift. It's a great night. I met Quelch.'

'He try to touch you up?'

'No. How did you know about that?'

'We have them in Poland also. He got anything for sale?'

'Three chickens.'

'Small fry,' said Piotr; he turned away from me and picked up a well-thumbed movie magazine which had pictures of girls in it.

'Pete . . . you and Grace?'

He kept his back to me, but his quiet return of serve had iron in it; 'No. Never.'

'Don't you like her?'

He turned to face me again. 'Sure, Charlie, I like her a lot. We all like her a lot.'

I spat out what was worrying me. 'So you don't mind that everyone has had her but you?'

'No, I don't mind. You must understand that if you offered me your tea mug to drink from, I would wash it clean first. It's the same thing.'

There was an answer in there somewhere, to a question that

had been worrying me. It was an odd answer, because I've told you before that Pete had shagged his way from Bawne to Bedford and back, whilst none of us got much of a look in. I didn't let him off the hook.

'At first I wasn't sure that I liked her. I wondered what she would do to the crew.'

'She's not a chop lady, Charlie.'

Chop ladies were the unlucky ones: every airman they went with got the chop soon after. You could spot them at parties dancing with each other; no one would go near them once the word got round.

I told him, 'I know that. But I suppose it would be a mistake to get too fond of her?'

'How old are you, Charlie?'

'You know – twenty. Why?'

'Then bloddy act it. First I thought she was anybody's. Then I know I seen her type before. she's nobody's. If you fall for her it won't last; sometime you'll get over it.'

He went back to his magazine. Ten minutes later he looked up and grinned. 'And don't *sulk* when an old man tells you the truth.'

I had learned early on with *Tuesday*'s people that there was little point in going to sleep with a couple of them adrift. You could doze, and get a bit of a rest that way, but they'd be sure to wake you on their way in; besides, I had to keep half an ear open for sniggers, and pissing in the fire bucket, didn't I? So I dozed. They weren't that late, but late enough to have to come in through the private gate. I didn't hear the Indian; it must have still been out the back of the Caxton pub. Marty came and sat at the edge of the bed. He had a graze across one cheek but I didn't ask. Instead I asked him, 'What was your land girl like?'

'Persuadable. Anna's an American who got caught over here at the start of the war. Her name is Anna Etta-something, like Plaice, or Cod. She comes from a farm in Missouri, so she's probably a bit of a find for the estate. She says that Etta Plaice is her mother's name: mother was once a schoolteacher, and the mistress of a famous American outlaw. She says that the outlaw has settled over here, now runs a perfectly respectable garage business near Godalming, and supports the war effort.'

'Do you believe her?'

'Probably.' Probably was probably our second favourite word. It was as close to a sure thing as you got in our world.

Marty had remembered what he had come over to tell me in the first place. He said, 'You *did* know that the radio you're fiddling with up at Crifton came from the B-17 that made such a god-awful hole in Old Man Baker's Long Ride?'

'Yes, he told me that. Most of the radio shack was bounced clear of the wreck.' I raised myself on my elbows, fully half awake now.

'It was smashed to bits when it hit. Some bits burned and some didn't. The tail section with the rear gunner was reasonably intact, but it had compacted up into the main frame. They heard him screaming above the fire for several minutes.'

'Thank you for that, Marty.' I was thinking of how long it would have taken anyone to reach the wreck anyway. Five minutes? Seven? Poor sod. 'Did anybody get out?'

Marty shook his head slowly, as if reporting a national tragedy. 'No: not a chance. Grace's boyfriend was the co-pilot.'

'I didn't know that. Nobody said.'

'Anna guesses that they were showing off. You know the way the Long Ride climbs away from the house? It's steeper than it looks. They must have dived into it and not left enough space to get out again. *Boomph*.'

'I just told you. I didn't know.'

'That's why I said you were such a tit about phoning Thurleigh from the Hall. I'm surprised the Yanks will even talk to you. I'm surprised that Grace will even talk to you.'

'Grace is fairer than that.'

Marty smiled a distant smile. 'Yes . . . she is. You're a lucky man.'

I thought, *What the hell do you mean by that?* but didn't ask. What I asked was, 'Where is she anyway?'

'She went back to the Hall on the bike; she's going north tomorrow.'

'I didn't know she could ride.'

'She can't, but it can't be too different from flying – if you let go of the steering it falls over. I had to start it for her from the pillion, and then hop off. I grazed my face on the ground.' At least he hadn't been in a fight.

'How's she going to stop when she gets home?'

'She says that she's going to go very slowly and point it at something. She's so drunk she could fall off the Eiffel Tower without breaking anything.' Marty stood up. A little unsteady himself.

'I walked back along the Drift. I met Quelch,' I told him.

'He touch you up?'

'No. That's what Pete asked. How come I'm the last one to know that?'

'Perhaps you're the last one he's asked,' said Marty, and walked away.

Bad Pyrmont

The following evening we toured Bad Pyrmont, which was a neat place to be found on the way to Berlin. I don't know what Bad Pyrmont had done to get a bad name, but there were 400 of us over it that night. There had been no special briefing for any of us, so if there was any particular purpose to the event we didn't know of it. Sure, they gave us the usual old guff about factories producing elastic bands which held the engines of FW German fighter planes together, but nobody believed that any longer. Anyway, as the Toff pointed out, FWs were mainly day fighters, they rarely bothered us; so all we were doing was making things easier for the Yanks, who bombed in daylight. When was somebody going to make things easier for us?

Fiver had got the QL crew bus, which was what we were comfortable in, and in the back I asked Piotr what there was at Bad Pyrmont worth going there for. He was pretty good at European geography, having come from around there somewhere.

'I believe they got a railway station,' he said.

'That's my primary tonight,' Marty said.

'There's got to be something else.'

'I believe they got a duck pond. A very good duck pond in the middle of a park.'

Conners said, 'Bombing ducks would be against the Geneva Convention. We haven't declared war on ducks yet.'

'Is all right,' from Pete, 'they are Nazi ducks. Party members.'

'That's all right then.'

'It may be Bad Pyrmont at the moment,' Fergal told us, 'but it's going to be a fucking sight worse in the morning.' Fergal didn't often swear.

You can see we felt all right about taking *Tuesday* to Bad Pyrmont.

At *Tuesday*'s dispersal Grease had a word with Chief Bryan, and I didn't butt in because I had no specific worries about her this time. Marty had definitely started to become odd about his bombs. He kissed his hand, and laid it on each bomb as he counted, and signed for them. Only in Britain would they make you sign for bombs before you took them to the enemy. What would happen if we dumped them somewhere? Would they dock their cost from our pay? Marty could count to nine, so that was all right – we had a 4,000-pound cookie and eight smaller blast bombs. No incendiaries that night, which was good. It was good, because if I was going to kill any civilian non-com types I wanted to blow them to bits, not roast them.

I think Marty read my mind, because when he ducked back out from the open bomb bay he grinned, and said, 'Wonder how many kids I'll kill with these tonight?' I noticed the Toff wince.

Piotr turned away from us, dropped his cigarette on the tarmac, and stood on it. Fergal was out of earshot doing his walk-round checks – he had more than forty to complete before we flew. I looked back at the QL and saw Fiver's pale face behind the screen: too far away to see whether she smiled.

Minutes later we had hauled up inside *Tuesday*, and were subconsciously registering the litany of checks between Grease and Fergal.

Their checklist *was* like a litany repeated night after night, flight after flight. It came out like:

'Ground/Flight Switch?' – '*ON GROUND*'

'Throttles?' – '*SET*'

'Pitch?' – '*FULLY FINE*'

'Slow running?' – '*IDLE CUT OFF*'

'Supercharger?' – '*M GEAR – LIGHTS OUT*'

'Air intake?' – '*COLD*'

'Rad shutters?' – '*AUTO*'

'Number two tank?' – '*SELECTED – BOOSTER PUMP ON*'

'Master fuel cocks?' – '*ON*'

'Ignition?' – '*ON*'

'Contact'

For thine is the kingdom, the power and the glory, For ever and ever. Amen.

You had your own job to do, of course. Bawne had changed its call sign to *Blackbirder*, which was something I had to remember, but was forbidden to write down. I've always had problems in the short-term memory department. Eventually I wrote it on a piece of rice paper sliced from the code pad, and tucked it inside my glove, vowing to make a last supper of it on the way down, if we copped it.

After I had done my business, while *Tuesday* was still climbing, and before I knew Grease would order me up to the dome, I moved up to his office like the last trip, and stood behind his seat. I touched his shoulder to let him know I was there. He didn't look up; just nodded. In front of us, and about one hundred feet above us, a lonely Lanc dropped away to port and turned back for home. I scanned it for its codes as it came back past us, and clicked the intercom.

'That was something, something, *kilo*, Skip.'

Grease clicked back. 'If it's the Boss, then he's showing some bloody sense at last.' There was a short pause, then he clicked again. 'I can see searchlights.'

'Enemy coast ahead, Skip. Four minutes,' Conners said.

Grease again. 'Take your places everyone. Overture and beginners, please. Watch the skies, gentlemen.'

For the first time I asked myself, *why are we doing this?*

We bombed on a group of wizard TIs put down by the Pathfinder leader. Marty said we were bang on for the station and a marshalling yard, but I still harboured suspicions that he was going for the orphanage and the duck pond. I was in the dome for the whole of the run in. I saw two bombers turn into roman candles and glide steeply out of the night sky streaming flame like torches, and another blow up with a great silent flash that shook *Tuesday* like a terrier shakes a rat.

I heard someone muttering 'Fuck, fuck, fuck, fuck' and realized that it was Grease cursing slowly under his breath, counting down the seconds until we released our bombs. As soon as *Tuesday* leapt like a salmon Grease stopped muttering. At that I thought, incongruously, *Out on you, owls! Nothing but songs of death?* – a line from *Richard III*, the last book I had studied at school.

I think that I told you that unlike most bomber pilots, Grease reacted differently each time we bombed a target – he was never predictable. I rather approved of this: if he was unpredictable to me, then he was even more so to the radar-led flak and searchlights down there. This time he caught *Tuesday* at the top of her bounce, turned her on her side, and made a flat fast turn to starboard without losing much height. I heard Conroy cursing as his maps and equipment slid into his lap, then Pete's 'Corkscrew port', and his guns begin to chatter, followed by the Toff's.

The move from starboard turn to port corkscrew nearly tore my head off. Grease allowed it two complete turns and then reversed them. I held on and shut my eyes briefly. When I opened them again we were flying in the dark, and I saw an angular mid-winged twin – certainly Mr Kraut – flying alongside on the right, and slightly below us: it was already burning inside, and in the cockpit you could see the crew struggling with their straps. A twin stream of machine-gun bullets reached out for it from behind; one of the figures stopped moving, and the flames burst out of the fuselage around the wing roots. The machine-gun fire hadn't come from *Tuesday*, it was from the front turret of another Lanc which had swarmed in behind it for the kill. The night fighter fell away, trailing fire like one of the stricken Lancasters I had seen minutes before, turning on its back as it fell, back towards the fires of Bad Pyrmont.

'Fuck-ing Henry,' said the Toff. It was a phrase he only used when he was moved.

'Rear gunner, Skip,' Piotr said.

Grease responded, 'Yeah, Pete,' and you could hear over the intercom his deep rasping breaths.

'I think that Lanc was with us through the turns Skipper.'

'OK, Pete.'

'I think it is Quelch. He's flying the focking thing like a fighter. I didn't lay a bullet on that 88.'

The Toff said, 'Toff, Skipper – neither did I.'

'Thank you, Toff. Keep your eyes open everyone. We're not out of it yet.'

Conroy had waited for a natural pause, and said, 'Course change in ten Skipper.'

'Thank you, Nav. When you're ready.'

There he went again. Sounding like a bloody officer. I don't know why, but his lonely chant of 'keep your eyes open everyone' had begun to irritate me.

On the way back Marty broke into the night and said, 'I think I get it.'

'What's that Marty?' asked Grease.

'It's Quelch. I know why he's always behind us.'

'Why's that Marty?'

'If he can't get up our arses on the ground, then he's doing it up here in a fucking Lanc.'

'Very funny, Marty. Now, keep your eyes open: we aren't home yet.'

Conners always knew when to say it. 'Dutch coast coming up in five Skip. Course change in fifteen.'

'Thank you, Nav. When you're ready.'

We flew over Manston on the trip north and the Toff remembered that he still had the Manston MO's walking stick. There was an old fire burning on the ground just beyond the airfield.

Grease offered Quelch the first shot at the runway as we landed, in a thick drizzle that pulled down vis to about sixty yards, and made the concrete greasy. Quelch went in rather heavily, and Grease, determined not to repeat Q's mistake, made one of the worst landings of his life: too fast by far. We were on the deck as we reached the hump in the middle of the runway, but were still travelling so fast that I thought we'd become airborne again. Anyway, Grease held her down. We'd launched nine aircraft for Bad Pyrmont. There was *Tuesday*, Quelch and the Boss, three other all-sergeant crews, one hybrid, and two all-officer crews. One of the sergeant crews had bought it over the target. The hybrid was down, so were the other two sergeant crews. So were we, and so was Quelch. The officers were not back yet, but we didn't know them anyway. The important question was where was the bloody Boss?

We debriefed with Harriet. The Toff asked her if he could debrief her one day, which earned him an old-fashioned look from the Pole, which was interesting. We confirmed Quelch's kill, and Piotr even used the same phrase he used at the time.

'He flew his Lancaster like a focking fighter plane.'

Maybe they'd get gongs out of it. Afterwards Grease, the Toff and Quelch went off from us, and talked in a corner. Then Grease came back to us and said, 'It *was* the Old Man we saw turning back; he'd lost all his boost and just couldn't stay up with us. He'd been falling back along the stream for half an hour.'

Conners asked it. 'Then where the fuck is he?'

'Nobody knows. He was heading for Manston to land on with his bomb load – I don't know why the stupid bugger didn't just ditch them. Manston's been shut because of a night fighter: they've had the intruder alert on since late evening, so nobody knows if he's there or not.'

'Didn't we see fire . . .?' I said.

Grease snapped, 'Yes, Charlie, we *did*. So best not think about it. If he's gone, then he's just bloody gone. Now, *I'm* peckish, what about you lot?'

Fifteen trips. Bastards. Halfway there.

We weren't maudlin. No one could accuse us of that. We just didn't like things or folk around us who reminded us of death. So when I awoke the next morning, and wandered lazily outside for the fire bucket the last thing I wanted to see was Bushes' horrible little saloon car. I probably haven't explained so far how proud of it he was: it meant more to him than all the bars on his uniform boards, or his DFC: he was the Boss, you see, and boss status demanded a WD car – even if it was a crappy little Hillman. So they gave him one. OK; so that was the second to last thing I wanted to see outside the hut on the morning after he didn't come back to Bawne from Bad Pyrmont. The actual last thing I wanted to see was Bushes' wife in her WVS uniform, behind the wheel.

She stepped out on the tarmac, as I tried to hide a yawn. That was probably a funk yawn: I always yawn when I get scared. It was about 0800. One of the things that scared me as she stepped out of the car was that she wasn't half as old as I had believed – maybe twenty-eight or twenty-nine – suddenly she was not far off the same age as Grace, and colossally attractive. Why had I ever thought her forbidding? She had old eyes, full of crying – huge and red. She opened her legs as she slid out of the car, revealing good stockings, great pale legs and pale blue silk knickers. I'm sure that it was unintentional, but I credited it to my memory bank current account anyway.

'You're Sergeant Bassett. Conny always said that you were the first to move in the morning. I was too shy to come in,' she said.

'Conny?'

'Connaught. That's the squadron leader's Christian name; didn't you know that?'

'No, ma'am.'

'I think that's strange . . . and if it's all right with you I'd prefer not to be called "ma'am": I'm not old enough for "ma'am" yet. Well, that's the way it seems to me.' She had a nice tired smile, and a shy way of not looking at you as she made it. She seemed less bereaved than we were. Perhaps that's how things are. You never know with women.

'Then . . .'

'Jennifer or Jenny . . . but strictly between you and me . . . and not when Conny's around: he gets touchy.'

When you don't know what to say to a woman try nothing, or candour. I wanted to say *call me Charlie*, but instead I said, 'It was just another bad night for some: I don't know what I can say to you about it, nor what I can do to help you deal with it.' Although I could always hope, I suppose. She was the first sexy widow I'd come across. And of course I had it bloody wrong again. She looked genuinely puzzled.

'Pick up my bloody husband from Manston, of course.' She wasn't putting it on because she continued, 'He landed there after 2300 last night, and has been kicking his heels ever since. He phoned more than an hour ago, and told me to come down to Sergeant McKenzie's crew. He said that you would know the form. He said that Sergeant McKenzie was dependable, and that Annie was available. Who's Annie?'

'An old Anson aircraft that we use as our air taxi.' It took me that long to understand what she was telling me; it was as if the world had stopped revolving on its axis, kicked over, and started again in reverse. If I gave her my good grin at least it wasn't some cheap come-on. 'They're alive then?' I said.

'Are these widow's weeds? Of course they are.'

'I'll shake the skip. He'll know what to do . . . and by the way, you can call me Charlie when the squadron leader's not around.'

The grin she gave me back was just as silly.

I don't know why we do these things, do you? Grease wanted everything carried out just so: with military efficiency and precision. Turd. He sent me cycling for Chiefy Bryan. The Annie had not only to be mechanically perfect in an hour – a difficult concept, because she hadn't been mechanically perfect for about four years – but clean and officerly for a Manston excursion. Then he said something about the honour of the squadron. Double turd. I doubted that Bushes would care one way or the other, but Grease obviously did. Conners Conroy was not only rousted out of his pit, but sent away in Pete's company to get spic and spanned. His new uniform was about to get its debut, because Grease would need a nav for the trip to Manston. We waved Grease and Connors off an hour later from the edge of the runway, standing beside the control caravan. I'd seen ground crews and off-duty WAAFs doing that for us: this was the first time *I'd* waved to a departing aircraft, and I felt as silly as a girl. The Annie was so slow compared with a Lanc, that you felt you could jog alongside her and still get to the perimeter fence first. My new friend Jennifer stood close to me. I could smell her perfume, and I had to shake my head free of the memory of her scrambling out of the car earlier. Of course she caught the movement, turned and asked, 'Are you all right?'

'Yes; fine. Just trying to dump a memory.'

'I keep trying to hold them. Too many faces don't seem to stay on the station long enough to be remembered these days.'

I could sense that I'd touched something, somewhere. A weakness or strength we shared. Or just lust. *Just Lust* would be a great name for an aeroplane.

'Do you want to go somewhere, or do something, while you're waiting for your husband?' I asked.

It was a code that I hoped she could read. This time she was the one to shake her head. She gave me the smallest of careful smiles before lapsing into sad and wistful again. 'Not at the moment, Charlie. I don't think that that would be a good idea, but thank you for asking me. I'll go back and get his food moving.'

I gave her the *no hard feelings* grin back and wondered *why not?*

'You're wasted on an officer,' I said.

She frowned, and walked back to the little Hillman parked alongside the watch officer's jeep, not far from us. I watched the cheeks of her bottom move against the WVS uniform skirt with every pace she took: and made a promise to myself. I would see her again. Two weeks earlier you could have counted the number of women I'd been with on two fingers of one hand. Since then there had been that American nurse, and occasions with Grace. Now I had a date to pick up with a postmistress I'd never met, and was chatting up the Old Man's missus like an old hand. When I had admitted my comparative inexperience to Grace, she had said something like, 'We'll soon do something about that,' remember? Was it really just as easy as that? She was halfway to the car before she stopped, paused as if in thought and came back to me with a finger against the side of her mouth as if she had remembered something. I think that she would have given me a chaste kiss if there weren't others around. As it was I had to content myself with what she whispered.

'It's because you believe that you're going to *live*, stupid.'

Then she was off again with hurried little steps, and that little swing of her hips that had captivated me seconds before.

Pete came over, hands in pockets: he was hard to fool where

women were concerned. He stopped his tuneless whistling, asking, 'What did she say to you? When she came back like that?'

'She gave me a fiver to buy us all a drink.'

'Can I see it?'

'When I cash it in at the pub you can.'

'Sure. I look forward to that.'

Didn't believe a bloody word. But he was usually discreet about his women. He couldn't complain if I had learned from him.

Marty took me to the station bar, at which we were still welcome. There were about twenty pimply faces I didn't know – new crews. We moved among them like pike among minnows. There was something essentially fresh and keen about them, which made me feel old, used up and nasty. I tried to explain it to Marty. He said, 'I know. Part of me wants to talk to them, and give them the tips that no one gave us. You know, the things that can keep you alive.'

'Yes.'

'And another part of me wants nothing to do with them. It doesn't want me to have any part of changing them into something like you and me.'

'What's that, Marty?'

'Infinitely corrupted, I suppose. It's something that bombs do to you.'

'That's a bit like saying that you'd rather they died now, as innocents, than turn into people like us.'

'We're not people, Charlie. Not any more. People are the

things we kill with our bombs every time we don't get a night off. I think we're something else now.'

It seemed that half the station turned out to see them back in. Hail the returning heroes! It did occur to me that we would not have been fêted for aborting a mission from mechanical failure, and bringing back a full bomb load. Mind you, given Grease's standard of touchdown they would probably have abandoned the airfield if we'd so much as thought about it. No one was scheduled to fly, and the wet murk lay upon us like a holy blanket, although it didn't seem to dampen spirits much.

There was an impromptu mixed ranks, mixed trades party in the T2 hangar that night. Not as unusual as you might think because that was the best way the officers could guarantee a worthwhile female attendance at their do's, not many of the WAAFs being rankers, you see. A couple of times I thought that I saw Bawne Billy, and once I caught a glimpse of Grace. Neither can have been there, but I raised my glass to each, and plunged back into the fray. Polish Pete danced nearly all of Harriet's dances, and I saw a couple of young pilot officers giving him resentful looks. It was just a marker, but something you had to take note of. Pete and Harriet slipped away before midnight and I don't think anyone else saw them leave. When Conners, Fergal and I got back to the billet an hour or so later the curtains were drawn firmly around old number eight.

Squadron Leader and Mrs Bushes had put in an early appearance, danced with others for a couple of hours, and left together like a happily married couple. Jennifer gave the station a democracy exhibition by asking a couple of sergeants for a dance, but not me. She met my eyes, then passed on to a guy close to me.

You ought to know that I left school earlier than I should because I've always hated being told what to do — you could describe it as a terminal disciplinary problem. Which was also a problem in my early months in the services. The RAF saved me by banging me up to sergeant aircrew where less people tried to boss me about. I hate it when someone's eyes drift over you with that *I'm in charge* expression behind them. That was what her look said. I made myself that promise again, but should have told myself not to shag above my class without accepting the complications that go with it. Grace didn't count: she had a class of her own, and nobody else was in it.

Peenemunde

Number sixteen was to Peenemunde on the Baltic, where we bombed an empty beach. Bushes didn't come with us, but Quelch did: we'd got used to him anyway. His sparks, a fellow named Fellowes who got a lot of ragging, and I, twinkled at each other after the target. Grease told me to shut up and keep my eyes skinned for fighters.

Peenemunde had been a scientific research station until mid August 1943. We should have left it alone in my opinion, because by developing unmanned flying bombs and V2 rockets it was in the business of making bomber crews redundant. If the war had been resolved by us flinging those at each other then we would have killed a damned sight less bomber crews, and a damned sight more home-based generals and air vice marshals. Which might have sharpened a few minds.

Anyway we had already clobbered it in '43. Several hundred Hallibags, Stirlings and Lancs with blockbusters must have come as a nasty surprise to them. The Germans moved their scientists out of our reach after that, but I think that the brainy little sods never forgave us for their first experience of a proper war.

We went back to Peenemunde in 1944 because some fool of a reccy photo interpreter convinced the Butcher that the Kraut was up to his old games, and making something canny among the dunes. They were wrong: all that was there were sandy beaches, pine trees and the mass graves of the people we had obliterated the year before. Perhaps I have it wrong. Perhaps we were just teaching the Kraut a lesson by disinterring all those bodies with even more high explosive than we killed them with in the first place.

We went home high, above 20 thou: the Kraut was so impressed by the danger to his war effort that *Tuesday* represented, that he didn't bother to put up one night fighter, or throw a flak shell at us. Grease asked Marty what we'd just bombed. Marty said, 'We just made some beautiful great holes on their best sea-bathing beaches. They're going to be *very* annoyed with us.'

Grease was yawning a lot, and I didn't think that it was funk yawning. I stepped forward, tapped Fergal on the shoulder, and conveyed by throat-chop hand-signal that perhaps Grease's O_2 supply was dodgy. I jabbed my fingers downward violently, meaning, *lose height fast*. Conners was also watching me intently, and gave me the thumbs up.

Fergal clicked. 'Skipper – Engineer.'

I heard Grease yawn into his mask before replying. 'Yes, Fergal. What is it?'

'I think the oxygen supply is a bit cranky Skip. We're OK, but it could affect the others.'

Conroy broke in. 'Safe to descend to 5 thou, Skip. English coast fifteen minutes.'

'Thank you, gentlemen. And Fergal . . .?'

'Skipper?'

'Don't be so fucking diplomatic next time: if you think that I'm going to sleep, bloody tell me.'

'You were bloody well going to sleep, Skipper.'

'No worries: bloody boredom.'

Looking between them I had watched the altimeter winding back and when it hit the tit called out. 'This is Charlie. Off oxygen.'

We all would have done the same then; unclipped the mask and let it dangle, relieved of the taste of dirty wet rubber at the back of the throat. If the mask had pinched your nose and cheeks it left indentations on your skin for hours afterwards.

Fiver came out for us in a small new Morris truck which was very comfortable, with bus seats in the back. It was probably less so for her: the cockpit had a canvas tilt, but was open to the wind and weather.

At the debrief Piotr suddenly threw us by asking Marty what height we bombed from.

'As briefed. Eleven thou, give or take,' Marty said.

Grease confirmed it, and said, 'Why?'

'I saw a man fall past my turret. He was falling fast.'

'180 feet per second per second, I expect . . . or something like that,' muttered Fergal, who then asked, 'Is that right? Why did I remember that?'

We ignored him. Pete's WAAF IO, who was doing the writing again, asked, 'You're sure? You saw a man fall past you?'

'Yes. I said it.'

'Was he aircrew? One of ours?' Grease asked.

'No.' Piotr was sort of short with his reply. 'He is Russian.'

'How'd y'know that?'

'He has snow on his boots.'

Ask a silly question. As it was, we couldn't shake his story on essentials. Pete said the man was in uniform but not dressed for flying, and fell almost upright with his arms and legs stretched out like an X. Pete said that there was something worse. 'He looked at me. His eyes to my eyes. And his mouth moved. I spoke back to him too.'

I always get to ask the obvious; it's my trademark. 'What did you say?'

'I said goodbye, Charlie; nothing else seemed appropriate.'

The story got around – a lot of debrief stories did, because the next time we went out to *Tuesday*, there on her nose, under the respectable row of yellow bombs which marked off her missions, and following the two small planes which recorded our credited kills, was another figure: it was the shape of a spreadcagled man.

'How is it that the focking officers get invited to our parties more often than we get to theirs?' asked Pete next afternoon.

'I wonder when Grace's getting back?' Grease said.

'I said, *how is it the focking officers—*' Piotr said.

'We heard you the first time,' said Fergal. 'They gatecrash ours because it never occurs to the patronizing bastards that they're disliked by we, the unwashed classes.'

'You be careful you don't turn into a Red,' Pete told him. 'Reds fall out of aircraft. I saw one once.'

It was then that I put two and two together. If there had been a cranky O$_2$ supply in *Tuesday* over Peenemunde, then Pete, stuck out at the back, on the end of the oxygen lines, would have had the worst of it. They call oxygen deprivation something like anoxia I believe. First you yawn a lot. Then you see things.

Grease was sitting in a utility armchair close to the stove, chain-smoking some American cigarettes that Pete had got hold of. You could smell hot horsehair from the chair's stuffing. He was studying my face throughout the exchange, and identified the exact moment when the penny dropped, because he gave a slow wink, and said over his shoulder, 'Why don't you put the radio on, Pete? Find some music.'

'OK. I got it.'

Seconds later Gracie Fields was in the hut with us, her high notes cracking like hearts, or ice on shallow puddles when a child steps on them. She was singing 'Sally'.

The officers had a wild party that night, and the only other ranks they invited wore knickers.

Grease had asked me, 'Fancy a wet tonight? I fancy walking to the pub to stretch my legs.'

I had money for it, for a change, and it wasn't a bad idea, although it didn't work out.

Some flashy fighter pilot gave us an unasked for aerobatic display late in the afternoon. Bushes had had his Lanc up on air test, and the Spitfire johnnie gave him the fright of his life, passing underneath him on the approach, and then zooming in front of him. Bushes almost stalled it into a field. When he got down you could hear him bellowing from the other side of the airfield: somebody was going to catch it. Later, while I was outside our hut smoking a cigarette into a rare warm dusk, an Erk cycled up and asked if I was in Sergeant McKenzie's crew.

'Yes. Bassett, the sparks,' I said, and he gave me a handwritten note.

I took it in to Grease. Our correspondent was the great hulking provost sergeant at the guardhouse who everyone called Bluto because he was the same shambling shape as Popeye's nemesis, and scary with it. The note said that Pete was in the pokey. That was more serious to us than you imagine, because until he got out we'd find ourselves flying with one-off rear gunners we didn't know well, or, by definition, trust. And we didn't know where Grace was. Not a course to be pursued.

'I'll cut along there and see what the score is. What the fuck's he done now?' I said to Grease.

I didn't want Grease with me for a reason. Most RAF types at that time loathed the gentlemen of the provost service. I actually knew Bluto passing well, and enjoyed his company – I just didn't want anyone else to know about it, that's all. It went back to my arrival at the station. Grease had been posted here with a complete crew, but their radio operator immediately went pat and mick with what turned out to be TB before they'd turned a prop in anger – I tell you, the pestilential Cambridgeshire climate had a hell of a lot more to do with our casualties than Krautie ever did. I was the replacement sparky and his magic piano, and I arrived about a week behind the rest. As I left the train carriage at St Neots station there was this great beast of an RAF sergeant at the next door along, who turned his ankle, and stumbled as he stepped down. I didn't see his trade flashes; they're not what you look for when someone is going arse over tit – I just moved in, caught him, and steadied him. The weight of the man was like having a horse lean on you. You could see that he didn't have a naturally cheerful face, but he forced a smile and said, 'Thank you, Sergeant.'

'You're welcome, Sergeant.'

We both saw the funny side of that. I laughed. He didn't, but there were some odd twitches in some of his facial muscles, which is as close to it as he usually ever got. Bloody provost marshal, wasn't he? Forget the Kraut, I'd just saved the real enemy a self-inflicted. He had been posted to Gransden, and me to Bawne; his people had sent transport for him – the provosts are good at that sort of thing – mine had not; so he gave me a lift.

We'd shared a beer a couple of times since then, by accident rather than design, and I liked his company. He knew me as Charlie, and I knew him as Alex. I had lost some of my family a couple of weeks before I reported at Bawne, and the odd thing is that the gigantic provost was the only person I'd told about it.

They had transferred his section to Bawne maybe three weeks past. He was a big man in every sense: slow thinking, I guessed, and scrupulously bent. Even the handouts he took and deals he made were fair after a fashion: he entered into working partnerships with his victims, rather than exploited them. He told me that he'd been a customs man at a distillery in Speyside before he'd joined up, and someone told me later that that was how they did things up there. I always suspected that Pete had negotiated the bottle deal with him, over our private service gate in the wire behind the hut. Anyway, if I was going to trade on a special relationship with the police, I didn't particularly want anyone else to know that I had one.

I rode over to the guardhouse on the Indian, and parked it carefully where it wouldn't offend the guard commander. Bluto looked out of a window and nodded approvingly, then opened the side door to admit me. I was waltzed through to his tiny office, which was almost smaller than he was. It had two doors; one you came in through, from the front of house, and one behind his desk, which opened on the office where his officer lived. His officer was his opposite: a crabby little sub-lieutenant about a thousand years old, who always had a hacking, chesty cough. That door was a couple of inches open: Bluto gestured at it with his thumb – which meant *I've got to watch what I'm saying* – and I nodded. I heard the distant cough. I've heard sheep with shagged-out lungs cough like that.

I said formally, 'Thanks for seeing me, Sergeant. Can you tell me what Pete's supposed to have done? He doesn't always understand English perfectly, and that sometimes gets him into trouble.' Lies, both of them. 'We try to look out for him.'

I heard the cough again. It sounded closer to the door. Some smoke curled round it. Had Bluto's officer lit a cigarette, or merely started a small fire?

'You can call me Alex in here. It's my office, and we're both sergeants.'

'OK, Alex.'

'I don't know if he's done anything, *yet*. A WAAF has been assaulted and the CO has had all the Polish servicemen – five sergeants and an officer – arrested. The officer is confined to his quarter, and the sergeants are all in here of course: Paluchowski is one of them.'

'Bushes has had *all* of the Poles arrested? He must have lost his marbles! That could cause a riot if it got out.'

The door behind Alex swung open at last, revealing the desiccated little stick of a man who had been standing behind it. He had a hoarse speaking voice with an Orcadian accent, and chain-smoked between bouts of coughing. His blue eyes sparkled with humour.

'Now, now, Sergeant. Speaking ill of your squadron leader after that fashion would be construed as blasphemy in some circles.'

'But sir—'

'And besides, it was not the squadron leader's order, it was the wing commander's, which probably means that it was delivered here on a tablet of stone.'

I appealed to Bluto. 'Can you at least tell me what's going on; what's supposed to have happened?'

His officer replied for him; I was beginning to think that the little Scot might be a good type. 'He probably shouldn't, but I don't see why *I* can't. You're aware that there's a do of some sort up at the mess this evening? It kicked off an hour and a half or so ago.'

'Yes. There was some talk.'

'I know about that. Something about the NCOs asking why the officers got to so many of their parties, when they rarely invite the lower orders to theirs.'

'I'd heard that too.'

182

'Well this one certainly started with a bang. When they opened back the dining room partition to let in the bold officer corps, they were greeted by the sight of a bewildered girl wandering around in the middle of the dance floor mewing plaintively. Apparently she had a potato sack tied over her head, and her hands tied behind her back.'

'That sounds like a cruel joke.'

'It could be regarded as such if she had had any clothes on. She hadn't. She was jay-bird naked,' – his clipped tones said the word as 'nekid' – 'and had that nice square Polish flag we're all so fond of painted on both cheeks of her pretty little bum, and the Polish colours painted like bullseyes on her titties. Nice little titties, too, I'm told.'

'Had she been . . .?'

'No, although she is taking it rather badly I'm afraid. She's in the medical unit. The doc says he can't smell sperm. Not scientific, I know, but he's a decent doc: he won't be wrong. She's insistent that she hasn't been harmed, except for some inappropriately intimate handling. The wing commander was the first through the doors. Soon after that he ordered the detention of the Poles. Is it clear now?'

It was not an appropriate time for me to say 'indubitably'. I said, 'What happens next?'

'They have instructed an investigating officer. He will investigate, I suppose.'

'Who's he going to be?'

'Me.' Then he sighed, as if life was becoming unnecessarily complicated, and added, 'Shut the doors, Alex, and get the bottle out. I need to think.'

'Is there anything I can do for Pete?' I asked.

'Sit here and think with us. *We* know what goes on at the periphery here — including where all the unofficial gates in the fence are — and we know who's stealing from whom, and selling it on. We know who's AWOL. That's just about the limit of what policemen know. *You* know what goes on in the bloody aircraft. Let's see what we can dream up between the three of us.'

The whisky was sweet and peaty and overproof. Alex told me to take water with it. After the first mouthful numbed my tongue, and fried my tonsils, I obeyed him.

Something was coming together in my brain. I said, 'Pete wouldn't hurt a woman. Nor would the other Poles. You've seen them in action. There isn't a woman in the country that they can't talk out of their knickers, but they never hurt them.'

Alex said, 'If, for argument's sake, there was an element of . . . tension? . . . between the NCOs and the flying officers at present, the Polish sergeants would hardly be likely to send a naked girl to an officers' party as a *present*, and sign it with the Polish flag, would they?'

Alex's officer said, 'Granted. To both your premises. So, what else is there?' He pushed out his glass for another dram. My friend Bluto poured another three. The little Scot sipped his, then said, 'There *is* another way to approach this . . . and this is where a complication manifests. Had it been a humble WAAF, or kitchen girl, or even a WAAF sergeant, we could have struck a deal with the girl and kept it under wraps, if you see what I mean. But she isn't. She is an officer. Is it possible that our gentlemanly Polish comrades were sending the officer class an unsubtle message – something like, "Stay your own side of the fence if you want us to stay on ours"? We have something like that between Catholics and Protestants in Glasgow. They call it sectarianism, but it's tribalism really. Annoying at times, but essentially harmless. As long as it's kept in perspective no one in Britain will ever get hurt because of it.'

Click, click, click. I said, 'I don't know if this means anything, but at the do up in the T2 a couple of days ago there was a WAAF officer who gave most of her dances to one of the sergeants – one of the Poles. I noticed that that didn't seem to rest easily with some of the younger commissioned types. They were pretty miffed.'

'How miffed, young Charlie?'

I didn't intend to gab, but maybe the whisky was doing something. Maybe it was supposed to. Alex poured us all another round. These bastards drank too quickly.

'I kept an eye on them. The sergeant and the girl. I particularly watched to see that no one followed them after they sloped off. I would have had to do something if that had happened.'

'You were genuinely *that* worried?' Alex asked.

'I was. I felt something.'

Alex's officer asked, 'I suppose that the woman *was* the WAAF intelligence officer?'

I mumbled, 'Yes,' feeling like a right little snitch.

'And I suppose that the lucky chap was your own gallant rear gunner?'

I mumbled, 'Yes.'

He pushed. 'I didn't quite get that, old son.'

So I said, 'Yes,' again, in a voice we could all hear. I felt even worse about it now. In for a penny, in for a pound, so I asked if the WAAF officer we were talking about *was* Harriet. They didn't have to reply; it was all in their faces.

The officer turned his back on us, and looked out of the tiny apology for a window. When he spoke again he had genuine regret in his voice. 'So it seems likely that some of our young gentlemen have been letting their high spirits get beyond control. If there was an unsubtle message involved here, then *they* were sending it to the girl and the sergeant. I was almost correct the first time. "Stay your own side of the fence." Indeed.'

'They most likely humiliated that girl for no other reason than jealousy. Pricks. They should be in here, not the Poles,' I said.

'NCOs get set in front of courts martial; young gentlemen have high spirits and get ticked off by the CO. T'was ever so.'

'It's not that easy,' I told him. 'Pete and Harriet had an understanding. It hadn't been going long, but it was going. Irregular, I know, and probably a disciplinary matter, but they definitely have something going on.'

'Make your point,' Alex said.

'When Pete finds out he'll go mad. Once he's seen her he'll go looking for someone with a gun. These Poles have guns everywhere, and a very touchy sense of honour.'

'Now that *would* cause a diplomatic incident, wouldn't it? What do you suggest?'

'You've got to keep him here until you've got rid of them,

or you'll have to get rid of him, and maybe the rest of the Poles when they find out – including the officer.'

'That would offend my sense of fairness,' from the little man. Then he sighed out a whisky-laden breath and said, 'I propose to put on my battered cap, and toddle off to make my report – *probable* cause, mind you – to the wing commander. He should have consumed enough beer by now to be amenable to a creative solution.'

'I imagine that he would ask you to cease investigating,' observed Alex.

'I imagine he would,' agreed his officer.

'I imagine that he will identify the high-spirited young gentle-men, and have them off the station by dawn,' said Alex.

'I imagine he would,' agreed his officer.

'. . . and he'll owe us a favour,' said Alex.

'I imagine he would,' agreed his officer.

'What about the girl?' asked Alex.

'I should imagine that Charlie will toddle off to the hos-pital, when he's finished his drink, and square it with the girl, wouldn't you?'

'Then we'll owe *him* a favour.'

'Yes, I imagine that'll be the way of it. Don't you?'

How can you deal with comedians like them? One thing I understood though: I asked them, 'How long have you two worked together?'

Alex smirked. 'Jim an' I have been partners for . . . almost ten years. We were in another service together. Any more questions, or shall we roll this thing up?'

'When can I collect Pete and the others?'

'Tomorrow morning at 0900. If they complain about being kept in for a night for something they didn't do, blame it on the paperwork. Takes a shocking long time to complete.'

'The Poles won't complain; they're not complainers,' I told him. 'They'll just get you back for it one day when you're least expecting it.'

'Then we'll just have to rely on you to watch our backs for us, won't we?'

I said it before. How can you answer a couple of comedians like that?

When I told the others the Toff asked me, 'How's Pete's girl?' I realized that I liked him enormously for the way he'd phrased that.

'Very angry. Humiliated. She didn't see who did it because it was a bag over the head job. She knew that her clothes were coming off, and reading between the lines they all copped a good old feel, but that's as far as it went. She felt the paint going on, but didn't know what it was or what they'd done. Or where they'd taken her. Even though it wasn't hurting her she was terrified that they'd disfigured her.'

Marty said, 'They probably have, it runs deeper than skin, doesn't it?'

'She's says that she doesn't want to come out. She told me that every room she walks into, every officer, every WAAF she sees, she'll wonder if they saw her, naked and with a bag over her head. I told her that she was amazingly attractive, and that I envied to death anyone who's seen her undressed, paint or no paint.'

'You smooth little bugger!' Grease said.

'She smiled. It was what she needed to hear. Pete should have been there to tell her, but he wasn't. So I did it. I don't think Pete will mind when I tell him.'

'Who *is* going to tell him?'

'Me. My next stop. Unless someone's got a better idea?' They hadn't of course. In fact most of them wouldn't look me in the eye. I was beginning to understand that there were some things I was better at than the rest of them. What is it they say? Horses for courses?

Toff had the last word. He said, 'We can't leave it there, can we?'

They let me sit in the cell with Pete. He had three blankets instead of the usual one and the empty plates said that he'd been fed. I told him all I knew from start to finish. He nodded from time to time as if there was some internal logic to the tale. If there was, it was something I had missed.

His first question was about Harriet. I said, 'She's all right. I promise you: all they did was paint her, and touch her. What's upsetting her most is the thought of getting you into trouble. She can't believe that she's not to blame for that.'

Piotr smiled. It's odd, but in that half-dark cell, that half smile made him appear older.

'Women feel like that, even when it's not their fault,' he said.

'And this time it *wasn't*, Pete, I want us to be quite straight about that. It was probably more to do with us than her.'

He nodded again. 'And they won't let us out of here until after the bastards have gone? That's what you said?'

'That's it.'

'And they won't be punished for it?'

'I didn't say that. In fact I don't think that that's the way it works. I trust the little Scotch bastard who banged you up. I think that he has something up his sleeve: something very nasty will be coming their way. He talked about a "creative solution" to the problem, and that doesn't sound like the Marquis of Queensberry's rules to me.'

'I don't understand the Marquis of Queensberry.'

'You don't have to, Pete. I'm just talking about a way the English sometimes have of reinventing justice. I'm sure it's out of your hands. I'm sure that the little Scotch bastard has sorted their futures out, and that they won't be long ones.'

'Truly?'

'Truly.'

This passing notes by hand was a First War thing, wasn't it? My father had an officer friend, who used to come to our house for tea after the parade at the local cenotaph each Armistice Day. He used to talk of having had two Runners killed under him, the way they would have talked of horses a hundred years earlier. Then they would laugh. Mind you, the bastard was a public schoolboy, so perhaps I was just too young to get the joke.

Anyway, Bushes had caught the habit. His decrepit batman turned up in the squadron leader's apology for a car the next morning, with a note for Grease. He had two notes in fact. The second one was for Sergeant Quelch, and he drove off with it as soon as he had delivered ours. He drove the damned Hillman like he was Nuvolari.

Grease showed us the note, which read:

Briefing at 1600. Just bring someone else to look at the maps. You couldn't read the scrawly signature. It could have come from the king for all we knew.

The Toff said, 'Fucking gardening again! If this is going to be a full mission without a formal briefing he's definitely not with us any more! He's not well.'

Grease asked, 'You OK for 1600, Conners?'

'Fuck no, Skip; I see maps every day of my life. Take someone else.'

Grease looked up at me. I nodded, then he said, 'You'd better go and get Pete; we're going to need him.'

Pete was sitting on the edge of the cot in his cell, in his underwear, when I walked in. The door of the cell was open: the other Poles had already left, quietly vowing vengeance apparently. Just as I had predicted. They'd all gone off to consult with their officer type, who had also been freed up. He was alleged to be a count or something, but a lot of Poles told you that. There must have been more counts than tram drivers in Warsaw before the war. He had been released the evening before, after the provost marshal had seen the wingco, but had elected to remain confined to his quarter until after the NCOs had been released. That was their way of things. One of the corporals in the guardhouse told me that a bus containing five young officers had slipped out in the small hours: he smiled as he told me that they all looked rather shook up. He said they'd been posted to a suicide squadron.

Pete said, 'Thank you for coming here, Charlie, but it's no use: I prefer to remain.'

'Don't fuck me around, Pete.'

'Look, Charlie. This isn't between you and me, it's between me and the English.'

'I don't care. I *am* English.'

'You're different.'

'All the girls say that. Now; get your bloody clothes on.'

He shook his head. Sadly, I thought. 'Listen, friend: I fought my way to England to join you, and your English RAF. All I wanted to do is kill Germans. I thought the English understood that. You send me to Krefeld again, and other places like hell, and I take it. I kill a couple of Germans for you, and what happens? Grease beats up on me for it; and I take it. You send me to Krefeld again, and I take it. Now my English friends have assaulted my English girlfriend, painted her body, and paraded her like a striptease . . . and what do the English do about that? You throw me, and every other Pole you can find, into prison for it. The fine English boys who did the thing are sent secretly away, without punishment, to avoid embarrassment. You proud of being English this morning, Charlie? I'm not proud of being Polish, that's sure. This time I don't take it. I am fighting for the wrong bloddy side, and it is time I stop.'

'You mean you want to fight for the Jerries?'

'Don' be stupid, Charlie, I'm not fascist like you English. I'm going to fight for the Americans. I won't wear your focking RAF blues again.'

'We're going over tonight. We need you.'

'Phone Grace Baker.'

When I moved towards him he flinched away. 'I'm warning you, Charlie, another step and I'll focking kill you.'

Part of me believed him.

Neither Alex nor the little Scottish officer was on duty. The duty man was a burly Yorkshire ex-copper we steered clear of in fights. He had common sense though, and called the doc. It took the cop and two provosts to subdue Pete without hurting him too much, and the doc gave him a shot which had him out of it in less than a minute. We dressed him, and they helped me lift him into the sidecar. That's how he came home; sleeping like a baby, but looking like a drunk. The Toff took a photograph of him in the sidecar, with his little box Brownie. Pete slept for so long that we weren't sure that he'd be awake for Bushes' next trip – whatever it was.

The Kiel Canal

Bushes told us not to worry, because the trip wasn't on until the next day, this was just a preliminary briefing – who'd ever heard of one of *them* before? The job was on in the next twenty-four hours, and it would be briefed properly. He just wanted our views. I hadn't heard of that before either. If democracy was putting down root among the officer corps it was going to be a more difficult war than I imagined. The operations board had just three aircraft on it, and there was a table covered with a black cotton sheet he had the six of us stand around. There was me and Grease, and Quelch and his mid-upper gunner, a grave Jamaican with prematurely greying hair (mine would be too if I had had to fly regularly with Quelch) who was called Francis or Francie. He was a great drinker. The nav from Bushes' regular crew, a Scot named Murray, was there as well.

Bushes looked at us, and barked at the skips, 'Didn't either of you think to bring your navigators?'

Quelch shrugged. 'Francis doesn't usually get to see the maps; I thought that it would be a treat for him, sir.'

Francis's teeth lit his face with a smile. He wasn't pleased;

he just thought that it was very funny. He was a quiet man with a cultured speaking voice when he could be bothered to speak at all; his father was a doctor with a pricy general practice in Wigmore Street, and Francis was a Classics First. He found most things very funny, particularly the English. This didn't win him many friends, and he got into a fair number of scraps. Quelch said that he was a ropey gunner, and mad with it. Privately I agreed with Quelchy and suspected that he was the maddest of the lot.

'Ours refused to come. He says he doesn't do maps this early in the day,' I said.

'He'll do what we fucking well tell him.'

'*You* tell him that sir; he'll probably listen to you.' That was Grease.

When Murray pulled the black cloth clear and kicked it under the table we forgave Bushes' testiness immediately.

A large-scale map of eastern England and northern Germany was pinned to the table: a single red line on it connected a small airfield in Cambridgeshire, Bawne, with a port in northern Germany.

'Fucking Kiel,' breathed Grease. 'The fucking bastards.'

There was no red line showing the return trip; maybe they didn't think we'd need one.

'. . . and you haven't heard the worst of it yet,' mumbled the squadron leader. 'They want us to piss all over the Kraut in public.'

Quelch said quietly, 'Explain please. Sir.'

'We're gardening at the end of the Kiel canal, and they want them to see us doing it. The idea is that if we're seen mining the entrance to the canal it will back up the canal traffic for a couple of days, while they sweep the channels. Which is just what is required, apparently.'

'Smack my doggie!' said Quelch. I think that the phrase must have meant something quite different in the circles in which he moved. In technical terms I thought that this was a precision job for maniacs. I mean *other* squadrons' maniacs.

'We are *not* the bleedin' Dambusters. Why don't they ask them?' I said.

'Apparently they're not too good at bombing water. Things sticking out of the water they can manage, but not water itself.'

You've heard the phrase *you could have heard a pin drop*, of course: well, after the initial skirmish no one wanted to be the first to speak. Then Quelch said, 'I've been to Kiel before, sir. It's the most heavily defended port in Germany. Worse than Hamburg.'

'The interesting thing is,' said Bushes, 'some silly bugger in ops obviously thinks that we can avoid Kiel itself, and just over-fly the sea locks.'

'Would they care to come with us? Do you know that they don't even bother to have too much flak around the canal basin itself – they just have three enormous armoured flak ships moored outside it. With us down on the deck, trying to fly between them, they'll mince us. It will be like the Charge of the Light Brigade.'

'Will it, though?' I asked them.

I had an idea: sergeants are allowed them, occasionally. This was one of mine. Have you ever had one of those scary moments when every open eye in a room looks at you? I spoke to Bushes. Might as well shoot at the top, if you're going to shoot at all.

'You tried to make us laugh by saying 617 couldn't bomb the sea if they tried, sir. Have *you* ever bombed the sea?'

Bushes growled. 'I fail to understand.' Then, 'What do you mean, imp?' as if his first four words had been too difficult for me.

'We actually bombed the sea on our third trip. We were already over the German border when the entire second force was recalled, and us with it. I remember it, because it counted as a trip even though we didn't bomb anyone. The whole mob of us had to ditch our bombs into the bomb box.' The bomb box was a designated jettison area of the English Channel. 'Fish-killing on a grand scale. I came up to the office to watch them. So did the nav.'

'And?'

'Have you ever seen a cookie explode at sea level? The shock wave is enormous. It's a very spectacular sight – like a small tidal wave running out concentrically, and fast, from the blast. Then there's the blast effect itself: imagine being down there inside it. What about somebody lobbing a couple of cookies between the flak ships, say two minutes before we arrive at a hundred feet? If they're still floating they won't have got over the shock before we're through them and away. The gunners can add to it by hosing them as we pass.'

Grease breathed out a long sigh and said, 'Give the little man a coconut.'

Bushes said, 'I'll put that up,' and to his nav, 'You can give us a route back now, Murray. We may even need one.'

'Better make that a dotted line. Now there's only fighters to worry about,' Q muttered.

Outside, I asked Grease, 'Mind if I lose myself for an hour or so? Someone will have to watch out for Pete when he wakes up. He has an odd look about him at the moment, even when he's asleep.'

'Someone'll do it. Where you going?'

'Over to Crifton – not to the house, although I could always call in and see if the Yanks left me a box of bits for the Boss's radio. Someone I nearly met. This time I'll do the job properly.'

'Stop being mysterious young Charles. Just say *bint*.'

'Bint, then.'

'Good for you. I'm pleased you've got the knack of it at last. I was worried when you met Quelch down the Drift.'

'That was a chance. A mischance. I've found out that I like girls.'

'Good for Grace, then. Tally-ho, as the fighter jocks would say.'

'Tally-ho.'

I didn't tell him that it was nothing to do with Grace. He could work that one out for himself.

No one had plans for the Singer, and Piotr was still out cold and snoring, so there was no reason not to use it. I was at the Crifton Post Office and Telephone Exchange thirty minutes later. A small bell chimed over the door as I stepped in. A woman's voice without a body to go with it called out, 'I'm sorry; we're closed. I've cashed up.'

Same voice, anyway. If she turned out to be ugly I still had room to bank to port, and get out at low level. She was behind

the high, dark wood counter, bent away from me, and fumbling
with the levers on a heavy old dark green safe. She straightened
up still turned away. Young. Yeah. That's what I had thought:
she wore a cream cotton summer dress that flared gradually to
the knee: it was printed with faded red flowers, and looking
forward from the tail I could see that most of the right pieces
seemed there. A good solid flier, I thought; probably not too
aerobatic. Not too tall; ruddy bronzy hair bleached by the sun,
and worn in some sort of a roll or pinned up in a bunch – it
would darken as the days shortened, like my sister's did.

'I almost hoped that you'd say that,' I said, and she swung
on me.

'I know your voice.'

'Good. I know yours too.'

'But we haven't met?'

'If we had, I'd have married you.'

Laughs. Tinkling sound. Like sleigh bells.

'You'd have been too late: I did that in 1939. You're the
RAF boy who phoned the Americans a few days ago.'

'You're right. That was me. I couldn't resist a look. Do you
mind?'

Behind the creaky little post office she had a small kitchen
sitting room, with a solid fuel stove, a square table and two
chairs, and a couple of cupboards. There were also two utility
armchairs, which had seen better days, either side of a cabinet
radio on a side table. The room was deliciously warm; I needed
to unbutton my battledress top immediately.

Sometime early she told me that her husband was also a
sergeant: a tank commander captured near Tobruk. Before the

war he had been Crifton's youngest postmaster, but had been in the bag, first in Italy and then Germany, since 1942. She wasn't keen on the Yanks, she told me, because they made all the moves. I didn't know what she meant, but she had her back to me whilst she juggled an old black kettle between the hotplates of the stove. I was thinking of some moves of my own. You could have played a fiddle on the crackling power in the air between us. She stood facing away from me most of the time, fiddling with the kettle, which seemed reluctant to boil. Not like me. We talked for a while about this and that, before it was time to fly or die.

I walked up behind her, slid my arms around her waist, and pulled her against me. She gave a sharp intake of breath, but then carried on talking as if I was still a mile away. She talked about keeping the post office and shop going herself, and finding that she was better at it than her husband had been: there was a little nest egg waiting in the bank for them when he returned. I kissed her neck where her hair turned up into its loose roll. Each time I kissed her she would pause between sentences, and then scurry on. Like a murmur, like a breeze. I breathed in her smell, which was fine and vague and resinous: *pine trees*. The Yanks, she said, thought women could be bought. They didn't know English women.

I said, 'I love your hair, and I love your neck,' and kissed the nape of her neck. Her skin was so pale that my lips left a faint red mark.

'Oh,' she said. It was a small noise. I was sure that it wasn't a *no*, so I slid my hands down to her thighs and gently began to inch her dress up. About then she stopped gibbering altogether.

My heart was pounding too hard for me to be able to speak at all, so she had done well to get this far. She suddenly twisted round towards me, and then held me, hard enough to squeeze the breath away from me. She spoke in a low voice, her eyes not meeting mine: I was learning that that was what women sometimes did.

'Let's have that cuppa afterwards.'

When I finally had time to look at her I couldn't help setting it against my picture of Grace, who I had thought freckled, but who had but a few lazy splashes of them by comparison.

'Who were you thinking of, just then?' Susan asked.

'You. I *love* the freckles on your body.' I leaned over and kissed her navel, and let my tongue linger. I tasted her salt.

'Liar.'

Her hair had partly come down. She pulled out the remaining pins and it fell around her shoulders. Her face lost its lightness, and she settled back in the big pillows and closed her eyes.

'Who are you thinking about?' I asked her.

'Sam. I tried to think of his face as I came, but I lost it just at that moment.'

'Does that make you unhappy?'

'Yes. Rather. More of a betrayal; but it doesn't matter. That was good, wasn't it?' When she spoke again the cloud seemed to have lifted. 'Do you want to do it again?'

This time she rode on top, like a Hussar on a galloping charger. I think that she'd done that before. I hadn't. Sam had been a lucky man, until his luck ran out in Africa.

After the second time I said, 'I can't believe that *that* was so easy.'

'Thank you.' She gave a low rueful laugh.

I said, 'No: not you: *it*. Wanting to go to bed with you, asking you, and then just doing it.'

'I knew it already. After I put you through to the Americans I warned myself that I would probably go for you if you ever walked through the door; and you just did.'

'What about the Yanks?'

'No. I don't know why. Pride probably: they seem to be able to have whatever or whoever they want. A lot of wives and widows do tricks for them, but I didn't ever think I needed to. Is another pair of nylons important?'

'What about the Yanks?' I asked again.

She sighed, and gave me a black look. That was a first. 'They flirt; and if they're good at it, it's hard to resist coming straight back at them. Sometimes I let them touch me. Then I wait for a two beat, and say, *I'm married*, and laugh behind my hand when they walk back out to their jeeps all crabbed over. That's the worst that I've done. Until you came along – as soon as you touched me I was finished.'

'Me too,' was all I could think of saying. 'Let's not talk about it. Can I see you again?'

She made me wait. 'OK, but not too often. I don't want talk.'

'Shall I telephone you?'

'That would be wise, wouldn't it?'

I had that feeling again: absurdly pleased with myself. Silly, really. In the car, rolling slowly back over the flat part of Bawne road, I imagined a woman sucking your soul out, and instead of breathing it back into you, breathing it out into the clear, cold air, to be lost forever. Somewhere over Germany maybe.

I caught up with Grease and some of the others at the NCOs' Poor Bar. There were several recreation shops open to NCOs: this was one of them – it didn't restrict you to the company of sergeants aircrew. When I walked in Grease and the Toff were on tall stools up against the bar, already three sheets.

'Remember we're working tomorrow,' I said.

Grease said, 'Don't worry. It's cool.' That was the first time I'd heard those words used that way. He gave me one of those looks – you know, his eyes were focused on me but the alcohol was getting in the way: he took a swing at me whilst I was still six feet away, and fell from his stool.

'What was that for?' I asked the Toff.

'Something to do with the fat guy who runs the kitchens. Apparently one of the girls has broken her arm, and you forgot to remind him of something.'

I bent to help Grease up. Initially he shook me off, but then let me pull him to his feet.

'Bloody Sparks! Are you my sparky bloody conscience or bloody aren't you?'

'No; I'm not,' I told him. 'I'm your bloody sparks, that's all. I can't help your bad memory.'

'Tha' little girl's got a broken arm now. Fat Guts says she's fallen down again.'

'What did *she* tell you?'

'She's off home, isn't she. I asked Fat Guts where she was, and he told me. Bloody smiling he was.'

'Are you going to do something about it this time?'

'If you bloody remind me.'

'We'll remind each other, Skip. OK?'

'Yeah; that's . . . cool.' He must have just learned the expression.

I walked them both out into the crisp air for an early night. Outside a car slowed to let us cross the road. It was Bushes. He was in the passenger seat, which probably meant that he was too drunk to drive, and his wife was behind the wheel in civvies. You could see her arms. (Our bold pilots, Bushes and Grease: I wondered if Quelch was drunk somewhere, too.) She smiled at Grease and the Toff and didn't even make eye contact with me. I learned then that a woman you wanted could pull out of you, and blow away all the pleasure from the woman you'd just had, no matter how good she'd been. Cow. Something like that. You know what I mean? Why was it that at exactly that moment I began to think about Grace, and wonder who she was with?

After we went to Kiel the MO was in need of a stress break. He had a nervous breakdown instead.

I was in the dome looking for the fighters that were bound to come after us, and was the first to notice it. I clicked, and said, 'Skip? It's Charlie.'

'OK, Charlie; what is it?'

'Quelch has lost his top turret. Like it was wiped off.'

'Speak to him.'

I twinkled to Quelch's sparks – Quelch was flying on our starboard side, and the Boss on the other, and we were all so close to the deck that swimming was the only other option. I fired up our Aldis lamp and asked him, 'What's your situation?' It was actually the one-letter code the squadron used unofficially, which was 'Q'.

He twinkled back. 'Flak. OK.'

His twinkling was slow. I thought that it might have been wrong handed, or maybe he was just out of practice. I turned my back on him, and twinkled that over to the leader's aircraft. I added that Quelch no longer had a mid-upper turret. What always impressed me about Bushes was his speed of thought: he immediately dropped back behind our twitchy little formation, and then surged up on the other side of Quelch so that we were bracketing him.

I saw the German fighter before anyone else, which made a first. I just happened to be looking aft from the dome.

'Fighter, Skip, above and dead astern.'

I didn't shout 'Corkscrew', in case he did. You can't corkscrew anywhere from fifty feet, except into the briny. Almost immediately I felt *Tuesday* shake as the Pole and the Toff poured .303 shit back at the Kraut. I became aware peripherally that Quelch's and Bushes' rear gunners were doing exactly the same. Piotr was shouting something in Polish which sounded extremely filthy, and which must have done the trick because then there was a big white flash: a quick, white wall of water from where the Kraut flew into the sea behind us. The poor sod never even got a shot off at us.

Pete stopped firing immediately. 'He's had it,' he said. I could hear him drawing in great gulps of breath.

Grease hadn't deviated from his course by a degree. He responded. 'Good show.'

I ask you: 'Good show' – what did he think he sounded like? I found that my hands were shaking, and held to the rim of the dome to stop. Bushes put Quelch into the circuit first, and then us. He did another low, fat circuit himself before coming in, which meant that we were off the runway and on to the track by then, and I had a rare chance of watching my squadron leader landing an aircraft. All those stories we'd heard about his ground crew strengthening his kite's undercarriage must have been true. He was even worse than Grease at getting back on to the deck: he bounced it like a football, and I reminded myself not to fly with him unless I was ordered. I was standing behind Grease for our landing. It became my place for what was left of our tour, unless I was working. Grease had said, over his shoulder, 'You can be a good leader without being a good pilot.'

I knew that he was talking about the Boss, but said, 'You can't be a good pilot unless you're good at landings.'

'But you can still be a leader.'

'Then there's even a chance for you, Skip.'

Conners had held Fiver back from Q's aircraft, but we could see the people clustered around it, and the meat wagon was by the square fuselage door. Quelch slouched over, dragging his heels and leaned into the Morris to bum a cigarette. That wasn't the real reason. The real reason was to talk to somebody: anybody, that is. There was dried blood on the back of his hand.

As usual, it was me who asked the question. 'What was it?'

'A Flak 88 we think. It came in under the sparks, and out through the turret. Just blew it clear away. Francie went with it. He's in several bits in there.' This was all delivered in a matter-of-fact, weary voice. If you didn't know him better you'd think he didn't care. He blinked, like someone waking from a deep sleep. 'One of the bits lived for about ten minutes. Told a damned funny story about Don Bradman, but for the life of me I can't remember it now.'

'What about Fellowes?' – that was his sparks,

'Shrapnel in his bum and legs, I think. He took a knock, and wasn't with us for a while. That was Henry signalling you. What did you think of his Morse?' Henry Horsefall was Quelch's flight engineer – Fergal's opposite number.

I said, 'Neat. Very easy to read. He can have my job any day.'

Fergal leaned over to me and said, 'I should learn how to do a bit of that.'

Grease said, 'Yeah. Good one.' Then he said, 'Sorry about Francie. He was a good type, wasn't he?' It was rhetorical, and for us all.

'Yes,' Quelch said.

We offered him a lift, but he said that they'd wait for their own transport. Because we'd only used three aircraft the intelligence people had arranged a one-off interrogation for us. They'd pushed twenty-two chairs around two tables angled together, and of course we left two of the chairs empty. I'd seen the empty chairs before, usually in sevens in the mess at breakfast, but for once these got to me. Before I could sit down I picked them up, and placed them against the wall, out of our sight.

There was just one intelligence officer for all of us together – a bent man; in his fifties I'd guess. I remember his long drooping salt-and-pepper moustache, like a Mexican bandit, big, unreadable dark brown eyes, and a languid manner which told you he was a proper bastard. He asked pointed questions, but wrote slowly. That suited us – our brains didn't seem to be working too fast. It was always like that after a job: either your brain moved at a funereal pace, or it raced like Wolf Barnato at Le Mans – there was no telling.

He had a brown cardboard file cover alongside his writing pad. I read the title upside down: it said *Barrett Bombing: Trial*. The cookie had been dropped between the flak ships by a volunteer Mossie from a Northampton Pathfinder squadron. Pathfinders could be like that. We over-flew the impact point three minutes later, unloading Marty's mines and flying through what was left of the shock wave, with seawater falling on us like rain. One of the flak ships had overturned completely. The others didn't get a gun on us. There was some desultory responsive fire from the shore side, and it was one of these that did for Francie. The last enemy shot of the night, as it turned out.

The four gunners who fired on it were each interested in who was to be credited with the unlucky night fighter. Piotr said, 'It was a single-engined radial. Must have been a 190.'

Bushes' gunner disagreed. 'It was a single all right, but it had a pointed nose. I reckon that it was a late mark 109.'

That didn't solve the problem of who was going to claim it: nobody liked claiming quarters – I mean, which quarter had you shot down? The tail assembly? The port wing? No.

The Toff came up with a solution; resigning his own claim he said, 'Francie can have my quarter.'

Quelch's rear gunner immediately agreed. 'Mine too.'

That settled it. The letter to Francie's parents would say that he got his Kraut, before they got him. That was our second fucking gardening trip, and our last. Someone's got to show the clever sods how to do it the first time.

Trudging out, tired to my bones, I found myself alongside Bushes, and asked him, 'Excuse me, sir, but what was that *Barrett Bombing* thing about, on the IO's file cover?'

'Your idea, wasn't it? Gotta call it something. Don't worry, you'll only be famous for about a quarter of an hour, until the next one comes along.'

There was a new Lanc in one of the blast bays when we got back, and Grace was asleep in Marty's bed. They must have moved into number eight sometime during the early hours in order to spare our blushes.

That was trip seventeen. Oh yeah. The MO was in need of that stress break because Q made him stitch the body of his mid-upper gunner back together again before putting it into the coffin. He went off the station the morning of the boy's funeral, and we never saw him again. He left a small Austin Seven Chummy, which Piotr bought from him before he left.

The sewn-together pieces of Francis Lambie, Francie, were buried in the small churchyard at Everton about ten miles from Bawne. The Everton church caps a sharp hill, and looks out over Tempsford airfield. Putting him there was a matter of RAF expediency; they were planting the five crew of a Tempsford Halifax, and their three unlucky passengers, on the same day.

Some faceless wonder must have figured that it saved official time, expense and effort to tag Francie on to them, rather than give him his own send off. After all, there was a war on. I didn't mind. Although he was further away from those alive who knew him, he was alongside good company. He's there still – he wasn't moved soon after the war the way a lot were: you can see the stone. Visit him sometime, he'd like that. He'd think it funny.

In the graveyard I noticed a marker stone from the 1700s which read something like *Joanna Giggle, beloved wife of Jonas*, and her dates, and *Peace, perfect peace*. It had been put there by her husband, and its homily made me smile. It would make Francie smile too. Maybe they could all giggle together in the hereafter. From the squadron there were five from Quelch's crew, and everyone from *Tuesday*. Grace came along, but stood away from us close to the church. It was a fine bright day, but the wind had a bone in it which brought tears to the eyes. It got to Grace more than the rest of us: her cheeks gleamed wet in the sharp light. That's what I chose to think anyway.

Quelch surprised me. His face wore a dangerous look as he stood over Francie's coffin, defying the whole damned world to say anything ungenerous about his boy. A Home Guard patrol provided the volleys of rifle fire, and a Boy Scout bugler sounded the last notes. I've heard that bugle call too many times, and in too many places, to want to hear it again, but it was never better than on that windy Bedfordshire hill top. Bravo, Francie.

When the practised service was complete, Grease and Quelch got us all together in a huddle near the lychgate and told us that we were all up for a week's leave: Bushes' orders, apparently.

We'd borrowed the Morris for the funeral so that we could all travel together. We'd even borrowed Fiver to drive it, although she had stayed away from the service and sat in the car. Grace hooked through my arm as we walked back to it, and asked me if I was going back to my folks for leave.

My stomach knotted immediately: I answered her. 'No.'

'That's sad. They'll want to see you; wherever they are.'

I said, 'They'll see me soon enough, if this lot keeps up,' and gave her the long stare until the penny dropped.

She just said, 'Oh,' as if she'd stepped in something a dog had left, dropped her hand from my arm and moved up to walk between Marty and Connors. After a minute she linked her arms through theirs, and I knew exactly what she was asking them. I hadn't realized that Grease was just behind me, and had caught the exchange. Now he moved up alongside. He didn't ask me anything, but his silence was saying it all. I told him.

'My mother, father and kid sister had a house south of London which got on the wrong side of a doodlebug. No one was hurt, but they decided to go up north to my father's brother in Hamilton in Scotland. They wouldn't listen to me.'

'I know where Hamilton is,' said Grease, 'we've one in Canada, too.'

'They were lucky. Dad got a job almost immediately, and they got a nice small flat for the duration. It was cheap: probably from someone at the Lodge.'

'What went wrong?'

'It was a tidy little tenement flat, with some sort of stove in the kitchen. Mum and my sis used to bank it up when the old man had a night shift, so the place was warm for him to come home to. There was never a problem with fuel: his brother's down the mines. What they didn't know was that there was a problem with the flue. Dad came home one morning to find the flat full of fumes, and them long dead. He told me they looked peaceful; like they were asleep, but with rosy red cheeks.'

'When did this happen?'

'The funeral was a few days before I joined you. It was such a silly way to go Grease; a bloody waste.'

'I wish you'd told us. It's all waste. Even Krauts in night fighters.'

'I suppose so,' I said.

'Grace'll feel bad — putting her foot in it.'

'She can live with it,' I told him, but I was thinking of myself.

The passenger seats in the Morris ran across it in benches. I climbed into the rearmost one, sat in the corner and leaned back against the canvas tilt. After some pushing and shoving Grace squeezed in beside me. A few minutes after Fiver lurched it into gear Grace let her head drop on to my shoulder.

'I guess that we're even now. I remember being so cross at you when the thing with the Americans came up. I was trying to forget them: to get myself away from them. Everybody has a secret grief these days and I've blundered into yours, haven't I?'

I think that I nodded slowly, taking in what she was trying to say, and said, 'It's OK. There are just some things I don't want to talk about.'

'My thoughts, precisely. Can we be friends again?'

'Does that mean I get to have you again?'

'Until bits start to come off, darling.' She put her arm around my shoulders and hugged me, like someone from one of those Red Army posters you sometimes see. OK, so maybe I loved Grace, but there's more than one kind of love, isn't there? Maybe that's why I asked Pete, who was sitting directly in front of me, to ask Fiver to drop me in the middle of Crifton as we drove through.

'I'll see you all later,' I told them.

The post office was closed. I walked around to the back door and knocked – I could hear dance music coming from the kitchen radio. It was Ambrose and His Orchestra, I think. Susan was wearing the same dress as before. It looked freshly washed and ironed. She smiled, and then stopped smiling, but let me in immediately.

I stepped past her and said, 'I know you said not too often, but something happened and—'

She surprised me by stopping my mouth with a kiss. Not one of real passion: there was something else in it. Something like *I'm angry, but it's all right this time because I'm also pleased to see you.* I lifted her dress, and had her against the wall. She was desperate for me not to come in her, but I was stupid. That must have upset her, but afterwards she stroked my hair, as if I was the one who needed consolation.

This time I stayed for the cup of tea she had originally promised: we sat on hard upright kitchen chairs on either side of the kitchen stove.

'One of those killed my sister, you know,' I told her. Then I explained about Black Francie, and how he laughed at the English and everything we did, and was never patronizing. I told her what had happened to him, and about his funeral. I told her about pointless death and my beautiful kid sister. I told Susan that the first time I had seen her I noticed that she had my sister's beautiful hair; that I knew it would gradually darken and copper over the winter months, and she nodded as if she knew what I was talking about. I told her.

'Look, don't take this the wrong way, but when I'm with you it's like she isn't quite dead. Not yet. But that's not why I wanted you.' I told her that when I had told Grease about my sister, I had thought of her instead. There had been nothing else in my head, and no logic to this, but I said, 'I don't know what I would have done if you had said no. You probably knew that.'

She blew on her tea and reached her free hand over to lay it on one of mine.

'I didn't. But a bit of notice would help, and . . .'

I knew what she wanted to say. I blocked. 'Yes. I'm truly sorry about that. It won't happen again.'

'No, it won't; and if there are any consequences this time, remember you're sharing them. My father's a solicitor. A vindictive one.'

I laughed.

Then, without warning she made me cry. She made me cry simply by asking my sister's name. My sister had been named Francesca, for my Italian grandmother. Everyone called her Francie, and her smile lit up the whole world. It suddenly made Black Francie's equally meaningless death impossible to bear. In front of that terrible shiny enamelled stove, on a hard chair with my head bowed to my knees, I cried myself to pieces in front of a woman I hardly knew.

Afterwards Susan asked me, 'Could you stay tonight?'

I couldn't think of a reason not to. I knew the pub the Morris was stopping off at, so I called there. Fiver eventually came to the telephone. She giggled a lot, and made disappointed little mews when I said I'd see them in the morning, as if I had been in with a chance. Who knows; perhaps I had been, I just didn't know it then. Anyway, birds and bushes sprang to mind, which was a signal my brain had re-engaged; I was straightened up and flying right again, to borrow one of the tunes the Andrews girls were trying out. Least I think it was them.

'Even if you never ever come back,' Susan said, 'let's have a decent romp tonight: one we won't forget.' She must have known something that I didn't, even then. Sex isn't always about sex, is it? That night I slept, and I think I began to let both my Francies go.

The next morning I requisitioned a GPO bicycle with Susan's blessing. She had five posties' bikes locked in a shed behind the little shop – they were redundant for the duration, but she kept their tyres pumped, and their chains oiled, awaiting the outbreak of peace, and the inevitable triumph of George Rex's General Post Office. I offered to bring it back later in the day in the back of our car, but she insisted I keep it, and donate it to the war effort. I thought it a useful bit of kit to add to our small land fleet.

Peter the Pole had not hung around. He had started early, and made for town in the Singer with Marty and Fergal, who were both heading for their families. Whenever you started to frame the thought that Pete was an unfeeling bastard who cared for no one except himself, he threw a googly at you. Mine was by way of an open note on the pillow of my bed which had his London telephone number, and a scrawled invitation to feel free to join him if I found myself at a loose end at any time during the week.

Grease was packing: he had a brother in the Wavy Navy who commanded some sort of patrol boat which operated out of Dover. He called it *Dover Patrol*, but I think that that was the old name for it. He was going to spend a week at the port so that they could see as much of each other as possible.

'You can come with me. They'd make you welcome – they're not like the regular Blue Jobs; they have a bit of class,' he said.

I said, 'Nah. But thanks. I'll stick around here, and see if I can get a shag.'

'Seems to me that you're not doing too badly on that score at present, young Charles. Is it your youthful good looks I wonder? Maybe you should give the pecker a rest for a week, and let it get its breath back.'

'Not that you won't be chasing some fat-bummed Wren around?'

'Steal the Blue Jobs' girls? Moi?'

We laughed, and he turned aside to see if he could get another shirt into his leather suitcase. Then he asked, with his back to me, 'You won't be going up to see your old man, then?'

'No. Don't worry though. I only blamed him for ten

minutes: we were OK before I left. The truth is that I don't want much contact with my former life until we're through the tour. It's like the Krauts we're facing are all Harold Larwood, and I know that if I take my eye off the ball, even for a minute, they'll have my stumps out of the ground. I can't afford to do that.'

Grease had his relieved smile on when he faced me. 'What about the bint you've being slipping out to see?'

I explained, 'Maybe I'll see her, but maybe not. She's nice, but only a plate of cakes.'

'A plate of cakes.' He said it slowly, as if he was trying to understand a retarded child.

'Yes, Skip. What do you do if someone puts a plate of cakes in front of you? You grab one — whether or not you're hungry. Christ; I sound like Pete, don't I? Don't worry about me; I'll make out.'

He grinned. He was halfway to being an officer already, without knowing it. Being asked to make decisions all the time can really shag your head up.

'I just wanted to know. I didn't want you sitting here going doolally because you had nowhere to go. If that's what you *want*, then it's all right.'

'It *is* what I want . . . and if I get bored I'll go up to town, and show Pete how to pull a couple of birds.'

'Pride cometh before a fall, and all that, Charlie.'

I touched his shoulder.

'Not for us Grease. When we fall it'll be for three or four miles, and pride won't come into it, will it?'

I sat on his case so that he could fasten it, and helped him buckle a stout leather strap around it for good measure. I needed two hands to lift it to the floor. To give you a better picture of Grease I'll tell you that ten minutes later he picked it up with one, and loped to the door of the hut as if he hadn't a couple of hundredweights hanging off his arm.

'Where's Conners and the Toff?' I asked.

'They've taken the Indian – Toff's going to drop Conners at the station for the early train: he's going home.'

'What's the Toff doing?'

'He's fitting a family visit in somewhere, and then heading to north Wales for a spot of fly fishing. He's nuts about it; he's never said a word to us before, but as soon as I said the magic word *leave* he gobbed on about nothing else. Fiver was practically undressing herself in front of him at Malachie's last night, and he never bloody noticed; just babbled about Wickham's Fancies and Soldier Palmers and the like – they're trout flies, apparently.'

'How did Fiver take it?'

'That's the fucking point. She got so bloody mad that she didn't take it from anyone. Flounced off with the lorry, and left us to walk back. I reckon that last night that prick she's married to got lucky for the first time in weeks!'

'Good for him. I'm all for young wives getting a spot of loving from their hubbies these days,' I told him.

'Explain.'

'Keeps them in practice for bastards like us. Want a beer before you go? There's a crate under Pete's bed.'

I showed Grease our new bicycle. He wanted it repainted in *Tuesday*'s colours, and with her squadron codes on the head tube. While we were discussing that, Chief Ryan drove up in our new Austin Seven Chummy, which he had serviced, and topped up with fuel, for one of Pete's usual considerations: it was a very smart little car – gleaming black and cherry red coach work with small dark red leather seats. The Chiefy rode off unsteadily on the post bike, saying he'd see what he could do with it before we came back off leave.

Grease asked me, 'Fancy driving me to the station for the midday train into town? Then the car's yours for the duration. I won't need it.'

'What time's your connection down to Dover?'

'1800. Plenty of time to get pissed, or pick up a tart at Lyons.'

Maybe he would. Maybe it would work out for him. I drove him to Cambridge for the noon train, and had a drink afterwards at a small dark bar which had probably seen the Wars of the Roses. I tried to imagine it full of students in peacetime, and couldn't. The only other customers were two quiet American aircrew in short brown leather jackets, who turned out to be what they called pursuit pilots – what we'd call fighter boys. They weren't like our fighter boys, who were generally obnoxiously assertive, and loud. These Yanks were quiet and reflective – devout Christian Scientists, they told me – which explained the cloudy lemonade they were drinking. They flew an aircraft they called the P 38: we called it the Lightning. That was its problem, they explained, although its range got it to Berlin and back as a close escort to the daylight bombers, it was just incapable of moving like lightning when the Kraut started shooting at it. Hence their casualty list was high, and morale low. I shook hands solemnly with them, and invited them to join the club. They told me their names, Bales and Winchester, before I left them, and that drinking alcohol would ruin my life. I told them mine, thanked them for their concern, and agreed to visit them in the USA after the war.

What I hadn't told Grease is that I didn't think that I'd be seeing Susan again, and the reason was that she wasn't like Grace. No; it didn't make much sense to me either. I didn't tell him because I didn't want him to laugh at me. I told God instead. He did what Grease would have done, and laughed at me. I didn't know that he had so much to laugh about: I'd seen the cities burning, remember?

It wasn't my last dance with the Yanks for the day, because Bluto stepped out of the guardhouse as I drove in, and waved me down. He said that an American airman was here to see me, and had been directed to the hut an hour ago. The American was outside the hut sitting on the bonnet of a strange little truck, leaning back against the windscreen, and smoking one of those large cigars they call stogies. The truck was a Dodge; smaller than one of our one-tonners, but with bigger wheels, and four-wheel drive, like a jeep. I had seen one before. This had a canvas tilt over the driver, but hard sides. The body stood high above the ground.

The chevrons on his shoulder told me he was a master sergeant, which meant that technically he outranked me, but he grinned when he saw me, and said in a voice from *Gone With the Wind*, 'Hi, Bud. Are you Mr Bassett?'

I walked over, and reached up to shake his proferred hand. 'Charlie Bassett.'

The American drew in a lungful of smoke. 'David Thomsett. Tommo. I got a lorry-load of radio spares for you to choose from. Compliments of Major Wynn, United States Army Air Force. He said that you were to take what you needed, and apologizes for not getting back to you about the darts match. Things are difficult for him right now, he says, but he isn't forgetting that the honour of the USA is at stake.'

Each of his sentences was accompanied by a puffball of tobacco smoke. They looked like small flak bursts.

'I'm moved, Sergeant.'

'Well, don't be, son. Moving is what I had in mind. Jest as soon as you've opened up out back, and made your choices.'

He explained that he was a quartermaster sergeant, who could turn his hand to working on an aircraft if he had to – 'I jest mend the buggers: I don't fly them' – and he owed Wynn a favour, and that this was it. He slid down from the truck, and walked me round to open its padlocked back door, revealing a mobile radio workshop with spares and tools in orderly kiosks, on either side of the interior of the rear compartment.

'Neat, ain't it?' he said. 'We almost never take a radio out of a ship these days. We just drive this little beauty out to them and repair them in situ.'

I took a couple of tuners, spare coils and valves, a box of universal connectors, and an aerial junction to replace the jury rig I had built. I also took US sizes of screwdrivers and spanners. At first Thomsett refused anything for his effort, but then I produced two bottles of Polish vodka, and a bottle of Spanish brandy from one of our lockers. He was delighted by what he said was their rarity value and the gesture, and by the time he was turning his curious little lorry in front of the hut I had bought a friend for life. He'd given *me* things as well, and said that if I could mend an American radio then it was time to Americanize me anyway. The gifts were a black stogie cigar, a .45 calibre Colt automatic pistol and a box of bullets. Life's like that; I'd started the day as one of Butch's bomber boys, and ended it as Wyatt Earp.

It wasn't until after I had laid out the spares and my new treasures on Conner's bed that two thoughts occurred in close proximity. The first was to wonder what had happened to Grace – she had been with us as we left the cemetery the day before. The second was the realization that if I did stick around for the week it was odds on that I would be shanghaied into a crew with a sick radio operator, for a trip into the unknown. Then maybe my luck would run out, if I believed in luck. I resolved to telephone the big house that evening, and take off, to wherever, in the morning.

Obviously Fiver wasn't the only one to hold back on her largesse the evening before because Grace answered the telephone – she had gone directly from Malachie's, leaving her small kit with us, and asked me to bring it with me when I came. Unless I was any good at washing knickers, she said. I said that I wasn't, but that was only to satisfy her prejudice; it wasn't true – I was quite good at it. You wouldn't want anyone but yourself rinsing out your underwear after a trip, you see.

I went to the mess that evening for a quiet beer, but it didn't turn out that way. There was a party on for a sergeant pilot who flew a Lancaster with our significant others – the squadron we shared the field with. His name was Peel, and he and his crew had just had the rug pulled out from under them after twenty-nine trips. They'd crash-landed their kite that morning, coming back from Dusseldorf. Peel didn't describe it as a crash-landing, he just said that his aircraft started to fall to bits as they lugged it over the perimeter fence. That was their T-*Tommy*, a nice old lady Mk 1 who'd soldiered on since late 1943. She was the oldest aircraft on the airfield by far, with more than a hundred trips chalked up on her nose. She wasn't going anywhere again, so Paxton, their CO, had decided that neither was her crew; they'd done enough – Peel had the twitch anyway, although not as bad as Bushes.

I was glad for Peel and his boys, even though I'd never got on with them, and sad for *Tommy*. So we gave them a send-off party together. Fiver danced on a table. They had the knickers off her, black woollen ones like schoolgirls wear for gym. Everyone clapped and cheered, and she did something like a Spanish dance, holding her skirt at her waist snapping her fanny at anyone who hadn't seen it before. That was when it went quiet for me. I went to one of the small round bar tables at the back of the room, and sipped at my beer, which tasted watery and weak. I was suddenly sober. I thought about Susan's husband, in some POW compound somewhere, and that led me to think about Fiver's husband sitting at home alone, listening to the radio. They were probably rebroadcasting Winston, from deep down in his bunker under the war, fat and safe.

Fiver must have seen me sitting alone, because after her dance routine she climbed awkwardly down from the table, and came over to sit by me. She crossed her legs and said, 'What happened to you last night? I missed you,' and blew out a long stream of cigarette smoke. She used to smoke Piccadilly untipped: you could still get those until a few years ago.

'I got lost.'

'I used to get lost like that when I was your age.' She can't have had three years on me.

'When was that?'

One of those silences that friends like. Then a frown; 'Years ago. Hundreds of years ago.'

My melancholy must have been catching. I told her, 'Get your knickers back on, and I'll walk you home.'

She stood up quickly, and gave me an old-fashioned look. She said, 'I think you got that back to front, Charlie,' and walked away.

I thought that was that, but I'm wrong most of the time when it comes to women, because she came back a few minutes later, gave me the eye-lock, patted her bum, and said, 'OK. Ready?'

On the way out we passed Bushes, his wife and several of the more presentable representatives of the officer class. They must have been Peel's guests. Bushes gave me and Fiver a quick glance, and a smirk. Jennifer's eyes met mine, and she frowned. It was the way her little mouth dropped into the upside-down smile whenever she didn't get her own way.

'Not staying, Sergeant Bassett? I was hoping for a dance tonight.' Cow. A chinless type on her arm scowled briefly before letting the grin back on to his face.

'No,' I told her. 'Not in the mood for it. I think there's a war on,' and then Fiver tugged me past.

The quickest route was around the peri-track, out through our hole in the wire, and along the Bawne road. It was a fine crisp night with plenty of light. Fiver started to drag her heels as we approached the shed I lived in, but I didn't slacken our pace, and took her out on to the road. There was an early ground frost, and our shoes clacked on the metalled surface. Fiver hung on to my arm as if I was the last boat on the *Lusitania*, and eventually told me, 'This is nice.'

'Yes. I suppose it's good to be good now and again.'

'You *are* a good man, Charlie.'

'No. You mustn't say that. I'm not.'

'Charlie Bassett you're a good, kind man. Why do you think you're not?'

I tried to put into words something that had been welling up in me for days. I could tell Fiver because I thought she wasn't that clever. How wrong can you be?

'I don't think I know the difference between right and wrong any more . . . or good or bad,' I said.

She gave a little laugh. She had a fine, girl's laugh; one that would remind you of a brook gurgling. 'You're such a *fool*, Charlie. Nobody knows that these days.'

She kissed me at the gate of the cottage she shared with her husband; her mouth was big and open and wet and moved with a wonderful sensuous sloth. Once kissed never forgotten. It had nothing to do with passion, and everything to do with companionship and greed.

'Come in for a cup of tea. Dougie won't mind — we don't get too much company.' she said.

I was introduced to the contractor in a small, warm sitting

room. He no longer had the Hitler moustache I remembered. Vera Lynn – and whatever you may have heard, we never called her the 'Forces Sweetheart': we called her something else altogether – was jumping off 'The White Cliffs Of Dover', from a smart new Bakelite radio.

'Is that live from the Troc?' I asked him.

'Aye. Have you ever been there?'

'Yes. Several times. You can always tell – it has an echo all of its own.'

'I've never been up to London myself. Maybe after the war.'

Close to he was maybe twenty years older than his wife, and wearing badly with it. There was a pipe on a smoker's friend beside one of the chairs, and a heavy scent of Navy Cut in the air. Fiver had greeted him with a hug and a kiss, and I had been unprepared for the obvious affection she had for him. She left us, and I heard water, kettle and crockery noises from another room. As soon as she left the room he offered me an expression which asked a question without words. I shook my head briefly and firmly, and said, 'No.'

I felt bad about the relief on his face. For him, I think, her going with those dead young men at the airfield was just about bearable . . . but if she had started to bring them home?

Fiver's tea was strong, and without sugar – they'd blown their ration the week before, she said. She warmed her toes in front of the fire, I talked about cricket before the war, and Doug talked of the first job he'd laboured on – repairing the Byfleet banking at Brooklands. He'd even raced there himself, in club events. Even although there were only the two of them, by the time I slipped away before midnight I felt as if I had had a glimpse of something I hadn't seen for months: something like a family.

I will admit to a slightly elevated pulse – as one of the RAF docs would say – when I saw Bushes' car outside the hut on my return. But it wasn't her. The Boss was sitting on the end of number eight in the dark. His head was resting on his chest, and he had taken his trousers off. You could have smelt the beer from him upwind forty yards away. I think that he was sweating it. He had an unhealthy pallor, but then, most drunks have, and I wasn't then the expert I have since become. The building was chill. He ignored my arrival, or didn't sense it, so the first thing I did was bank up the stove. When I walked back to him he stirred and muttered, 'Where d'ye get all the coal?'

'The same place you get the tyres for your banger, Boss. Them that asks no questions . . .'

'Poetry. You must have gone to a good school.' Then he coughed a deep and liquid cough: I wondered if the MO knew about that. Then I remembered that we'd just lost our doc.

'I did.' I told him, 'Grammar grub. But it was wasted on me, wasn't it – that's what you think, anyway. Bloody hated it.'

I moved behind him, and turned the sheet and blankets back. For a moment I smelled Grace – expensive perfume, and sex.

The squadron leader asked, 'What ye doing now?'

'Putting you to bed, Boss; you're as pissed as a fart.'

It was easy to topple him back, push him into the bed, and

remove his tie: I didn't want him to strangle himself in his sleep.

As I pulled the blankets over him he said, 'Odd expression that. How does a fart get pissed? It just gets farted. Don' go away: sit there for a moment.' He gestured vaguely towards the next bed; Fergal's, as it happens.

'I'm fagged out, Boss, I want to get my head down.'

'I wanna tell you something.'

'OK. What is it, sir?'

'It's about the wonderful taste of fish. It's something I found out.' He had reached the running-one-word-into-the-other stage, and his eyes were already closed. I wondered how many pints of the watery ruin they were serving in the bar a man needed to drink to get as drunk as he was.

'I went to a public school, you know: a cheap one, but a good one. All the juniors talked about sex all the time, an' never got any of course. You listening to me?'

I nodded, but he would have gone on anyway.

'. . . unless one of the seniors buggered you. There was this fat one called Carrington – got the MC last year; a sapper major would you believe? – I remember him telling me that if you licked fanny it tasted of fish. He was the first one to tell me that.'

'I was told that when I was a kid, too.'

I lit a Players, and remembered the sweet tobacco smell in Fiver's front room. Maybe it was time to take up a pipe. Some of the fathers of the squadron smoked them.

'You don't follow me, Bassett. The point is, that in my sort of school an awful lot of jacking off went on . . . and if it really made you blind, half the fucking men in the world would be blind by now, wouldn't they? Well, I soon learned that if you didn't wash yourself clean afterwards you began to smell. And what is more is that smell was distinctly fishy. You foller? I remembered that again today.'

'That's very profound, sir, but I really don't need this.'

'You still don't understand, do you, ape? What *that* means is the next time you go down on a woman and she tastes of fish, all you'll be doing is licking out what the man who was there just before you left behind him. See? This "girls taste like fish" crap is just something the women made up in order to get away with murder.'

'Thank you for that, sir: but I told you; that's something I didn't need to know.'

'You're a cocky little snot, Bassett, but a handy sparks.'

'Thank you, sir.' Then I stood up, and said, 'Goodnight.'

'G'night Sparks.'

I walked away from him to my own bed. I turned off the light, and undressed unsteadily in the glow of the stove. I've told you before that I didn't like banking the stove: it reminded me each day of my mother and sister. I couldn't help wondering what they were doing, even though I knew that they were dead. I'd never see them again. Or maybe I would.

Just before I closed my eyes Bushes said quite distinctly, 'My wife, you know – her name's Jennifer; sweet Jenny. She *is* sweet, but she tastes of fish lately.'

I said, 'You don't mean that, sir. It's just the beer doing your thinking for you.' It was ridiculous, but at that moment I felt older and wiser than him, and added, 'We'll talk about it in the morning.'

But we didn't, because when I awoke he was gone, and the bed so neatly made that I wondered if I'd dreamed it.

Driving the little saloon was almost a restful experience, because driving it anything other than sedately would have been really stupid: with its high centre of gravity it would have overturned if cornered at more than about fifteen miles per hour. That's why the battered jeep with two Americans in it caught me up so quickly on the run through the trees to Crifton. One of them fired a pistol in the air to attract my attention – at first I thought that they had had a blow-out. I stopped, and they pulled in behind. Maybe it was a stick-up.

When the passenger walked forward to me I said, 'I suppose you're going to ask me to throw down the money box, and stick up my hands. Sorry to disappoint.'

'What?' Then he grinned. 'Oh. I get that. *Stagecoach*. Sorry. We couldn't get past because the road is so narrow, and couldn't think of another way to signal you – there's no horn on that thing.'

I held my hand out to him. 'Charlie Bassett: I'm on Lancs at Bawne. This is my week for meeting Yanks.'

'I'm Harold Manley, and the stiff driving me is July Johnson. We're from Thurleigh.'

'I know a couple of guys from Thurleigh. Dave Thomsett, and a pilot called Peter Wynn. Do you know them?'

Manley groaned, and rubbed his hand over his face. Sackcloth and ashes.

'Shit. You know Bandit and the Major. You won't tell them about the shot, will you?

'Not if you ever get round to telling me why you wanted me to stop in the first place.'

'OK,' he said. Then he called back over his shoulder to the jeep. 'Come 'ere July, an' hide your fucking piece: this Limey knows the Major.'

They were both navigators from the 306th, and one of their good pals, another nav, had flown into the Long Ride at Crifton in the B-17 which had never come out again. They wanted to know if they'd get permission to see the spot their friend had fried in. The thought of them putting the same question to a frosty Grace stopped me. I got them to park up alongside the cavernous coach house, and agree not to leave their jeep unless I called them forward. I did something right for a change. Grace had come out to greet me, but stopped as soon as she saw the Americans. She was wearing riding pants, a crisp white blouse and an expression which would have dropped an elephant at a hundred paces.

'They knew the navigator on your B-17,' I told her, 'and they just want to see where their pal died. They were driving down to ask permission.'

'Just tell them yes, and get rid of them.'

'Do you want to meet them?'

As I turned away she touched my arm and added, 'Tell them to come back when they've finished. For a glass of lemonade, or something.'

I nodded. 'OK . . . and Grace?'

'Yes?'

'You've never looked lovelier.' I blurted out exactly what I meant. Grace blushed. Bullseye.

She looked up at the crisp blue sky momentarily, then back at me. 'It's really autumn,' she said.

'"No spring, no summer beauty hath such Grace, as I have seen in one autumnal face." It is Donne this time.'

'You will have to stop doing that, Charlie.'

'Can I stay? If I don't, they may make me fly.'

'Stupid. Your bed's been made up since yesterday.'

They had put a hefty table, with a two-inch marble slab on top, and four heavy old chairs in the stone basement room where I had challenged Grease with his mountains of murdered birds. The room was clean and cool. Mrs Barnes had taken to her bed ('with an indisposition' Mr Barnes told us). Consequently one Mrs Coates would serve tea.

'I take it that Mrs Coates is of the same vintage as he is?' I asked.

'No, she's about twenty years younger than the Barneses . . . say, about fifty. And frisky. Tim came across her with someone in the woods off the Long Ride once.'

'Who's Tim?'

She walked away and looked upwards through the long narrow window above our heads. From that angle there was nothing to be seen except sky. Grace gave me the significant pause before she replied, 'He was co-piloting the B-17 which made the hole those two boys have gone out to see.'

When we heard the high-revving jeep engine Grace asked

me to pull hard on an iron hand grip attached to a wire which hung down alongside the door.

'I take it that I've just rung for tea?' I said to her.

'Yes, you have. Don't blush, and don't think of it as an imperative. You've just tipped off Coates when to serve. You've saved her a trip; if you hadn't done that, she would have had to come all the way down here to ask us, return to the kitchens, and then come down here again with the tea. You don't understand because you weren't born to service.'

'You're definitely not a socialist then?'

'Nor a prig like you, Charlie Bassett, if that's what you mean. The only difference between socialists, Liberals and Tories, is that Tories are more likely to stick it up the wrong hole when they're pissed.'

'I wish I had your experience of life, Grace.'

Her face fell. 'No you don't. Really you don't.'

She put the bounce back as the two Americans walked in, followed by Barnes, who was serving our tea himself. Perhaps Mrs Coates was having a little lie down. The man named July Johnson looked less at ease than the other, Manley. He didn't meet Grace's eye as he spoke to her. 'Hi, Miss Grace. You won't remember me.'

'Yes I will. You're July Johnson' – she put the stress on the first syllable of July. 'You flew with Tim a few times when Roger Graham was sick.'

The boy looked sick with embarrassment. He ducked his head.

'Do you still carry that damned pistol everywhere with you?' Grace asked him.

He grinned back. Looking at her this time. Then a shadow passed, and he said, 'I'm sorry . . . we're all sorry about what happened to *Good Golly* . . .'

'That was Tim's plane,' Grace explained for my benefit.

Johnson ploughed on as if she hadn't spoken, 'but I'm not going to stand here in front of you and pretend that it wasn't anything other than plain stupid. Stupid flying.'

I gave Manley a brief warning glance and waited for Grace to explode. The thing about Grace is that she has this infinite capacity to surprise: she moved quickly to Johnson's side, laid a hand on his arm, and spoke very gently to him. 'It's all right, July. I know. It was stupid flying, but they're all gone now, and now we have got to get on with it. Tim would be pleased to think of you and Harold here; making sure I'm OK.'

'Yeah; he'd say that was nice.'

Grace said, 'Are you two ready for tea and a sandwich now? Charlie and I are starving.'

Johnson said, 'Am I just! Sitting down to tea with the daughter of a Sir, in an ancient English country pile: who's gonna believe this back home?'

Later that evening Grace and I ate our supper in the kitchen. This made Barnes uncomfortable, but Mrs Barnes bustled around us like a mother hen with her two favourite chicks. She was a heavily built lady who chuckled a lot. I smelled 8711, and the stale wine on her breath, as she bent over me to serve a thick brown spicy soup, which was followed by a cold cut of lamb, heavy with fat, and small, sweet golden potatoes and a steep hill of cabbage. The cabbage tasted so good that it must have still been in the ground that morning. Barnes unbent enough to agree to himself and Mrs Barnes joining us at the table for a mug of tea, and a glass of whisky: Mrs Barnes would have killed him if he had refused. Barnes had laid a fire in the grate in the library, which is where we finished the evening.

At some point I confessed, I told Grace, 'I fall in and out of love with you every few days. I'm just like a yo-yo.'

'I know. The trouble is that we aren't synchronized. You're on the way down, as I'm moving up. When you're in love with me I can hardly stand the sight of you: I can't bear being fussed over. Then as soon as you've gone I'm so desperately unhappy. I simply can't wait until I see you again.'

'What about the others?'

'Sometimes I love them too. Do you mind?'

'Not awfully. It's a bloody strange war, if it does this sort of thing to you, isn't it?'

'I suppose so.'

'What about tonight?'

'Would you mind terribly if we didn't, Charlie? It's not terribly convenient.'

'I can always ask Mrs Coates.'

Next day Barnes woke me with tea and a wad.

'Excuse me, sir. There's a gentleman to see you. Miss Grace asked me to call you, but she said you weren't to hurry,' he said.

'I heard a woman singing: before I went to sleep.'

'I don't doubt it, sir. But there's no one living in this wing now — apart from yourself. Might you have been dreaming?'

'I might,' I told him, but I didn't believe it.

Grace and Bushes were sitting opposite each other in leather chairs in what Barnes had called the smoking room. It was probably because the fireplace smoked. Bushes was wearing an elbow-patched tweed jacket over service trousers, shirt and tie: he looked too tired to get up, and didn't. I had automatically stiffened to attention in spite of my natural inclination, and my civvy clothes. Grace was wearing a silk, pink, slinky thing, with a sash tie, which slid over her figure like liquid. She was giving him oodles of leg.

Bushes said, 'Morning, Bassett. Sorry to break into your leave, but two types in long coats have been stooging around asking for your bloody tail gunner. That Polish pig. Our honourable receiver of stolen property.'

'Who are they?'

'Won't say, but they have ID cards which claim Ministry of Works, and have large open numbers stamped on the face of them, like bus tickets. One of them's one of us, and the other's another bloody Pole I think. Don't believe a bloody word of it, because they're bloody policemen of some sort, of course.'

'What do they want?'

'I don't know. They wouldn't tell the wingco either, so he had them booted off the patch. That is quite literally; but I'm sure that they'll be back with all the right papers.'

'Did they search the hut?'

'Funny thing that. Nobody seemed to remember where Paluchowski was billeted.' That made me smile. 'I thought that if you had a telephone number for the Pole you could give him a bell, find out what it's all about – that sort of thing.'

'I'm sorry: Pete never leaves me a contact number when he's away.'

'Course not. Just a passing thought.'

'Thank you, sir. *Tuesday* will appreciate it. What did you have for Miss Baker, or is that private?'

Cab Calloway was belting out 'The Mermaid Song' on the radio. Grace stretched out a hand at waist level, and studied her fingernails. She said, 'Conny's told me that I won't be flying any Lancasters for a while. They're going to deliver the last five in a oner; this week, while I'm away. And he's apologized for having me grounded.'

'Grounded, sir?'

'Yes although it was a bit of a mistake actually. She was flying that ruddy Spit which almost wiped my nose last week. I complained to the War House – they found out that it was an ATA delivery flight: my bad luck was that it was Grace who was flying it. Back to some OTU.'

'Bravo, *Grace*. Bravo, *sir*.'

Bushes squirmed in his chair: he had never looked comfortable in it anyway. 'Don't worry: I'll fix it,' he said.

Grace said, with a captivating little smile which put the world right, 'Don't you worry, too. I already knew, and it's already fixed; the grounding's only for eight weeks. I've been ATA flying without a proper gap since 1941, so they've sent me off on eight weeks compulsory leave. I'm sure that I'll be back in the sky after that.' Then Grace told him, 'Now you're here, you'll stay for breakfast, even if you've already eaten. Charlie and I are starving.' That was the second time she had told someone how well she was feeding me.

Afterwards we walked the Boss to the front door, and saw him into his grotesque little tin box. Grace was being a good hostess, whilst I just wanted to see him off the premises. I followed her up the wide dark wood staircase to her room, feeling that I was climbing through history. Her bed was an enormous four poster with black wood posts polished by a thousand hands. It had rich, green brocade drapes.

'I wish I could have seen his face!' she said.

'When?'

'When I flew the Spit underneath him, and popped up in front. I bet he had to stand on his pedals. Hasn't much of a sense of humour, has he?'

'He's got the twitch. He probably filled his trousers.'

'I'll forgive him.'

'You were flying dangerously. Grease would have reported you as well.'

'Grease can be very po-faced about flying: you all can. I was flying it like a Goddess, and probably for the last time. There aren't that many Mk 1s left. Imagine how you'll make love to me when we know it's our last time, Charlie: it was like that.'

'You think too much.'

Grace lay back on her bed and flashed herself at me; nipples like ridged brown bullseyes.

'Wanna bet?' she asked.

*

238

I recognized the voice of the girl who answered the phone, but couldn't place her. She sounded sleepy. I tried again, because I was sure I knew the voice, but the picture of a face wouldn't come. Pete sounded wide awake. He moved effortlessly between sleep and complete alertness.

'Did I wake you, Pete?'

'No. She did.'

'There's been a couple of coppers, policemen, up at the station asking for you. One of them might be a Pole; are you in some sort of trouble?'

'Me? No. What did they want?'

'It didn't get as far as that. The wingco and the Boss gave them the bum-rush, but the Boss thinks they'll come back.'

'Must be some political thing: some mistake – I told you we had Nazis on both sides of the Channel these days.' He sounded breezy and unconcerned. 'I make some calls, Charlie.'

'That's probably a good idea, Pete,' and I gave him the telephone number of the Hall if he wanted me to do anything. If he recognized it he didn't say.

'Hey, Charlie; you think we'll go back to Krefeld next week?'

If I had been as po-faced as Grace thought we were, I should have said something about careless talk costing lives. Instead, I said, 'Probably. We've made a fucking mess of the job every time we've been so far. Sooner or later Butch is going to want it done over severely.'

'I thought that too,' said the Pole. 'Thanks for calling me. Don't worry. This is nothing I can't fix.' Then he put the receiver down. You got no hallos or goodbyes with Pete. And I agreed with him: there was nothing that a Pink Pole couldn't fix – that's what I believed when I was twenty, anyway.

I worked on the radio all day, and by the time I had finished I could have talked to the moon, if the Yanks could have flown a B-17 that far. In the late afternoon I tuned into the traffic coming from a daylight raid the Yanks were mounting over the Kiel canal. It was a terrific signal. Chiefy Bryan would have liked this radio – it was better than *Tuesday*'s.

That night Grace wanted to go to the pub in Crifton. She was well known there. We drank too much Tolly Cobbold beer, which was dark and sweet, and drove the Austin slowly back to Park House for that, and another reason – the air was thickening. That night there was a dense fog.

Grace wanted me again, but her mind wasn't engaged by what we did, and part of me was secretly glad when she suggested that we sleep apart, and get some small benefit from the night.

I was awoken about 0300, but not by the woman who wasn't singing in the corridor outside. It was a rude awakening, with a torchlight shone in my face. For a moment I was back on the squadron, but then Barnes dragged me back into the real world.

'Mr Charles. Please wake up. There's something bad happening outside,' he said.

I sat up in bed, and pulled on a sweater I had thrown down over the end of it. Barnes went over to the window, turned off his light, drew back the blackout and opened the small frame.

Tendrils of khaki-grey fog licked in at him immediately. I had seen this stuff before: it hung in the air like a living wet moss. You could be fooled into thinking that it had a sentient malevolence. Then I heard them: Merlins, their sweet music ebbing and flowing. Some nearer, some further away, then some nearer again. They were in the circuit.

I joined the old man at the window, asking him, 'How long has this been going on?'

'More than an hour.'

'Shit. They'll be dying out there soon.'

'I think that they already are, sir, which is why I came for you. After the first one went down. Is there anything we can do?'

'Not a damned thing, Mr Barnes.'

I switched on the big green radio in its battered case, and searched for the radio profile they were using. It was my trade: too easy really, and the one occasion I wished otherwise. It wasn't the squadron, but our stablemates on the other side of the station, and they must have had a lucky raid, or an easy one, rather; there's no such thing as a lucky raid. It seemed too cruel that they'd dragged their bombers back from Germany, only to have to fly in circles over their home station – until their engines stopped, and they began to die in their own back yard.

Barnes had a cat's whisker radio of his own, and listened in to the radio operators each night as our fleets set out for Krautland, and then limped back. In his head, and through his cheap earphones, he came to Germany with us. After he'd heard the first one go in he'd seen a distant glow in the fog.

Then he'd come to me, because he understood the tragedy around him, and thought that I would know what to do about it: all I could do was share the nightmare.

We drank his employer's whisky, and listened to the voices of the WOPs reporting dwindling fuel reserves, until each of their aeroplanes became their coffins. They took more than an hour to go. Most of the skippers ordered their crews to abandon, but it was evident that most of the crews had refused: no one wants to jump blind if they can help it. So we heard them go off the air, one by one. Barnes knew them by their voices better than I ever could – he'd been listening to them for weeks. He'd say, 'That's L-*London*,' or 'That's Andrew Thomson's crew.' Then he'd take another sip of the whisky and stare out of the window.

We thought we heard two distant *crumps* as thirty tons of steel and aluminium buried itself nearby, and on one occasion we definitely saw a brief orange-yellow glow, a flare in the fog a few miles away. The last one took ten minutes to go on its own, after the rest had ploughed in. I had met the sparks a few times, although I couldn't remember his name. His last words were, 'One engine gone,' followed by, 'both port engines out,' and finally, after a pause of about a minute or so, he shouted, '*tim-ber!*'

Then all we had left was static. My speciality. I switched off the beast which had brought the war into our room. What was left of the whisky was in our glasses. Barnes swallowed his in an impressive oner, and asked me, 'Exactly what happened there, sir?'

'They lost the lot, Barnsey. They lost the whole fucking squadron.'

'I see.' He moved unsteadily to the window, closed it and drew the blackout curtain. His torch beam seemed blindingly bright after the gloom. Then he said it again. 'I see, Mr Charles.' Then, 'I think that I'll be getting along now. Thank you for keeping me company.'

'Thank you too, Barnsey.'

I stood in the doorway and watched his torch beam waver along the long narrow corridor, bouncing off the dark panelled walls. Somewhere far away a girl began to sing. But she wasn't real, so I went back to my bed, and lay on my back staring at the ceiling until the whisky overcame me.

In the morning everyone in the great house found an excuse to be in the kitchen. Six of us: we were like rabbits huddling together after the Death Fox had completed his night's work. Grace even cleared some of the dishes. No one said much. I dropped one of the windows to catch the last heat of the year: then I slammed it up again, because there was smoke on the wind.

When Grace sat down alongside me I asked her, 'Did you sleep through the racket last night?'

'Yes, 'fraid so. Mrs Coates told me this morning.'

'Glad it's not me.'

'I wonder if you *are*?'

Sometimes Grace punched straight for the balls. 'How many?' she asked.

'I'd guess at about sixty-five. There are always some miracles, statistically. I suppose that's why you always get back in the plane. You're always going to be one of the miracles.'

'I think that you will be, Charlie.'

'I know. So do I. I'm just not sure that I want to be any more, but don't tell any of the others.'

'What will the RAF do – now they've lost a whole squadron?'

'Talk lots of guff about national pride, the honour of the squadron, bravery and endurance – you know the form. Then ship in twelve new kites and about ninety bods, and start all over again.' Grace gave a bitter little laugh, and I asked her, 'What's that for?'

'I was just thinking. They might need you and me back sooner than they thought.'

'You fancy driving over to Bedford tonight? We could see what's being served at the Lamb, and maybe see a flick – as long as it isn't *The Wizard of* bloody *Oz* again!'

'OK – but you're on your own for the next few hours. I'm going to ride the whole of the estate boundary.'

'Don't damage any serfs.'

'Piss off, Charlie.'

Mrs Bassett's son doesn't need more than one time of telling. I sat in the library and read in the end-of-year sunlight, which streamed through the deep windows, consuming cups of tea, coffee and sandwiches brought to me at regular intervals by Mrs Coates. There was a radio in the corner, the bloody place seemed full of them. I found an Anne Shelton programme, and then Big Hearted Arthur took over for half an hour of silliness.

He sang 'Kiss Me Goodnight, Sergeant Major' and I wondered again why the Germans had ever thought they could conquer a nation which could see the funny side of the war.

Barnes came to find me at about 1600. 'Miss Grace is back, sir. She's still down in the stable block.' There was no mistaking the tone of his voice. Orders are orders: befehl ist befehl.

I noticed that she had a black smudge on her forehead. When she lifted her right hand to wipe it away I saw a red weal, like a burn, on the back of it.

'What do you do in 1944,' she speared me with, 'if you want a couple of your very own Lancaster bombers?'

'I don't know. What *do* you do?'

'You buy a small estate in Bedfordshire . . . and you just bloody wait.' When I didn't bite she added, 'We have two new ones out there since last night, although they're not much bloody good any more.'

'Anybody get out?'

'Don't know.' She sniffed, and I realized that she had been crying. 'Shouldn't think so. They just look like the remains of rather enormous bonfires.' Then she started to cry again. I felt awkward doing it, but I hugged her.

When she could speak again she said, 'There's a field they call Alan's Field, for some old reason. It's just a thirty-acre hump in the land. When you stand in the middle of it the ground drops away from you on all sides, and you can see three counties – it's my favourite place. We deep-ploughed it last week.'

I wasn't going to like whatever came next, but I asked her anyway. 'Is that where the wrecks are?'

'No.' She shook her head. 'They're a couple of fields to the south. No: there is a *man* standing in Alan's Field.' She suddenly buried her face in my shoulder, and muffled her words, 'They told me he was a radio operator, just like you. He's upright, half buried in the top of the hill, just like a scarecrow or a statue standing there. His parachute had opened but it was all tangled up. His eyes were open, and he was smiling. Oh Christ, oh Christ, oh Christ, oh Christ . . .' She punched weakly at my chest as if it had been my fault. I thought of what his body must have been like below the waist if he'd plunged feet first into the field. Then I pushed the picture away. I held her as tightly as I could, as if I could squeeze the horror out of us.

Eventually I asked her, 'What's being done?'

She stayed in my arms, but leaned backwards away from me, tapped my chest twice with her burned hand, sniffed, and told me, 'I've sent Anna Etta up there, with two of the older men. They'll dig him out, and bring him down on the handcart. Bawne says that they're rather busy, and if we can keep him overnight they'll collect him in the morning. Ghoulish.'

'Ghoulish,' I agreed, and turned her so that she was beside me but with my arm still draped around her shoulders. That's how I walked her back into the house; Grace needed a bath, and we both needed to get inside a bottle of her old man's whisky.

The film was a Will Hay film: I can't remember much about it, or its title. It had rained again just before we sat down, so the auditorium was hazy with smoke and steam. A few weeks ago I had looked on the flicks as my best shot at getting my hand inside a girl's blouse – now it was different: there was no desperation. Is that what happens to married couples, I wondered? Anyway, I could relax, hold hands, and enjoy the Fat Boy on the screen; he always made me laugh

We had a couple of pricey drinks in the old pub on the High Street, and then Grace led me across the road to the American Red Cross Officers' Club. Strictly speaking the club was off-limits for me – I hadn't been touched by the magic dust which made me an officer or American – but Grace seemed to know the guys on the door, and they guested me for the night. The air inside was pungent with the smell of American toasted tobacco, and maybe something else that I wasn't as familiar with, but had been shown RAF educational films about. A quick look round indicated no one going mad in my near vicinity, so maybe the films had got it wrong. It was mainly a place to sit and drink in, although a lot of the guys seemed to be stuck on coffee. There was a small dance floor served by a small combo of four musicians, probably moonlighting from one of the big USAAF bands. They did 'Begin the Beguine', and 'Moonlight Serenade' and things like that.

Peter Wynn drifted past on tiptoes, dancing a girl two sizes too big for him, but his eyes unglazed momentarily when he noticed me.

'Hi, Charlie. You still around?'

'Hi yourself, Major. Guess I am.'

'You got Grace with you?'

'Yes.'

'Great. Tell her I'll get that dance from her later.'

Grace was a great dancer, fast, flowing and exquisitely balanced – and consequently in constant demand. I only had one dance from her. I moved over to part of the club where three huge leather Chesterfield settees were arranged D-fashion to a fireplace, like the chairs in the smoking room at Crifton. A smaller group of mainly older officers were bunched there, standing around a woman in the dark uniform jacket and skirt of the American Red Cross, with its bright round shoulder patch. I noticed her noticing me, and she waved me over, patting the seat alongside her. She was somewhere in her early thirties, and had thick dark short hair. Her speaking voice was both feminine and mannish at the same time, and mid-American; like Lauren Bacall after she was famous, and halfway through the day's first pack of cigarettes.

'We don't see many RAF boys here: you must be honoured. Like a coffee?'

'Yes please.' She waved over a coloured waiter. 'I'm with Grace.'

'Ah, Grace. She's a great dancer isn't she? Hang on to her, and you've got a ticket into anywhere you please.'

'I'm Charlie Bassett.'

'Pleased to meet you Charlie Bassett. I'm Emily.'

'Are you a nurse?'

'Hell no. I just run this joint. Leastways, the entertainment side of it.'

'Just checking me out?' I asked her.

She laughed this absolutely great laugh. 'Just checking you out,' she agreed. 'Do you know any of the guys here?'

'I know Major Wynn, and most of his crew if they're around.'

She said, 'You know Peter?' Then she gave me a shrewd eyeball-to-eyeball look. It was like she was seeing clear through to the back of my head. 'When d'you last see him?'

'A week ago . . . maybe a bit longer.'

'He's lost a couple since then. I wouldn't ask about them if I was you.'

'Thanks.' I gulped my coffee. It was still scalding hot, but I took it like a man, feeling my palate crisp. Across the smoke I saw the waiter suddenly grin. I grinned back.

'Where did you meet him?' Emily asked.

'My crew ended up in a drinking competition with his in a London club, a few weeks back. Then I met him again at the Wellington in Bawne village. That's about twenty miles away from here.'

'Yes. I know it. There's a maze in the church there, isn't there? That drinking competition in London? The winners didn't get to end up across a bunch of American nurses by any chance?'

I don't think that she could see my blush in the poor light.

Grace danced in and out of view from time to time, always with a different partner; once with Peter Wynn. She was more his size than the Amazon I had originally seen him with; they looked good together. After an hour or so I caught a glimpse of her leaving the room through another door, with a different airman. They were holding hands. I watched for her coming back between the gaps in conversation with Emily and a serious USAAF aviation doctor, who had wire-frame spectacles. It took about fifteen minutes, then Grace danced with someone else. She blew me a kiss as she moved past.

We left half an hour later. Emily entered my details in a 'permanent guest register', and asked me to drop by any time. There was something about the way she and Grace exchanged greetings, right there at the end. Grace kept her chin up, but whatever it was, she got the worst of it.

In the car she told me, 'That place is not so much fun any more,' then chewed her lip.

I drove the little car very slowly, on account of the drink and the blackout, and we smoked cigarettes from the deck of Luckies someone had slipped her. We had the car windows wound down just a crack, so that the smoke was sucked out into the night.

Some time after we passed St Neots I asked her, 'Why did you do that? Go out with that Yank? If you're feeling that randy all you have to do is ask.'

'And you'll come panting? Really, Charlie?'

'No. Be serious, Grace: *why*?'

'Because he asked me, if you must know. He told me that he was going to die tomorrow and that he wanted me. Why not?'

'And if he doesn't die tomorrow? How many times has he used that line?'

'Who cares? He's going to go soon, that's all that matters. He's a dead man; it's all over his face. He *is* going to die. Believe me.'

'What about me?'

She sighed as if in exasperation. 'I've told you, Charlie;

you're going to make it. You and the *Tuesdays*. That fact alone makes you quite an attractive proposition in some light.'

'Thanks Grace.'

'Grow up, Charlie. You make me feel old.'

Snap, I thought, but didn't speak aloud.

After a mile's silence she asked, 'Anyway. What were *you* doing?'

'I was talking to that woman Emily. I liked her.'

Grace's riposte was quick and bitter. A rapier thrust. 'Oh,' she said, '*everyone* loves Emily.'

After that she turned in her seat away from me, and showed me her back for the rest of the journey.

Breakfast the following morning was a small mountain of nature's bounties. Where did civilians get that decadent heap of food from? It was a year's bacon and egg ration for a small family. I told Grace that I would leave later that morning.

'Do you remember Conners asking me how I navigated as accurately as I do?' she said.

'Yes; you told him you followed the railway lines, and showed him a railway map of England. We do that sometimes now if we're low level over France or Holland: Pete got us a pre-war railway map of north-western Europe from somewhere. It's a bit tatty, but Conners loves it more than his charts.'

'Well, I lied. Or didn't tell the whole story, rather.'

'What's the rest of it?'

'There was a book I read before the war, while I was learning to fly. It was called *The Old Straight Track*, by a travelling salesman named somebody Watkins. He had travelled all over England, by horse and trap, and early car: he said that if you look along alignments of significant features in a landscape – hills, church steeples, very old trees, gaps in hedges and old lanes – you could see the remains of ancient straight trackways that date from before the Romans: from even before the folk who laid down the Drift. He believed that these invisible tracks linked some sort of prehistoric religious centres: he called them ley lines or something. I think that the religious centres bit is a load of old tosh, but the lines are there; you can see them clearly from the air. I use them as well as my railway atlas to navigate with. All you have to do is look at the landscape with a big eye for the patterns on it, instead of a small eye for detail. From above 700 feet you can see for about three miles.'

'What's this to do with me leaving?'

She sighed and gave me the *look*. I felt like an idiot again.

'Absolutely nothing, Charlie. Do drop in again the next time you're passing.'

She stood up and left the kitchen immediately. I realized that for the first time I had experienced a flounce, in all its flaming glory.

Barnes gave me a wink which was so slow that I almost mistook it for a full side facial tic: he said, 'Ye are fallen from Grace: Galatians 5.4.'

I suppose he was used to it.

As soon as I stepped into the Nissen hut and dropped my bag on the floor I was aware that something was wrong: it wasn't as cold as it should have been. Someone had been at the nutty slack, and the stove was still warm to the touch. Either one of the boyos was back from leave early, or we'd been occupied. Maybe the Nazis had landed, and Mr Churchill had forgotten to tell us.

The Boss bustled in shortly after my arrival: I knew it was him by the hideous squealing of his car's brakes outside – only his Hillman made that noise, and only he drove it badly enough to produce it. He was embarrassed, as well he might be: either he had been slumming it, up to no good with a floozy, or had been subject to a spectacular demotion – it was *his* spare clobber spread on and about old number eight. He could never have cut it as an other ranker, you know; he was far too untidy – although he had made the bed. When I saw him in the midst of the mess he had created – which included used clothes, empty beer bottles, and beans and corned beef cans – I felt almost sorry for him: the word *slob* sprang to mind. Verily.

He said, 'Sorry about the mess. I moved in for a couple of days to get some peace.' Then he added more truthfully, 'Small falling out with the memsahib.'

'Nothing to do with the taste of fresh fish, I trust, sir?'

'Fucked if I know, Bassett. Same as all of our arguments. We're both probably arguing about something different, and neither of us can quite see what. Don't get married, Bassett.'

'I think that I'd have to ask your permission anyway, sir.'

'And I'd bloody well say *no*; what's more, you'd thank me for it, later.'

At least he was lobbing the ball back over the net to me as far as this conversation went. His face had stopped ticcing for the time being. I looked at his spread of detritus and told him, 'I don't want you to think that we begrudge the space, and all that, sir, but haven't they created something called an officers' mess to provide persons of your station with accommodation among other persons of your station?'

'Yes, but if I went there then people would know.'

'People will know *here*, sir; or don't NCOs count as people any longer?'

He looked uncomfortable, as had been my intention: I wanted rid of the bastard.

'Anyway,' he said, 'it's all over. Storm in a teacup really.'

'I'm really pleased about that, sir.'

'Don't be such a patronizing little git, Bassett.'

'OK, sir.'

'I'll send someone over to get my things.'

'OK, sir.'

'What's this "OK, OK"? You're mixing with too many Yanks, Bassett. I hear things as well, you know.'

'OK, sir.'

Then a copper of mean rank cycled over from the guardhouse with a message from Alex. The note he handed me was sweat damp from his progress.

I asked him, 'What did you do to him to deserve this?'

'Beat him a game of Chaser, didn't I, Sergeant.'

'Dunno; did you?'

He wasn't amused, and couldn't follow the conversation: he would make a good high-ranking cop after the war, I thought.

I said, 'Yeah. He's not a good loser, is he? Thanks for the note. Take it easy on the way back.'

Alex's note read: *Please phone woman named Emily – American Red Cross Officers' Club at Bedford. This is the provost service, not your bloody messenger service! Speak to me about P.*

He hadn't signed it. People like Bluto don't.

I walked into Bawne for the exercise, and used the new telephone call box near the church. When I got through to the club at Bedford, Emily said, 'Hi. Thanks for getting right back to me.' It took me a few seconds to try out the words in their new running order. They seemed to fit, so I filed them away. She continued, 'You *do* remember me?'

'Of course I do. You joined me up in your club as a gesture of solidarity with the working class.'

She laughed that great laugh I remembered.

'No. It was nothing to do with that commie claptrap – it was because I liked you. Listen: Lee Miller's staying here tomorrow: have you heard of her?'

'Glenn Miller's wife?'

'Christ no. Glenn stays here all the time, but he never brings Helen.'

'Who's she?'

'Glenn Miller's wife. Look, are you following this?'

'I don't think so. Hang on.' I put more change in the telephone and pressed the button.

'Still there?' Emily said.

'Yes. Go on.'

'Lee's a famous war photographer. Probably the most famous in the States. She's over from Europe for a few days to do a series of aircrew photographs for *Vogue* magazine: she's going to change her sponsorship to the AAF and promised them some army publicity shots of British and American aircrew together. Guess who got the job of rounding up some Brits? I thought of you first.'

'And I'm the Chinese Emperor.'

'Seriously Charlie; and there's a party here afterwards with a special bar.'

'Then count me in. I shall be proud to represent my country at competitive drinking with my American cousins. I'll put it in my logbook as essential liaison duties.'

'Call it what you like, brother; just *be* here. I'll send you transport at, say, 1500 tomorrow.'

'Quite the organizer, aren't you? What's the rest of your name?'

'Rea; and, yes, organizing's what they pay me for.'

Bushes' bag of bolts was outside our hut when I returned: the car was untenanted, but the hut wasn't. My irritation at Bushes' return was mixed with relief that he was moving out: it turned to wariness as soon as I saw that it was his wife, not him.

'Mrs Delve?' I said.

She was back in WVS standard sexless dark blues, standing between the beds, looking as if she couldn't make up her mind about something.

'Don't be a pain, Charlie. I told you to call me Jennifer.'

'I think that I prefer Mrs Delve. That way I know where I am with you.'

'You're in your billet, and so am I – although technically I should imagine that I'm out of order; unchaperoned.'

'*I'm* here,' I blurted out, cursing myself inside.

'So you are. Which bed is yours?'

I pointed at the one nearest to her. 'That one: you were right.'

'You don't keep much, do you? No photographs of family, or pin-up girls?' She paused as if a thought had just occurred to her. 'I say, you're not one of that ghastly Quelch's little catamites, are you?'

'No. You're the third person to ask me that.'

'Sorry. No photographs of girlfriend or family?'

'No girlfriend. Nearly no family. Most of them were killed a couple of months back.'

'Sorry.'

'Don't be: I'm killing other men's families in Germany every night, after all.'

'That's different.'

'I wonder . . . I shouldn't imagine they'd think so.' I wanted to change the angle of the conversation. 'Did you come to see me, or to collect the squadron leader's things?'

She looked away from me as she answered, which was disconcerting: it was if she was speaking to someone who wasn't there.

'Both. Conny asked me to clear up after him. He's like a child about everything except running a squadron – it's the only thing he *can* do. He said that there was just you here, and that it would be less embarrassing for him if his stuff was cleared away before the others came back from leave. *I* thought it was a chance to clear the air – between us, I mean. I don't know what happened to make us so uncomfortable and snappy with each other, but I'm not enjoying it. I find myself plotting a course around the station in a way that ensures you and I don't bump into one another.' She gave a bitter little laugh – it had a very feminine and vulnerable ring, compared to Emily's.

'If it helps, *I'm* not enjoying it either. You either snub me altogether, or play the grand duchess,' I said.

'I know. I can't seem to help it.'

'For what it's worth, I'm glad you came here: it was brave.'

'Me too.'

'You didn't have to say that.'

'Neither did you.'

She was obviously one of those good-at-pauses people. She turned slowly, then sat on the edge of my bed, facing me across the aisle, which seemed about as wide as the Rhine. She nodded at Pete's cabinet radio on the shelf behind his bed. 'Does that work?'

'It's probably one of the best in Cambridgeshire. We picked up Tokyo Rose on it one night.'

'Put some music on.'

The radio seemed inappropriately loud in a room virtually empty of people, so I hurriedly racked the volume back. It was the Orpheans playing dance music from *Afternoon at the Savoy*.

Jennifer stood up, decision made. 'Dance with me,' she said, and we met halfway, in the corridor between the beds, dancing two slow numbers with her head against my shoulder. One of them was 'Stardust', and the other was 'Serenade in Blue'. The singer sounded like that Frank Sinatra who used to sing with Tommy Dorsey.

Afterwards I sat because my legs were shaking. Eyes down.

She said, 'Thank you. When this war is over, I'm going to

spend thousands on pretty, frivolous dresses, and live at parties. I will dance with all the boys left alive. Have you thought about after the war? Most people do, but they don't like talking about it.'

'Only that I want my possessions to be few, and wholly functional. I don't want to be weighed down by things that don't do anything.'

'Such as?'

'I want a jeep rather than a car: no frills — they'll be cheap after the war. Nothing soft, silly or decorative like that Austin Seven I've crawled around in all week.'

'I rather like it.'

'I think that you're supposed to; that's the point.'

She had made no move to collect up her husband's debris.

'I sat down because my legs were trembling. It's like flying over Hamburg,' I told her.

'I know. You didn't have to tell me that.' She did the pause thing again, then asked, 'I suppose that this is just plain old fashioned lust, isn't it?'

'Yes. I hadn't really thought about it,' I said. Liar. It sounded cool until my voice began to shake.

'Well, you'd better have me then, hadn't you?'

But there was something resigned about how she said it, and perfunctory about what we did next.

I don't know how long I took. Not long enough, I suspect. Being given total freedom to do as I pleased with a grown woman's body was a recent discovery for me. Within my narrow range of experience, I thought hers quite splendid.

Afterwards I sat on the edge of the bed beside her, running my fingers around her stomach, and stroking her navel. I thought that I had never seen a person as beautiful, or as deliciously wanton, and said so, aloud, without intending to.

I helped her pile Bushes' things into the old kit bag he had brought them in. I found it under number eight. We didn't exchange more than half a dozen words before she drove off, but I couldn't help smiling a lot, and eventually neither could she. After that I switched frequency on the radio to pick up an American jazz programme, and whistled away with a black singer named Fats Waller. I even cleared away the Boss's empty tins and dirty plates.

I tell a lie: there was something else. Before I closed the car door for her I told her, 'The Boss thinks that you're fucking the other officers, and it's making him unhappy. Tell him he's wrong.'

'What if he's right?' In four cheeky words I had a glimpse of a woman I hadn't met.

'Then *lie* to him.' But would she?

'I'm not having sex with anyone else.'

'You are *now*,' I told her.

There it was again. That smile. Later that night, with the hut blacked out, and the Pink Pole's wireless set burbling away in the background, I picked out 'Serenade in Blue' again – only this time it was Glenn Miller's people. I lifted my arms and danced alone in the corridor formed by the eight beds. It must have looked pretty odd, but I was feeling pleased with myself.

*

The transport that Emily Rea sent for me was piloted by a familiar figure: the same Master or Technical Sergeant, Thomsett. This time he had a covered jeep.

'Hi, Tommo. You come here more often, and they'll give you a pass,' I said.

'Got one.' He held up the buff cardboard ticket, and added, 'You never know when it'll come in handy. I cut a deal with some big policeman you got.'

'What for?'

'Meat. Quarter of a smoked pig – for delivery tomorrow.'

I laughed. That would be Alex.

'Come on. I'll show you why you don't need a pass,' and we drove out of the gap in the wire behind the Nissen hut. I closed it carefully behind us because that was the deal; we were never to rub the provos' noses in it.

Thomsett wasn't impressed. 'Yeah; we got a few of those,' he told me.

In the jeep I said, 'I was with some of your guys recently. They seemed to think that you're some sort of gangster. Al Capone or someone like that.'

'Shucks.'

I laughed at that. 'That's what Gabby Hayes always says in Westerns, isn't it?'

'Yeah. Those guys at Thurleigh Field: they're some comedians, right?'

'They seem to think you have it all sewn up.'

Tommo chewed on his dead cigar in silence for a few heartbeats, then he asked me, 'You get their names: these comedians?'

'I don't think I ought to tell you that, do you?'

He grinned at me when he should have been watching the road. 'No: you better hadn't, I guess.'

There were three Sherman tanks parked in the road outside the ARC Officers' Club in Bedford. The road around one of them was cracking up where it was sinking into the storm drain, or the sewer. A small old man in a pinstripe suit circled it nervously carrying a clipboard. He had the drooping moustache and look of a local council officer; he was far too late to prevent the damage. The club lobby was crowded with young American tankies in fatigue suits, and something like soft leather flying helmets. Emily Rea emerged laughing from the scrum, dragging one of the soldiers with her. He was at least six feet four.

'Hi, Charlie. This is Albert Grayling. He and his boys are moving south. They're going over soon. When he phones me for accommodation he forgets to say that they'd be bringing their tanks along with them.'

Albert said, 'Hi,' and shook hands. 'I'm Albie.'

'I'm Charlie. One of your tanks is settling into the drain in the road outside, I think. You'll find a council official with a clipboard out there. He's got you surrounded, but I think that you've got him worried.'

Emily laughed the laugh. 'I'll get him in here, and get one of the girls to buy him a drink.'

Albie had a nasty fresh gash in his forehead, just below the edge of his leather helmet. It had obviously bled hard and long, and was just beginning to congeal. I pointed at it.

'Goddamned Ronsons,' he said, 'were never made for people my size: Texas boys joined up to ride horses, not iron boxes.

Would you believe that the American Red Cross Club can't produce a nurse or a goddamned medic?'

Emily said, 'I'll make a note of that. Get through to the bar Charlie; I'll catch you later.'

'What's a Ronson?' I asked Albie.

'Goddamned Sherman tank. Krauts call them Ronsons after the cigarette lighters, because they burn so well if they hit them with a decent anti-tank shell. We also burn, but not so good.'

'What can you do about it?'

'Make sure there's another tank between you and the Kraut gun; apart from that, getting legless a lot seems to help.'

Emily said, 'Don't you believe him Charlie.'

'I'll think about that,' I said, not because I meant it, but because it was better than saying nothing.

There was another scrum at the bar, and I recognized Sandy Lyon, who flew with Peter Wynn.

'Is the galloping major here with you?' I asked him.

Lyon looked at me, looked away, then looked at me again. 'No. He's got a lotta letters to write. He's on a pass from this.'

I tried again, but the guy had something like the twitch, and definitely didn't want to talk about it. So I changed back.

'Who's Lee Miller?'

'I am,' came a voice from somewhere round about my right ear, so I swung and found myself with a woman about my size. She had a French cigarette, a tobacco-bashed-up voice, and a battered green overall that matched it: it had a patch saying *War Correspondent* sewn sloppily on one shoulder. She had a nice mobile mouth, but crooked teeth, and although you could see that she had been very beautiful not so long ago, her face was now a bit used up, and she sported a cold sore where her lips joined port side. 'You're one of Emily's Brits; I'm gonna make you famous.'

'You're Lee Miller?'

'Pleased to meet you, Biffo,' she said, and stuck out a hand. It had a glass of bourbon in it. Her hair was probably a fine blonde when it was clean – it didn't look as if it had been in several days. Maybe she was also telepathic; she added, 'You're gonna have to wait an hour. First I get outside this drink, then I get inside a tub – then I get you on a roll of film inside my camera. OK?'

I grinned. It was a free bar: I could cope. Two other Brits at the bar were also aircrew: I guessed that we were all flying the same trip. There was a tall, brown-haired French Letter type with full wings, and a furlong of coloured ribbons all over his left tit. He had a huge moustache that made Bushes' splendid effort look like eyebrows. On Bushes, I thought, the moustache looked impressive: on this fellow it looked ridiculous; deranged – and I wondered if anyone had had the heart to tell him that. His colleagues sported the N badge with single wing: navigator.

Moustaches spoke first, 'Hello, old boy,' but he didn't like the look of the stripes on my arm, so turned back to the American officer he had been talking to, leaving me with his navigator, a flight sergeant like me, who glanced briefly at the ceiling as he handed me a drink. Yeah; I could cope.

'Charlie Bassett,' I said to the nav.

'Bourne. George Bourne,' he said.

'I fly from a place that sounds like that. Who's your fool?'

'I fly with Braddock. He flies brilliantly, but he's the dumbest thing they've sent into the air for England yet. VC material, and so vain you could drown a pig in him. Refuses to use his Christian names – practising for his earldom. He already has enough gongs to have spare ones to wear in the bath.'

'How many trips you got left?'

'It doesn't work like that in our mob. You just fly until you have no more left in you.'

'Pathfinder then?'

'Yeah. Still can't believe we volunteered.'

Braddock turned back to us: the Yank who turned away from *him* had a look of relief on his face. 'You talking about me again, George?' he said, and held out his hand to me, saying, 'Braddock, old boy.'

'Bassett, old boy.' I put back. 'They named me after the dog.'

'Oh, I see. Bassett what?'

'See?' said Bourne.

Braddock told me an interesting story when he found out I was stationed at Bawne. A week earlier they had lobbed a cookie between a couple of Flak ships outside Kiel, so that three kites from our squadron could creep through the gap and lay magnetic mines into the sea space. He told me that the clever ploy had been their wingco's idea, and that it had worked so well that the old man was sure to get a gong for it. That was interesting. I said that I'd heard about the op, but I didn't tell him my part in it. Gongs seemed to feature often in his conversation, and well up in his personal value system. When he looked pointedly at the ribbonless space above my left pocket I explained.

'I had the offer, but I sent it back. We're pacifists in my squadron: we don't believe in the war.'

The photography in a side room – like a chapel without the paraphernalia – was a sombre affair. Emily Rea mixed us up with five Americans: they all looked bone-tired, and embarrassed. We made meaningless conversation whilst the lady with the lens moved around us shooting. She made no demands on us at all – at first she recorded what was there, not what she made up. I couldn't see what she was looking for. The camera – it was probably a solid Rolleiflex – looked big in her small hands, and her washed hair shone like cloth of gold.

Then, just as it all seemed pointless, she went to the smallest and youngest of the Yanks. He was a co-pilot who looked barely old enough to be out of school. She kissed him, then stood back off us and clicked her shutter at him again and again. That must have been too much, because soon after that he started to shake, and then to cry, and it all broke up. The camera carried on clicking, even as Emily was hugging the kid out of the room to somewhere private to clean up.

'You got sniper's eyes, Lee,' said Peter Wynn, who was standing in the doorway with a mug of coffee in his hand. He noticed me, and said, 'Hi, Charlie – can't you leave our women alone?'

I had a drink with Lee Miller. I told her a bad joke about Don Bradman, and then I told her about the dead radio operator standing up to his waist in Alan's Field at Crifton.

'I wish I had shot that,' she said.

I was bloody horrified. 'Then what would you have done?'

'I would have gone somewhere to throw up. Then I would have gone out and done it again.'

'Why?'

'It's my best job. What's your best job?'

'I talk to people on a radio.'

'Nice job. Don't give up on it.'

'Nor you.'

She smiled when I said that. I knew that there was no chance she'd give up. A small American with thick black hair, receding hairline, big nose and bigger spectacles fitted himself alongside us at the bar. He had the *War Correspondent* shoulder flash as well, but he was wearing a tailored uniform. Lee introduced him as 'My conscience, Dave Scherman.'

I told him that my boss, Grease, occasionally tried to stick that label on me, but that I didn't let him get away with it. He had a gentle speaking voice.

'Your boss probably doesn't need a conscience. Lee does.'

After that they told me about their work, and seeing the world through a lens. Lee said that she'd been some sort of a photographer's model years ago so that she also saw things from the subject's point of view. They exchanged a glance between them that said there was more to the story than that, but that I wasn't getting it.

'For a few years 1928, 1930, Lee was the best known clothes horse in America. Her face was all over *Vogue* magazine. Now she's their most famous photographer,' said Scherman.

'Dave's better. I get the art, but he gets the story,' Lee said.

I didn't know what they were talking about. 'I was four years old in 1928,' I said.

'. . . and I was already 400,' said Lee, suddenly moody.

They unwound later, and told me outrageous stories about artists and photographers I'd never heard of: Lee seemed to have lived several lives already – which put something into my memory. She held her hand with its drink in a heavy glass protectively across her body, and although her body stance looked relaxed you could sense the sprung tension in her – like a cat, fight or flight was written all over her. And so that's how I'll always think of her. I will never forget either of them: they had carved old love in the spaces between to a shape you could almost reach out and touch.

I awoke, scared, at 0215 – I've always instinctively known the time. The woman I hadn't really heard at Crifton was outside the hut singing 'The Man Who Broke The Bank At Monte Carlo'. One thing I wasn't going to do was get up to let her in. I threw a couple of shovelfuls of slack into the stove's gob, and left the air slide open to roar it up. While I was doing this the singing stopped, or faded rather. Think me daft if you like, but the next thing that came into my mind was Grace – a surging roller of unselfish affection, and simultaneous shame at the way things had been left between us.

What happened to me then was sudden and unexpected: what happened is that I grew up a bit – *just like that*, the Great One would have said. I know that some people mature slowly, and that some never mature at all, but I can still recall the odd feeling of sitting alongside the stove – one side of me roasting hot, and the other cold — suddenly finding myself to be something approximating an adult. And I thought that the new me was going to turn out to be a lot more sensible than his predecessor, because he fancied a piece of toast, and went looking for the makings.

I dreamed, or I awoke just once again before morning, Black Francie was standing at the end of my bed. All his bits were back together again. He didn't say anything, just grinned like the Devil. I grinned back and rolled over: he didn't scare me. Just as I was sliding into sleep I had the oddest of thoughts: I knew that I was ready to fly again.

In the morning I breakfasted in the sergeants' mess for the first time in weeks, it seemed. The young girl was back serving tables, one-handed because her arm was in a sling. I decided to tell Grease about it before he found out for himself. The girl looked more waif-like than ever: younger than my sister, and *she* was still going to school — or would have been. I was relieved to see several faces I knew, and at least two complete crews I had seen before: it must have been a good week.

Hodges, the sergeant sparks on X-*X-ray*, wandered over with a huge wad and jam in his hand. 'What ho, Charlie. What you been up to?'

'Leave.'

'Yeah, but what you been up to?'

'Give me a clue, Hodgo.'

'That big bastard of a provo has been in here nearly every day looking for you.'

'That's all right. It's not about me.'

'Good show. He looks a mean bastard to cross. I should sort it out if I was you.'

'I will. Don't worry.'

You took things like that from Hodges because he was the oldest operational flier on the station. His father was a chief air raid warden somewhere on the south coast. Soon after we had been posted to Bawne Hodges had got the CO's permission to show his old man around. What I remember most easily about the officious old bugger is that he wore his dark blue ARP battledress and white warden's steel helmet throughout, as if the Kraut was going to visit us any minute.

In the mess lobby, alongside the rows of hooks for coats and caps, there were two telephones in man-sized three-ply boxes, which gave the impression of a degree of privacy. One was only connected to phones on the station, and on the other you could dial out: that one was locked off whenever the station went to war – say every other afternoon. On the internal one I phoned the guardhouse, got Alex, and told him I'd be in later that morning; with the latter I phoned Crifton.

Barnes answered. He told me that the body had been collected from Alan's Field, and that a salvage crew had dug a huge pit where they were burying what was left of the two Lancasters.

When I asked to speak to Grace he said, 'I'm pleased about that Mr Charles. She isn't down yet. Shall I call her, or could you telephone again later?'

'Get her out of bed, Barnsey.' Bombs armed.

'With pleasure Mr Charles.' Bomb doors open.

It seemed a long wait: I managed to whistle most of 'Minnie The Moocher'.

Grace yawned, and said, 'Yes; what is it?'

'I just wanted to tell you that I love you, and will always love you. That doesn't mean I won't behave badly, or stupidly from time to time. It just means that I love you – just as you are; can't help it. It's something that's fixed in me, and I can't do anything about it. I just wanted to tell you that exactly as it was, with no other words in-between.' Bombs gone.

She didn't react immediately, and when she did her accent slipped.

'You mad fool, Charlie Bassett.' I guessed that the accent was Durham, near one of her father's first factories, where she had been born. Then she laughed, but not unkindly. After that she said, 'If I hadn't laughed, I would have cried. I'm very glad you called. Is this your last day?'

'Yes. There'll be a formation fly-past in the bar tonight.'

'Are you coming over?'

'Maybe, but probably not. I have to see the police about Pete – fuck knows what he's been up to this time – and I wanted to clean the hut up before everyone gets back: like a fresh start. I may not have time after that. It doesn't matter: there'll be dozens of other times.'

'Yes. I know there will.'

Neither of us knew what to say after that. Then Grace sighed and said, 'I'll be here alone all day. Daddy's gone off to London; to help Winston with something, I think. If you can't get away, you can phone me later.' It was odd to understand that Crifton's servants didn't count for anything. Even with a dozen of them there Grace still thought of herself as alone.

Bluto was testy.

'I've been looking for you all bloody week.'

'Hodges told me this morning.'

'He loves giving the bad news, doesn't he?'

'Don't be hard on him. He's a good sparks, and almost old enough to cop off flying altogether. Give me some char, Alex, and tell me what's the matter. What's Pete actually done?' I loved the glass-house tea: they made it strong enough to dissolve an EPNS spoon in; I'd noted the steaming mug in front of him.

'Get it yourself.' He indicated a stained urn standing on a stove in the outer office. 'And don't nick too much milk or sugar. We're short.'

'*We're* not,' I told him; 'I'll send some round.'

It was good to put the knife in sometimes.

'Nobody seems to *know* what he's done,' Alex told me. 'That's why I'm asking you. There's this copper, who's probably Special Branch, and a fellow from the Polish Government in Exile in Scotland who looks like a comic-strip spy. Dark felt hat with a big floppy brim: the guv'nor says he's watched too many Conrad Veight films. We think that if it was a simple case of thievery, black market or a paternity suit then the local police would have been round here, and we could have fixed it. We think that it's got to be political.'

'Correct me if I'm wrong, but we still don't lock people up for their political opinions in this country, do we?'

'Not unless they're Fascists, although Winston had some

Scottish Nationalists detained last year. We've a small camp full of them somewhere: heedering and hodering away to one another.'

'I didn't hear about that.'

'You wouldn't, would you? You haven't heard it now.'

'What were *they* doing?'

'Trying to negotiate a separate peace deal – it is *alleged* – with Adolf.'

'Bollocks! Nobody's that stupid!'

'I'm just telling you that we live in trying times.'

'*Pete* is not a Fascist: he loathes the Germans. That's at least 150 per cent true. He loathes them in a way that you couldn't understand. He would eat their babies.'

'Yes. That's what everyone else says. He almost got you killed, hating the Germans, didn't he?'

'You heard about that?'

'Your CO told my boss by way of illustration. We are reasonably certain of his anti-German credentials.'

'So, what *do* you think, Alex?'

'I go along with the political theory. No matter how much he scares the Axis, for some reason he scares his own people even more. You'll have to keep an eye out for him.'

'Since when have I been doing anything else?'

When I returned to the hut I found the post bike, cleaned, greased and repainted in a proper camouflage scheme propped against it, and a neat new sign, in RAF stencil on the outer storm porch door. It read *The Grease Pit*. I guess that the skipper must have commissioned that from Chiefy Bryan before he left. Cleaning the Grease Pit was easier than I anticipated. Everyone had managed to make their beds before they left, so it was a matter of piling the chairs on them, opening all the doors, and sweeping the shit out. I had let the stove die, so I was able to clean that as well, and set it up for the active winter already running down on us. We could be well into it before we finished the tour, I realized. Soap wasn't a problem – although it was for the rest of the population. Pete had a sweet-smelling box with half a hundred bars of it under his bedside locker. I cut one of the bars in half, and dropped them into the two toilets. If they were left to dissolve long enough the first flush would do the business. Barnes's little team would have been proud of me.

The place was Bristol fashion when Jennifer Delve walked in. I hadn't heard her drive up because she had cycled. She didn't say Hello or any of the other things which people say when they meet: she only said, 'Charlie.'

I looked up from making my own bed, which I had left until last, in order to air the sheets and the two coarse wool blankets. I probably did do the hello bit, but I can't remember. I know that I asked where Bushes was, and she said something like, 'He's had to go over to wing all day. I think you might have a busy week.'

'Good. The quicker the trips come on, the sooner they're over. Roll on the end of the tour.'

She said that she wished Conny would stop flying, and then she asked me where the others were, and I told her that they weren't due until later.

When a woman has made her mind up, I found out then, she's like a B-17 with two engines out: she's going to go down on you, however hard you try to keep her flying. As a consequence of that . . . how would Jane Austen, or one of the Brontë women have written it – *reader, I took her*? Don't knock it. We'd mashed my bed up between us, and she remade it before she left. That was a nice domestic touch, I thought. She fucked me from underneath, her skirt around her waist again, with a keen, noisy abandon, and hated herself for it afterwards just the way I wanted. I thought I could go back for more of that. She shed a couple of tears – just the one on each cheek. I was interested to note that it didn't move me at all. I licked them off: they weren't even salty to the taste.

We were sitting around the big oval table in the pub at Eltisley, the name of which always escapes me these days.

'You get your end away then, young Charlie?' Grease asked me. I had to be careful because a straight yes would lead to a guessing game around the table, trying to flush the fox from his den.

I settled for a half-truth instead, and said, 'I ended up in an American club in Bedford. Do you remember those nurses we met in London? There were loads of them there.'

'Jammy little bugger,' the Toff told me.

Everyone had got in early enough for an end-of-leave binge. Grease had been first home, but I hadn't wasted drinking time bringing him up to date, except to tell him about the state's new interest in our Pole.

'No point in asking you, Pete. When *didn't* you get your end away?' Grease said.

'Not before I was eleven years old.'

275

'So tell us why these secret policemen have been snooping around asking questions about you? Are you in trouble?'

'No,' Piotr said, and when no one else said anything, sighed and filled the space with, 'You will have heard of Sikorsky?'

'Yes,' Marty said, but Grease shot him the shut-up glance; he wanted Pete to go on talking. Pete did.

'My *General*; Wladyslaw Sikorsky. Poland's torch. He died in a plane at Gib. More than a year ago. It blew up just after take-off, and fell into the sea. Such a small bomb: so discreet, so British. Four people drowned, and two people survived: the pilot and another passenger: your friend Piotr was the passenger: his survival was unexpected and they don't like witnesses. Witnesses worry them sometimes.'

'OK,' said Grease.

'Also the Government in Exile is rich in luxury goods, through the good offices of our American allies, but kept deliberately short of real spending money – also because of the influence of our allies. They keep us dependent. I convert one product into the other for them. I know how to buy and sell. I balance supply and demand. I know who gets what, who sells it, who buys it, and how much for. I know whose fingers are in the honey pot, and how far down. Because I do it with them. That will worry them . . . sometimes.'

'OK,' said Grease.

'Also before the Germans came, 95 per cent of the land in Poland was owned by 4 per cent of the population. When I was a student I wrote a small book saying that that was wrong; that things would have to change. You see, I am that unusual Pole who hates Germans more than I hate the Russians. Most Poles hate the Russians more than they hate the Kraut. That worries them sometimes too.'

'OK,' said Grease.

'And also I know which pretend countess is fucking which pretend duke, or which minister in the Government in Exile, because I am fucking her also.'

'OK,' said Grease, 'you can stop now; we get the picture.'

'There is something else. When your honourable RAF officers painted Poland's flags on Harriet's tits, my people think that is political too. I think that also worries them.'

'Are you saying that the authorities are investigating you for all of these reasons, Pete?' I asked.

'No. Only one of them probably: difficulty is deciding which one.'

'Just so long as we know that you're not a rapist or a murderer,' Grease said.

'I am not a rapist,' Piotr said very firmly.

It was then that I remembered the voice of the woman who had answered the telephone when I had called Pete to warn him. Her name was Jean Shore: Abbot's girlfriend. Pete had said that she was really Abbot's wife, and that he was going to buy the Singer from her.

Piotr was looking at my face as this memory jelled. Maybe he saw something there. He spoke directly to me. 'That is right Charlie; I am not a rapist, but if God provides me with an opportunity, he expects me to take it. You will understand: isn't it the same for you too?'

I probably blushed as I said, 'Yes. It's the same for everyone these days.'

For once Grease didn't know what we were talking about, and I enjoyed his brief frown. It was time for a change of course.

'What about you, Skipper?' I asked Grease, 'Did your brother line you up a big, bouncy bed wearing a Wren's uniform?'

'One day, Charlie, I'll tell you all about Portsmouth girls.'

Yeah. Eat, drink and be merry, for tomorrow we fly. That was always our excuse.

Just before we all turned in I went over and sat on the edge of Grease's bed because I didn't want any of the others to hear.

'That kid in the mess is back, with her arm in a sling. She smiles, but nearly jumps out of her skin every time anyone looks at her. The fat bastard must still be knocking her about,' I said.

Pete had overheard: in truth, he missed very little. 'Perhaps some women like it that way,' he said.

Sometimes you became aware that Pete lived on a different fucking planet to the rest of us.

'Don't be so bloody soft,' I said, 'she's English,' and spoke loud enough for the others to stop what they were doing, and look up. Pete bastard-smiled at me. I've told you before that I never liked it when Pete smiled his bastard smile at anyone like that.

'Put it in the can,' Grease said. 'Hit the sheets everyone, and no farting. Air test tomorrow.'

The weather front swept over us in the middle of the night, and then stopped dead – just as if God had targeted Cambridgeshire for a taste of eternal wrath. One of the things that Cambridgeshire taught me about God is that he is inordinately fond of rain. Like old man Heinz, he has at least fifty-seven varieties of it.

I was woken by the water drumming on the Grease Pit's curved iron walls. I got up to bank the stove, and went back to bed. I thought of *Tuesday* standing out there in the rain, and hoped it wouldn't get under her skin as easily as it did mine.

Grease came back from his run soaked to the skin, and with news. 'No flying. Probably for two days: there's a lot more of this shit out in the Atlantic waiting to wash over us.'

In the red brick palace the New Order Board bore an Order of the Day which said that the discipline officer would conduct PE for all ranks. The DO stood alongside it in his small kit. Then he ran away after Quelch ate the notice and tried to kiss him.

'No flying today I guess,' Quelch said.

'We could have a dance tonight,' I said.

'Why Charlie, how nice: I didn't think you cared.'

'No. I mean all of us.'

'Better and better,' said Quelchy.

Grease said, 'Leave Charlie alone; he's ours. You'd better scram. I can see the DO on his way back with a couple of coppers.'

Alex in his police uniform, complete with glossy white battle bowler, had brought his smallest provo with him. They looked like that Victorian print of the two dogs, *Dignity and Impudence*, which always hung in your front room. They were as rainswept as the DO: the water streamed off them.

Alex, tense, asked Grease, 'Where's this bloody OOD, Sergeant?'

'Dunno,' said Grease. 'Never seen one. One was never here.'

'Where's that fairy Quelch?'

'Dunno. Who's Quelch? Don't believe in fairies sergeant.'

'You're fucking well under arrest,' snarled Alex.

'What about me?' the Toff asked him. 'I don't believe in fairies either.'

'And you.'

'And me,' I said. It had been a calculated gamble, but about another thirty voices began to chime in, and chairs began to hit the deck as aircrew got to their feet.

'Goodo,' Grease told Alex, 'if I'm under arrest, perhaps they'll let you fly our kite to Berlin tomorrow instead of me.'

'Fuck the lot of you,' Bluto said. I think that was the end of the mutiny. If he had in fact arrested us, in a legal sense, then I guess that I'm still a fugitive from justice, because I was never unarrested. I don't know why, but eventually we were the only crew left in the mess.

We were only mildly concerned when Alex and buddy came bursting back into the room.

'Charlie, I need you quick – I need aircrew; anybody,' he gasped, then turned and ran out of the door again. Grease looked at us and shrugged, but led the discreet stampede in pursuit. The rain had eased, but only just, and there was a Thorneycroft lorry outside. Alex was in the back buckling on a side arm, and making a mess of it. His nervous sidekick was cocking and uncocking a small machine gun, which was either a

Sten or a Stirling: I never did learn the difference. We piled in alongside them: I fixed Alex's holster belt for him as the lorry careered away in the rain.

'What's the problem?' the Toff shouted.

Alex's dwarf said, 'I think we been invaded, Sarge.'

'Fuck that,' murmured Grease. 'I want to get out again.'

He was too late. The lorry was already pulling up after less than half a mile. We were at one end of the cross runway. So was an aeroplane, which we approached gingerly: that is to say that we all stayed behind Alex. The kite was painted in a light grey wash and decorated with hundreds of dark green squiggles. That was new to us, but the big black crosses on its sides, and the swastika on its tail were a dead giveaway. Visitors. As we closed in on it, trying to avoid the standing water, we could see brown-clad occupants moving about behind the perspex.

'If any of those bloody machine guns move, just hit the deck and stay there,' Alex muttered.

Grease ignored him. He walked past to stand looking up at the cockpit, and waved up at it. The pilot slid back a small square window, and shouted a spiky improbable something in weary German. Getting no response from anyone below, he tried again in French, and then accented but clear English.

'Yes? What is it that you want?'

'We surrender,' Grease said.

'No *we* surrender.'

'I said it first. You must take us to Germany. It rains too much in England.'

'This year it rains too much in Germany also. Is this England?'

'Definitely.'

281

'This is a pity. I thought it might be Holland.'

'Holland is 250 miles in that direction.' Grease pointed roughly to the south-east, and added helpfully, 'We think that it's raining there too.'

'That also is a pity,' the German said, 'perhaps you could spare me some gas?'

'I'm afraid not. We need ours for bombing Germany.'

'That also is a pity. We are German, you see.'

'I had guessed that.'

'Do you think that I should shoot my navigator? He is an offizier, you know.'

'That would waste a perfectly useless officer. We could exchange him for one of ours if you liked? Fair swap.'

'I think not. I suppose that your offiziers are stupid also?' It figured: a lot of German pilot types were sergeants, like Grease.

'You got it, Fritz. You keep yours: Lufthansa will need him after the war.'

'For what? Flying passengers to the wrong countries? I think not.' Then he said, 'I was not trained for this. Probably the war is over for me. I still think perhaps I should shoot the navigator.'

'Why don't you come to breakfast instead, and think about it?'

'OK.'

He slid the perspex shut again. Germans are good decision makers. The crew of five dropped down through a trapdoor under the nose of the aircraft, on to the wet tarmac of Old England. Except for a gunner of forty or so they all looked like scared children. So did we. Alex's pal's hands were shaking, and the automatic he held was shaking with them: I gently pushed down the barrel until it was pointing at the ground.

Grease shook the pilot's hand and said, 'Welcome to England, and thank you for the aeroplane.'

'Think nothing of it, Sergeant. Consider it recompense for those you leave in Germany every night.'

Who said the Kraut doesn't have a sense of humour? Although I don't know why Grease didn't thump him for that one. One of the crew had a big black eye already; it was closing up on him. I think that he was the nav. Conroy moved forward to look after him.

At this point Alex decided he was able to speak again. 'Well, fuck me gently,' he said.

'No, that's Quelch's job,' I reminded him, and when he gave me the look, added, 'Cheer up, Alex. You've just captured a Junkers 88. Bound to get a medal for that.'

We didn't get to keep the Jerries for long: the officers came and invited them to breakfast in *their* mess. Which was more than they'd ever done for us.

Then some serious gentlemen from London spirited them away to the aircrew interrogation centre. We hung around the main gatehouse to see them go, but the lorry they were transported in had its tilt laced tightly shut. I threw the departing lorry an exaggerated Nazi salute, which annoyed our cops, and said, 'Silly sods.'

The Toff whispered, 'Bye-bye, Krauts,' but because we were inside, they wouldn't have heard him anyway.

Later someone told us that our bold Bushes was so pleased

that he went into the small washroom alongside his office, and shaved his moustache off. Bush-free and as mad as a fucking daisy.

Back in the Grease Pit, relating the story to Marty and Pete, Fergal pointed out that we would need a new nickname for Bushes.

Pete shrugged and said, 'Try Bushless.' Then he asked me, 'You still fancy his wife, Charlie?'

I can't remember what I answered. I hope that I didn't let her down and blush.

At 0730 I shook them awake individually — except Marty: I realized that there was no point. Grease was surprisingly good at weather for someone who wasn't a native: he sniffed the drizzle while my head was in the fire bucket, and as I emerged said, 'It'll clear: we'll get an air test in today. Loosen everyone up and be ready for ops tomorrow.'

'I'll get things moving. When do you want to fly?'

'We'll have half an hour on the ground at 1000; find out what the Chiefy has been doing to her since we've been away. Take-off at 1030 unless the Old Man says no: I'll ask him: I want to see what he looks like with naked lips.'

Breakfast.

'This is no bloody way to run a hotel,' Fergal said. He was referring to a breakfast of spam fritters, bread and marge, and jam so old it was impossible to identify which fruit it was made from.

'How is it that mine host here grows fatter and fatter, like

Winston, while we're eating this shite and growing thinner?' Grease asked.

'Obvious,' said the Toff. 'He's eating something else, isn't he? I'll bet he never sits down to powdered egg and mashed potatoes.'

'I thought you were going to do something about him, Skipper.'

'Would you shut up if I came across with enough bacon, eggs, fresh vegetables and enough of a variety of meats to last us a month?'

'*Can* you Skip?'

'Depends. What have we got for barter, Pete?'

'Mainly spirits. A load of vodka, some Portuguese brandy that came from a blockade runner, thirty of those white wool sweaters the underwater Blue Jobs wear . . . some parachute silk – not made up. Some car tyres. Give me a few days, and I'll see what else Glasgow and Edinburgh can come up with. Will that do?'

Grease asked, 'What's it got to do with Glasgow and Edinburgh?'

'When they say *Polish Government in Exile* they bloody mean it! They exile us to Scotland. Didn't you know that? Half Poland lives in Scotland this year.'

Air test. *Tuesday* was damp. Like all good whores, she was a bit clammy on the inside, and would be until the heater had been run full throttle for twenty minutes. That was a problem for me, because the heater fed from one of the Merlin engines, and its port into the aircraft interior was alongside my radios. I was going to have to cook inside my flying clothes, until we had the old girl dried out. I did have the option of wearing less, of course, but then what would happen if I had to bale out over the North Sea?

There was a click on the RT, and Piotr asked me, 'Can you turn the heater right up when we get going, please, Charlie? There's as much water inside the turret as there is outside: I can't see a focking yard.'

'OK, Pete – I've already set it to max.'

With my spare ear I heard Grease tell Fergal, 'A rookie called Whittaker took *Tuesday* to Merseburg – never heard of it before. Apparently the Yanks are stonking hell out of it by daylight, whilst we stoke the ovens for them at night. We lost Porterman's crew there.'

'Never heard of him.'

'Hey, Pete. Where's Merseburg?' Grease asked.

'South of Berlin, Skipper, and not as far as Dresden: popular with the Yanks. There are a lot of guns at Merseburg. I think that they make things there. Better we go some other place.'

We heard Fergal and Grease reciting the prayer. As they ran the engines up Fergal clicked and said, 'Starboard outer throttle, Skip: it feels a bit odd. As if it's moving through the gate fractionally slower than the rest. It doesn't feel smooth.'

'OK. Watch it.'

The leave must have done him good, because he was calling for gear up before we crossed the boundary fence: a really flashy take-off. Then I was free to unplug, and climb up to the front office, and stand behind Grease. I felt happier these days, being able to see where we were going. I bent down and asked him where we were cleared for.

'Northampton and East Anglia, but I thought we'd stooge over to Thurleigh, see if there's anyone about and give them the old two-engine routine,' he shouted.

The two-engined joke consisted of finding an American B-17 on air test, and flying up alongside him. The B-17 was underpowered compared with the Lanc, and we would demonstrate our superiority by cruising up behind, feathering two of our props and turning the taps off. Then we'd cruise past on only two engines, with two propellers windmilling in the breeze, but still overtaking him. Match that, baby. I moved back to the astrodome and watched the sky.

We were on a south-westerly leg when I caught a brief flash of light on my right and about four miles away, I'd guess.

'Unknown, Skipper – three o'clock; our height, say three miles out now.'

'OK, I can see him,' Grease said.

I felt the gentle changes of trim as Marty, the Toff and the Pole swung their guns to cover the newcomer even though they had no bullets, and the corrections to compensate that Grease and Fergal made.

The unknown grew into a large, friendly B-17, just as we had hoped. It was flying an enormous lazy flat circuit centred on Thurleigh. We did the two-engine thing, but they must have seen it before, because just as we began to pull ahead everyone in the American pointedly looked in the opposite direction. So Grease throttled back, and he and the Yankee pilot then played chicken – they tucked in so close that one wing tip was under the other, and then they would alternate: first the Yank on top, and then Grease, then the Yank again – like that playground game where you put one fist over the other. Eventually they tired of that, and their top gunner began gesticulating at us. First he pointed at *Tuesday*, then he would point at his own ship. Then he would jab his fingers in a downward motion, and finally mimic a man drinking from a glass.

'What's he saying?' Grease asked.

'I think that *Tuesday*'s being asked out on a date, Skipper. He's asking if we'd like a drink.'

'That's what I figured. Tell him yes will you?'

How do you signal yes except by putting your thumb up, and nodding your head like a demented pigeon? He didn't seem to get it. Eventually I twinkled him. *Be glad to: after you.*

The reply read *Me no sabby*.

When I told Grease he said, 'Fucking Indian,' but by then he had his hands full, because the American had done a very smooth wingover and was descending in a shallow dive towards his base. England's best, a Canadian, an Ulsterman and a Pole, tucked in behind and followed him. We sang 'Foller Me home' and 'Home on the Range', until Grease yelled at us to shut up.

I told *Blackbirder* at Bawne that we were slightly unsure of our right rudder, and were landing short at Thurleigh to check it out. *Blackbirder* believed me, and sounded concerned, but he was an officer: you'd be surprised what some of them believe. As if to make up for his exceptional take-off, Grease's landing was an absolute boner – we bounced down Thurleigh's main runway like a jack-in-the-box.

Their control tower came on air and said tartly, 'Hey, Lanc, mind the real estate.' Then, 'Ride 'em, cowboy!'

I didn't reply: I was too scared. Grease was holding *Tuesday* down like a bucking bronco, and breathing very deeply from the effort. Even with all the noise of Conroy's kit flying about the aircraft, and my helmet on, I distinctly heard the Toff drop one of his super-farts. The last time I had heard that, a Kraut had been shooting at us.

What we didn't want was exactly what we got – an RAF officer with as many rings as Mata Hari on the end of his sleeves was there to greet us at the foot of the tower. I expected a grade-A bollocking, but he laughed.

'You lot still alive? Where's my bloody walking stick then?'

The American lieutenant who had jeeped us over to sign in, asked, 'You know this guy?'

The Toff said, 'He's met my foot, and Charlie's fingers. Then we got drunk, slept in his hospital and stole his walking stick.'

'An' he's still speaking to you?'

'He's a doc,' said Grease, 'we adopted him: he's almost one of us. Especially if we give him his walking stick back. We'll drop it over Manston on our next trip, Doc.'

The fat doctor sniffed into an enormous red handkerchief, then said, 'I wouldn't bother, Sergeant. I'll be hitching a ride to Bawne with you anyway, if that's all right. It's my last stop, they tell me. Is it true that your last MO ran away?'

'Was a mistake,' Piotr told him. 'Some focking gunner comes back in three pieces, and they make the MO sew him back together before he is buried.'

'Why do you keep saying that it was a mistake, Pete?' Marty asked.

'Should have offered him money for the job. Doctors understand money.'

'Don't they half.' The big MO laughed: maybe it was his big laughing day. 'You boys thirsty?'

The crew of the B-17 we'd followed down had got there before us: a long, low, rectangular billet at the edge of the field, up close to the hedge and wire backing the Backnoe road. It was about twice as big as ours, full of off-duty airmen, and had the name 'Snake Pit' painted sloppily in yellow above the door. Inside it was lined with three-ply, and the roof was supported by a thin iron frame. The walls were smothered with wonderful pin-ups, and across one set of end panels they had painted the names of all the targets that the hut's many passers through had visited. It was a word-map of France, Holland, Belgium and Germany. These boys had done the Grand Tour all right. I noticed that their stove was smaller than ours. Pete noticed it too, and was soon in animated conversation with a couple of the inmates – I guess he was cutting a deal. Grease had seen 'Snake Pit' and laughed aloud: one of the Yanks had asked him why, and Grease told him about the Grease Pit. 'Home from home,' is how Grease put it, looking around – you could always rely on him to come out with something original. I found myself with a stubby bottle of light American beer in each hand, in conversation with one of their flight engineers. I asked him why

'Snake Pit' and he told me that one of the radiomen was a full 'Injun', and kept a pet rattlesnake. In Bedfordshire.

Grease nearly stepped on it about an hour later. He was being very easy on the juice, intending to fly us back to Bawne for dinner. The snake glided from under one bed, near me, across the central aisle and under another: its movement was slow, smooth and lazy. It must have been about five feet long, and as fat as my arm at the middle. I froze. Grease stepped back and nearly stood on it. The snake ignored him. Oh yeah, that's right, it had a big, fat, bony rattle above its tail wheel.

The engineer, Anderson, told me, 'Don't worry. He's always full of rat: this place is stiff with them. That means he's never cranky – hardly ever bites anyone. We got some serum flown in anyway, just in case.'

I suddenly felt I understood that doc who sewed Francie back together. When the fat MO started harrumphing, and looking tactfully at his watch, Grease said our thanks, and moved us on. While we were still beside the Snake Pit about six American aircrew cycled past along the Backnoc road. In among them was a smaller woman in dark blue duds, who waved, blew me a kiss and shouted, 'Hi Charlie,' then stood on the pedals as she pulled away to catch up the others; her dark hair stood up stiffly in the breeze.

'My, my,' Conners said, '*somebody's* stock just went up.'

It had been the American woman, Emily Rea, but I didn't tell them that: let them dream.

The MO rode up in the office, in the place I had made my own, for the short flip from Thurleigh to Bawne. I had to ride at my station, and didn't like it. Grease fooled the Yanks with a lumpy take-off, but made a damned near perfect approach and landing at Bawne. If I had to choose, I preferred it that way. The sun came out from the clouds and kissed the runway at the same time as we did. What do the Yanks say? Geronimo!

At take-off we had queued behind two Fortresses, and the Doc explained the afternoon while we waited. 'I bummed a ride with an American pilot named John Morgan, from Manston to here. He wouldn't take me on to Bawne because he's actually cleared for Twinwood, the satellite airfield just round the corner. He flies VIPs around a lot – he says he's flown Glenn Miller.'

I've already told you that everyone had a Glenn Miller story in '44: the guy had obviously been shooting a line.

'What in?' Grease asked.

'Ghastly little American job: I think they call it a Norseman. Bloody rattles all the time.'

'I know them: underpowered. So you were stuck at Thurleigh?' Grease said.

'Then our American friends came up with an enterprising wheeze.'

'Tell me, sir. Although I suspect I won't like it.'

'Some major in the tower, waiting for his birds to come home I suspect, said they'd tune their spare into *Blackbirder*, wait until they heard one of ours go up on air test, and then send up a Fort to trail its coat in front of it. They said that once you spotted the B-17 you wouldn't be able to resist bumbling over here to play the two-engine trick; once you were in that close they'd get you down for a drink, and I'd get a free lift. Taxi! They weren't far wrong, were they?'

'No they weren't bloody wrong,' Grease told him through clenched teeth: not a good loser, our skipper. We'd got an MO again, and a pretty senior one at that. Although I'm not sure that we were going to like it. The next morning he paraded me, Grease and the Toff in his office for medicals. He got reacquainted with the damaged bits, and grinned at me afterwards.

'I didn't do a bad job, did I? I was worried about your fingers at the time.'

'You might have told me, sir!'

'I'm too good a doctor for that.'

Maybe he'd be worth hanging on to after all.

Merseburg

So it was our turn. We were going to Merseburg. I didn't like the colour Pete's face turned when the curtain was pulled back and he saw the map. Grease usually shifted around in his chair during a briefing because it was too small for him. This time he sat still. *Like he was dead*, I suddenly thought, and a nerve twitched under my left eyelid. Then I thought, *Fuck it!* and started to pay attention. The only thing I liked about the target was the predicted weather – we were supposed to have layers of cloud to duck in and out of all of the way back, but enough clear over the target to clobber it. They told us it was some military shit or other, but I had begun to believe that they made that up. We were just bombing German people in their homes until the Kraut soldiers at the front had had enough, and went home. The senior intelligence officer at the briefing – he was the one with the Mexican handlebars – always told us about the cumulative effect our bombing campaign was having on the morale of the civilian population. I remember cornering him at a party at Lavenham, and pointing out that as far as I knew the more bombs the Jerry dropped on Liverpool, the angrier and more determined our civilians there had become. He said, 'There you have it, old man. That's *why* we're going to win the war. We can take it, but the Jerry can't. Every day Butch tells Winston that their morale's crumbling and the end is just around the corner: LMF, the lot of them.'

Yeah. That would be right! So why the hell were they still shooting back at us? For the whole of the briefing Piotr viewed the stage with left eye only, through a circle he made with the first finger and thumb of his left hand. As we shuffled out I asked him why.

'To ward off the evil eye: old Polish trick. Some other bugger get flames out his arse tonight.'

'You don't believe in the evil eye, Pete. That's an old wives' tale.'

'Lots of old wives in Merseburg. Merseburg is a witchcraft city.'

'Don't talk wet.'

Quelch was behind us in the press. That wasn't always where you were comfortable with him placed. He said, 'He's right you know. Forget the gibbery guff about marshalling yards and tank turret factories: all Merseburg has got going for it is a hell of a lot of witches. Always did have.'

'See!' said Pete.

'Don't bloody encourage him,' I told Quelch, 'he's windy enough already.'

'And you ain't? Piss my blankets!'

If you've never been to Merseburg, don't: not even in peacetime. It had little to recommend it even before we and the Americans started to do it over, and has even less now. Pete was right. It had a lot of radar-predicted flak – heavy guns. As usual we were about a third of the way back along the stream, which was Grease's favourite place: Squelch was thirty yards behind us, which was his. Even from twenty miles away when we broke from the embrace of the cloud, we could see accurate flak converting Lancasters instantaneously to flame above the target. Merseburg itself *boiled* with flame, like a wild cauldron, and as we flew into it the smell of burning even got through our masks. It had been burning for a week already I'd guess. What else was there left to bomb? How could anyone still be alive in that? We bombed on red target indicators that winked up at us.

Grease was steadily whispering, 'Fuck, fuck, fuck – fuck.' His consistency was reassuring somehow, and it was good to know that he'd figured out some way to count off the seconds.

Marty was very good; very calm; like an angelus tolling. 'Up, up . . . left; left again.'

'Get on with it, Marty' – that was Fergal.

'Steady . . . steady . . .' Then he used the words of power, and *Tuesday* leapt up and forward, for freedom.

Only one bad thing happened. A Lanc that was below us must have dropped its load and simultaneously hit an updraft, and I reckon it rose clear through 1,000 feet. Marty saw it coming, and Grease had to weave to make room for it, which spoiled our aiming-point picture. I was in the dome looking upwards, when suddenly this Lanc lifted alongside into my field of vision like magic. Grease was cursing it, but I guess that its pilot had been caught by surprise as well. I saw him look across at me in the red glow, and distinctly saw his teeth bared in a grin. He was a pro all right, because he immediately put his ship's nose down and dived away from us, gaining speed. He must have been a hundred feet ahead and another hundred lower when a flak shell burst directly in front of him. With a smoothness of motion which belied what must have been happening inside, all four of its engines stopped, it turned over on its back, and in that configuration swan-dived gracefully into the hungry red sea beneath us. There was a flash of yellow as it struck, as if Merseburg had swallowed it, and belched.

Marty reported calmly, 'No parachutes.'

'Thank you; got that,' Conroy said.

When its pilot had turned and grinned at me I could see that the Lanc had had pictures on its nose, the same as *Tuesday*. But it wasn't the same as *Tuesday*, of course: I couldn't read the name, but I saw it's cartoon clearly because it was large and outlined in white: a wickedly grimacing witch on a broomstick. I decided not to mention that at the interrogation.

Grease did an odd thing on the way back. Conners had routed us back to the coast avoiding the hot spots for flak, but instead of staying down on the cloud, or close to it, Grease climbed and climbed, up in the clear, cold air. You could see the stars for a million miles. Grease clicked. 'Sorry about this chaps, you'll be late for breakfast, but I just didn't feel *safe* down there tonight.'

I don't know what the others thought, but that was all right by me.

I heard a conversation between Grease and Fergal that went something like: 'Fergal?'

'Skipper?'

'What was our rate of climb?'

'Fucking amazing, Skip. Either we left half the kite back there, or we have four very enthusiastic motors.'

'That's what I thought, too. Fuel consumption?'

'Bang on. You might even have some to spare.'

'Curious. I wonder what Chiefy did to the old witch.'

I wished he hadn't said that.

Conners said, 'Navigator, Skip. Dutch coast in three minutes.'

'Thanks Nav; course?'

'Second star from the right, and straight on till morning.'

'Arsehole.'

Some time later Marty, crouching behind the front turret guns, reported a fading, red glow in the cloud a couple of miles below us: somebody had bought it. Grease's shoulders slumped and he dived for the coast and the open sea, gaining speed as the clocks unwound. When we had no further essential use for our masks he began to whistle. It was the old march tune 'Lillibolero'.

In the Morris driving back from dispersal, I sat in the front next to Fiver because she asked me to. She held my hand between smooth gear changes: we didn't talk; I was bone-tired, but very alert. I heard Grease say, 'That was meant to be us. Some other poor sods got burned for us tonight.'

'Some other poor sods didn't have no skipper half as clever as ours,' said Piotr, and I heard the rasp of a struck match as he lit his fag.

*

We got the IO with the Mexican handlebars because Harriet hadn't returned yet: I asked myself if she ever would. The Boss moved restlessly from table to table, crew to crew, during the interrogation. We were one short; an all-officer crew that had ditched their Lanc in the Wash. It was our B-Flight commander. Air-sea rescue had located their dinghy and remarkably all seven of them were recovered, but I suppose you can't get lucky all the time. The flight commander tended to leave us as alone as much as we did him: I couldn't remember having seen him for a couple of weeks, except at squadron briefings. Fergal explained that officers always floated – drowning wasn't a good way of getting rid of them.

The IO had to put up with this conversation and frowned a lot. Bushless was touching his lip from time to time, where his moustache had been. He seemed to listen to the debrief with interest, particularly when we described the Lanc we saw lost in front of us over target, and he told Grease, 'That would have been Porterman. He's not back yet.'

According to Chiefy Bryan, Porterman's crew had been lost the week before. The IO caught my eye and shook his head briefly; better not to say anything.

The Boss was back by the door as we filed out, with a word for every crew. Seeing him touch his lip again I found a tired smile from somewhere and asked him, 'Miss it, Boss?'

He grabbed me by the arm, and pulled me out of line. 'No. But it makes me look too bloody young – I wouldn't want to be mistaken for a sprog like you, Bassett.'

'No, sir.'

Grease turned and gave me a sharp questioning glance, looking over his shoulder. I was embarrassed. I didn't need an officer's personal bloody revelations.

'It's probably the novelty. I'd leave it off, if I was you, sir,' I said.

'Y-e-s,' he said, pronouncing the word slowly, as if some thought was required, then something strange happened behind his eyes and he said, 'Porterman's crew is overdue.' His tic flickered alarmingly.

Instead of reminding him that Porterman was dead, I said, 'Yes Boss.' Was I turning into Peter Wynn: twenty years old from the neck down, and a million years old above it.

Piotr was waiting for me at the door, and like Grease had been listening to every word. I've told you that sometimes you hit the bed weary to your very bones, and that was that. Well, that morning we lay there for a long time before anyone snored.

When I staggered out of my pit in the morning Grease was already outside. I asked him what the Thurleigh visit had been about. Grease's egg and bacon plan had been the two-engined trick to get *Tuesday* invited to Thurleigh, and once on the deck do some illegal exchanges. Once he had a beer in his hand he forgot. I told him, 'I have a contact there. Why don't you leave it to me?'

'OK.'

'Did you notice the snake?'

'What snake?'

'Forget it.'

Grease said something else, but I didn't catch it because my head was in the bucket.

When I lifted it out Grease was a hundred yards away already, stretching out into the long, loping strides that seemed able to carry him on forever. I went in to shave, and then sneaked out to phone Grace, using the post bike to glide down into Bawne.

'Hi. It's me.'

'I know, Barnes told me. I was dressed this time, so he didn't get a treat.'

'Apologize for me.' Grace giggled. It was good between us. 'I miss you.'

'I know. It's wretched, isn't it? Can you come over, or meet me somewhere?'

'I don't know. I'll call you later if I can.'

'That's good. If you're not flying on Thursday night we could go back to the ARC at Bedford.'

'You told me that it wasn't fun there any more.'

'It isn't, but there's a pianist playing there I want to hear. A blind man from the East End; he plays his own sort of jazz but it's not like jazz you've ever heard: it's softer, smoother – Grease would say that it's cool. It's the sort of music they would need to play to calm me down if I was stuck in a lift. That's one of my big fears by the way; I don't think I told you that before.'

'You didn't, and I'll remember.'

'I know you will, Charlie. By the way, Daddy's back, but he looks tired.'

'Tell him I repaired his radio.'

'He already knows; he was up there for hours last night listening to you – I think Barnsey was sitting with him: they both looked hungover this morning.'

It was a difficult conversation to end: the telephone did it for me as the money ran out.

I remembered overhearing an odd conversation that Fergal and Grease had had about *Tuesday*'s engines the night before, and mindful of the fact that the others would not have surfaced yet, and being nosey, I cycled back to dispersal to ask the ground crew. Maybe I could bum a bacon sarnie out of them as a bonus. Grease had beaten me to it, of course. He was there in his running outfit, gently steaming in the cool air. He stuck his head back into the old railway wagon as I slithered to a halt alongside him.

'Make that two sarnies if you can spare them – we'll swap you half a bottle of brandy if you like – Charlie's just turned up. We all owe him a thank you anyway.'

I didn't rise to it.'

'What did they do to her while we were away?' I asked him.

'Gave her an extra ten knots maybe, and she climbs like an eagle.'

'How come?'

'Why don't you ask the Chief yourself, he's up inside working on the Toff's turret. Did you know that it jammed on him last night?'

'No I didn't.'

'Me neither. The sniffy little bastard didn't tell anyone.'

I always liked the way *Tuesday* shifted slightly as you climbed on board and moved around her. It was as if she was alive. I had two sandwiches, bacon grilled on their coke brazier between tombstone-size slabs of bread: one for me, and one for the Chief. He nodded as I handed his up to him, and said, 'Mind me tool box.'

'What's the problem?' I asked him.

'I think a bearing's collapsed. I haven't seen that on one of these new turret rings before. Could be that bloody grease which did for the doors.'

'Can you fix it?'

'No problem. But it'll take us a couple of hours. She'll be ready for tonight.'

It was often like that. They knew before us if there was an op on: it wouldn't have surprised me if he knew the target as well. I never did get round to asking him what they had done to boost *Tuesday*'s motors.

Freiberg

The station was shut down by lunchtime, and by mid afternoon we were being told how to evade the defences of somewhere in southern Germany named Freiberg. We landed at 0520 the next morning with empty tanks and brown trousers. One of the squadron ditched in the anchorage at Southend when they ran out of gas, and two more chose Manston, because they would never have made it to Bawne. The one who ditched was the same B-Flight commander who had ditched the night before. This time we got lucky, and they drowned the bastard, although the rest of his crew made it. They were picked up by an Australian Walrus team, whose seaplane was so heavy with bodies it couldn't take off: they taxied it damned nigh fifteen miles on to the customs launch station at the end of Southend pier.

The Boss flew this trip with us, and the strained faces of his regular crew afterwards told their own stories. He had the twitch at debrief, and I thought that he was carrying one shoulder above the other like Richard the Third.

We sat around the stove and ate baked potatoes: Piotr had

produced a half-pound slab of butter to slap in them. Nobody spoke much, but Conners said, 'We can't keep calling him Bushless. It's a negative: doesn't mean anything.'

'What about Samson? He lost his hair too,' said Pete. So, Samson it was to be.

Later, in the dark, we heard Conners chuckling madly. It was a worrying sound. Piotr asked quite icily, 'Why is it you are laughing, Conners?'

'I just imagined telling my mother that I was still shitting my trousers at twenty-one!'

Fergal had dropped into the serious gear he sometimes found just before he went to sleep. 'Listen chaps; I just thought of something. Say some of you make it, and marry, and have children – do you think your kids will be fighting the Kraut in twenty-five years? Or will we have kissed and made up, and be buying cars from him by then?'

Piotr said, 'No: if there are any Germans left alive by the Russians, we will still be fighting them. Anyway, no Englishman will be seen dead in a German car for a hundred years. The Krauts build industries on the bones of dead Jews. Millions of them. This country got a conscience – you British will never forget that.'

'You really believe that?' I asked him, but Pete answered the wrong question. While he believed that the British would never forget what was happening inside Germany, I thought that maybe our process of forgetting was already under way.

'I been there, Charlie. You remember that.'

I remembered something that Quelchy had said in his cups in the pub one night. He said that the Poles killed more Jews before the war than the Germans had since it started. Quelch was never any good at maths. Pete had given him the bastard smile, and asked, since we'd declared war on the Kraut for invading half of Poland, why we hadn't declared war on the Russians for invading the other half seventeen days later. Pete was never any good at politics.

Grease told us to shut up. He sounded all officerish and snappy, like the prefect in charge of the school dormitory. As I went to sleep I was running over in my mind something the runway maintenance johnnie had told me that I hadn't told the others. He said that the squadron would be going back to a small town named Krefeld later in the week. He hadn't looked encouraging as he had said it: in fact, if I was a perceptive man I would have said that he was gloating.

On Sunday morning I wanted to see the doc, and Grease was summoned over to see Samson. We wandered over together. Grease looked more or less presentable, but he insisted on wearing his top tunic button undone, like a fighter jock, and I knew that would drive The Boss crazy. I shouldn't have worried – he was already as crazy as he was going to get. We could hear him shouting at his sergeant clerk from outside the red brick office block he was caged in. I waited in the roadway while Grease went in, but soon they both came outside: they ignored me.

'We lost your flight commander again last night, McKenzie: that's two you've got through by my count.'

'Mine too. Sir. I don't remember this last one too well: I don't think he liked talking to other ranks. He sent me notes sometimes.'

'Did you read them?'

Grease looked pained. 'Yes, sir. Always.'

'Good show. I'll remember that when I want you to pay attention to me.'

Grease looked pained again. He said, 'You sent for me, sir.'

'Yes, I did. I have to replace your flight commander. Should be you, because you're exhibiting a curious longevity, your nav seems to be able to find his way around Europe in the dark, and your gunners aren't bad. Only you're a sergeant, aren't you?'

'What about his radio operator, sir?' I asked.

'Fuck off, Bassett,' he said, in a friendly, weary way – as if I was the source of a persistent headache.

This time Grease looked properly alarmed. I understood why. 'You aren't going to break the crew, sir?'

'Thought about it, but decided against. I'm going to rejig the batting order. You're the number two in A Flight from now on, and you can tell the fairy that he's number three.'

Grease asked the natural one.

'Who's going to lead the flight, sir?'

'*I* am; when I'm flying. Now fuck off and get things organized. Pay attention to the notes I send you.' He stumped back into the admin block, slammed the door hard behind him and started shouting at his clerk again.

I looked at Grease and said, 'He's as mad as a fucking bat. What is there to organize?'

'Fucked if I know, old son.'

Grease hopped a lift on a small Bedford – he wanted to tell Chief Bryan about the changes. Grease wasn't prepared to lose *Tuesday*'s best dancing partner over an administrative movement.

I went to our pal the doc, who was hungover, and not best pleased to see me. After I wandered around the problem for a few minutes he said, 'Look, Charlie, there are three types of patients that come through my door voluntarily. Type one wants something for the shits, type two wants me to write them a ticket away from flying, and type three are the mad buggers who want Benzedrine so that they can party all night long, and still go flying. Which are you?'

'I'm a type one, Doc, definitely. Although I'll probably be a type three by next week, and a type two the week after.'

'So you get the shits from time to time. Have you considered that shitting yourself might just be the appropriate response of a normal man to people shooting bullets at him all night long?'

'That doesn't help, Doc.'

'Neither can I. All I can do is give you a bottle that will stiffen your crap up a bit. You'll still shit when you get scared – the only difference is that you'll be sitting on hard lumps of it all the way back, grinding it into your clothes. The smell will be ten times worse, your clothes that much harder to clean, and you'll get a painful rash which you'll eventually bring back to me. Stick with the runny stuff – your long johns will absorb it and it rinses out easier; and I'll give you some cream to take out the soreness: I take it that your old ring's a bit tender?'

I nodded.

'Don't let Quelch or his brethren see you with it. We also prescribe it for catamites with overactive arseholes.' I looked up glumly and he said, 'Cheer up, young Charlie. I know it's not the romantic sort of thing they tell you about when you sign up, is it?'

I shook my head.

'I'll get the pharmacy to give you a big bottle of bennies as well. That will save you coming back as a type three next week. Run along now.'

By the time I returned to the Grease Pit so had Grease, and he was fuming, because he had had his first note from Samson. The Boss had examined our last three aiming point photos and pronounced them crap: we were off operational flying until we had completed three days practice over the target ranges in the Wash. We bounced Grease in a blanket and scragged him until he saw sense – if Grease wanted to take this sort of competency judgement personally he should have applied for a commission in the first place: we all knew that he was thick enough to be an officer.

I sold my bottle of pills to Pete for a brand new fiver,

I telephoned Crifton, but the woman who answered said that Grace was in London for a couple of days; then she laughed in a deranged sort of way and hung up on me. It must have been the mad woman they kept in the attic.

We hung around *Tuesday* all day with the ground crew, bumming her up. She was like new when we had finished. Chief Bryan enjoyed ordering about a crew twice his normal size, and thought that taking over the Boss's flight was quite the thing. If we weren't careful he'd become insufferable.

Chiefy and Grease took the Toff to one side and told him his fortune. Turret problems were to be reported immediately and without question. His head was down when he came back, but I don't think they laid a glove on him.

We went down to the Wellington, put my fiver from Pete behind the bar, and made a start on it in the middle of the evening. I remember that beer – Fordhams – sharp and hoppy. Grease was a brake on us that night: insisting that we didn't get too upside down, because he intended us to get it right on the ranges the next day, and be back on the ops board by Tuesday. We pinched a wheelbarrow from the garden of the house nearest the police station and wheeled Grease home in it.

Back in the Pit, Pete began to pack. 'Don't need no tail arse for practice bombing,' he said. 'I find some Poles. Some duchess to shag.'

He and Grease argued outside for half an hour, but whatever was said, Pete won. He threw his bags into the back of the Singer and was away through the fence before midnight. I just prayed that the Boss didn't come up with some silly ideas for gunnery practice.

The first practice day worked like this: we reported to the briefing room after breakfast in full kit, our squadron bombing officer – our master bomber, an old flight lieutenant of about thirty-three – briefed us for what he called 'the shoot', and gave us a short lecture pointing out that how good a job our bomb aimer did depended on our getting him over the bleeding target in the first place. Then he turned us out, and briefed just the bomb aimers, whilst we mooched about *Tuesday* waiting for Marty.

There was a new woman driving the Morris. She was older than Fiver and looked severe. A large mole on her chin had a long black hair growing from it. We sat Grease up alongside her because he was the bravest. I wanted to ask where Fiver was, but I hadn't that much courage.

There had been four other crews at the morning briefing. Quelch was one of them, and the others were the new B Flight. One of the pilots shuffled over to Grease, held out a paw for shaking and said, 'Hello: I'm Whittaker. I put a few holes in your kite's tail last week. Sorry about that.'

Grease must have been feeling generous. He said, 'No worries, bud,' a mixture of the Australian spoken by the other squadron, and American from Thurleigh.

When Marty joined us at the dispersal he had fifteen minutes to brief us, and then it was away into the wide blue yonder. Only it wasn't blue: it was grey, as usual. *Tuesday* had been bombed up by the grumbling Erks with inert practice bombs, and small smoke floats – a much lighter load than she was used to. Which was useful as it turned out, because the starboard outer engine blew itself to pieces as we crossed the perimeter fence.

Fergal pumped the fire extinguishers, but there was no point: there was fuck all engine left to extinguish. Grease got the flaps and gear up, and found something like flying speed, but the truth is that we were staggering around the circuit like a wounded duck. I told the caravan to hold back the buggers behind us, because we were coming straight in on one of the cross runways: Conners said afterwards that my voice was as high as a choirboy's. I was so scared that I forgot to shit myself. In order to fly us on to the end of the short runway Grease had to get us in a tight figure of eight, which he accomplished with

311

the minimum of fuss and bother, and most of poor old *Tuesday* was on terra firma again within five minutes of taking off.

'I don't suppose they'll count that as a trip, will they Skip,' said Marty, and had us all laughing. The fire truck and blood wagon had started after us, but Chief Bryan's lorry beat them both to it, and we trailed all three down the runway behind us as if they were the tail of a comet. After Grease had pulled us on to the grass and Fergal had turned all the taps off, Grease slid open the small perspex window by his head and spoke down to the Chief. 'We dropped something, Chiefy.'

'I can see that. Where's the bloody engine gone?'

'In the next field, I think. There were a lot of big pink pigs standing around watching us.'

'I'll send Dobbo to collect it: he's good with animals. I'll tell you what happened to it this afternoon.' The old fellah looked concerned.

'Don't bother Chief. It bloody well blew up, and fell off. I can see that for myself.' Grease slammed the window shut. You could have seen the anger shining off him thirty yards away. Up in his office he undid his straps, and took one or two deep breaths, then he turned to me and Fergal and grinned. 'I wonder what's for lunch. I'm starving.'

During lunch one of the mess boys came over with a note for Grease. It said that the squadron leader was outside, and would like a word.

'If you think you can skive off work by breaking your bloody aircraft you've another think coming. Find another one: there's enough of them around: Paxton's mob dropped them all over the county last week,' he said.

Grease came back in and told us what Samson had said.

'An inspirational and caring leader,' Toff observed.

'For that you can swallow your char and find us another kite: Chiefy will come up with something.'

All they had for us was the old Anson: at least Grease and Conners had flown her before. She had no bomb shackles rigged, so the Toff and I had to balance the practice bombs on the sill of the fuselage door, and push them out when Marty shouted '*Now!*'. The bastard creature was so slow as to almost stop in the sky, like a blimp. It was the first time I had seen bombs fall almost vertically: dropping them on the floating targets in the Wash was like playing vertical darts. It had about as much similarity to dropping bombs on German school-children at night as powdered-egg custard has to the real thing. We got back on to the deck about half an hour after the rest of the group.

Grease taxied the heap up to the hangar into which they had towed *Tuesday*, and we climbed stiffly out to confront our ground engineer. The Toff and I were frozen stiff; my fingers ached again. Chief Bryan's lorry was parked just outside and contained most of *Tuesday*'s errant engine: one piece containing the block, a heap of smaller pieces, most of the screw, the cowlings, one exhaust shroud – and a large dead pig.

'Where's your man Dobson?' Grease asked.

'Down at the MO – pig bit his finger off and swallowed it; wedding ring and all,' the Chief said.

'*This* pig?'

'Fuck, yes. It was bleeding from several wounds when he climbed into the field: we think it's full of engine. Had Dobbo's finger off, then dropped dead in front of him. That's what Dobbo said: then he requisitioned it for a mechanical autopsy: the RAF wants its bits back. He told the farmer to bang in a bill to the Ministry.'

'While we were in the air that was my engine, so the pig's *my* kill,' Fergal said.

Chief Bryan looked downcast; 'We reckoned halfers.'

I could see the sudden weariness hit Grease. That happened at times when a combination of physical exhaustion and absolute absurdity got to you together. His shoulders went down. 'Yeah, why not?'

The next day was the worst day of the war for me. I spent most of it lobbing practice bombs out of the Annie's door with the Toff. I hadn't been mistaken the day before, my fingers *were* hurting, and they've been oversensitive to cold ever since. What made it worse was that the old radio receiver in the Annie was small and fuck-all use to beast or man: as I got progressively colder all of its controls seemed to get smaller and stiffer. I used the palms of my hands on the Morse key. Eventually the Toff had to press the tits, keys and buttons, and wind the trailing aerial in and out, while I did the talking. When we climbed down from her at the end of the afternoon, tired and dispirited, Grease gave my shoulders a squeeze that nearly fractured my collarbone, and said the sincerest 'Thank you, partner' I ever had out of him.

The others wanted to get over to *Tuesday* before they called it a day because the Chief had promised her to us for the next day; I couldn't be fussed. The ugly wench happened to be parked up by the stand we left the Annie on, delivering a box of spares: not that the Annie needed them – what she needed was putting out of her misery. Anyway; I cadged a lift back to the Grease Pit with the ugly driver, and sat on my hands all the way back in order to get some warmth into them. Perhaps she thought that it was the only way I could resist the urge to ravish her. In the romantic half-light of the late autumn afternoon she looked absolutely no better.

When I asked after Fiver she smiled a coquettish parody of confidentiality, showing canine teeth which would not have shamed Bela Lugosi, and said, 'Women's problems.'

I nearly threw up.

It was just as well I didn't, because then there would have been nothing in my stomach to throw up a few minutes later. Somewhere on the ride one of my monosyllables must have been the wrong one, because at the end of it the hag was grinding the bus into gear and moving off while I still only had one foot on the ground. It unbalanced me and I staggered, then cursed her for her clumsiness, but she was already fifty yards away. It was because I was unbalanced that I noticed a light on at the far end of the Pit showing through a window. Good: that meant Pete was back. Even in the Annie I didn't like flying one short: it felt unbalanced.

Several of Pete's suitcases were on his bed. They were thrown open, and the contents – mainly Pete's off-base wardrobe – were leaking out like blood from a corpse: a bad simile, as it turned out. One of his lockers had been broken open – the door was hanging askew, and someone with their back to me was leaning forward over Pete's bed, leafing through magazines and papers. I never for a moment thought that it was Pete. As the man turned I gained the impression of a tall thin film-star type, with black, slicked-back hair. His expression was young and old, and he had the face of a corrupted child. He was wearing a long, dark overcoat with the collar turned up, over an expensive dark grey suit, and ridiculous tarty two-tone shoes, like a golfer; a white shirt fronted a Guards tie. As he turned towards me his coat swung open, and I saw a pistol stuck in his waistband, just like a gangster would have in a George Raft film. He made eye contact with a big open, apologetic smile, and simultaneously moved his right hand for his pistol, and I knew with certainty that he intended to kill me, and that I could reach neither him nor the door in time to prevent it. So did he. Then his hand stopped moving, and his fingers flexed, just about at the time I heard a small noise just behind me, and Pete's voice, calm and even.

'Take a step to your right, Charlie.'

I probably took several, and turned to look at him. I had always noted how quietly Pete could move, it went with his inch perfect dance steps, I suppose. Now he had adopted the classic gunfighter's pose: side on to the stranger and looking along his straight left arm, at the end of which was a bleeding great automatic pistol pointed at the man.

'Who . . .?' I asked.

Pete just shook his head. I looked at the stranger again. He was eye-locked with Pete. When he flexed his fingers again Pete shot him – he didn't even get to touch the butt of his pistol.

The explosion was so close to me that it temporarily shut down my thinking processes, and deafened me. The bullet took him between his eyes and slightly above the brow ridge, with the result that the whole of the top and back of his head blew away in a splash of brains, bone and hanks of hair. Most of it seemed to adhere to our curved roof above and behind him . . . and then drip. I didn't realize that a single pistol shot, which was somehow still ringing around the Pit, could generate as much noise and smoke. The dead stranger flopped back on Pete's bed, over his clothes, in the attitude of a crucified Christ, with what remained of his head over the edge and running on to the floor. Pete didn't break his pose until the man stopped moving: the last movement was in the outstretched right hand, which trembled and twitched momentarily, and then was still.

Then Pete said, 'Goddam,' just like they do in Westerns.

As he moved down the room to look at the man he kept the gun pointing at the body: I edged along behind him. As we peered over the bed and into the man's head I saw that what was left of the brainpan was completely empty – you could see the clean white bone inside.

Peter said it again: this time he whispered in some kind of wonder. 'Goddam.'

I quickly retraced my steps, and threw up outside the Pit.

When I returned I found that Piotr had already laid a blanket on the floor, and between us we tipped and rolled the body down on to it, and wrapped it up. Just like the dead radio operator who Grace had described to me, he had died smiling. Pete had taken the pistol from the dead man's belt. It was a heavy revolver with a barrel so wide you could push the whole of your index finger into it, and still have room to move it about.

'Is a special Izhmekh. Russian: focking huge bore — say twelve millimetres. You can load it with shotgun shells if you shoot close. If he hit you with that he blow *all* your head away, not just part of it like I do,' said Pete.

'Where did you get your gun, Pete? It's not issue.'

'It's yours, Charlie. I saw it when you left your small locker open one time. I borrowed it to go away with. I went to find the men who came to find me. What do they want, I ask? Maybe I need a pistol: maybe I don't: I didn't take a chance. Here, have it back now.' He tossed it on to the bed alongside me almost as if it was an object of disgust, adding, 'I only used two bullets.'

'Two?'

'I met the other one also.'

'What did they want, Pete? Was it political, or something else?'

'I don't know that, Charlie. They never said properly: they just tried to kill me. So I killed them back.'

Then the end door banged open and the Toff burst in, the voices of the others not far behind him. He paused, and scratched his backside through a hole in his silks: he had an expression on his face that said that he was trying to remember something.

'Hi, Pete. You been letting off fireworks in here?' he asked.

Grease did not do his nut; you had to give him that. He prowled up and down the Pit like a hungry panther, while Pete told us his side of the story. The rest of us sat on the ends of our beds like naughty schoolboys, and tried not to look in the direction of the thing in the blanket. Not that there was a lot to

Pete's story. Because he couldn't be certain to get to Scotland and back in two and a half days, he had decided to tackle his contacts in London. Maybe he could find out what had gone wrong. He based himself at Abbot's wife's flat in North London. He told us it was a bourgeois little affair; part of an Edwardian house at the southern edge of Hampstead Heath.

When Marty asked him why anyone would want to live there, he replied, 'They don't get bombed all that much.'

Yeah. I could go with that. He hadn't warned her he was coming because he no longer trusted telephones, and when he walked in he interrupted her in the task of mopping up the blood. Hers, that is: she'd been visited by the two policemen the day before, and had been so badly beaten that she hadn't moved for six hours afterwards. Not only beaten, either, said Pete.

The Toff asked him.

'Were they policemen, Pete?'

'Secret policemen, I think. In Poland that's not the same.'

'Nor in England,' muttered Conners. 'You'd better tell us the rest of it.'

One of the two was a Pole, Pete told us, and having enjoyed the main course the day before, came back an hour after Pete had arrived, for dessert. He pulled a pistol, and got a shot off at Pete as soon as he saw him. Pete took his time about it, and didn't miss. His shot didn't kill the man, but did enough to make him drop his pistol and fall down.

'Same pistol. Izhmekh special. Big bastard.'

'At least you didn't kill him. In Belfast they would have killed the sod,' said Fergal.

'That was later: after we talked.'

'So at least you know what they want you for.'

'Not exactly, Fergal. He said it was for the black market. Which wasn't true – all the Poles I know are in the black market, and most of the Englishmen I know buy from them. No: it's not that. I wished I talked to him longer.'

Grease did me a favour by asking the obvious. 'Why didn't you?'

'He starts to scream. Jane takes a pair of her knickers from a drawer and pushes it down his throat with a poker. He chokes. We watch him choke. He dribbles a lot when he chokes: did you know that? I don't know how that works. Jane smiles. You ever seen a woman smile that way?' He was looking at me. I shook my head. 'I got no future with a woman like that, Charlie.'

I told you that Conners was always the sensible one; he asked Pete, 'When the body's found, will anyone recognize the knickers?'

'No. Parachute silk. Half the girls in the world wear parachute silk.'

Before he started screaming the dead Pole told the live one that his English friend was coming north again. Pete had flogged the Singer up the Great North Road, and beaten him to it. After seeing him through the wire, Pete went in through the main gate, and phoned Jane to say that he was safe. Then he walked over to the Pit wondering if he had a strong enough hand to deal himself out of the trouble he was undoubtedly in – even if he was unsure what it was. Then I blundered in first, and the dice started rolling again. Pete hurried in after me, still rehearsing his arguments in his head, but by then it was too late. The film-star type lost his head, and then lost his head. It was a story so simple and incomplete; so full of holes, it had to be true.

Grease stopped pacing and gave one of his great whistling exhalations of breath. He asked Pete, 'What did you do with the *first* body?'

Pete looked embarrassed. 'Is in the Singer; parked by the guardhouse, near the telephone I use.'

'Fucking hooray,' murmured Marty.

That was the first flaky tactical decision I ever knew the Pink Pole make.

I was sent to collect the Singer because I knew Alex, and there was just the chance he'd go easy on me if we were discovered. That was bad reasoning, but it wasn't tested that night: I doubt that anyone saw me steal up to the car and drive it away. It took three swings to fire the cow up, and I was sweating inside my shirt, out of fear, when she spluttered into life. There was a hump on the back seat covered by a large GWR tarp, and when I got into the driving seat and looked back over my shoulder, the first thing I saw was a clenched white fist sticking out. I had to lean over and tug the tarp over it, and couldn't resist the urge to touch it: it was cold, like my hands after Krefeld; how could I have expected it to be otherwise? Grease told us that we had to get rid of the bodies, and Marty told us how. His solution, born of his profession of dropping things on people, was theoretically straightforward.

'Dress the bastards in scraps of our old service clothing without ID marks, and pop them out over the ranges tomorrow.

If they drift in, then they're dead aircrew. If they smash to pieces and don't; they don't.'

The Toff said, 'I think that what we're doing is called "compounding a felony".'

Grease said, 'No. What we're doing is covering Pete's arse: just like he's covered ours for eighteen trips.'

Good old Grease, I thought; straight to the bone. Pete sat on the edge of his bed, put his hands over his eyes and sobbed silently: but it wasn't because of what he had done. Seeing as I had taken the risk to recover body one, I was excused the job of washing the gobbets of head off the Pit, as long as I helped Conners strip and dress the corpses. After that we laid them on the floor in one of the latrines, and closed the door on them. It was a tight squeeze, but they fitted. The worst one was the Pole Pete had brought down from London, because he had stiffened into a foetal position, and his shirt and trousers were hard with dry blood. Pete's shot had taken him through the pelvis, but I imagined what he had done to the girl the day before he died, and hoped he'd died in agony. That is one of the things I will have to confess to God, if He comes down and makes me a Catholic on my deathbed.

I told you that Toff was a fisherman – well, we gave him the job of recovering Jane's panties packed deep down in body one's throat, and he did it with a long piece of bent wire. We put them, and the mangled .45 calibre bullet Marty found against the wall, into the stove. I think that they arrest people for that, and call it 'interfering with evidence': damned if I cared. We didn't ask Pete to join in: he stayed sitting on his bed, and after he had stopped crying, chain-smoked American cigarettes. It was as if he was already separated from us. I remember that we all seemed to take a long time scrubbing ourselves clean that night, before we turned in, and that we locked all the doors to the Grease Pit. That was unusual.

I didn't get off to sleep easily, and I'm not sure that any of the others did. After a while Pete got up, moving quietly, and dressed himself in fresh civvies: he lit one of Grace's candles and knelt in front of it for some time. Then I saw him moving slowly about filling two suitcases. He must have sensed that I was awake because before he did his runner he came over and touched my shoulder, and smiled at me. I smiled back, feeling as awkward as I always do working in the realm of emotion. Then he turned, took up his bags and left as quietly as he could. I heard the car move away, waited a few minutes, then got up and locked the door after him.

He had left the light burning on his bedside locker. As I moved over to extinguish it Grease said, 'Leave it, Charlie. Turn the radio on, but keep it down.' His voice was muffled. I found a US army station playing Tommy Dorsey: at that time in the morning it was the slow numbers. 'Lonesome Road' was about right for Pete just now.

Then I heard the scrape of a match, and smelled tobacco smoke from over the room, and registered Fergal's soft bushy voice. 'Anyone fancy a cuppa?'

He made tea for all of us, and brought round the mugs on a tin tray made from a Lanc's floor panel. I turned on one side and, propped on one elbow, smoked one of Pete's cigarettes, drank the tea he'd bartered for us from somewhere, and listened to the sound of America from his wireless. As the candle burned down it flickered wildly from time to time. There were a couple of whispered conversations, but not with me. The last tune I heard as I drifted into sleep was 'Smoke Gets In Your Eyes'. That would be right: it must have been the smoke that did it.

Grease surprised the master bomber that morning by rousting him out of his room before breakfast, and requesting permission to fly a reccy over the practice targets before we took bombs out there again. Samson had been passing the door, overheard, and intercepted Grease as he left. Grease told us he said, 'I heard that, Sergeant: very impressed: very professional.'

And you've gathered by now that keeping his gob shut was one of Grease's problems.

'Then you should make me an officer, sir.'

'Consider it done: too many sergeants in A Flight anyway. All-sergeant crews get bolshy.'

So, in order that we could ditch the mortal remains of Pete's two cops, Grease had to request an additional training sortie, and because bold Samson heard him asking, it indirectly won Grease his promotion. Just one of God's little jokes.

We drove out to the Annie crammed in the boxy little Austin, with the two corpses propped up between Conners and me in the back. Grease drove, and Marty huddled alongside him, still half asleep. Fergal and the Toff rode shotgun on the running boards. Fergal did the business with Annie's reliable old Cheetah engines, which rousted out Chief Bryan from the hangar. He was rubbing his hair with one hand when he spoke to Grease: he must have been asleep.

'Thought you wanted *Tuesday*? We've been up half the night with it.'

'We do. Don't worry – this is just a reccy: back in an hour.' That was optimistic. I was crouched behind him as he slammed the perspex shut. When Grease wasn't in the mood to argue, you didn't. Even crew chiefs had figured that one out.

We flung the corpses into the North Sea, beyond sight of land, from about 2,000 feet, after first flying a fat, flat circuit to check for surface vessels. We didn't want them fished out too quickly. The first one, hardened into a curl, spun like a googly as he fell: the one who had had designs on me caught the trailing edge of the starboard wing, and windmilled away from us more sedately. The Toff and I saw neither hit the ocean in the grey half dawn before we wrestled the fuselage door shut.

Fergal shouted, 'That was wrong: we should have said something. A few words.'

'OK. I'll come round again. I know some words,' Grease said.

As he banked the Anson in a lumbering circle, looking down at the grey into which the bodies had been launched, he said, 'Death to the pigs. Fuck the lot of them. Amen. There: that'll do,' and pointed the old girl back towards England. It was better than no words at all, I suppose.

On the way back when we were on finals, just when he should have been concentrating on what he was doing, he looked over his shoulder at me, and said, 'I'm getting bored with this, Charlie. It's time we killed some of the real enemy again.'

I thought, *yeah, butchers, park-keepers and kindergarten teachers: the* real *enemy.*

Grease's landing was so bad that my teeth rattled in my gums.

The Boss must have thought so too, because the morning shoot was cancelled – they wanted us to do the real thing again that night. Bastards.

We all sat around the stove drawing lots for who was to go and tell Samson that we'd mislaid a rear gunner, even though we all knew that Grease would do it in the end. We were still there when, preceded by the sound of a motorbike, Grace walked in with a suitcase in each hand.

She dropped them noisily to the cold concrete floor, and bleated, 'Sanctuary, sanctuary. If I have to spend another day with mad stepmother I'll shoot the cow!'

We probably all looked at each other, which is why no one said anything immediately, so Grace stared and asked, 'What?' defensively.

'Grace; I think I love you,' Grease told her.

'And me: I love you too,' said Fergal.

'Absolutely,' said Conners. 'Until the seas and mighty oceans run dry.'

'How could I not love one so glorious, and a decent shot into the bargain?' the Toff said.

'Oh sweet, attractive Grace,' said Marty. I think that line might have been from Milton, and wondered what other lights he had under his bushel.

That left just me, but before I could say *please* or *no*, Grease blundered in with, 'Charlie's always loved you. Right from the moment he first saw you, and dried up in mid sentence.'

Grace tried again, and put her props in coarse pitch; 'Just what the fuck is going on here?'

Grace giggled when they asked her. I stayed out of it, and tried to look disapproving. I probably just looked scared.

The question was whether to put our invisible Pole problem to Samson – whose Flight we were nominally in – or to the master gunner, who was nominally Pete's boss. Grease reckoned that we went direct to our *own* master, because he could overrule the master gunner if he felt like it, and he was mad anyway. We drew lots with matches, and I lost. They sent me away to redbrickville in the Austin, to wait outside until I saw the bastard in his office. I watched him drive up from off-station, in fact, and wondered if he'd been with Jenny. I gave him a couple of minutes to settle, and then breezed in past his man, who didn't even have the time to half-arse rise out of his seat, knocked, and headed straight into the inner sanctum. The squadron leader was sitting at his desk staring with slightly glazed eyes: he was waiting for a benny to kick in, so when I asked him if he had a couple of minutes and kicked the door shut behind me, all he said was, 'Eh?'

That was all right.

'We have a problem with the Pink Pole, sir.'

He yawned, and his eyes focused on me. They were more or less synchronous. 'I told you that a couple of weeks ago. Mad buggers, all of them.'

'And your decisive action that day probably saved his bacon, sir.' My tongue should have turned brown.

'Glad you think so. What's happened now?'

'He's found out what they want him for, sir. It *is* the black market – something to do with buying and selling car tyres, and drink. These coppers are prowling about all the time, and Pete has gone to earth here on the station. Sergeant McKenzie sent me over here to seek your advice, sir. We don't want to lose a decent rear gunner this near to the end of our tour.' I produced a bottle of black-market whisky from beneath my battledress jacket, and placed it on the desk between us.

'You seem pretty bloody sure of yourself,' he said.

'I'm anything but, sir, although we have come up with a plan to make the best of a bad job . . . but Grease won't hear of it unless you give it your blessing. Do you happen to have a couple of glasses, sir?' I think I was overdoing the 'sir' bit; overegging the pudding, because that was the first time I had ever heard him laugh: *really* laugh.

'Christ, Sparks, your mob do me over good: they really do.' He poured us two half glasses. 'So what are you going to do about it?'

'The way we see it, sir, is that what we are about to propose could not have happened in the service say, two or three years ago. There were still a lot of regulars around then, everyone knew where they stood, God was in his heaven and the discipline was tight.'

'You're telling me that things are different now?'

'Indubitably.'

'Stop saying that, Bassett. I hate it. Sound like a public schoolboy.'

'Sorry, sir.'

'Go on.'

'The old air force is dead: it will never come back. The regulars we started with in 1939 are dead, or out of it, and we're overrun with Aussies, New Zealanders, Poles, Czechs, Belgians and what have you. They have as much discipline as a fart lost in a fairground, sir, and most of the Brits left flying are either children fresh from school, or completely doolally . . . flak happy.'

'Thank you for that analysis, Bassett. It is reassuringly consistent with my own. Pity about the Brits, ain't it? Continue.'

'That means that colonial behaviour is tolerated just a little more than it used to be, as long as we get the job done.'

'I deplore it, but agree. I suppose that you are proposing some aberrant form of colonial behaviour appropriate for your mad gunner? Gone to earth, you say? Like a fox?'

'Nothing odder than he's already done, sir. He'll just disappear. You won't see him at briefings or interrogations, inspections or parties. You won't see him at all, except in the rear turret of a Lancaster shooting pieces off a Kraut – which is where you really need him to be. Apart from that he will go underground – he's used to it; it's how he got out of Poland. He'll cease to exist, until those coppers stop snooping about for him, and bugger off.'

'They're back then?'

'I saw them a few hours ago.' Not a lie.

'And Paluchowski *will* fly? You're not pulling the old plonker by any chance?'

'On my honour as the worst that the grammar-school system

can produce, there will be a gunner in that turret on every trip, even if I have to carry them into *Tuesday* in a sack.' My 'them' was not a grammatical error. It was a word I chose with care. Not a lie. He blinked slowly; the tic under his eye made an exploratory move – the benny had finally hit.

'You want him to be excused every fucking thing except flying?' he said.

'Yes, sir. We do. You can leave the rest to us.'

'At least that makes a change. Most NCOs who sit where you're sitting agree to do anything else, *except* the flying. Bizarre.'

He swirled the remnant of the whisky in his glass around moodily, then swallowed it in a oner. He closed his eyes, held it for a beat of three and then opened them. Both of his eyes looked at me at the same time.

'Ah shit; let's have the other leg,' he moaned, and held his empty glass out. He observed that the bottle was half full when I left – *my* philosophy, exactly. I left it on the desk.

Krefeld

We climbed up into *Tuesday* and went back to Krefeld that night. Maybe Pete knew a thing or two after all. We had a fat cookie and eight sharky 1,000-pound blast bombs, and a large pink pig painted alongside the spreadeagled man under the bomb mission markings on the nose. At the aircraft Marty had stood up with his head in the bomb bay, and tried to give one of the blast bombs a blowjob. Chief Bryan stood there shaking his head; his oppos sniggered, and no one saw Grace precede me up the ladder and into *Tuesday*. As we climbed in, over the lip, I was supposed to turn right and head for the lights, whilst she turned left for the turret; instead we turned to face each other, holding up the crocodile for a minute or so. We hadn't spoken in the bus. Either of us. We leaned towards each other, didn't kiss, but rubbed noses like Eskimos. Grace smiled and whispered, 'Don't worry. See you in a few hours.'

Heaven or hell? I asked myself, but didn't say it. I smiled too, and turned away from her.

I know some old bomber types who walked away from the RAF at the end of the war, and walked away from Europe too.

They never left the shores of Great Britain for the rest of their lives. I suppose that if you asked them what towns in Germany looked like they'd reply something like, *usually black except where they were on fire*. That was Krefeld on trip twenty, with Grace in the back.

Grease's take-off was lumpy; you could feel *Tuesday* rising and falling like a gentle rollercoaster as she slowly gained height. That was probably because we took off too close to some slower old sod in front of us, and were squashing around in its wash. The old sod was the Boss's kite – he had insisted on taking up with P-*Peter*, the oldest Lanc on the squadron, only now it was designated P-*Papa*. Quelch's wagon, which his ground crew called *El Disgustivo* because of the state it was always left in, was M-*Mother*. Anyway, I distinctly heard Grace's snigger, and Grease asking, 'You said something, Pete?' and Grace replying, 'No, Skipper. Sorry.'

At about 200 feet I wound out the trailing aerial – a job I hated, because to do it I had to crouch in a ball on the floor, which was an awkward, hot job in full flying clobber. When I stood to climb up to the office, Fergal, sensing my movement, looked over his shoulder, and waved me back. Then he cupped a hand over each ear, which told me that Grease wanted a listening watch. That meant he feared a transmission giving us a recall or a route change.

That night the signal was particularly bad, drifting in and out: I flew the first hour with my hand on the tuner. Grease did his usual job on the rendezvous point, flying slightly wider circles than the briefing asked for: Fergal and Conners between them would later have to find a way to save the extra fuel this used.

The reason for this happened about a mile away – there was a sudden fire in the sky, which fell like gobbets of molten lava, illuminating a small village below. I found out later that a late Lanc from Linton, playing catch-up, had climbed through a squadron of Halifaxes, and clipped one of them. Two wickets down, in Grease-speak, before we even got over the sea. I listened in through the static and the garbage, and whistled a silly Arthur Askey tune under my breath. I couldn't get it out of my head.

When Conners called out the old faithful 'Enemy coast ahead', Fergal leant back, and waved me forward to the astrodome.

When I stuck my head up into the glass bowl I got one of those clear dark nights that I so disliked. There was nowhere to hide out there if the bogeyman came after us. I suppose that the advantage was that you had a chance of spotting the Kraut before he had a visual on you – unlike the cloud and the murk that could sometimes give you a fine illusion of safety, until you remembered that he was feeling for you through it with his radar set. They talked about giving us something similar, but it never came to anything whilst I was on the squadron.

Anyway, it was nice to be of use for once: I saw the Kraut like a shadow off the starboard bow, flying parallel to us and way out on the edge of my night vision. Sometimes he was lost in the stars.

Click. 'It's Charlie. There's something off to starboard, maybe twenty degrees. He's about 1,000 yards away. It's not one of us.'

Click: that's Grease. 'What's he doing?'

'Nothing. Just shadowing, but I don't think he's being friendly.'

'Upper gunner. I got him.' That's the Toff.

'Bomb aimer: me too. Do you think he's homing the rest of them in on the stream?'

Click. That's Grease again. 'Could be. You stick with him Toff. Charlie, you watch port and above, Marty just look forward.' We rogered, and then he asked, 'You OK, Pete?'

'Fine Skipper.' Grace's voice seemed deeper in the O mask. 'Can't see anything yet.'

'Can you see Quelch?'

'No, Skipper.'

'I know he's there somewhere: my ring is twitching. It always twitches when he's out there.'

'I can see a Lancaster now. It's closing from dead astern, and slightly above.'

'Thank you tail. That'll be him.'

'He's half rolling . . . he's turning to starboard. He's going like hell, Skipper.'

Grease clicked. 'Aw no,' and groaned, 'not again.'

Quelch had dived gently towards us from astern and above, and then turned fast and sharp to starboard, to draw an interception course with the Kraut. He was on top of him before the Kraut knew what was happening. Q's bomb aimer must have let him have it with the two machine guns in the front turret from about 300 yards. The night fighter turned in towards us to cross the stream, but Quelch was having none of it. Wrenching *Mother* hard port, he flew across the triangle at it: once he had pounced I don't think that any of his bullets missed their mark. Bomber against fighter shouldn't have been an uneven contest like that, but it was — the Me 110 (I saw it for that as it closed) dived away under our nose streaming fluids, smoke and small pieces of aeroplane. He wasn't going anywhere else tonight. Quelch zoomed, breaking off the pursuit rather than ram *Tuesday*; we wouldn't hear the last of that at interrogation.

About half a minute later Grace sang out. 'There was a flash down there: very red. I think it broke up.'

Grease told her, 'Thanks, Pete: now watch your lower quadrant, that's where they'll come from.'

I don't think that she needed telling, but a boss always has to have his say, doesn't he.

Shrapnel has this characteristic sound as it collides with aircraft aluminium: it's like hailstones striking a metal shed when you're on the inside. The next one was too close. The bastards coned us with radar-controlled searchlights during the run-in, and Grease refused to run away. I actually saw the glowing red and blue microbes of steel, like humming birds on automatic pilot, zip in through *Tuesday*'s skin at one side, and out through the other. They left a scent of burnt air, which got in under my mask. I looked frantically round for the fire that wasn't there.

Conners called out. 'Yow! Something just burned my bum.'

'Nav's been hit, Skipper,' I told Grease.

'OK, Charlie, shut up.'

Marty intoned, 'Left; left a bit. No, right a bit. No steady. That's it . . . steady.' He was a single-minded bugger once the bomb run started. I hated flying with the bomb doors open: I felt very vulnerable then. Like living one of those dreams when your pants are around your ankles, and everyone's pointing at you. Marty never seemed to mind. He told me that dropping the bombs was like shooting your load, but better. Then he said those words of power I told you, and *Tuesday* leapt. After the photograph Grease took us away in a flat curve to starboard, gaining height and heading for the black. I had the chance for a quick glance down as we swung away. There were supposed to be two aiming points but four distinct enormous fires were burning. The old guys who told you that it was like looking into the maw of hell weren't just falling back on some tired old cliché – they were giving you the literal.

'Lancaster on fire and going down,' Grace called. Her voice was higher this time.

The Toff clicked. 'Whereabouts?'

'Left. My left. His starboard inner is burning like a blow-torch.'

'I've got it. Four parachutes. Five . . . gone. Five parachutes Nav; you got that?'

'My arse hurts,' Conners said.

Click: Grease. 'Did you get the five parachutes, Nav?'

'I wrote them down. Can we go home now, Skip?'

Grease said, 'Charlie, once Conners has given us a heading, go back and slap a dressing on his arse if he needs it. No morphine until we no longer need him, though.'

Fergal stood up to the dome for me while I tended to Conners. A piece of flak had sliced cleanly through the cheek of his left buttock about an inch deep. It was very bloody, and by torchlight the open wound looked like a piece of steak: after I had poured sulphur powder into it, it *did* need a dressing. In fact I used three on top of each other before the blood flow slowed. I roped it tight, pulling the edges of the wound together, with three rolls of narrow bandage looped tight around his waist and leg, and gave him the morphine over Holland. Because Conners didn't have his mind wholly on the job, we drifted too close to Meppen, on the border of Krautland, and got another peppering of radar-directed flak. The flak storm was lighter, with spent energy this time – that was because Grease had given up on low cover and had taken us high again. The metal shards clattered around *Tuesday*'s tail.

The surprise must have led Grace to click the RT because we all heard her say, 'Ouch!'

My heart lurched.

'You all right, Grace?' the Toff asked.

'Yes. Sorry. It startled me.'

My heart unlurched again. I think everyone else's did too. This wasn't going to be as easy as we thought.

I never got back into the dome on that trip. By the time I had given Conners his jab it was time to weave a little magic in the ether again. I knew the RT was OK, but put a call through anyway. Everyone answered promptly, except Conners, who leaned towards me from the navigation table and gave me a great beaming smile. Old Conners was always a big fan of morphine.

I don't have to tell you that by the time we made it home it was raining, nor that Fiver was waiting for us at dispersal. Situation normal again. For once the signal to Bawne was as true as an arrow in flight, and they gave Grease the OK for a straight in, because he had wounded on board. Grease pulled off a beauty: only three heavy bounces, and a smart skid. The meat truck was parked alongside Fiver's little Morris bus at our dispersal pan, and the doc was sitting on the step in the drizzle.

We carried Conroy out sitting, because I didn't want to start his wound flowing again. He was too stoned to be embarrassed about it, calling out, 'Gee up, gee up,' and pounding Grease and the Toff's shoulders as he rode. They put him face down on a stretcher in the ambulance, and later the MO told us he was asleep before they got him to the surgery. In all this to-do, no one noticed Grace, with Pete's old off-yellow survival suit hanging around her, slip into the back of our transport. Just before we boarded Grease put his face very close to the Toff's, and whispered forcibly.

'As long as Grace is in *Tuesday* then her name is *Pete*; no mistakes − savvy?'

'If you say so.'

'I *do*.'

In the back Grace gave Grease the eye, but it was the Toff she leaned over to kiss, all the time with her eyes on Grease, who grinned at her and said, 'Yeah, OK . . .', and it was him who broke the eye contact.

I walked around to the front, and got up alongside Fiver. She'd gone white when we told her that Conners was cut up, but relieved when we told her where. Even so, she was clumsy with the gear changes.

'I'd like to hold your hand, like Conners does, but mine has got his blood all over it,' I said.

'He is going to be all right?'

'Of course he is. We wouldn't lie to you.'

'Then ask me again another day, after you've washed.'

She was smiling. It was a wonderful smile.

I asked her to stop off at the Pit; I needed a leak, I said, and the flak had pranged *Tuesday*'s Elsan toilet. When I slipped off the wagon and into the Nissen hut, Grace, swaddled in Pete's overalls and with her head turned away, came with me. I washed my hands in one of our two precious sinks, and came back alone.

Fiver gave me an old-fashioned look as I climbed up beside her, which I countered with, 'Don't even ask. And get used to it.'

'Is Pete in trouble?'

'He will be, if the cops catch him.'

It wasn't exactly a lie, was it?

The next morning Grace went running with Grease. That wouldn't raise too many eyebrows. A lot of people must have known that she bunked with us between ATA delivery flights. I reacquainted myself with the fire bucket, refreshed by the night's rainfall. Everyone surfaced eventually, and Conners said he couldn't feel a thing, although he looked a mite tottery.

Chiefy came round at about 1030, and when we asked if there was anything on, shook his head, and said, 'Naw.' Then he asked Grease, 'What the hell were you playing at over there? She's got more holes than a pepper pot.'

'Anything serious?'

'Naw. She'll be looking pretty again tomorrer.'

He had actually come round to sort out the pig. We settled

for a gigantic leg – port, rear – dressed and ready for the oven, or the pot, and a front quarter that the Chief was going to have smoked for us. Even after that he looked unsure of himself; you could just tell that there was something else coming. He said it all in a rush:

'Look. You know we had some real bad luck with Dobbo; the funeral's at 1300 today. The lads would be really chuffed if you could come. We'll stand you a beer afterwards of course: these things ought to be done properly.'

There was Grease, Grace, Marty and me around him when he said this, and he must have taken our immediate silence for a refusal, because his shoulders slumped down.

'Lummy!' Marty said. He sounded stunned, which is how I felt. Grace put her arm around Chiefy's shoulder, and kissed his cheek. He didn't pull away this time.

'Christ! Yes. Of course. We'll all be there. Best bib and tucker. I'm so sorry, Chief,' Grease said.

Chiefy Bryan gave a little frown. 'Thought you knew about it, anyway.'

I asked him where the burial was.

'We thought the little graveyard where they put Black Francie. There's been a visiting parson there for a few weeks now, and we've kept his car running for him, so he's agreed to say a few words.'

He'd better do a bloody sight better than that, I thought, but I kept it buttoned.

It was Marty who chatted up the motor pool and won us Fiver and the Morris, and it was a sober mob that piled into it at 1200. Fiver drove us unhurriedly back to the friendly little graveyard at Everton. The sky was overcast, but at least it wasn't raining. Before the war that single dead bell from the church tower would have rolled out across Bedfordshire, but for the moment it was silent. All we had was the sighing of a damp westerly wind, because the Ministry of Fools had requisitioned church bells, for invasions, the signalling of – of which we hadn't had any proper ones yet.

We saw Chief Bryan and his martial huddle against a grey stone wall at the far side of the churchyard: some distance from where Francie had already begun to rot. Grease dressed us into line, and marched us slowly in to face our bereaved ground crew. The parson stood over the grave, between us. Fiver had joined us this time, and I sympathized with her when she giggled nervously: the parson scowled at her. I know why Fiver giggled. For a start, there was something wrong with the grave: it was less than a foot deep, and less than six inches square. My first thought was that there *must* be more of him left than that.

Then I looked up to find Dobbo watching me mournfully from the line of Erks and fitters. He looked about as serious as you can get at your own funeral. Panic, but by then the Parson cleared his throat and began.

'Brothers and sisters in Christ, we are gathered here today to lay to eternal rest the left ring-finger of Aircraftsman Dobson . . .'

I had to steady Grace, who, out of control, momentarily slumped against me. Or maybe she just turned her ankle. I don't know. The coffin and the grave marker had both been fashioned out of an old ammo box. Dobbo blew the 'Last Post' himself, on a kazoo he held in his good hand. A small dog had got in from somewhere: it wandered over to raise his leg to piss over the temporary marker on Francie's grave. Someone had laid a bunch of late violets on it, I noticed.

They have a wonderful pub at Everton within a fast ground loop of the churchyard – the Thornton Arms: it's still there; heavy with memories of Tempsford. You should try it. We did. We got totally out of our heads, and chased the parson out into the road after he tried to french both Grace and Fiver. I still don't know if he was a real parson, or a deserter on the lam they'd found somewhere. That night Grace and I took the Austin over to the ARC Officers' Club at Bedford and listened to a very smooth piano player named George Shearing. He was just a kid in dark glasses to me, obviously blind, but I didn't spot his stick anywhere. I can't remember many of the tunes he played, but Grace and I danced to all of the slower ones, including 'Honeysuckle Rose'. Emily Rea wasn't there – she'd pushed off to take in a Glenn Miller concert at Twinwood. Neither was Peter Wynn nor his crew. Without them the place seemed untenanted.

Vechta

The next day was a Friday, and at night we went to Vechta, south-west of Bremen. We were carrying a covey of 1,000-pounders and incendiaries. Grease made a great take-off and a fair landing: we'd become connoisseurs of Grease's touchdowns by then. Oh yeah; and Grace got her first Kraut.

What happened was this: Grease wrong-footed both Quelch, for a change, and the flak downstairs, by attempting to run across the target a full ten knots slower than briefed, which wasn't easy for Marty. That brought *Mother* up alongside us and about 250 yards out. She took a flak hit that shredded her starboard wing tip, and the blast threw her on to her beam ends: on her side. I thought for a moment that she'd flip over. As Q did that, Grace saw a single-engined Kraut — a 190 — sliding in under *Mother*'s tail, into the blind spot, so she gave it a liberal hosing with her four .303 machine guns. She had the dubious satisfaction of seeing the fighter's canopy blown to smithereens, and the pilot slump instantly over the controls as it nosed down. A goner. Then it spun out of sight.

The Toff shouted, 'Attagirl! Grace got one. I saw the bits coming off him!'

'You OK, Pete?' That was Grease; the good shepherd.

'Yes, Skipper.' She sounded subdued. That's how people should sound when they've just killed somebody. That's how I felt after each raid latterly. Pete had never sounded subdued – he was just a tradesman doing a job.

Coming in low over the Wash, where we could see the whitecaps in the crackling dawn, *Mother* twinkled us: *Thank Pete. We owe him beer*.

I twinkled back *Two good turns deserve one other*.

We were in the circuit when Quelch landed. *Mother* kept on trying to drop her damaged wing tip, but Quelch made a copybook three-pointer. I forgot to wind in the trailing aerial, and we left it in a tree somewhere along our approach. Ah, hell. It was twenty-one, wasn't it? So was I. Nearly. The Toff and Grease had a row outside interrogation about Toff forgetting to call Grace 'Pete'. Toff backed down. I could see Fiver trying to work out what they were arguing about. She looked mystified. We had to tell the languid IO about the Kraut our rear gunner got, because Quelch's crowd would report it. He still didn't ask us where our gunner was when he looked around the table. Maybe he couldn't count: he had to be bad at something.

Back in the Pit I was worried that Grace would take it badly, but she was tired, and shrugged.

'To be honest, Charlie, I didn't even think about it. I just *did* it. I think that's how most of the killing's done these days: we aren't fully human any more, are we?'

I gave her a hug and said, 'You're something better. You do it with a better *grace*.'

'Who was that?'

'Shakespeare, I think, *The Tempest* or *Twelfth Night*. We're all proud of you. You saved Quelch tonight.'

'Let's hope it was worth it.'

Just about then the others started to pile in. Not noisy. They were drained, like us. Grace slept in Pete's bed again that night. She made no move for old number eight. She was a part of the crew now.

PART THREE

Out of the Blue

Celle

According to our logbooks the next trip was to Celle, north-east of Hanover. There was probably a garden gnome factory, vital to the Hun war effort, that needed a bit of a seeing to. We put 350 Lancs and fifty Hallibags over Celle in twenty minutes, and turned a vertical example of Man's achievement into a horizontal one. As part of the deal we started a number of random fires as well. The year was drawing in, and Butch probably wanted to save the beleaguered citizenry fuel. I can't say much about the trip because there is damn all about it in our logbooks.

One of the reasons that there's damn all in our logbooks is because we didn't see another aircraft from the time we took off until we were back in the circuit around Bawne. Not even Q. The vis that night was absolutely awful: it was like flying through diarrhoea, so I was on listening watch for most of the outward trip.

After debriefing we trooped back into the Pit to find that Grace had roared up the stove. She was sitting on Pete's bed in uniform issue silks two sizes too big for her, hugging her knees. The smell of bacon was hanging in the air.

We weren't flying for a couple of days: Butcher's orders. The squadron must have done something to please the old sod for once. Of course, it wasn't us that they were worried about, it was the aircraft. All of A Flight's and most of B Flight's crates were due about ten hours' work: engine-out jobs in some cases. They could still poke us into spare kites, but Samson must have gone down the easier route.

By now some of the new guys were pointing us out in the sergeants' mess and whispering the number of trips we'd done. They tended to come up and make conversation, as if our longevity could rub off on them: it rarely did. By October '44 the squadron average aircrew life was eight trips a piece before you copped it. Oddly enough for the actual aircraft themselves it was nine: I've never got my head around those stats. Anyway, it meant that you were reluctant to get close to anyone off the crew. Quelch and his gang were the exceptions; they'd attached themselves to us, and there was nothing we could do about that. For us the good side of it was that, for two reasons, the bosses tended to be just that wee bit more economical with the experienced crews: firstly the experience itself was valuable, expensive and hard earned – why throw it away? – and secondly the impact on squadron morale was worse when a crew close to screening got the chop. To use Grease's cricketing metaphor, getting the chop was a bit like coming to the top of the batting order as the blokes in front of you got out. Whereas, if a tyro crew copped it in the first couple of ops, so what? That's what everyone expected anyway.

We were third top in the squadron's batting order: there were two crews with more trips against them than us. One was an all-officer crew who'd got through twenty-five trips without leaving a mark on their aircraft. It creaked a bit, but looked as good as the day it left the factory. They were all upper-class tools: we all knew they'd never make it. The other crew was a mixed mob, both by rank and nationality: they had had so many prangs that nobody knew how they'd got to twenty-seven. They were drunk nearly all the time now, and I had the feeling that they might just complete their tour and get clear. If we were behind them at take-off Grease always used to let them get airborne before launching *Tuesday* after them. The way he put it was that he had no intention of *Tuesday* falling into the damn great hole in the ground they were going to make one day. I reckoned he was wrong.

I suppose *some* questions were asked about why we had an ATA girl in tow so frequently, although none got back to us. Everyone knew that she was one of us, but no one outside the crew knew by how much. Grease worked out that the best we could do was never appear anywhere on the station as a complete crew: that way, with a bit of luck, no one would work out that we'd cast off a Polish rear gunner in favour of an English lady pilot.

Have you ever had a late autumn's day off, when it failed to rain, and the sun gave the last of its life to the ploughed fields? I have. Grace and I took the bicycles down the Drift, and walked out to an old oak tree that reared from a grassy hump in the middle of a field. She lay with her head on my shoulder as we soaked up the air's last heat. I opened my battledress jacket, and she her uniform jacket.

'This is heavenly,' she said.

'What is?'

'Being with you. Sun shining. Feeling good with all of you. Peace.'

'In *Tuesday*, what we do, Precious, isn't peace.'

'It is for me. Nobody's called me Precious before – do you mean it?'

I could have said 'indubitably', I suppose, but I didn't. I thought about the question as if it had meant something, and said, 'Yes. I do. Very much. I'm scared to death when you're in the back of *Tuesday*.'

'So am I. But it is much better than when I waited in the hut for you all to come back. Are you scared for yourself as well?'

'Of course I am, and for Grease and each of the others. But it's something we don't talk about. If one of us said "Let's go home" when we were halfway to Lubeck one night, there's a fair chance that the rest would agree – so we don't talk about it. I won't let them down if they won't let me down. It's something like that.'

'Not long now,' Grace said.

'No, not long now,' and I closed my eyes and felt the sun on my face.

I think that it was about 5 minutes later that Grace suddenly sat up and said, 'I nearly forgot; I've brought you a present.'

She opened her gas-mask case and produced a lumpy parcel. It was inexpertly wrapped in brown paper and tarred string, as if a child had done it. I wasn't used to gifts. They weren't my family's thing. Inside the paper and string there was an unused straight briar pipe, three large tins of RN issue Light Navy Cut tobacco, and a couple of boxes of matches. Her voice told me just how much she wanted me to be pleased; I didn't disappoint her. She said, 'You talked about starting a pipe; I hope the tobacco's all right. Daddy got it for me from a friend in the service.'

'It will be wonderful. No one's given me anything like this before. Where on earth did you find the pipe?'

'I went up to London to get it. There's a wonderful shop on the Strand – you should smell the tobacco and cigars in there: only you need a ration for them. The pipe shape is called a straight billiard. I didn't know what to get as a starter.'

I gave her a kiss that went on for hours, but stopped at the lips.

'Does that mean what I think it means?' she asked me.

'Yes.'

'What? Tell me.'

'I love the pipe you brought me.'

She squealed, and pushed me off. 'Bastard. You know what I wanted you to say!'

'I love you?'

'Do you?'

'Yes.' I said.

'Good,' she said, as if something had been settled, and smiled an odd inwardly directed smile.

Later she asked me, 'When your tour's over the crew splits up, doesn't it?'

'Most likely: unless we volunteer for the Pathfinders or special duties as a complete crew. Even then there'd be no guarantee that we'd stay together, so I'm sure that we won't be doing that. We'll go our separate ways – mostly as trainers to operational training units.'

'I've delivered more clapped-out aircraft to OTUs than you've had bad breakfasts.'

'Sorry. Why did you ask?'

'So I can explain something.' It was the first time I'd heard her wander around a subject until she found a decent glide path. I meant to ask her about that sometime.

'Explain away, then. I'm going to sit up and fill my first pipe.' We disentangled.

'I'm in love with you, Charlie, and I want to make love with you. A lot. I think about it often; especially when you're not around.'

'That's not a problem.' I had difficulty with the pipe.

'I've seen Daddy do it,' Grace said. 'The art is rub the tobacco between your palms until it's shredded, and then pack the pipe neither too hard or too lightly.' Then she said, 'I don't want to sleep with anyone else any more.'

'That's not a problem either.' I had the pipe about right, I thought, and managed to light it from the first match, with my hand cupped around the pipe bowl. It felt wonderfully natural.

'You're such a mule, sometimes, Charlie. Don't you see that it wouldn't be fair on the others if I suddenly say to them Charlie's my man: he gets me from now on, and you lot don't. How will they feel?'

'So you're going to carry on shagging the lot?'

'Don't be so stupid. What I'm saying is that I'm going to do it with no one; not even you.'

'Not even me?'

'That's right: no exceptions. I'm part of the crew now. You don't have sex with the rear gunner.'

'Never?' I had the pipe going well now; the tobacco tasted warm and sweet in my mouth.

'Not until the end of the tour. Then as much as you like, for as long as you like. Just you. Can you wait that long?'

'Yes.' I let a great sweet cloud of blue smoke into the air. I think I grinned at her.

'If I have to.' Then I let the silence hang, before asking, 'Will you marry me?'

Grace's mouth dropped open. She laughed a scared laugh. I persisted.

'After the war: will you *marry* me?'

She made me wait. The laughter dried up. Eventually she gave me the eye-to-eye and said, 'If you can find me. Yes.'

On the way back we stopped at the end of the Drift, and were buzzed by a strange grey and green Spitfire with American stars where its red, white and blue should have been. I leaned the clumsy post bike I was riding over to touch hers, and kissed her again. Why do your lips feel so heavy and sensitive when the sap's rising? She laughed with pure pleasure. She made me believe that someone cared for me.

Marty was on his own in the Pit with one of our well-abused Olympia Press books – *The Nun's Tale* – and I asked him where the others were.

'Some Yank Spitfire – I didn't know they had any – turned up ten minutes ago, and Grease's nose bothered him.'

Five minutes later Grease came in with a small box tucked under one arm. He tossed it to me; it was heavier than it looked.

'That's from your pal Peter Wynn, but you'll not get near him: the officers have got him. Like flies around a turd. He asked me to give you the box; it was his excuse for coming over. He says that Quelch has bought it from some bloke called Tommo.'

Grace said, 'I think I'll just go over and say hello,' and left us.

'I wonder what the Quelch is up to?' Toff said.

I turned over the box, reading its legends. The contents were the property of the United States Eighth Army Air Force. There were a lot serial numbers and a description.

'What's he got now?' said Grease.

'An illuminating deflection gunsight for a fighter plane,' I told him.

'What for?'

'It's *Quelch*. Who knows?'

Something was eating at Grease, and he wasn't ready to tell us yet. I hoped that it was nothing to do with Grace.

I received a letter. It was on the letter board in the mess, secured beneath pink criss-crossed elastic that had been designed for knickers. On the back of the pale blue envelope a small neat hand read *From Jane Shore*. It was delicately perfumed.

Quelch was there first. He said, as I reached for it, 'Mistress

Shore, no less. Wasn't she the whore of one of the Edwards? The Third or the Fourth? In our case, the late lamented Abbot's beautiful lady. If you're doing what I think you're doing young Charles, it's close to necrophilia. Following in the cock steps of a dead man.'

A couple of the big, younger sergeants were hanging around: they sniggered. When I gave them the stare they looked away quickly, and when Q screwed up his mouth with a kiss for them, they shuffled off.

I grinned at Quelch. 'That was good. Two months ago they would have mouthed off at me.'

'It's your twenty-odd trips. They look at you, and remember not to speak ill of the dead.'

'Is that how they see me? Already dead?'

'Of course. Isn't that how you see yourself?'

'No. It's what I see when I look at *them*.'

'You are not our typical aviator, Charles. Dead men walking; all of us.'

The girl's name and the perfume were a cover, of course. It was from Pete: addressed to me, but meant for the whole crew. Reading between the lines he said that he was well, and that we were to use all the *spare things* we were minding for him: he didn't think he'd be back. I read it standing on the roadway. Quelch stood in front of me, and didn't try to get a look at it. It was the sort of thing you liked him for. He had the wooden box in his hand: I had put it in the top space of his locker, which he never locked.

'Good news, was it?' he asked.

'Very,' I said, 'she's a trooper; a good sort.'

He gave me a push, suddenly acting like a pantomime dame. 'Oh, Charlie,' he said, 'you are a *one*.'

We shared the road until it split: him to the main gate; me to the peri-track and the Pit. When I asked him what he was going to do with the gunsight, he became serious, and gave me a peculiarly sensible explanation: 'Shoot at the Kraut, of course.'

'Explain.'

'Pluke' — he was Quelch's bomb aimer — 'is a bloody useless front gunner.' I nodded: we all knew that. 'So we've locked the front turret gun barrels exactly parallel to the forward fuselage: they can't elevate, depress or traverse. All they can do is point forward. So instead of him doing all of those nervy things, and missing every time, I just point *Mother* at the Kraut, fly up his arse, lay a bit off for deflection if he's crossing me, and tell Plukey to press the tit. Bingo: Kraut in a state of advanced combustion. The point is, we aim the kite, not the guns. The Kraut isn't used to hulking great Lancs chasing him around the forests of Bavaria with machine guns: quite a shock to his old system, I'd guess.'

'And the gunsight?'

'If my chiefy can get it mounted and working, it will mean I can get the job done with less bullets: shorter bursts.'

'Have you told the Boss, or the master gunner?'

'What do *you* think?'

'I think that I'm glad I don't fly with you.'

'Another two or three of Mac's touchdowns and you could change your mind.'

'Yeah,' I told him, 'he can get kinda lumpy, can't he?'

I didn't tell everyone about the letter at first. Just Grease. I waited until the Pit was empty before I showed him. Grace hadn't come back. Grease got in first, before I had a chance. He looked shifty.

'Grace had a word with me,' he said.

'Uh huh . . .'

'While she's in the turret she doesn't want any of us in *her* turret . . . if you see what I mean.'

'You mean . . .?'

'Yep. She says she can't be one of the team unless she stops screwing the team. She said that you'd understand, but the others might not. What do you think?'

'I think that Grace is keeping us together and alive. For that reason, if she told us to go to church parade in girls' dresses every Sunday, and whistle in the communion cup, we'd do it. I think that the others will see it her way as well. I think that you'll explain that to them and that I'll back you up, although you won't need me to.'

'Thanks, Charlie.' He still looked uncomfortable.

'Is that it?' I asked.

'I just notice the way you look at Grace sometimes. She might even look back at you the same way. Have you gone soft on her?'

'Maybe a bit softer than you have, Grease. Will that do?'

'And you'll still not . . .?'

'Not until the tour's over, Skip. Then it's every man for himself.'

He put his arm around my shoulder. 'You're a good man Charlie Bassett.' I wished that folk wouldn't keep saying that.

I handed him Pete's letter. Grease read it twice. Don't get me wrong, he was a great skipper, but academically not the sharpest arrow in the quiver.

'Should we have a look at what he's left here, or wait for the others?' he asked.

'You tell me; you're the skipper.'

That was unfair of me, because on most other occasions outside the aircraft I was at pains to point out to him that he held exactly the same rank as the rest of us. He gave me a strained look that said as much.

'Let's do it.'

There were three shiny black metal cabin trunks under Pete's bed, padlocked, and three upright battered personal lockers filched from the flying rooms. I suspected that the six keys on a key ring I had found on my bedside locker after Pete had pissed off would provide an easy answer. There was another thing I found. I found that my .45 and the box of bullets were missing again. We lifted the boxes on to Pete's bed. One was already jemmied by Pete's late visitor. It contained a three-inch layer of papers – mostly signed-off bills in Polish. Underneath that it was packed with booze; nearly forty bottles of spirits of all types and strengths. I wondered where the vodka had come from, and promised myself a taste. The second box contained cigarettes and hand-rolling tobacco. I was disappointed to find no pipe tobacco. The truth is that although Pete had kept us supplied, we had kept our noses out of his affairs. That meant that neither Grease nor I had ever seen as much loot together in one place. There was enough here to fling a couple of decent parties, keep us in smoke until the end of our tour, and then some, and some left over to flog. I remembered that Pete always used the word 'convert' – he never thought of himself as a salesman.

Grease suddenly turned away from the last of the boxes with a grunt; I asked him, 'What's the matter?'

'Don't know, Charlie. Let's look at the lockers: I'm trying to work out what we can safely keep, and how much of this stuff we've got to get rid of.'

The lockers were much the same. Crammed in alongside Pete's uniforms – including that of a Czech army corporal, a ruse de guerre previously unknown to us – were innumerable bottles of whisky, boxes of butter and cheese, cartons of cigarettes and small motor parts. There were also neatly folded squares of parachute silk. Whatever Pete had been up to, he'd got too good at.

We were still unloading them when the Toff, Marty and Conners blew in. They had this word we all used at that time. Toff used it. '*Strewth!*'

Years later, after he had become intelligent, he explained to me that he thought it had derived from the medieval middle English, and meant 'God's death'. It wasn't God who had died for this stuff, but two nosey coppers who weren't quick enough on the draw. We sat on the beds around our mountain of what was undoubtedly ill-gotten gain.

'What's in the other box?' Marty asked.

I watched Grease, who watched me. Finally he nodded to me, and I stood up to open it. It was full of money.

It was Grace who put it all into context later when she came back a bit squiffy from officer camp. 'No matter what you think, the money's not as dangerous as all these bills and letters,' she said.

We were counting the money: bundles of notes in elastic bands. I think we had more there than you'd find in the bank at St Neots after the Saturday market. We had counted about a tenth of it before we gave up, and got to nearly £1,000. It was like looking at ten good pools wins, I thought.

Grace was leafing through the papers bundled on top of the spirits in the first box we'd opened. 'I can't read Polish, but I know an invoice when I see one – that was the end of the business Daddy started in.'

'So?' I was the only one paying any attention.

'If Pete was some sort of one-man Mafia, which I can't believe by the way, it looks like he kept reasonably meticulous records of his ill deeds. There are dates on these bills going back to 1941 . . .'

'When he arrived here. He got in through Spain.'

'. . . and names that I recognize. I reckon you've got half the exiled Polish government, assorted English dukes and countesses, not to mention MPs, generals, colonels, group captains, wing commanders and dozens of others. It looks like he was once an aide-de-camp for some Polish general. Since then Pete has been feeding the black market with goods obtained by crooked Polish functionaries: he was like an agent or a go-between. And he took a cut, probably both ways. All of his customers could be here.'

When you're twenty, and looking at the biggest heap of

money you're ever likely to see in your life, the implications sometimes escape you. Not so Conners.

'Pete was mad to keep records.'

'Or maybe wiser than you think,' said Grace, 'because if any of those persons know that they exist they'd shift heaven and earth to get them back.'

Grease gave a great sigh: I think that all along he'd known it was too good to be true.

'I think we'd better talk about this,' he told us.

Marty and Conners made us real coffee: there was plenty of that too. What Grease did next was lead off the discussion by asking me, 'Are you sure that Pete wants us to have all this?'

'That's what the letter says. I was happy with that before I saw the money, but now I'm not so sure.'

After that he sat back, and let everyone have their say. Then he asked questions and summarized what was coming out of the sausage machine at the business end. It finished like this: 'We've about nine or ten trips left, and we could knock them off in a month, or get knocked off doing them.'

We nodded. This was the skipper.

'And we've more booze, fags and money than we need to get us through.'

Not one of us dissented.

'And what's more the whole lot is likely to be, if not hot, at least decidedly warm, and recognizable when the cops come back looking for it.'

That was the bit we didn't like. I answered for all of us.

'Yeah.'

'So first, we split the booze and fags from the dosh. Nobody gets to know about the dosh except us.'

'OK,' said Marty: he had perked up a bit. We were all extremely depressed about our good fortune; it must be the way it takes you.

'The only risk we take is getting someone already into the black market to take everything else off our hands.'

I said, 'I already know someone. That Yank Tommo who sold a gunsight to Quelch. He's a big black cheese at Thurleigh: you want it, he's got it. That sort of guy. I met some navigators who said that he was a gangster or something. They were really leery of him.'

'Coloured bloke, is he then?' Grease asked.

'No. Black as in black market, as in Al Capone.'

'Oh! Do you know him well, Charlie?'

'No; only a bit. Just a couple of deals. But Major Wynn obviously trusts him: better we trust him than a complete stranger.' The only two people who knew about the .45 were me and Piotr: I decided to keep it that way. 'What do you want me to ask him?'

Grace had a head for business. 'Ask him to take everything off your hands. Everything. Replace it with enough to get us through the month, and give us the rest in money, less his cut. Don't argue over the pennies.'

'And you've got until 1300 tomorrow to get it done,' the Toff told me.

'Why?'

'Because they could be marching us in for a briefing to God knows where soon after that.'

For the life of me I can't remember the name of the pub in Thurleigh. It's called the Jackal now, but I'm sure it was different then. There's something going wrong with a man who can't remember the names of the pubs he's drunk in. It was late evening. There was a quiet group of USAAF men up at the bar. Something must have happened, although Tommo said that all the ships had come back that afternoon.

He hung up the conversation for a beat of about five before saying, 'We can sit here all evening making small talk, but you ain't got the time, an' I ain't got the time, so why don't you spit out what you drove over here to tell me?'

So I did. The whole story. It was a two-pint tale: we bought a round each. Afterwards he stared out the window for several minutes before replying.

'Normally I don't do real business with folks I don't know real well.'

I nodded; it was better to let him talk it out.

'That business we done was just favours for friends, and getting to know your price, you know?'

Nod again, Charlie.

'You could be a pig for all I know.'

'I told you: we've just dumped two of those in the North Sea. I can show you their pistols: in fact, we'd need you to get rid of those too, if you can. Pete left them.'

'Big Russian jobs? I can unload them in London no problem. Officers will soon be looking for souvenirs to take home to mummy and daddy.'

'I'm not a policeman Tommo; and I'm not working with them. I've got a couple of hundredweight of black market goods that I didn't ask for, and I'm scared to death a copper's going to walk through the door any minute. I didn't know who else's advice to get.'

He nodded this time. 'An' the deal is, I take your stuff into my stock, an' it disappears. I give you enough of my stuff to get your team through to the end of your tour, and give you the difference in dough? About how much was you thinking about?'

'Haven't a clue, Tommo. I don't know the going rates. You give me what it's worth: less your commission – you set that too. We can't do this without you. Want another pint?'

'I want my head examining.'

'Thank you.'

'Where you got the stuff?'

'In the car around the corner. It's all in there – packed full.'

'Aw *Christ*, Charlie! You got a death wish? I knew there was someone doing it on your station. There's someone like me at most camps. I just hadn't got round to meeting him yet – it's a sort of floating network; you plug into someone when you need them.'

'Pete would have agreed with that.'

'When Major Wynn sent me over with the radio spares you wanted, I figured it must be you; that was until I met you. Then I knew you hadn't got the savvy.'

'Thanks for that, Tommo.'

'No offence intended, pal.'

'None taken.'

'What happened to the dough?'

'The dough?'

'The *money*?'

'Yes, I know what it means. What money?'

'Your pal's working capital. He took off and left you with his business – he will have taken all the money he could use, but that still left his working capital.'

'Yeah. I see. He *did* leave some cash behind. We haven't made up our minds what to do with it yet.'

'How much?'

'About £2,000.' Oh, Charlie.

'Don't flash it around fer Chrissake, OK? Don't draw attention to yourselves.'

'OK. I'll tell them.'

'I'll wash it for you, if you like. Say for 5 per cent.'

'What do you mean?'

'I'll give you US dollars for it, less my 5 per cent. That's a handling fee. Then I take you up to my good pal the captain who runs the cash accounts at PX store – he's a trained accountant, you know – tell him you won it in a crap game, and he exchanges it for nice clean British money.'

'Less *his* 5 per cent, of course.'

'Maybe.'

'I'll tell them. Thanks for the offer.'

'When you start smoking that pipe?'

'Yesterday. My girlfriend gave it me.'

'Maybe I'll start. You can't get a decent cigar in this country any more.'

'I know; the Yanks have got them all.'

He paused before he laughed at that.

I drove back carefully, sitting on £475 15s in my back

pocket. Tommo said he'd send over English cigarettes and whisky in a day. The laugh was that by the time I got back, the Pit had run out of cigarettes, so they had to beg a packet from another crew.

Lubeck

Lubeck. Fucking Lubeck. We air tested *Tuesday* late morning. Grease was almost caught out by the take-off; I don't know why. At one point we had our starboard main wheel a couple of feet off the runway while the port main and the tail wheel were still happily landlocked. That also meant that we were about to turn left, or ground loop. I still don't know how he got it off the ground. He selected wheels up in a hurry as if to make out he'd done it on purpose.

We were on RT, and Fergal click-clicked. 'What the hell were you *doing* there Skipper?'

Grease sounded unconvincing. 'Just trying something.'

'Fucking *don't*. Whatever it was. Engineer out.'

You can't say I hadn't already warned the Boss: discipline was going to hell.

'Pilot to navigator. Where are we going?'

'I thought Frinton-on-Sea, Skip. It's nice at this time of year.'

'Course? If that's not too much bother.'

'You're so fucking low, Skipper, in case you hadn't noticed,

369

I didn't think you'd need one. You can follow the A1 south, and then take the Colchester road at Bishop's. Make sure you slow down for the tight corners and S bends.'

Grease snarled. 'Anyone else wants to complain about my flying?'

There was another double click. It was Grace, and I could hear her drawing a deep breath before she spoke.

'For the first time in my life I'm feeling airsick. Sorry.'

Grease pulled us smoothly through 3,000 feet, climbing at about 155 knots. The engines had never sounded better. I suddenly realized I had forgotten to trail out the aerial, and got down on my knees winding like crazy. I thought that Grease hadn't noticed, but he said, 'No matter, Charlie.' Then, 'Sorry everyone. I don't know what I was thinking about back there.'

I did. He was thinking about the same as the rest of us, which was about a tin box full of money locked in one of our two latrines, and wondering what he would say if Alex or his ferret found it there. I think his apology pulled us back into line. We did a triangle on Bawne, Frinton and Orford Ness, doing the last leg deliberately at low level, particularly over the airfield at Woodbridge. We ploughed their outfield at about 220 knots, scattering Erks in all directions.

'You *do* realize that they'll complain?' Conners observed.

'What are they going to do?' That was from the Toff. 'Ground us? Suits me. I've already been to Germany too often.'

Grease asked, 'Who's at Woodbridge these days? Used to be Mosquitoes, but I've got a feeling the Yanks may have moved in. What colour were the uniforms you saw running?'

Marty: 'I only saw their bums – they looked brown, to me.'

We did the next twenty minutes professionally, with Marty calling back landmarks against Conners' charts. Grease put us into a wide circuit above Bawne, enjoying his flying I think, but just before touchdown Conners told us, 'In the bar yesterday that bastard Quelch asked me if my arse still hurt, just like that! In front of everybody. The bloody place erupted.'

So did we, and as a result Grease dropped *Tuesday* ten feet on to the runway. We didn't feel the runway hump over the small ridge, because we jumped right over it. Grease was still laughing when Fergal pulled the throttles back on him. It wasn't the police waiting for us at the pan, but Samson, his face as red as a plum, his cheek muscle ticking like a metronome. He shone with anger. Sparkled with it. And Grease made it worse by sort of shambling up to him, and we made it worse by unconsciously copying Grease. I was suddenly aware of how big Grease was, and how small the Old Man was. The squadron leader put his hands on his hips and when he spoke his voice was quiet and even, which must have taken him some effort.

'I saw your take-off, Mac, which is why I came down to speak to you. Now I've seen your touchdown.'

'Bloody dreadful, weren't they, sir?'

'Did you *ever* go to a flying school?'

'In Canada, sir.' You'd have thought from Grease's tone that that explained everything. Perhaps it did.

You could see the fires of Lubeck from forty miles out. There were no defences that night, because the Yanks had been at it for two days, and Butch had sent 400 aircraft over it the night before. I think that the local Kraut defence organizations were probably exhausted. We inserted from the North Sea at 22,000 feet through what looked like broken stratus clouds between Cuxhaven and Heide, avoiding a prickly little town named Itzehoe. That's when we saw Lubeck burning. No Kraut rose to give battle anywhere along the track, and only two or three searchlights wandered the sky above the city. They should have turned them off, they only served as signposts for the bomber stream. I didn't see a single casualty over the city. We bombed into the sea of fire on yellow and green target indicators. Marty took the best target photographs of his life; they proved that *Tuesday* was precisely where she was supposed to be as the bombs fell away from her. On the way home we saw a ground explosion just north-east of Gravelines, which could have been one of ours going in, and then we were over the sea.

Conners and the Toff lit fags, although we weren't supposed to until we were back on the deck, and as we were approaching the friendly isles again Grease clicked to ask me, 'What's the matter, Charlie? Not your chirpy self tonight.'

I didn't know how to reply to him. When I tried, my voice didn't sound too good.

'That felt too much like murder, Skip.'

No one spoke again, apart from Conners and Fergal doing the business, until we were back in the circuit. That was fucking Lubeck. A verb, not an adjective; if you see what I mean this time. Twenty-three.

We were last home again. Fiver dropped Grace at the Pit again, thinking it was Pete skulking off: she had got used to the routine. Fergal had told her it was some cloak and dagger thing. Well, it was, but not in the way she thought. Our intrepid squadron leader had bagged the IO with the Viva Zapata, and all we had left was Harriet. She was very businesslike; I had forgotten what a good IO she was. Pleasant with it, as well. It felt distinctly weird. The Boss's team was still around the table when I slunk out last, and because I had a nose for trouble I hung around in the locker room waiting for them. Something had bloody happened because they were one man down, and that one man being their sparks I had a proprietorial interest in the matter. Eventually Samson drove off to his office to write up the delivery report for the Butcher. I ended up outside in the road, sharing a fag with their nav. I remembered his name just as I opened my mouth.

'Difficult one, Don?'

'Fucking lunacy.'

'What happened?'

'The skip switched off, and flew us into the sea just off Hollesley. Ripped off the bomb and under cart doors. Fucking near drowned Holland and Worsley. We skipped along the surface like a pebble before we got airborne again. Must have lifted a couple of tons of seawater. You've never seen anything like it.'

Holland was their sparks, and Worsley the rear gunner.

'Where's Holland now?'

'Fast asleep I should imagine. He had a fit of the screaming abdabs. We had to tie him down on the rest station. The doc's taken him away to meet the big syringe in the sky.'

'Take care,' I said, as I trod on the cigarette stub.

'How?'

As I turned away from him, towards the slight yellowing of

the horizon which said dawn, I noticed just a slight movement from the door of the parachute shed where we'd hidden Pete on the first night Grace had subbed for him.

Grease was in there with Harriet. I could see most of her short legs, so I guessed that her skirt was around her waist.

'It's not what you think, Charlie,' he said.

'Yes it is. You're shagging Pete's officer.'

Harriet laughed. I hope that there was a little embarrassment in it.

'She's not Pete's officer any more, she's mine,' Grease said.

I sat alone for aircrew breakfast. I don't know where the others got to. I could have joined some of the Boss's team, but that would have sent out the wrong vibes if they started to look for a replacement sparks later in the week. The little girl was doing the serving, and there was something the matter with the food, because the eggs were real, and she gave me an extra. She looked bright and sparky, and her arm was no longer in a sling. The fat sod was nowhere in sight, and it looked as if the grizzled sergeant who was usually in charge of the galley was supervising things. I waved him over.

'Anything the matter, mate? Where you bin tonight then?' he asked.

'Fucking Lubeck. No, nothing's wrong: bloody marvellous grub in fact. I'm just too tired to make the best of it. I was just wondering where the fat bastard was.'

'A lot of us are wondering that, Charlie – it is Charlie isn't it?' I nodded; my mouth was full. He stuck on, 'Nobody's seen him since the day before yesterday, and allegedly his quarter weren't slept in last night. I think that the provos will give him another couple of hours, and then make it an official AWOL. First time I seen someone with a number as cushy as his do a runner.'

'Me too, but I'm not complaining. Disliked him on sight.'

'So did the rest of us; so don't worry about it. Enjoy your breakfast now.'

Lubeck and back without a casualty, the Boss flies his kite away from a mistake which would have killed anyone else, a decent breakfast and Fat Guts had done a bunk. Maybe God was in his heaven after all.

Back at the Pit everyone was snoring, except Grease, who wasn't there, and Grace who was sitting on the edge of Pete's bed wearing her baggy long johns. She looked a little pale, and about as feminine as a bowser.

I sat alongside her and asked, 'Are you OK?'

'I don't think that my stomach recovered from the bouncing Grease gave us this morning. I'm not used to sitting at the rear end of an aircraft.'

'You could be right. It's where you sit, out on the tail. Every movement of the plane is exaggerated. It's OK for me: I sit over the centre of gravity. Do you fancy a walk? Get some air?'

'Would you mind? You must be tired too.'

Now it was true dawn. Half dark, with great gashes of dull yellow and pink pushing back the heavy greys still in the west. We walked around the peri-track not saying much, listening to the dawn chorus start up. No war messes up their lives. I had my arm around her shoulder, and hers was looped around my waist. Our hips rubbed together as we walked. A Mosquito night fighter that had been an impromptu nocturnal guest took off, and droned south. A straining old Halifax, short of fuel no doubt, and unable to reach its own base, flopped thankfully on to our runway. The dispersal pan it was directed to was not far from where we stood watching, but we were in the dark and they didn't see us. We heard the banter as they dropped out on to the concrete: they sounded like a good crew. Fiver drove out to meet them, and take them to the sergeants' mess. I hoped that they'd appreciate her. It was like the privilege of being able to watch yourself at a distance.

'I'm OK now, and tired. Let's go back,' said Grace.

I looked back over my shoulder at the Hallibag as we walked away. There was an airman still there in the shadows, looking up at it. I think that he wore a long flying jacket and riding trousers, but I may have been wrong.

I was awoken by the bell on the fire engine, and got to the window just in time to see a small lorry, the meat wagon and the fire tender crest the hump on the runway, hare over the ridge and across the field. Outside I dunked myself in the fire bucket, and spoke to Grease who was limbering up. I wondered where he'd spent the night.

There was no smoke from the direction the vehicles had aimed at.

'What's up?' I asked him, 'I didn't hear a crash.'

'And I didn't see one. Buggered if I know. Nothing's arrived while I've been here.'

'Nothing to do with us, then.' I shrugged off what was sitting in the air between us: Grease didn't; it wasn't his way.

'Charlie, we've got to do something with Pete's money.'

'*Our* money.'

'OK. *Our* money, then. In case the cops come looking for it.'

'I know.' I was irritated. Probably because I didn't know what to do either.

'That was Alex and his Blue and White Jobs who just flew over the hill in their Dinky lorry after the fire tender. Some day soon they're going to be coming here.'

'I told you. I know.'

Grace said, 'Split it. Break it down into smaller amounts. It won't arouse as much suspicion then.' She had stumbled out of the Pit after me, and now followed me into the fire bucket: she made a lot more noise than I did. She had pulled on a pair of faded American fatigue trousers over her silks: when she bent over the bucket they followed the contours of her bum. Scratch what I said about last night, she looked so sexy I could have laid her down on the cold concrete. Grease seemed not to notice. The small provo lorry reappeared trundling over the hump on the runway, then made a right to head in our direction. Grease pretended not to notice, but said, 'Balls.'

The police lorry parked up about twenty-five yards off, and Alex stepped down from behind the wheel. They have this conceit in military police circles that the senior ranker always drives. I reckon it's because the others are too dumb.

'Morning, Alex,' I said, and gave him my innocent smile. I never even got close to fooling him.

'Charlie. Morning, Mac; Miss.' He actually touched his cap. His black curly hair boiled out around it.

'Fancy a cuppa?'

'No thanks, Charlie. I got the squad in the truck waiting for me.'

'Ah.'

'Excuse us, please,' to the others, put his great arm around my shoulders and walked me out of earshot.

'What's up this morning?' I asked him.

'They found the late catering officer in the old latrine pit the other side of the field. The one that was there when everyone was living in tents apparently. I don't know if you've been over there lately.'

'No. I deliberately stay away. We sometimes get the niff of it over here when the wind's in the wrong direction. Horrible.'

'Even more horrible to drown in.'

'Fat Guts had only been here a couple of months: you *could* have walked into it if you didn't know it was there. The grass had grown over it just like the rest of the field. Wasn't it marked out with tapes and a couple of warning signs?'

'Yeah, Charlie: you *could* have walked into it, with your hands tied behind your back and a sack of cement tied to your belt. But then again; unlikely.' He let that sink in. 'One of the runway maintenance guys was over there ferreting, and noticed that something had gone through the surface.'

'Can't say we'll miss him: he knocked his people about. What happens next?'

'The group captain will try to keep it in-house, but my guess is that they'll soon have an HQ special team crawling all over us. Supercilious bastards.'

'You don't like them, then?'

'What do *you* think?'

'Why are you telling me this, Alex?'

'Because for me and my boss this will have to take priority over anything else we've been asked to do. For instance, if we'd had a signal from HQ last night telling us to turn the station upside down, looking for an elusive Polish rear gunner with a penchant for dabbling in politics, and any illegal black market materials associated with it, we won't be able to do it until after the flap over the fat man has finished, will we?'

I turned away from him. I hope that I didn't blush.

Later, Grease asked me, 'What did he say?'

'He said they've found the body of Fat Guts from the mess in the old latrine pit on the other side of the field.'

'Ugh,' said Grease, 'what a way to go. Saves me a job, though.' I was relieved that he said that. I had immediately wondered. Even so, I was far from sure he hadn't had a hand in it. 'What else?'

'I'm not sure, but he told me to get rid of anything embarrassing before they come for it, I think. Tomorrow at the latest.'

Krefeld

We were on. Would you believe Krefeld again? What was left to bomb there? We saw something that pleased and depressed me simultaneously. What pleased me was seeing the whole crew get out of a cripple of a Lanc. It was nice to know that the parachutes sometimes worked when you needed them. We were over Holland on the return trip, and plugging for home at our best cruising speed. Two night fighters had had a sniff at us just after target, and twice Grace and the Toff had driven them back with a withering concentration of fire: they were getting quite good at putting all their bullets in one place. It must have been discouraging for the old Kraut. The second one got one or two bullets on us as it dived past: I heard them zip through *Tuesday*'s sides, and one of them, almost spent, whanged off the main spar. Everyone answered the call-through. We caught up with a damaged Mk 2 straggler in Holland: it was lower than us and skipping on top of the cloud base. It had nothing burning, but its big fat starboard inner was trailing dense black smoke as if either it had caught fire, or wanted to. The prop was just windmilling in the airstream. Great chunks of the wing surface

380

had been ripped away. It looked like flak damage over the target to me; bleeding miracle she'd got that far.

Fergal stood up to look over Grease, as we came up on its right. 'She won't make it, Skip,' he said.

'Why?'

'They've smashed up all the fuel cells in the starboard wing. Even if she doesn't burn, or fall to bits, she'll run out of juice before we even get to the Channel.'

I could see their sparks in his astrodome looking at me over about fifty yards of cold dark air. He drew a gloved finger slowly across his throat. I clicked. 'They know. Their sparks just gave me the finger.'

It strained up for another hundred or so feet above the cloud layer, and then the bodies started to leave; first of all two from under the nose, quickly followed by one from the rear door. The sparks gave a brief wave and then ducked out of sight. Within half a minute three more bodies came through the rear door, just like that: one, two, three. That left just the pilot, and that was always the sod of these big bombers. As soon as he took his hands off the column they spun, or just dropped out of the sky, pinning the poor bugger inside before he had the chance to get out. He flew on alone in the empty aircraft for about another four minutes; what must that have been like? Probably trying to decide which exit to jump for. When you were caught in one of those, up above the dying Reich, there was no usherette with a torch to show you the cinema door, believe me. Then the wing went. It didn't break off, or fold back — I've seen that before — it simply disintegrated into whirling pieces, and what was left of the old girl flipped straight over on her back. As that happened the last body dropped out of the emergency hatch above the pilot's head. How he didn't clart himself on the rudders I'll never know, but the bomber dropped away into the cloud, and his chute showed before he did as well.

'Seven parachutes; did you *see* that?' I told Conroy, for his log. 'Seven lovely bloody big parachutes.'

Fergal clicked, and said, 'Engineer. Are the natives below friendly, Nav?'

'Maybe. They might have come far enough,' Conners said.

Marty had said it first; some things are better than sex. Seeing all seven bodies get clear of a stricken Lancaster is one of them. It was the first time on ops that I had been prompted to pray. I filled my lungs with ox and thought *Thank you, God*, but must have said it aloud instead, because the Toff, and then Grace, said, 'Amen.'

'Pilot to crew: don't lose it, people. Keep your eyes open, we're not home yet,' Grease said.

What depressed me was that the Lanc had been one of ours. It was D-*Dog*. Whittaker and his crew called her *Der Dog's Bollocks*. It depressed me because I had started to like the Whittaker team: they'd racked a good few trips in a short period, and were starting to look safe. We could have kissed Grease for his landing that morning: you get medals for touchdowns as smooth as that.

Alex was waiting for me at the door as I left the interrogation hut. Grease and Harriet were still talking together across the table: she leaned over and squeezed his hand.

Dwarfed in Alex's hand was a small buff envelope. He thrust it at me, and said, 'I warned you about this.'

Oh Christ. Give me one more day, please, God!

'What?'

He took what was simple fatigue to be truculence.

'Using my office as a personal bleeding messenger service. Here.'

Eat humble pie time, Charlie.

'Sorry, Alex. I'm bushed.'

'Bad, was it?'

'So-so. Hey; but listen to this. I saw *Dog's Bollocks* go down over Holland, and all of the bastards got out!'

'*All?*'

'I counted the bloody parachutes, Alex; isn't that just marvellous?'

He put his arm over my shoulder, just like he had done the day before, and steered me to the mess. I wasn't always sure about people touching me uninvited. Perhaps I should introduce him to Quelch. Then I realized that I hadn't seen Quelch, so I asked him if he'd heard anything.

Quelch was the night's second little miracle. He'd ditched *Mother*, dead empty of fuel, in a flat, calm swell off Brighton Pier, miles off track to the south, and they all rowed ashore. Confounding their evil sea-worthiness reputation, his Lanc was still afloat the next morning. Then the Blue Jobs chopped off its tail with a minesweeper while they were trying to get a line on it, and it sank half a mile from the shingle, despite their efforts. Q was livid when he got back: he said that she knew where she

383

was going, and left to herself she would have made the beach alone.

The envelope containing the phone message had a single sheet with a single typed line on Alex's typewriter.

Phone me tomorrow, if you can.

It's nice to have a choice, I suppose, except when you are as tired as I was. I showed it to Alex asking, 'Who was it?'

'The American bird who left a message before. I didn't know that there was more than one.'

Tomorrow was the today during which we had to get rid of the money. I phoned the ARC Club early. Emily Rea wasn't there, but I recognized the voice of the girl who answered the telephone without being able to place her. I told her who I was, and she said, 'Hang on a tick; I'll just look at the list.' Then she said, 'Yeah. You're one of the Brits. Can you come to Major Wynn's party tonight? We'll kick off at about 2000.'

I relaxed. 'What's Peter done? Won a Congressional Medal?'

There was a beat of five or six. No response. Then, 'No. Nothing like that.' She suddenly had a quiet voice: a little girl's voice. 'He's being buried at 1030 at Madingley. It's an all-American send-off, but he wanted you to be at the party. He left a list.'

What would Mr Cooper have said? *Just like that?* Probably.

We split the money into seven amounts of £1,300. That still left more than £3,000. Then we drove around Cambridgeshire and Bedfordshire opening up bank accounts like Bradford millionaires. I took a chance with just one. Conners split his into three – that was serious motoring. The Toff kept a couple of hundred in his pocket, despite the warnings, but opened two accounts. Marty and Grease opened two apiece in different banks. Fergal put his in an envelope inside an envelope, and at St Neots station gave it to the stationmaster, another Mick. He told us that it would be with his mother and father in Belfast before a letter could get there.

It was my first experience of the grown-up world of banking. The manager didn't fancy me much, although he quickly reached out a claw-like hand for my money. He'd send me a cheque book, he said, in a fortnight. I told him that it was compensation for property taken over by the Americans. Everyone believed stories of places leased to the Americans. Grace dropped off at the local bank in Crifton, and paid £1,000 into one of her accounts. The time-expired cashier treated her like an old friend and ignored the sum, with which you could have bought a fair house, as if it had been her petty cash. Perhaps it was. Something odd passed between them: he counted the money but no receipt or signature changed hands, and when he asked, 'In the usual account, Miss?' she beamed and answered, 'Why not?'

That left about three grand which the blokes wanted passed through Tommo. I phoned him, but he was close-mouthed. 'See ya tonight, pal,' was all he'd say, 'at the Major's do. Bring that stupid little car, will ya?'

If you thought that Wynn's do might have been a subdued affair it just goes to show that you were never on the loose in the forties. That wasn't our way to party. The joint was jumping. I put on my number ones and Grace helped me to spruce up. She put on her ATA bests, and partnered me. This time it was me that talked *her* over the threshold, because she wasn't on Wynn's list, whatever that was. For two people who had looked ready to set claws into each other a fortnight before, she and Emily treated each other kindly. Just a gentle hug that was held for a three beat. Then Emily did the same to me. She said, 'You haven't missed much. You know where the bar is Charlie; Grace and I will see you shortly.'

Befehl ist befehl again. I think that it was girls' room stuff.

That man Braddock and his nav, Bourne, were propping up the bar again. Braddock had taken off about four inches of moustache at each wing tip. He touched what was left nervously, and asked me, 'What do you think?'

'Terrific. Like Douglas Fairbanks. Why did you do it?'

'Got bored.'

Bourne shoved a glass of that cold, sharp American beer into my hand, and said, 'He's lying. Tell him the truth, Guv.'

'Saw a movement out of the corner of my eye, and thought it was the Jerry. Turned tight into him, and we went arse over tit into a spin. Turned out to be the end of my whiskers. Lost damned nigh 15,000 feet before I pulled out of it. Bloody silly.'

'Now tell him the rest.'

'Well, we *made* it, obviously, although the wings were in a funny attitude when we landed: the Mozzie looked as if it wanted to clap hands with its wing tips above the cockpit roof. Deuced odd.'

'Deuced,' I agreed.

'And because George is turning into a windy old sod he said he wouldn't fly with me any more if the same thing was going to happen again. Bloody old woman.'

'So you gave them the chop?'

'Don't have the time to train another nav, do I, old boy?'

I noticed that they both had fresh ribbons. 'Collecting gongs again?'

'Just Bars.'

'What for?'

'Bringing the kite back without ripping its wings off, of course! What's the matter with you Bassett; you were sharper than that a couple of weeks ago.' Braddock had lost none of his charm.

'I keep on expecting Peter Wynn to walk in. Do you know what happened?' I said.

'Someone shot us a line, but I don't believe it. Ask one of the brethren, then come back and give us the gen.' He turned away to the coloured barman and asked, 'Another three of your delicious beers, my dear.'

The barman looked horrified, and showed the whites of his eyes, but produced the goods, which is why I had my second beer in my hand when Grace walked up. She looked as if she had had a small cry, but wasn't unhappy with it. In fact she gurgled an unstable little laugh, and squeezed a few more tears out. A couple of the Yanks crowding the bar near us also laughed, probably at Grace's laughter, but quickly looked embarrassed, and stifled it. I didn't get it.

Emily pushed through the throng dragging Tommo behind her. 'I tried to keep this type out but he threatened to buy the place from under me!' she said.

'He was probably on the Major's list anyway,' I said.

'First name. Peter never forgot his friends.'

'What happened?'

The black barkeep had put a big glass of bourbon in Tommo's hand without being asked. For an NCO in an officers' club I thought that that wasn't bad going.

Tommo grabbed me by the elbow. 'I'll tell ya,' he said, and steered me away to an austere little side office with a grey filing cabinet, a neat small utility desk and a plain chair. 'Secretary's office,' he explained when he shut the door on the hubbub outside.

There were framed photographs in a line around the walls. In the last one I was posed with Braddock, George Bourne and some USAAF aircrew from that session with Lee Miller: we all looked suitably weary and martial at the same time. A small combo outside had started to play 'Coming in on a Wing and a Prayer', and it sounded as if half of Bedford was in the chorus line. The sergeant sat in the chair whilst I perched on the desk.

'When did the Major draw up this list of people to attend his wake?' I asked.

'When he knew he'd bought it. He dictated it to an ARC nurse. He had a few hours.'

'I'm sorry.'

'Not as sorry as the Major was. That mad redskin got chopped over Lubeck. The Major went into his billet to make sure his things were cleared out, sat on the fucking rattlesnake, which bit him on the fucking arse. They gave him the anti-venom when he got over to the doc's, but by then it was too late: an' you can't throw a proper tourniquet around an arse, can you? The serum just gave him a few hours longer, that was all. Everyone who loved him came in to say goodbye.'

'This wouldn't be a line, would it, Tommo? Just winding a Brit up?'

'I wish it was Charlie. The Major would have liked the turnout tonight, but he sure would have preferred to be here in person, I'd guess.'

'Yes.' It seemed the only appropriate thing to say.

Then Tommo laughed a little, and I think that I did too. 'Those B-17s he flew have armour-plated seats for the pilots. He didn't have an armour-plated seat the one time he really needed one.'

'That's how it always happens.'

'You got some dough you need changed, you said?'

'Thanks Tommo. It's a bit more than I thought. The boys really appreciate this.'

I held out my hand for his before we reached the door.

'Nice doing business with you Sergeant,' I told him. His handshake was like Iron John.

'And with you, partner,' he said.

Was it my imagination, or did I feel the fish hook go straight in through my upper lip?

Grace was dancing with someone I recognized as one of Peter Wynn's crew when we moved back into the bar, but she stopped when she spotted us, and her partner walked her across.

'Hope you don't mind, Sergeant,' he said.

'No, of course not. Thanks for looking out for her. Sorry about the Major.'

'Yeah. Fine guy; great captain. Pity about his arse.'

'What happened to the snake?'

'Major made us promise not to kill it. It's in a big glass box in the PX: it's gonna be the base mascot.'

After he left, Grace asked me, 'What was that all about? That boy was genuinely scared of you.'

'Not me,' I told her, and ruffled her hair. 'Just the company I keep.'

She was just about to return serve when she followed my line of sight, and saw Tommo. He smiled back at her, showing his teeth. She looked at me, with new interest I thought. 'I see what he means,' she said.

Bourne and Braddock saw me through the cigarette smoke, and the latter had a question on his face as, with his drink-free hand, he animatedly pointed at his backside. I raised my glass to him and gave him the affirmative nod. He shrugged, and turned his attention back to an ARC nurse at the bar alongside him. I put a face to her voice now: she was the plump little redhead I'd met in London a million years BC. The band began to play 'Blue Moon', and Grace said, 'Dance with me. We're not going to stay too long, are we?'

Emily shook hands with me, and gave me a hug as we left. She said, 'Everyone on the Major's list gets to be a full member of this club from now on, Charlie. You tell them that when you get back to your base and they'll have to make you an officer.' She gave me an envelope, and said that some of Lee's photos were in there for me: Grace took charge of them.

I gave Emily a chaste sort of kiss, which is the only thing you can do to *some* sort of women without they say so, and told her, 'See you soon.'

In fact, I never saw her again.

The back seat of the Austin was stacked up with tins of Royal Navy, Player's Airman and Craven A cigarettes, and cases of scotch and gin. It started on the second swing. Tommo came outside just as I was about to pull away. I let the window down on the strap, and he shoved a heavy parcel bound up with tarred paper and string at me.

'I nearly forgot. I got no use for this,' he said, then walked back into the club waving, but not looking.

On the way back Grace said, 'He can wrap a better parcel than I can,' as she opened it for me, and then, 'Wow, Charlie! About twenty tins of pipe tobacco. All kinds.'

'The blokes will be expecting us to spend the night at Crifton, and go on in the morning.'

'Which is why we won't. I told you. Fair's fair, Charlie.'

I did the big sigh, but ended up laughing. So did Grace. We could see a big bright star in the sky to the south, through the trees lining the road. It kept the same elevation and compass bearing to us the whole way. It shouldn't have done that. I had seen stars like that when we were off flying somewhere, decided not to say anything to Grace, but she noticed anyway.

'What's that star? The bright one?' she asked me.

'That's Peter Wynn,' I told her.

*

On Monday morning we moved one of Piotr's lockers to stand by his old bed, labelled it 'G Baker' and with her ATA number, and stowed all the party goods in it before locking it and giving Grace the only key. Highly unofficial, but we reckoned that was our best chance.

A little later, Alex, two of his boys and a civilian contractor came down the outside road, and rewired the little gate we had been using for three months. Alex shrugged. The body in the bog had changed things. Provost heavies from London were coming, so it was back to bullshit and weekend passes.

I had told Grease about Peter Wynn first thing. I was having my head dip, and he was bouncing up and down on the spot. I must have eventually told him about the snake in the Snake Pit, but I couldn't remember when. He shook his head and smiled; he told me that he had never believed the story.

Treuenbrietzen

We went to a target which had been named Treuenbrietzen; noted, before we got there, for two beautiful wooden medieval bridges. Marty had scribbled *For Dobbo's finger* on the 4,000-pound cookie we carried. The rest of our load was racks of incendiaries.

They tried another battle plan for Treuenbrietzen: the bomber stream bunched up and passed over the city centre in a broad carpet, ten or twelve aircraft at a time releasing their bombs every minute. The result was beauteous fair to look upon – the usual sea of red calamity was broader, longer and less dense, but rippled with concentric blast rings.

That night Grease thought the Brits around us were a damned sight more dangerous than night fighters. Not all the pilots took the same view, which is why most of the casualty list that trip read *Collision over target*. That is why the Butcher and his barons never tried it again.

After Marty muttered the words of power, *Tuesday* leapt like a breeding salmon, as usual, as did the aircraft around us; but whereas their pilots held them down after gaining 500 feet,

Grease let us go on climbing for another half thou with Quelch somewhere astern. Connors gave Grease the return heading and warned him that we would pass between two night-fighter stations.

Then Grease did things differently, of course: after ten minutes he took us down on to the deck in a steep descent, flying so low that we had to lift for church steeples and power cables. Quelch's bus stayed with us as if attached by a tow rope. Until we reached the northerly of the two night-fighter airfields, for which Grease had steered deliberately, then Q pulled up alongside and we swept over the base together. I reckon that we were at less than fifty feet, and now I knew what we had been doing over Woodbridge a few days earlier. Grace plastered a twin-engined job as we swept over its dispersal pan: it was beginning to burn before we were away. Quelch caught a single-seater trying to get off, and consigned it to the burning fiery furnace. The airfield exploded with flak as we left it, but they had no idea where the attack had come from and were just shooting the sky.

The skipper didn't lift us into clear air again until we were in Holland, and did the *after you* bit with Quelch once we were in the circuit. We both waited in the air while priority to land was given to two from the other squadron who been beaten about a bit over there. *Tuesday* seemed to accept the runway with gratitude and relief. She felt like the rest of us, poor cow.

Fiver seemed slightly drunk, and very chatty. Conners sat with her again; they giggled a lot, except when Conners leaned back and asked Grease, 'Precisely *what* were we doing with Quelch, over that Jerry airfield in the middle of the night, Skipper?'

'Target of opportunity. You heard them at briefing tell us that we were free to go for targets of opportunity.'

Fiver crashed the gears: Conners ignored her.

'That's with our bombs, Skip. In case we can't find our primary or secondary targets we're released to find a target of opportunity elsewhere. They don't expect us to go haring all over the Reich looking for Krauts to shoot up with our machine guns, and you *know* that! If you're looking for a target of opportunity next time, why don't we find out where Butch lives, or just make for High Wycombe?'

Then Grease stunned us all by muttering, 'This tour's almost over: I want a medal to take home.'

After a long pause the Toff said, 'Oh shit!' He was identifying exactly what we were in. Bright fellow.

After the debrief, when we said that we rather liked that method of bombing, the squadron leader leaned over our table and said that's why we'd never do it again.

I phoned Braddock at his Mosquito station near Pickering. I remembered doing the Yorkshire Ridings in geography classes at school, wondered which one Pickering was in, and tried to envision it on the map in my head. Some fool had obviously made him a squadron leader too, because that's what their duty officer called him when he asked me if it was really necessary to wake him. I was awake; why shouldn't the rest of the bloody Air Force be?

Braddock didn't *sound* awake: 'Ye-es, Braddock.'

'No, sir, *you're* Braddock. I'm Bassett. One of the Bawne Bassetts.'

He picked up on that. 'What is it, Charlie?'

'My pilot wants a medal before the end of our tour, and we're scared shitless that he'll kill us all earning it. I wondered if I could buy him one of yours?'

He took so long to answer that I thought his tongue had fused to the roof of his mouth. 'Do you know what time it is, Charlie?'

'About 0530 by my watch.'

There was another long gap. His nav was right about him: he wasn't too quick over the ground. I heard him yawn. Twice. 'How does he think he's going to get this medal?'

'By being very brave, we think, sir.'

He yawned again. 'Then I think that you're deep in the shit, Charlie. Goodnight now.'

The heavy, black Bakelite handset buzzed in my ear. The bastard had hung up on me before I could tell him that we already knew that.

Grease was summoned to see the doc, who said he wanted another look at his arm. We knew it wasn't about that. Privately I wondered if the doc had been slipped the word that Grease was gong happy, and wanted to get to him first. Anyway; I went with him. He did Grease's arm, and then asked for a look at my frostbitten fingers. I actually had no problem with them, except three were still dead at the very fingertips, and had lost their fingerprints. That might come in handy later in life.

The way the MO um'd and ah'd around what he wanted to say was uncharacteristic, and worrying. We ended up discussing the weather. I remembered what Tommo had said to me in similar circumstances.

'Doc. It's been great chatting with you, but *you* haven't the time, and neither have we, so why not spit out what's on your mind?'

Grease gave me a sharp look. That was not the way he wanted an officer addressed by anyone except himself; he was going to be one, one day, remember? And the doc had about thirty rings on his sleeve.

However, the doc smiled sheepishly. 'Well said, Sergeant Bassett. I will remember you.' We didn't help him any further, so he said, 'It's difficult talking about a fellow officer.'

'To other ranks, you mean?'

'Precisely, Bassett.'

'Then don't.' I half rose to leave. His cheeks flushed: anger or embarrassment? Grease pulled me back down into the chair.

'Squadron Leader Delve also flies as your flight commander?'

'Yes,' Grease said. He spoke with a quiet exact voice. I had heard that before. It happened when his loyalty was being tested, which was something to which he did not react well. The MO said what he had to.

'Half his crew were wounded last night. One of them seriously. Were you aware of that?'

'No.'

'They told me that he made a mistake, and flew them back over Zetel. The inside of *Peter* was like a butcher's shop.'

Grease scowled, and shrugged. 'His nav should have told him; mine would. There's more flak around Zetel than in most of the rest of Germany put together. No one can tell me why.'

'He *did*, and was threatened with an LMF posting for his trouble. Delve could be heard chuckling as the flak was hitting them, apparently. Did you also know that he's set his heart on a round hundred trips?'

'We know about that.'

'He has two more to do.'

'We know that too.'

'I think he'll kill the lot of them before that.'

'Ground him.'

'I can't. None of them will say a bad word about him, or his atrocious flying.'

'Nor will we, so what do you want us to do about it?'

'I don't know, Mr McKenzie. All I can do is pass the buck.'

'Not to a humble sergeant you can't, sir.'

'Perhaps not. But I can pass it to the number two in his flight, can't I?'

'Cunning old buzzard,' I told Grease once we were outside again.

'Wanker!' Grease said. He had this thing about personal responsibility; then he muttered, 'Not much bloody urgency about the place today, let's see if a pub's open,' and spoiled it.

We went into the Cock and Bottle in Bawne. Its four-square shabbiness always appealed to me. Grease complained about the beer. He wasn't wrong. Everyone said that Phillips Royston beers had gone down hill since the brewer's eldest son had been killed. He had been RAF like us, so I made a thing of drinking a few of their pints every week if I could. A point of honour you might say, and bad as it was, it was a million times better than the piss in our station bar.

I decided to ask Grease the question outright. 'Did you have anything to do with the Fat Guts's death?'

'What d'you take me for Charlie, some sort of gangster?'

'We *are* gangsters, Grease. The Krauts call us "Terrorfligers". We kill dozens of civvies every night we go over there, old men, women and children, or hadn't you thought that one through yet?'

'Don't patronize me, Charlie, please.'

'Then don't bloody patronize me back. Buy us another glass of this swill.'

I noticed that there was a small pack of grey prayer cards behind the bar. Perhaps the chaplain had slipped around the pubs and consecrated them, just in order to keep everything above board with God.

'I met someone when you were away in Bedford that evening,' Grease said. 'I came here. I think now that he might have been following me. Not me personally; anyone from the crew would have done. He said he was Czech, and a pal of Pete's.'

'Did he prove that?'

'No, but I believed him.'

'Prune.'

'I think he was telling the truth; the ways things turned out.'

'How?'

'He said that someone had informed on Pete to the authorities, and that he'd been asked to find out who. The phrase he used was "grassed up". It sounded oddly authentic – like something that Quelch would say. He was some sort of private detective. He looked a bit of a thug.'

'Surprise me! A Czech private detective wandering around loose in Cambridgeshire in the middle of a fucking world war. Who walked in next? The seven dwarves?'

'He said he was looking for someone developing a local unofficial market of their own which would face competition from Piotr. Pete, getting virtually unlimited supplies from the Polish government, was always going to win that one. In those gangster stories you like it's called a "turf war". So this guy tells on Pete, and gets him investigated, maybe removed altogether, and takes over his customers. His turf.'

'That's possible.' Then it dawned on me. 'You didn't tell . . .?'

'Fat Guts was the only one I knew about. Some of the other pilots go to him. We never needed to; we had Pete. It seemed like killing two birds with one stone.'

'Killing was certainly the right bloody word for it, and I don't know whether that was fucking inspired, or just plain fucking daft, Grease. Did you do anything else to facilitate his sordid little murder?'

'No. I just gave him my opinion. He thanked me very courteously, drank up, got up and drove away. He had Pete's Singer by the way. He offered to buy me a drink, but I turned him down.'

'I suppose that made you feel a lot better about it?'

'Fuck off, Charlie.'

'You knew nothing else until the bold Bluto drove up and told us?'

'No.' He wouldn't meet my eye, but I'm sure that that was because he felt stupid. That was not an unusual state of mind for Grease. I put my hand on his shoulder and waved the barmaid for two more glasses of beer.

'Good. Let's keep it that way. I don't want to end up drowned in the cludgie as well.'

The latched door to the bar opened, and then banged shut behind someone. Before I could turn Gerry Brookman said, 'Hello, Mac. Hello, Charlie. What are you chaps drinking?'

I had put him out of my mind since he bumped *Peter* down on the runway at Manston. The odd thing is that this was a *different* Gerry Brookman: he had a bit of a limp, and I instinctively liked him, whereas I had loathed his predecessor. He got us glasses of swill. This had all the signs of turning into a session.

'When did you get back?' Grease asked him. Grease had this thing about never calling flight lieutenants or pilot officers 'sir' off the station: he would rather have swallowed his own urine. Even Grease had picked up on Brookman's change, because he seemed genuinely friendly, and interested in the reply.

'I didn't, yet. Came here first. I need a couple under the belt before finding out what Bushes has in store for me. They broke my crew, you see.'

'We don't call him Bushes any more,' I explained. 'He shaved it off and he's called Samson now.'

'Over a woman, wasn't it?' Brookman had a hooting laugh, like a hunting owl. Then he asked, 'How's that pretty little wife of his? Still teasing the titties off the squadron?'

'I haven't seen her around much. Perhaps he's sent her away.' I had snorted into my beer at the question, and Grease

401

gave me a brief quizzical look, which he immediately wiped. I don't know why, but I felt moved to offer Brookman my hand.

'I'm glad you're back,' I told him.

'Gerry. Call me Gerry,' he said. 'With a "G". I don't want everyone to call me "the Kraut".'

Brookman had lost a chunk of calf muscle in his starboard undercarriage leg. He told us that for the moment the doctors had bridged it with a metal pin and a length of chain. We decided we didn't believe that just as the landlady's daughter moved behind the bar. So of course he had to take his trousers off.

Quelch walked in with a grey prayer card in his mitt, took in the scene, and pronounced, 'Dead, and gone to heaven. What are you chaps drinking?'

Marty and Fergal drifted in from somewhere. Marty told us, 'That new police squad are turning the whole station over. They came to the Pit, but Grace stood in front of her locker. She said that it belonged to the ATA first, her second, and that they had no jurisdiction over it. Turns out she went to something like a finishing school in Switzerland with the tit of a lieutenant in charge of the squad. He has fond memories of a younger Grace, so he agreed with her, naturally.'

'Where is she now?'

'She's borrowed the Austin, and they've gone over to see her father; apparently he remembers him as well. At first I asked her to take the Indian, and bring us a bag of spuds back.'

So her old man was back from London. I wondered if he would need a lesson on his American radio, or whether he could work it out for himself. And she'd taken some old pal back to meet him.

'Good idea.' I blew the thin froth off the head of my new pint. I was irritated, and knew exactly why.

'You can borrow mine if you like,' Quelch offered helpfully.

'Your what?'

He looked blank for a couple of seconds, then he said, 'Indian, of course.'

Black Francie's replacement wore a turban: that had interested us for about ten minutes.

Later I recall Marty fixing Brookman with a basilisk stare, and telling him, 'You know Brookie, we always thought you were a nasty cunt. You're not a nasty cunt at all: you're a decent cunt.'

'Thank you, Sergeant. I always thought you a snotty little swot, or a swotty little snot; I forget which, but you're not. You're probably a half-decent bombardier – isn't that what the Yanks call your trade?' The officer thing was always there. 'I drink to you. Thanks for your part in saving our lives.'

It didn't faze Marty. 'Think nothing of it, Brookie old boy. It's what any swotty snottie would do for a decent cunt. Any day.'

Brookman's laugh turned him into an owl again, but he fell off his chair, and made a hard landing on his arse. 'Totally pissed,' he told us. '*Now* I can report for duty.'

As we wandered back mid-evening the rain hit us halfway between Bourne village and the main gate. It was falling like stair rods: no visible cover in either direction. Grease's voice was masked by the sound of the rain bouncing from the road. He told me a dirty joke that ended with the word *lictionary*.

That sort of thing still passes for humour in Canada. After a minute I started to laugh. After another so did Grease.

We had to squeeze between the barbed wire behind the Pit. It wasn't late, but if one of the new provos had seen us in that state we would have been in the slammer for the night. Later I heard that Brookman had managed to get himself arrested before he could report for duty. Maybe he had a better brain than we credited him for.

I remembered something, and stopped Grease before we dived in out of the wet. 'Pete.'

'What about him?'

'He always believed that the police were after him for some political thing, not the black market. You don't go looking for someone for a spot of black marketeering with a gob-sized pistol in your pocket, do you?'

'Does it matter?'

'Someone should tell Alex.'

'You volunteering?'

'No.'

'Then forget it. Pete'll sort it out, or he won't sort it out, and by then we'll all be sleeping on feather beds with a bit of luck. If you worry, you die; if you don't worry, you die. So why worry?'

'All those papers of Pete's. They probably kept him alive and in business for three years.'

'And then they nearly got him killed.'

'That's what those two dead coppers were looking for: what are we gonna do with them? We'll have to chance our arm one way or the other.'

I've told you that Grease could be officerly and decisive when the mood took him, and this time he wanted to get out of the rain. He said, 'Give them to the Germans: they'll know what to do with them. Clever fellow, the Kraut. The next time we start a fire in Germany we can dump them out on top.' Bravo.

The rain had passed over by lights out. Grace and I took a short walk around the Pit and had a snog. Our shoes squelched in the grass.

'Did you . . .?' I asked her.

'What do you think? No, I didn't. I told you I wouldn't.'

'That was with the boys. He's not one of the boys.'

'But *I* am, stupid! That's the point. Pleased you're jealous, though.' Then she gave me a hug.

'Isn't your old friend going to ask awkward questions about why you're living with a bomber crew on an operational station?'

'No. Not a chance. It wouldn't occur to him that there was anything odd about it: that's why he's a policeman. He's so thick that he needs to read a Giles cartoon three times before he gets it. Daddy was on good form.'

'He's the sort of man your father would approve you marrying.'

There was one of Grace's little frozen, golden silences. You have to go to a school in Switzerland to get them exactly right.

'Firstly, if Daddy feels like that, let *him* marry him! And secondly it just goes to show how little you know my father. Now; apologize.' I sensed that there was a grin on her face, but that she was also deadly serious.

'Sorr-ee, Grace,' Conners whined from a part-open window of the darkened Pit before I had a chance to answer.

'Sorry, Grace,' Fergal echoed.

'Sorry, Grace,' I said loudly and firmly. She gave me a big soft kiss, hugged me again, and we returned to the Pit's front door hand in hand.

Nearly Berlin

OK. So we were *supposed* to go to Big City again. Nobody gets it right every time. Not unless your name's Cheshire or Gibson or Reid. Frau Berlin was never the same place twice anyway, so you didn't get bored with the experience of rogering her. This time Grease went blind, and stayed that way for about ten hours. He said he'd never been blinders and sober at the same time before.

We filed in for the briefing early, because we were carrying non-standard bomb loads to drop on non-standard TIs, and they wanted to get in a detailed brief to the bomb aimers afterwards. I found myself sitting on the end of our crew line, with a wizened Welsh mid-upper from another crew alongside me. He was called the Goat, and not because of his success with women. His personal aroma occupied a space about three feet around him, like an aura. He must have caught my instinctive movement, because he whispered, 'Sorry. It's my feet you see. Terrible bad smell.'

'You wash them?'

'All the time: doesn't seem to help. My wife told me not to bother to come home until I get them fixed.'

'See the MO.'

'He refuses to see me. Says that my feet smell too bad; anyway, where's your Pole? I haven't seen him for a week. Our skipper says that he murdered Fat Guts, scarpered, and that all those new cops are looking for him.'

'Silly bloody rumour. Pete's in the shitter. He gets the squitters something terrible before each op these days.'

'He got me two cigars for my Da's birthday: we hadn't seen any in years. Bloody good bloke.'

'We think so, too.'

'THOSE MEN THERE!' Samson yelled. I looked up. He was jabbing a pointed finger directly at the Goat and me. 'Take their names and put them on a charge. Failing to pay attention during an operational briefing.' The buzz in the rest of the hut dropped to a murmur.

The Goat stood up: rather smartly, I thought. 'I didn't know we had started, sir,' he said.

'. . . and insubordination, and for smelling so bloody horrible.' The murmur swelled to a sniggering laugh, but I knew that it wouldn't alter anything: I was still on a charge and liable to get my pay docked. It didn't occur to me that I was rich, and that the charge didn't matter because I could pay a fine out of my pocket money these days.

Samson ploughed on. 'I'm going over the Big City tonight, chaps. Who wants to come with me?' He guffawed.

Brookman was sitting in the front row. Even with only a view of the back of his head I knew he was grinning: he was flying as a spare dick with someone. The group captain, who was the ranker on the station, had put in one of his irregular appearances, and it was him who said primly, from one of the dining-room chairs on the stage, 'For heaven's sake, *sit down*, Conny, we haven't got to that bit yet!'

He was right, of course: they hadn't even pulled back the sheet over the route map, and already the groaning was suppressing the laughter. The Boss did exactly what I had seen Brookman do the night before. He trailed the left wing of his arse as he sat down, and demonstrated the first and second laws of gravity. As he sat on his backside on the stage, grinning foolishly, I realized that he was drunk.

The group captain stood up and smiled thinly. 'We've told you the punchline before the joke, gentlemen. Very bad form. Can we get down to business now?'

Fiver swung the Morris past the storm door of the Pit, and Grace scrambled in, out of Fiver's line of sight: I thought that Grace looked a bit pale, but she was cracking jokes right and left, and on great form. I wasn't sure whether Fiver knew exactly what we were doing, or whether she still thought we were smuggling Pete on to *Tuesday* each trip. The way she positioned the vehicle for Grace's pick-up made me think that she didn't *want* to know; which was for the best if you think about it.

We had two 1,000-pounders and two cookies. Marty scampered over and started to caress the four bombs, but the rest of us engaged the ground crew in one-to-ones, which enabled Grace to slip past them with her head down.

I shared a fag with Dobbo, who told me, 'Your gang have got a lot more chatty lately, you know that?'

'It's getting the wind up that does it.'

'Nah. It's not that.'

'I could get all sloppy, and say that it feels as if we're all in the same team.'

'Nah. Don't do that. I know what you mean, though.'

'How's the hand?'

'No problem. The doc has given me some blue bombers that take the pain away: two a day. I have to be careful because they have me away with the fairies for a while after I've taken them. Where we going tonight, then?'

I was not supposed to tell him, but he could guess from the fuel load, and anyway I liked the 'we' he'd used.

'The Big City. Adolf-und-Eva-ville.'

'Drop one on him for me, will you? Personal.'

'Sure thing, Dobbo.'

Grease was still angry because the Boss had asked him if he wouldn't mind flying the same trip as the rest of them this time. I know that it was on the tip of Grease's tongue to reply that we felt much safer further away from them; but he held back. He had carried a large cardboard box, bound up with string, on to the Morris with him. Now he took it to Chiefy Bryan who was with Marty in the bomb bay.

'What's that?' Chiefy asked.

'Propaganda leaflets. They asked us to poke them out down the flare chute, but that would take too long, and be too fucking dangerous. I want Charlie looking out for night fighters, not pushing out yards of paper. The Kraut will only use it to wipe his arse with anyway: there's no point dying for that.'

'The brass do come up with doolally ideas from time to time, Mac. Do you want us to get rid of it for you?'

'No. I thought I'd rope the box to one of the bombs. Whether it falls off on the way down, or blows up on the ground, the same thing will happen. Bits of fresh bog paper spread all over Berlin.'

'Is that where you're going tonight?'

'You didn't know that?'

Chiefy pulled his lower right eyelid down with a fat finger, then let it click up again. 'Course not. I'll get some string for you.' He noticed Marty stroking his bombs, and crooning Benny Goodman's 'Flyin' Home' to them, and added, 'I wish he wouldn't do that.'

We all settled into our places in *Tuesday*, and I put an RT call through, and the ground WT checks. Grease seemed in no hurry to get started, and when he did he said to Fergal, 'The prayers will be conducted in silence tonight. Just tap the gauges and only call out if anything's fucked.'

'Roger, Skip.'

It was oddly peaceful. You thought you could feel *Tuesday* shift on her legs as we moved about: apart from that, all that came from Grease and Fergal were a series of grunts and taps and scraping sounds. I missed the usual litany, but paid far greater attention to what was happening: which had been Grease's purpose all along, of course. Then one engine burst into life, and another, and another, and another, and *Tuesday* was trembling around us like a dog fresh from the village pond, shaking the water from its coat. All twelve of the squadron Lancs waddled on to the perimeter track to queue for the main runway. Then they held us there for five minutes, and then it was switches off. What is it that the poem says? *Not tho the soldier knew, someone had blundered.* Chiefy came round in a light Bedford petrol tanker, and topped up *Tuesday* and the new *Mother*, who was in the line behind us. From Samson's kite, *Papa* the message. *No loose chat. Walls have ears* twinkled back down the line. He was frightened of the German listening stations. About time.

The Toff called down to me, 'What was that?'

I told him, and he snarled back, 'Walls! What walls? We're in the middle of a fucking airfield! There are no walls for fucking miles! Fucking twat!'

He was twitched. Grease leaned back and told us. 'Cut it out, you guys. Calm down. Toff – walk back and see that Pete's all right, and knows what's going on. They could scrub the raid.'

It was just to give him something to do.

Scrub it? Yes, mein herr, and I'm a Dutchman. Half an hour later we started up all over again, and again Grease did it without words. He had told us that he'd met a submariner on the leave he had in Pompey, and that submarines had this thing they called the *silent routine*. Grease was never one to be outdone: now we had one too. Samson was leading: we were number five on the track because we'd been slow getting out: we'd close up on him later. Again he was held back at the threshold, but just when we thought it was a scrub he got an orange flare followed by a green, and gunned it along the runway, weaving slightly under full power. We all got off. I asked Grease if I could ride up behind him for the off. He said, 'Why not. If they don't want us to use the fucking radio there's fuck all else for you to do until listening watch.'

In front of us was F-*Freddy*: its crew called it *Foxy* and had painted an outrageous bit of bint on the nose behind the front turret. The Goat flew as its top gunner, and I noticed that it weaved violently under acceleration – even more than Samson had done. I leaned forward to listen to Grease, who said, 'I think that it's these funny bomb loads. They've affected the c of g.'

When we got the light from the caravan Grease and Fergal pushed the throttles up to the gate, and were rewarded by *Tuesday* giving an almighty lurch to the left. Grease heaved her back, and she crabbed over to the right.

'Fucking hell!' he said.

Marty, lying full stretch on the bomb aimer's rest at the front called back, 'Right, right, left a bit,' in a parody of the flying instructions he gave over target.

'Shut up, Marty!'

'Right a bit.'

'I said SHUT UP, Marty.'

'Then fly the cow in a straight line, Skipper; you're giving me the shits.'

We were lucky. *Tuesday* had good engines, and the closer to flying speed she made, the less she yawed. We were going in a straight line by the time her wheels lifted from the runway. Grease sulked; he barked, 'Silent routine; silent running,' at us.

Nobody replied. I'm not sure if that is what he meant. We lost contact with the main squadron within five minutes, and Grease asked, 'Course please, Nav.' Naturally Conners didn't answer. Grease tried again. 'Course please, Conners.'

After a suitable pause, Conroy replied.

'Permission to secure from silent running, Skipper?'

You could have heard Grease's sigh back in the caravan at Bawne.

Conners followed up with, 'Steer 030, Skipper. That should cross the circle and put us up behind Samson in about ten minutes.'

'Thank you Nav. Anyone seen Quelch?'

Grace answered him from the rear turret. 'Yes; he's about six feet away.' She sounded under strain.

It was a wonderful night for taking those romantic moody aircraft photographs that the aeroplane manufacturers love: above a rolling flat brown cloud layer we bathed in half moonlight. I hated it, and also Conners's calm call of, 'Enemy coast, Skipper.'

All my friend Fritz had to do was lurk in the fringes of the cloud, and wait for us to cross over him. The squadron was flying in a loose flat diamond spread out over a large patch of sky. It hadn't been planned that way, it just shook out as we set course for Krautland. I don't think Samson was even aware that we had been missing during the climb in. He was flying at the point. There were about eight squadrons up in front of us, and maybe double that number behind us. Some of those would be stacked above us too.

'Charlie. Keep your lamp to hand, please,' Grease told me.

Fucking Grease was up to something again. If I hadn't been wearing a canvas helmet my hair would have stood on end. He pushed the throttles up out of cruise, and we swam up to Samson's kite. Like the rest of us he was rising and falling gently on the disturbed air left by the aircraft which had preceded us. His sparks twinkled us.

'He wants to know who we are.'

Grease said, 'Tell him, and remind him that he asked me to stay close.'

When he twinkled back, Grease asked, 'What did he say?'

'I'm not telling you, Skipper. But maybe we'd be better off pulling back to a safe distance.'

'I *hate* indecisive officers,' he said, and nudged *Tuesday* in so that our wing tips appeared to overlap. *Papa* lurched suddenly to the left to avoid us, and of course, everyone else, loosely flying on Samson, did the same.

'That was good,' Grease said, and did it again. A dozen aircraft twitched to port like a laboratory frog wired up to a car battery.

I clicked. 'For God's sake, Skipper.' There was a rapid stuttering burst of Morse obscenities from our leader. I guess that Grease had made his point.

'OK,' Grease said. 'Just for you, Charlie.'

Grease dropped us back and down away until we were skimming in and out of the cloud tops: *Foxy*, and the Goat's bad feet, were ahead of us and roughly about 150 feet up. Quelch was diving in and out of the cloud behind us like a mad porpoise following a boat.

'Listening watch, please, Sparks. I'll call you forward when I need you,' Grease said. I gave him the thumbs up, and moved back to strap in: Dobbo had attached a decent webbing harness to my seat after I complained about falling out of it so often.

He'd won it from a Mosquito that someone had wrapped around a tree a year ago. I heard them immediately: Kraut fighters and their controllers. So many of them that it was as if we had disturbed a swarm of wasps which was homing on us.

'Skipper, this is Charlie.'

'OK, Charlie.'

'There are dozens of the little bastards out there. So many that I can't pick them out.'

'OK, people. You heard what the man said. Watch the skies.'

Twenty minutes later life became a little more tricky . . . as Alec Guinness would have said. Deep inside *Tuesday*, behind and below Grease and Fergal, and behind even Conners, the interior was suddenly illuminated by a brilliant yellow light, followed by the sound of a distant thunderclap. There was a shock wave we lurched through, and a pattering sound as *Tuesday* flew through something. Marty and Fergal shouted out together, but it was sounds, not words, and *Tuesday* was crabbing a bit, with cold air whistling through her – although not too much of it. After the flare of light Grease was the first to use real words.

'Pilot. I'm blind,' he said.

He had been looking directly at *Foxy* when it blew up. Just a quick glance to check his station keeping when it vaporized just ahead of him.

Fergal clicked. 'I've got her.' Then, 'I may need some help up here.'

The cockpit was a bit of a mess. Grease was sitting with his hands over his eyes, and Fergal was crouched alongside him.

The steering column gave the occasional small twitch: George the invisible autopilot had us in hand for the time being. None of the perspex windows had actually shattered but those to the front and above had crazed over, with one or two small holes through which cold air was spearing. Here and there they were streaked with thin threads of oil.

'I'm OK,' Grease said, 'except I can't see anything. Total blackness. I'll be OK in a couple of ticks.'

But he wasn't, and after a couple of minutes someone touched my back. I thought it was Conners, but it wasn't.

'Get out of the way Charlie, and get Grease out of the seat will you, Fergal?' Grace said.

It was obvious really. I don't know why nobody thought of it. We sat Grease on the floor of his office. He was worried that we had an empty tail turret, but I told him that Quelchy was still out there, which seemed to help. With his help we worked out the best switch. The Toff took the tail turret, and I was to climb into his whenever my radio skills weren't needed. Marty had also hurt his eyes, but the sight came back in five: he had been looking away from the explosion. Once the Toff crawled into the tail-arse turret, and gave Quelch's bomb aimer the thumbs up, our consort sheared off. When he came up alongside Fergal stood up and blocked his view of Grace, gave him the OK sign, and then a circular motion with the right hand. We were for the dark, and then home. There was a problem with that because we hadn't dragged *Tuesday* this far in order to lose the trip completely. In crude terms that meant not abandoning until after we were over the Black One's homeland.

Not shy of fuel now, Grace climbed us hard in wide circles

until the altimeter was reading a questionable 29,000 feet. That can't have been right, but *Tuesday*'s engines were gasping for breath every now and again, so you never know. The rim of each circle took us a little further into the Reich, and although we were high in exposed sky at least we would have the luxury of actually being able to *see* the Kraut climbing towards us. 10,000 beneath us the shadow forms of four-engined bombers streamed towards Berlin. We called it the Big City, but it wasn't as big now as it had been on the day a year or so ago when we started on it.

At 29,200 feet *Tuesday* said 'no'. Grace held her straight for long enough for Marty to say grace – if you'll forgive the pun. God knows what he was bombing: some Kraut chicken runs no doubt. All we cared about was that the bombs fell directly into Germany, and we got another trip out of it: so much for Dobbo's personal message to Adolf Hitler. *Tuesday* immediately gave us another couple of hundred, but we didn't need them: Grace half rolled us over in a gentle dive towards the cloud in the direction of south-east England, taking a chance on her damaged screens by letting the speed build up to 320-plus knots. She flew with goggles on. By then we'd guided Grease back to the rest station, which was a canvas stretcher on to which you could strap a body. I offered him mother morphine, but he turned it down, insisting that he wasn't in pain, that he just couldn't see.

We saw one Kraut night fighter climb to offer us battle over the Dutch coast, but he got nowhere near us, because we were close to the end of the long dive across Holland. I would have loved to have been a fly on the wall as he tried to explain to his controller how a Lanc pissed past him at nearly 400 knots. To make matters worse the Toff gave him a quick burst from the tail turret in passing, and laid a few bullets on him. It was good to be first home for a change.

Grace made a long flat approach, and I gave the Bawne caravan all the right challenges and responses. Sometimes a bomber coming in to the circuit was like a stranger coming in to a Lodge meeting. An old Defiant night fighter had picked us up over Woodbridge of all places, and flew an escort above and behind us all the way. I had the chance for one or two scans out of the window. Although relatively undamaged *Tuesday* still looked in a bit of a state. Great areas of paintwork on her wings had been scoured clean, and one wing tip glistened for six feet or so with some of *Foxy*'s oil: about twenty feet of what I thought was parachute tape was caught across the other wing, and trailed out behind it.

We got Grease up to the office again for the approach because, as Conners pointed out, someone was going to be up for a gong for this, and if we made Grace the hero someone was going to ask what the fuck she was doing up there with us in the first place. Then they'd ask where Pete was. When the medics came to collect him, Grease had to be sitting in the gaffer's seat again. You won't be surprised to learn that Grace gave *Tuesday* the sweetest, gentlest contact with the runway.

As for the switch: it shouldn't have been easy, but it was. The big man with the stethoscope slid swiftly through *Tuesday*, and moved Grease around as gently as he would have done a child. There were tears streaming from beneath Grease's fingers as they led him away.

419

I led the debriefing, which was a novel experience for me. Harriet coached me through it, but was very rigid as I described what had happened to Grease. She would have to worry for a few more hours yet because she wouldn't be leaving her seat until the rest were back. I improvised like blazes, and told them that Grease's vision had been impaired by the flash of the explosion in front of him, but not entirely lost: *that* happened on the approach, and then Fergal crouched beside him talking him down flying blind: quite literally. Grease was the genuine all-Canadian hero.

Because there was no one else back, the IO with the Zapata moustache, who we favoured, came over and sat in on the debrief. He made me go over again what had happened to *Foxy*. I told him again that I didn't know. He was pressing about night fighters when Marty said, 'They hadn't reached us yet, although Charlie was tracking them in. I reckoned they would have got into the stream about five or ten minutes later. *Foxy* blew up: one of her own fucking bombs simply blew up.'

There was an uncomfortable pause, which I concluded by telling them that the Toff had laid a few bullets on a night fighter on our way home. I had to transpose him back into his top turret for the story of course, otherwise it wouldn't have worked. This was getting too bloody complicated. Then Harriet took us back to what we'd bombed. Marty insisted that it was a small airfield, but how he saw it from 29 thou God only knew. Conners said that it was just over the Kraut border on the way to Meppen: even with her attachment to us I could see that Harriet didn't believe us. We'd dropped off Grace at the Pit, of course, after a quick motorized recce to make sure the Blues weren't waiting in ambush. Either they hadn't yet worked out that Pete was signed on for trip after trip, but couldn't be found between them, or they didn't give a toss. Perhaps they really *were* here just for the body in the bog.

The other four sloped off to be first at the breakfast table. I didn't; I sat on a chair by the door and waited for some of the others to get in. I don't know how it had happened, but it was obvious from everyone's attitude that with Grease down, I was the number one man. It wasn't rehearsed, and it made me nervous about the war, and very tired.

I must have fallen asleep, and when I awoke Brookman's face was close to mine. He was squatting down in full flying gear, facing me with a hand on my shoulder. His grimy face was as kind as my father's.

'OK, Charlie?' he said.

'Yes. Sorry; nodded off.'

'What about the others?'

'Grease hurt his eyes when *Foxy* blew up. They're trying to say it was a night fighter, but it was her own bombs.' Then something occurred to me, 'Have you got a new crew?'

'No. I was flying with the Boss as a spare dickie. Batting myself back in again.'

My mind wandered. 'Grease thinks that it's like cricket, too,' I told him.

'Why don't you get some kip Charlie, you're beat.'

'OK. Where's Quelch?'

'He's not in yet.'

'OK.'

I should have looked in on Grease, but was too whacked, so

I borrowed a station bike without permission and weaved slowly to the Pit. For the first time since Grease had laid down the rule I trudged into the hut in all my clothes. One of Grace's candles was flickering somewhere. I lay on my back on my bed like a spent fish, and was asleep again in seconds.

I had just finished shaving the next morning when an airman cycled up with the usual ticket. This time it said that the squadron leader would appreciate a few minutes of my time, although that's not how they put it in the RAF.

'When? Now?'

'No. He didn't seem too concerned.'

'He going soft?'

The airman smirked: he knew something.

There was a fresh face in Samson's outer office, a new corporal. We were in trouble if he'd got himself a clerk who actually knew what he was doing. Brookman was also there, staring out of the window, looking taller than I remembered. He was smoking a straight pipe like mine.

'Hello, Charlie. Thanks for coming over. Take a pew,' he said.

This was new. I sat and waited.

The corporal came in as if on cue with a couple of mugs of tea.

'How's Mac?'

'I don't know yet, sir. I was going to go on to see the MO after coming here. Where's the squadron leader?'

'Afraid you're looking at him, old boy, temporarily of course. Mr Delve had a bad turn last night. He might be back,

but he might not. I understand the doc's sent him on to Ely.'
There was a hospital at Ely which specialized in RAF cases. He
seemed a little lost for what to say next. Then there was his
hooting laugh again. It was quieter this time and self-mocking.

'Now that I *know* your lot, it seems very strange to be
"Gerry" in the pub, and "sir" here. You can laugh at me if you
like, Charlie, but although I know I can do the rest of the job,
I'm worried about that.'

It was time to bring this conversation back on track.

'Needs must, sir,' I said firmly.

'Thank you, Charlie.'

'Was there anything else, sir?'

'Yes; 'fraid so, and I'm only discussing this with you because
your skipper's laid up. Comprenez?'

'Absolutement.'

'Don't take the piss yet, Charlie, it's not fair. Do you want
a waxer in the tea? The new bloke I've got out there is a bloody
wonderful clerk, but his tea is as strong as pig piss!'

I nodded. Probably grinned too. The waxer came from a flat
pint bottle of bourbon in the top drawer of his desk. Then it
came out of the blue: 'Quelch never came in last night. We'll
need a new number three for A Flight, and because I've been
away I've lost touch with the squadron, so I don't know who to
pick. I would have asked Mac's advice, but he's not here either.'

'There's that guy Whittaker . . .'

'He's gone too, Charlie; several trips back, last week some
time – you must have forgotten.'

'Yes. I must have.' I tried to concentrate, but although
unconnected names and faces swam into view I couldn't decide

whether they were alive or dead. 'It's difficult. I think that Grease would have told you to take whichever replacement crew arrives next.'

'Why?'

'It's a confident sort of thing to do; everyone will look up to you . . . and if we find ourselves nursing them for their first couple of trips, we'll probably be looking out for ourselves at the same time. That won't be a bad thing.'

'You should be an officer, Charlie.'

'No. I couldn't be arsed.'

'Did you know that the Boss has put Mac up for a commission?'

'Did he ask him first?'

We both grinned, I think.

'Think about it?' he said.

'Is that a direct order, sir?'

'Yes, one of my first, in this job.'

'How does it feel?'

'Distinctly odd.'

Then I realized what we had almost stopped talking about.

'What happened to *Mother*?'

'I don't know. You climbed up out of the stream, and circled to the north? Out towards Meppen and the Stadskanal?'

'Yes, I think so.'

'He turned south. I think that the nearest fighters were gathering south of the stream: he turned and offered them battle. Bloody insane. No one knows what happened next. There are no reports. I've asked all the right questions of all the right people. Nothing yet.'

'Quelchy'll be back. I shouldn't start sending the telegrams yet, if I was you sir.'

I started to sweat. It was time to get out of the seat. I never liked long conversations with officers: you always felt as if you were getting sucked into something. Anyway, he waved me down, and pushed a couple of photographs across the desk at me. One was a target photo.

'That's yours from last night. Congrats.'

'What for? What is it?'

'Luthersberg. I think they pronounce it "Lootersburg": it's a Jerry airfield near Meppen, just like Martin Weir said. You can just make it out. Usually we hit their airfields with small-scale stuff, and rockets, but you flung a couple of cookies at them! They must have wondered what the hell they did to deserve that. The other one is a nice recce photo taken by a low-level Spit this morning. Be careful; it's still damp.'

It showed the usual small airfield configuration of a main runway crossed obliquely by a secondary, ringed by a peri-track. The Kraut didn't have too many concrete airstrips, so he was particularly fond of them. There was a massive black splodgy figure-of-eight shape obscuring the area where the runways crossed. It was big enough to launch a destroyer into.

'Was that our cookies? What a bloody fluke.'

'Yes. Well done. They won't fly off there for a week. The bosses are very chuffed.'

'What about the 1,000-pounders?'

'There's a field alongside with several dead cows in it.'

'Probably Nazis. That's what Pete says about German animals. He was there before the war.'

'There's more. One of their night fighters fell near the Dutch coast, just about where and when you crossed it last night. One of the new Dutch radio stations reported it. We've claimed it for you. Congrats again. That was your mid-upper gunner, wasn't it? The one you call the Toff?'

'Yes. That was the Toff's.'

'Care to tell me what he was doing in the tail turret then? The guns in the mid-upper were hardly fired. Only enough for a gun test. But you got off a full ten-second burst from the tail. I went out to see your kite this morning I'm afraid.'

Ah.

I visited Grease in the medical block. The others were already there.

'I think that Brookie is going to be brighter than Samson,' I told Grease later, 'at least for the time being.'

'Will that be a problem?'

'It might be. He could be a blighter.'

Grease was sitting up in bed wearing a set of those sepia-glazed goggles they use to train people to night-fly during the day. His sight was mostly back, but the doc was taking no chances. He was wearing sky blue silk pyjamas, and had filched a Brown Job's tin helmet from somewhere. It crossed my mind that he was working his ticket with the doolally trick.

'He's Welsh,' Grease said.

'Who is?'

'Old Doc is. . . . and drinks like it's going out of fashion. He says that there are three teetotal Welshmen for every one that drinks: it's the Chapel, you see. That lays a great responsibility on the drinkers to keep up the national batting average. We got stocious last night. Good bloke.'

'I think he's a sweetie,' Grace said.

I hadn't missed her last night, but she had changed into ordinaries before I got back, and had jogged over to the small ward that Grease was sharing with an Erk who had broken his leg, and an Australian flight sergeant with bad burns. He'd spilt a bottle of bootleg hooch on himself, and fired it up by accident with his cigarette. What is it the Kraut was supposed to say? For him, the war was over. They would move him to Ely soon. Grace had pushed an empty bed alongside Grease's and spent the night on it, holding his hand as he slept. He said he realized his eyes were almost working again when she was the first thing he saw when he woke up. Grace told him that that was hardly a unique experience.

Grease peeped out from under the goggles: his eyes looked very bloodshot. He put the goggles back in place. 'Does he know about the agreement you came to with Samson, about Pete continuing to fly as long as he doesn't have to parade, or show his face outside *Tuesday*?'

'He knows about it, but he doesn't believe in fairies either.'

'So why are you looking so worried, young Charlie?'

'Because he didn't push the point. He saw I couldn't answer him, and left it at that. He'll come to visit you today with a bottle in his pocket like the one I've got in mine. Make sure you're bloody careful about what you say.'

'How did the conversation end then?'

'A little strangely. As I was leaving I turned and asked him how Samson's missus had taken it.'

'And?'

'He looked at the desk, and said, "Very well. Relieved he's off flying I think. She's gone to Ely in the car with them. I don't think that she'll be so . . . restless, now," and when he looked up I swear he was blushing.'

'You've got a dirty mind, Charlie,' Grace said.

'I wonder who I got *that* from?' We all laughed together, for all the world like brothers and a sister.

'Where's that bottle, Charlie? I'm gagging for it,' Grease asked.

The bottle I produced, and its twin, were flat pints of bourbon from Tommo. Grace and I got the Erk into an old wheelchair with wooden wheels, and brought him over to party with us. The Australian was covered in bandages and tied to the bed. He groaned piteously when he worked out what we were doing, so we did the kind thing . . . and left him where he was.

Eventually the MO reappeared and kicked us out. Grease tried to bribe him with Grace's body, and I was glad when that failed. He was worried about *Tuesday*, and extracted a promise from me to find out what she was like. Grace and I walked back to the Pit. I left her there, and trundled the Indian up the hill to where Chiefy Bryan had *Tuesday* on the hardstanding outside the T2 hangar. They were scrubbing down both upper wing surfaces, and replacing the cockpit glaze.

'She was in a hell of a bleeding mess when you finished with her last night,' he said accusingly.

'She's been worse. All the engines were still there. The bomb doors were there. Any holes were *small* ones.'

'Ah'm talking about the *mess*, sonny. You should have told us about that. It weren't fair.'

'Chiefy, you're losing me. All I know is that the new squadron leader sloped out here this morning, and you let him examine the guns without warning me about it first.'

'That weren't why he came out, Charlie. He came out to look at the mess, and then he cleared it up himself.'

'What the hell are you talking about, Chiefy? What mess? We flew through a Lancaster which had blown herself up. We got covered in her unburnt oil, and the explosion burnt off our pretty paint. All we came back with was bits of parachute webbing that some poor sod didn't have time to use. Don't tell me what she was like: I was out there with her!'

He turned away from me, took a couple of paces, then turned and came back.

'They weren't his bits of parachute webbing, Charlie, they were parts of the poor sod who didn't have time to use it. You flew back with five or six yards of guts over the wing. The CO came here after the lads didn't want to move it this morning, and the MO was away in Ely. Brookman took it down, and washed off where it had been . . . and I'm sorry about the guns. We didn't know there was a problem.'

It was my turn. I touched his arm with my hand and said, 'OK, I'm sorry. There's no problem about the guns. Nothing I can't deal with.'

Grease was let out that night and had 20/20, which he proved by getting out of his brains and driving us back from the Fox on the Huntingdon road. It was the pub of choice for Grease; he swore by the Wells and Winch's Biggleswade beer, and not many aircrew used the place. I liked it because you stepped straight off the road into one of the bars: there was nothing drink-time-wasteful like a garden or car park in-between.

Late on, Chiefy Bryan slouched in. He looked frazzled and dirty. I called him up a pint immediately. He nodded at me when I placed it in his huge mitt and said, 'She's ready,' then turned his back on me and joined a noisy group of ground engineer types who had taken over one corner. Grace sat on everyone's lap in turn, and sang with us – 'Roll Out The barrel', 'Don't Dilly Dally', that sort of thing. Then she sat alongside me and held my hand while we let the others sing. Trying to remember that night now, all I can recall them doing is, 'We're seven little lambs, who've lost our way . . .'

Squashed in the back of the Austin with the Toff and Marty, Grace said, 'I had a signal today. They want me back. Sometime next week they want me to pick up a Beaufighter at Twinwood and take it up to Ringway.'

It put a bit of a dampener on our mood.

It seems hard to credit now, but I was actually keen to get back in the air. We hadn't got many left and I wanted to get them flown. Then I wanted to get away from bloody Germany, and not go back there for a good few months. On the other hand there was also the break-up of the crew coming in a couple of weeks, and I wasn't sure that I could cope with that. I sloped over to the ops block, and hung around there until Brookie chased me away.

Back in the Pit I gave them the news. 'We're going bloody

nowhere. It's because of what happened to *Foxy*. They're emptying the bomb dump, and taking all the bombs back to the shop where they buy them. Then they're bringing us brand new ones. It will take at least a day; maybe two.' Then I remembered something, and told Grease, 'There's a note on the letter board for you, says there's a parcel for you to collect. I asked for it at the squadron office, but they say you have to collect it in person.'

'It'll be a Red Cross parcel from your folks. They don't think we're feeding their little boy enough,' Fergal said.

Grease flung a pillow at him. I flung one at Grease, and then we all started in. Grace sat by the stove with a face like Queen Victoria, and ignored us. It was scary to be in love with a girl who could be easily satisfied with a mug of tea and a newspaper.

When Grease came back he didn't say anything, so we had to pump him. He was curiously uncomfortable. Then he pulled a small, flat, expensive-looking box out of his pocket.

'Did you know that Brookie's going to put me up for a gong for the Berlin fiasco?' he said.

'Congrats. Someone had to get one for it, and we couldn't tell him Grace had flown the trip – they would court martial the lot of us.'

'Well, the thing is . . . I don't need one any more. Someone's just sent me one; out of the blue. A mad sod called Braddock, from Leeming or wogga-wogga land up north. Somewhere the Yorkshire people hide. His name's on the back of it, with his number.'

He opened the box and showed us a pristine DFM, and the scrap of ribbon which went with it. Braddock had stuck a note in. *All you have to do is collect ten gollies from the jamjars, and they send you one of these by return. I've got dozens, and I heard what you did — so I'm passing this on. Pretend I picked your name out of the hat! Braddock.*

I said, too casually, 'Who's Braddock? Maybe he *has* heard of you . . .'

'Yeah. That's what I'm scared of.'

'Anyway. You can take us all to the pub tonight to wet it.'

Grease looked mortified; still thinking like a working man. 'I can't: I'm a bit short.'

'We could always go to the bank,' the Toff said.

Grease started to spring the slow-on-the-uptake smile he was developing. Finally he remembered. 'Yeah. Why not?' He was definitely command material.

The party was in full swing in the Wellington the night they took our bombs away. Marty sulked: he told us he felt impotent without a live bomb within cycling distance. The pub was packed to bursting point, the blackout was being ignored and uniformed customers had spilt on to the pavement, the road and into surrounding gardens. There was a familiar girl heavy-petting a guy as small as me in US uniform. They were on a love seat on the rectory lawn.

When she looked over his shoulder and caught my eye she laughed, and waved. 'Hi, Charlie!'

'Hi yourself, Susan.'

Grease tut-tutted, and said, 'I don't know how you do it.'

I looked nervously around for Grace, but remembered she was in a scrum in the snug. The American disentangled himself, glared, and then grinned. He said, 'Hi,' and wandered over. 'Is that your girl?'

'No. My girl's inside.'

He held out his hand. 'Joe Stalin.'

'You've got to be joking,' I said.

'That's what everyone says. But I *am* Joe Stalin. People call me . . .'

'. . . Uncle,' said Susan.

'Susan made me a cup of tea on a bad afternoon. That's how I know her,' I said.

She picked up the drift, ruffled his hair, and said, 'He's just my Joe. He's a genuine four-O Yank.'

'What's that?' I asked deliberately.

'You *know*: overpaid, overfed, oversexed and over here.'

Ye*ah*, I thought, *and I know a field not far from here, where 3,000 of the poor sods are lying six feet under the grass*. But I didn't say that. Joe and I exchanged grins like winces, but let her off with it. You could detect the edge of something under her gaiety.

Joe said, 'My Sue is like all of your Limey women. Never there when you want them, and too quiet when you want to hear the old *hello sailor*. A genuine four-U British broad.' He gave her a hug to take the sting out of it, but I came in on cue.

'What's that?'

'Unseen, unheard, undernourished and under us.'

Too far. Susan burst into tears, and slapped ineffectually at Joe's face. He put his mitts up like a boxer covering himself and crouched and weaved, laughing all the time. Then she said, 'Bastards!' and ran into the pub.

'Broads!' the Yank said. It was that kind of a party.

I asked him where he was from.

'The repple depple. Some place called Bovingdon. I was only there a week.'

'Repple depple?'

'Replacement depot. They sent me to replace some bonehead of a major who got snake bit. You knew him?'

'No.' I shook my head, and apologized to Peter Wynn inside it. Then some of his old crew, Sandy Lyon and David Kovaks, the Jew, wandered out. 'Hi, Charlie. Your team here tonight?' Sandy said.

I nodded.

'You know this guy?' Joe Stalin asked.

'Hell, yes. We been promising to beat hell out of his crew at darts for a month. I guess tonight could be that night.'

Stalin gave me the look, but didn't pick up on the lie I told him. If he lasted a month maybe he would understand. It wasn't a case of not speaking ill of the dead. It was one of not speaking of them at all. Period.

Grace pushed out. She had a fresh pint for me in her hand. Nothing is lovelier than the woman you desire, walking towards you, carrying your beer.

'This is Joe Stalin,' I said.

Grace didn't bat an eyelid. 'Was that your girl who just rushed in crying?'

'Yes, it was.'

'Then go straight after her and make it up. Life's too short.'

I thought that he was going to protest, but he straightened

up, and repeated, "Life's too short",' as if the concept had just occurred to him. Then he said 'Yes, ma'am,' and dived into the bar after Susan.

'What was all that about?' said Grace.

'Lovers' tiff. Our new cap doesn't waste much time,' said Sandy.

'Who's got time?' the Jew asked.

None of us had an answer. It was the nearest we got to saying anything about Peter Wynn all evening.

Grace said to me, 'You don't know that girl. She's from the Crifton post office. She just heard that her husband died in some prisoner of war camp in Germany.'

'I didn't know.'

'Why should you? Someone told me that she held out long after all the other war widows around here had taken up with servicemen. Have you heard of the domino theory?'

'No.'

'Never mind, Charlie.' She pushed my quiff out of my eyes, and made me feel loved. There was something brittle about Grace too, tonight.

Wynn's old crew had a new B-17 G. It was called *Remember the Alamo*, was an unpainted shiny silver, and had a picture of a naked broad, they said, wearing a coonskin cap whose tail stretched down to tickle her arse. We were stumbling drunk by the time I had rounded up the others in front of the dartboard, and besides, there were ten of them to seven of us, including Grace . . . so they whipped us. Their little ball-turret gunner was so drunk he had to be held upright, but even so if you called out a spot on the dartboard he could stick an arrow in it. They said he'd been credited with four German fighter kills.

Later I sat squashed in a corner with Grace and a group of unhappy-looking Brown Jobs of mixed rank. They were as outnumbered as Custer's command had been at Little Big Horn. Their fat major had a raft of stained medal ribbons on an old battledress jacket: old Braddock would have loved him. I asked him where they were based.

'Here; for a couple of days. Living upstairs with my legion of the lost. We heard the racket, and thought we'd join in rather than try to sleep through it. What do you do?'

'Fly radios about over Germany. How about you, sir?'

'Take bloody bombs to pieces. Usually *theirs*, but we heard you had a problem with some of yours, and were posted up to make the blighters safe before you moved them.'

'*I* couldn't do that: much too nervy,' Grace said.

'It's all right. Whenever I get scared I think of something else.'

'Like what?'

'Like a horse race when I picked up a packet. I rerun the race in my head.'

'Does that steady your hands?' I asked.

'Haven't got a clue, old boy. I just do it so that the last thought in my mind is going to be a happy one. I say, I was hoping to meet an old pal of mine here tonight, but he hasn't turned up. Conny Delve? He's a squadron commander or something. Know him?'

'No, sir.' Grace gave me her sharp look, then glanced away.

I added, 'Maybe the RAF sent him away. It does sometimes. Secret squadrons and all that.'

'He was an odd cove. My fag at school, you know: God knows how he got to be a ranker.'

'In the RAF they give you the rank if you live long enough.'

'In my lot they give you it first, because you never do.' He slurped and spilled his beer. His hand shook from time to time.

'I'm sure he'll be sad to have missed you, sir,' I said.

'Maybe, Sergeant. I'm here for a couple of days anyway, I suppose.'

'I'll tell him, if I meet him.'

'Thank you, Sergeant. Good beer.'

I wondered what the hell he had been drinking all his life, if he thought so.

First Susan, then Peter Wynn and then old Samson. I had denied knowing all three in the course of a couple of hours: St Peter would have a thing or two to say to me, when we got face to face. Grace must have read my mind: she put her head on my shoulder and said the words again.

'Life's too short.'

Duisburg

The next morning it was Grease who got the note. We were both at breakfast when it was delivered by the girl he had always worried about. She smiled, leaned over and kissed his cheek, and said, 'Thank you, Sergeant.'

'What was all that about?' he asked me.

'I think that *she* thinks you fixed Fat Guts for her. Someone told me that girls go all gooey over you if you fight someone to protect them.'

'Christ, I hope no one else thinks so. All it will take is for someone to gossip to the coppers . . . they still hang people over here, don't they?'

'Yes, but don't worry; you've got loads of alibi, all we have to do is all tell the same story.' I nodded at the open message form in his hand.

'It's Brookie. He wants to see me,' he said.

'His Master's Voice. He probably wants to know why you drowned Fat Guts.'

'Fuck off, Charlie.'

I noticed Samson's car draw up in the road outside. Jenny

was driving. She wound the window down to talk to a WAAF officer: I decided to wander out and find out what gave. Besides, it was more or less what Grease had told me to do.

Afterwards, back in the Pit, Grease said that it was a bit odd, being consulted by Brookman like that, but he didn't feel uncomfortable,

'Course not,' Fergal said, 'you're almost an officer yourself. That's what being an officer feels like.'

'Like what?'

'Being a complete prick but not knowing it. It goes with the funny coloured stripes on the end of your sleeves, and the medals.'

'Then get used to it yourself,' snarled Grease. 'He's put us all up for one.'

I think that the following silence could fairly be described as 'stunned'.

'Fuck me!' said Fergal. 'The old man will be ashamed of me.'

I think that the rest of us laughed. I wondered if there was an address I could send the Pink Pole's to.

'So what else did he want?' I asked Grease.

'Oooh . . . sort of squadron stuff. Who flies with whom. That sort of thing.'

'"*With whom*",' repeated Conners. 'My my!'

'Where we going next?' Marty asked.

'I can't tell you: sorry.'

Fergal lifted a pillow from his bed, and sort of hefted it to get a feel for the weight.

'Duisburg,' Grease said quickly.

There was something else he told us.

'Quelch's lot are OK. Brookman got a signal from the Big House this morning: the Red Cross told them.'

'I told him they would be,' I said. 'What happened?'

'They obviously tangled with the Jerry night fighters. You know Q; it might even have been deliberate. Anyway they're claiming another one.'

'From where?'

'Bloody Switzerland. He just kept flying south until he ran out of airspace. The Swiss flak had a go at him, but they're bloody awful shots, and he shot back at them anyway. The Swissies weren't best pleased: violation of neutrality and all that – apparently they've banged them all up in pokey until they deport them. The War House is going to try to sneak them back on BOAC flights. Less embarrassing to simply give us them back apparently. All except Quelchy.'

'What's happened to him?'

'At the moment he's refusing to come back. He's claimed some sort of refugee status under the Geneva Convention. I think that they call it political asylum.'

'The Swiss are very keen on the Geneva Convention,' Conners said.

'Shut up, Conners. He's claiming that if he comes back we'll stick him in an aeroplane over Germany, and nasty people will try to kill him all over again.'

'He's too bloody right,' I said.

'The Swissies seem to agree with him for the time being.'

'Did they say thank you for the gift of his Lancaster?' Fergal asked.

'Apparently not. It seems they have more than enough already.'

There was something else lurking under all this. I could sense it.

'There's more, isn't there?' I asked Grease.

He nodded miserably. 'All the new coppers who were stirring things up have crept back to their lair: gone. Crime solved, so they won't be coming back.'

'Good.'

'No. Not good. The padre and the adjutant jumped the gun. When they went to clear out Quelch's crew's things they found a sack of cement, and a bundle of rope, under his bed. They matched those found on the body in the bog.'

Conners asked, 'What's he want with cement and rope?' For someone who could do sums Conners could be surprisingly slow on the uptake.

'Christ! Quelch killed Fat Guts.' I said.

'Why?'

'Because Quelchy *does* things, instead of just talking about them. It's an East End gangster tradition, and that's what his relations are.' I must have sounded rather bitter: Grease shot a reproachful glance in my direction, but kept his trap shut.

'Poor Quelchy,' Grace murmured.

'And Brookie says that now the cops have scarpered we've got to produce Pete.'

'Balls.' I said it. I guess we all felt it.

*

A fine rain clung to the outside of our new cockpit glazing. Grease had been singing, 'I Love Paris in the Springtime', putting particular emphasis on the word 'sizzles'.

'Orange and green. That's the off,' Fergal said. 'Did you get that, Skipper?'

Our load was wholly incendiary bombs. Hundreds of the little bastards. I hated flying with incendiaries. It was like sitting on top of a box of fireworks. I'd seen Lancs with incendiaries hit by flak and fighters. They never exploded: they burned all the way to the ground, like enormous aerial candles. I once saw a rear gunner bail out of one without his parachute, just to get away from the flames. Even Marty hated incendiaries: he said they weren't precise enough. He clicked. 'I *hate* this. I wasn't cut out to be a cook.'

I was standing behind Grease, looking out towards the control caravan. It's Aldis Lamp twinkled *long-short-long-long*. Which was a 'Y'.

'They're playing our tune, Skipper. It's time to go.'

Fergal pushed the four throttle levers forward, held them with both hands and *Tuesday* gathered way, out into the dark again. She was as straight as a die along the centre line with this lighter bomb load, tried to get airborne over the hump, touched down for another twenty yards and then soared away. Marty clicked again. 'Oops a daisy! Well done, Skip. You're really getting the hang of this, aren't you?'

Even Grease chuckled. We were second to last to take off out of eleven. Brookie had changed the routine; probably to stir the squadron up a bit. We were out here as number ten because Brookie chose to go last. He wanted to see his squadron in the air in front of him, so that he could tidy them up if things got ragged. Once we were in the air he would work his way to the fore, with us (and the replacement A-Flight crew, when it arrived) dogging him. Well; that was the theory and that's what he and Grease had been working out in the morning.

That night there were six more collisions over the target; more than twice the usual accidental losses. Twelve aircraft. Eighty-four men. Apparently Butch wasn't fit to be lived with the next morning, and fired two of the met officers who failed to predict it. As it was, flying through broken cloud, in a little moon, we only saw five aircraft for the rest of the night. That's not counting two of the collisions we saw as we ran in to Duisburg: they were just huge lights in the sky, followed by gouts of falling fire like molten larva. Minutes later we were in the same place. Marty had been telling the truth about his feeling for incendiaries: he sounded almost disinterested as he announced, 'Bombs gone. Bomb doors closed.'

Tuesday gave her usual salmon leap, but without the abandon of dropping a heavier load.

We had bombed on green and red TIs in the usual sea of fire. The Toff must have seen it as we banked away, because he clicked. 'What's the point in dropping incendiaries into *that*? It's like pissing into the sea!'

One of the aircraft we did see was a Kraut fighter just after we turned away. Before the Toff could call a corkscrew the Kraut did a wing over and dropped away from us.

The Toff clicked. 'Kraut to starboard, Skipper. But he pissed off before I could say anything.'

'Maybe he thought we were Quelchy!' said Fergal.

Grease clicked. 'Skipper, everyone. Maybe he'll come around again. I'm going to weave, and lose a few hundred. Keep your eyes open.'

Everyone rogered. Out in the tail Grace's voice sounded peculiarly small.

It's remarkable just how often God can catch you with your knickers down. We had crossed over into the North Sea, and Grease was nosing us gently down to England, Home and Glory when I heard a curious gobbling sound over the RT.

I clicked. 'Skipper, this is Charlie. What was that?'

'Dunno. Anyone else?'

'I heard it, Skipper. Sounded like a turkey.' That was the Toff.

'Call through, Charlie,' said Grease.

When I called Pete, Grace failed to respond. I tried again. Nothing. Grease came on immediately with, 'Toff . . .'

'Forget it,' I told them, 'I'm on my way.' With my heart in my stomach, I was over the main spar feet first with a spare ox bottle in my hand, and my RT lead trailing: I hadn't realized that you could move that fast inside a Lancaster. The rear turret door was hard to open: they often were as soon as they got cold, but as soon as I moved it aside Grace flopped back into my arms. Her right hand was on her O_2 mask, touching the mike plug. She made that odd gurgling noise again. It's the noise that someone makes as they are choking to death. I dragged the mask from her face; vomit ran out of it. I put my fingers into her mouth, found her tongue doubled back, and pulled it forward. Her head fell to one side: she coughed and a thin trail ofvomit ran out of the side of her mouth. When I removed her canvas flying helmet and her goggles, bile ran down her face and matted into her hair. Kneeling now, with her head in my lap, I pushed my mike plug into the remote jack.

'Skipper, this is Charlie. Grace was choking. I think her mask froze up. It's knocked her over.'

'Has she been hit?'

'Don't know. Wait one.'

I asked her, 'Grace?' three times, before she opened her eyes. 'Are you hurt?'

She whispered, 'No,' shook her head once, and closed her eyes again.

'Skipper from Charlie. She says no but I'm not sure.'

Grace opened her eyes again. She said, 'No,' but more firmly this time. Underneath us, and around us *Tuesday*'s aluminium skin trembled.

'She says no,' I told Grease.

'Can you get her forward to the rest station, and strap her in?'

'I think so. Give me a minute.'

Grace stumbled to the canvas stretcher, with me half carrying her. She did it with her eyes closed, feeling for the bulkheads and formers around which *Tuesday*'s skin was bound. As I tightened the strap around her she gripped my hand, still without opening her eyes, and whispered.

'Always there, aren't you, Charlie?'

It was more a statement of fact. I was also numbed by a desperate fear, but it wasn't the appropriate time to go into that.

When you go on to automatic pilot you don't make mistakes. That's why we made no mistakes. Conners did what he was supposed to do, which was to nav us on to the end of the runway at Bawne yard perfect. After that it was Grease's turn: he made a half decent job of the landing: we ran over the hump in the runway instead of leaping over it. I had got it right, and had made our problems and intentions unambiguously known to Bawne's caravan, who had the meat wagon and the doc on standby at our dispersal pad. Chief Bryan and Dobbo had turned out too. Once we were in the circuit there was nothing left for me to do, so I went back and sat on the floor alongside Grace, and held her hand.

When *Tuesday* was on the flat, and grumbling around to the hardstanding, Grace leaned towards me and whispered, 'Tell Grease that was a very good one.'

When I opened my mouth to reply she reached out, and barred my lips with a finger. I kissed it. Grease left Fergal to shut the taps and switches, grumbling something about the mags as he made his way towards us. Then I opened the door, dropped the little ladder, and let the doc in. In the half light he still didn't realize quite what he was dealing with.

'We'll get him down into the ambulance. Charlie will travel with you,' Grease told him.

The MO paused, and squinted up at him. 'That won't be necessary. I can cope.'

The doc had the rank, of course, but that doesn't count for much with someone as big as Grease in front of you. When he said, 'Charlie will travel with you,' again, there was something nasty in his voice. He scared *me*, and we were on the same side.

The MO shrugged. His voice became more Welsh. He said, 'As you wish,' and turned away. He was already in the back of the ambulance when Grease and I carried the stretcher in. Grease shut the rear doors on us: his face looked pale and pinched in the approaching dawn light. In the back of the wagon the doc must have noticed Grace's face for the first time. Game over. Grace smiled painfully at him, and after a long pause he said, 'Well, well, well. What have we here then?'

I have had a bad few hours after some trips. Life was like that. The doc was more assertive on his own patch, and had me sit on a hard chair in the corridor outside his examination room – which was conveniently alongside his small mortuary: the RAF thinks of everything. His examination took more than an hour. When a female member of his nursing staff turned up after five minutes I didn't know whether to be relieved or worried. I dozed on the chair to the sound of murmuring voices in the next room. I couldn't make out what they were saying.

When he popped his head round the door the doc's first words to me were, 'Hello, boy; you still here?' He beckoned me inside. He sat me in the patient's chair as if it was a consultation. Grace had been spirited out through another door, and surely not the one to the morgue. 'I suppose that there *is* an explanation for all this?'

I was dog-tired: out on my feet.

'Yes, sir. But I can't think of it at the moment.'

He nodded wisely, but I think that it was all an act: he didn't know what to do either.

'Your rear gunner appears to have suffered a spontaneous sex and nationality change. I've never seen that before. Fascinating. It will make an interesting footnote for the medical text books. Probably rewrite a few of them.' His voice told me that he was enjoying himself. I leaned forward, clasped my hands together as if in prayer and looked at the floor. Eventually he put me out of my misery, and laughed. As he did so he found his bottle and a couple of grubby little glasses from somewhere. It was navy rum.

'What happened to her?' I asked him.

'Just as you thought, but back to front. She must have begun to pass out, vomited into her mask, which *then* froze. When it backed up she began to choke on it: swallowed her tongue.'

'Only partly,' I told him.

'You undoubtedly saved her life.'

'Don't tell her that.'

'Too late. She knows.'

'So there's nothing seriously the matter with her?'

'I didn't say that. Another one?'

I held out my glass for the other leg.

'She does have a medical condition, Charlie, and it *will* prevent her from flying for a while, eventually.'

This time it was me with the closed eyes. I seemed to be floating. I spoke to the floor. More of a mutter, really. 'What is it? What's the matter with her?'

'It's called . . . it's usually called a bloody pregnancy, Charlie. Your rear gunner is pregnant, and if that ain't a bloody miracle, what is, eh? About five or six weeks gone, if I'm to guess. Another?'

It was the combination of fear, I suppose, being tired, and the booze: I was very drunk. He said he was keeping Grace in overnight just in case there was another problem, but that we could have her back in the morning: after that it was up to us how we sorted it out.

Outside it was half dawn; it had stopped raining, and there was a bright star low down on the horizon. When I stumbled into the Pit there was a party going on. A lot of noise, and laughter and music. Cab Calloway was doing 'Chattanooga Choo Choo', and everyone was doing it with him: it was a much better version than Miller's.

Pete was sitting on my bed, dressed in his number ones, and with a glass in his hand. He jumped up immediately and gave me a hug. Nobody was embarrassed by it. He said. 'Hello Charlie; how's Grace? Not bad, no?'

We didn't get to bed after Duisburg. It turned into a fair old bash. At one point I saw Alex, wearing only his policeman's white steel helmet, dancing with Fiver; he was an erect, impressive figure of a man. I wondered where his clothes were. Her husband, Dougie, was deep in conversation in a corner with Chief Bryan. Fuck knows where everyone had come from: but word of a party gets around. I watched Dougie and the Chief: fuck knows what they'd do to *Tuesday* next. After an hour or so it got too hot for me, and I wandered outside for some air. I must have walked right past the Singer as I came back from the medical block, without noticing it was back, or realizing its significance. The top was down; I sat in the passenger seat, let my head flop back and closed my eyes.

Pete woke me up getting into the driver's side. He had a glass of Scotch in each hand.

'Cheers, Pete. It's good to see you,' I said. I was surprised to find that I meant it. 'How long are you staying for, this time?'

He laughed ruefully. 'It's good to see you too, Charlie. Maybe I'll stick around this time.'

'You got things sorted out?'

'Yes. I got things sorted out. It was political, like I told you. The Poles in Britain are a small community. There are factions; competing factions. You understand?'

'Not completely. But I'll take your word for it.'

'I know you will, Charlie. That's why I can't lie to you as easily as I can to others: you make it difficult for me if I can't tell lies every now and again.' He collected idiom like stamps. 'They are already planning the new Poland, Charlie.'

'What makes you think that it'll be any different to the old one?'

'It will be. Some want to go back to living under a monarchy, and keeping the peasant in his place. Some, like me, want a communist republic; a free socialist Poland – it's what I fight for. There are others working to keep the Russians in charge in Poland after the Nazis are thrown out. Sometimes I hate the pro-Russians more than I hate the monarchists: more than I hate the Kraut, which is very odd. They are already working to eliminate anyone who doesn't think like them. They tried to stuff me.'

'What happened?'

'No matter: we have an understanding now. They understand

that what I could leave behind me when I die, will embarrass them more than I can by staying alive.'

'You mean all those bills and invoices you kept?'

'Partly.'

'You don't have them any more. Grease dumped them in Germany, tied to a 1,000-pounder. We thought we were protecting you.'

Pete gnawed at his lower lip for a few seconds, and then grinned. '*We* know that, but *they* don't. Isn't that so?'

'That's all right then.'

'It is a pity. Maybe I could have traded them for a post in the new government.'

'They would have killed you instead, Pete.'

'Maybe. But first they got to catch me, eh?'

'You still fucking Abbot's wife?' I asked him.

'No. It was boring. It was better when she was still married to him: it was like *stealing* then. You still fucking the Boss's wife?'

'No. I think it was a chance thing. Only a two-chance thing. Anyway, Brookman's the Boss now.'

'I heard that. What's he like?'

'Clever. Losses will go down if we keep him.'

'You still fucking Grace?'

'No. No one's fucking Grace. She's as celibate as a nun: she said that it was not appropriate for the crew to fuck the rear gunner. You should take note of that. She may relent now you're back, but I don't think so. Things move on: things change.'

'In what way?'

'She's pregnant. Doc just told me.'

'You tell the others, Charlie?'

'No; not yet.'

'Better you don't, Charlie. You let her work it out.'

'On her own?'

'Grace is never on her own: you *know* that, Charlie.'

'Yeah. I do, I guess.'

'So you fucking no one any more?'

I grinned. 'Yeah. That's right.'

'Better get your finger out, and your dick in, Charlie; life's too short.' I suppose that everyone was saying that.

'Why did you come back?' I asked.

'I told you. It was all fixed. Anyway, your man Alex, the policeman, he came and found me: I can't have been difficult to find, can I? He said you couldn't get through your tour without me: so I come back. Why do you all call him Bluto, by the way?'

'Someone in the Popeye cartoons at the pictures; same sort of guy. A thug. What did he tell you?'

'He told me that you couldn't hide me AWOL for ever, and when you were found out it was trouble for all of us. Better for everyone if I come back with him. No records made of it, he said; no harm done. No names – no pack drill, he told me it was something like that, and least said, soonest mended. That intelligence girl still here? Harriet?'

'She's with Grease now.'

Pete shrugged. 'OK.'

'What about the two policemen you killed?'

'They were unofficial policemen. I think they worked for the Polish Russians some of the time maybe; all your English secret policemen work for the Russians – don't you know that?'

Then he asked, 'When will we go to Germany again, Charlie?'

'Tomorrow, or Tuesday maybe. Let's go back to your party first.'

As I was about to get out of the car Pete asked, 'Do you think the world's gone mad, Charlie?'

I didn't answer him. I don't think that I cared any more, and that would have been difficult to explain. Back in the Pit Alex was still dancing with Fiver. He was fully clothed now, whilst she wore his steel bonnet. Dougie had disappeared, but Grace had arrived and was sitting on a bed with Fergal and the Toff. She had a drink in a long-stemmed glass. It could have been a G&T, or a Martini. She smiled when she caught my eye. It was like doing a jigsaw puzzle. The closer you got to finishing it, the faster the pieces fell into place. I thought that because there was only one worrying puzzle left in my life: had Quelch really killed the fat man? Grace didn't count as a puzzle: she was a variable; you just played the cards she dealt you as they fell.

Grace and I didn't speak about what we'd learned from the MO, and she didn't tell me why she had discharged herself from his care. I awoke on the floor in the corner. I had a split lip so I must have had a fight with somebody, but couldn't remember who with through my hangover. Pete was back in his bed, and Marty was under his. Conners, Fergal and the Toff were having a snoring competition, Conners and Fergal from on top of their beds, and Toff from the old armchair. Grease was missing, probably out for his run. I was still in my flying jacket. It was as if Grace had never been among us.

The door of the locker she had used hung open: it was empty. I remembered then the puzzle I had been trying to solve when the fight started: would we last another three or four? If the others felt as ill as I did, the answer to that was, not if we had to fly today.

Grease wasn't running: he was flat on his back in the dewy grass outside, looking at the sky. 'Grace took the Austin, and all her things. I said that that was OK. I think that I asked her to marry me.'

I could see the narrow indentations in the grass where the car had recently stood. 'What did she say?' I asked.

'That it was out of the question.'

'Good; because I asked her too.'

'What did she tell you?'

'She said that she'd marry me if I could find her.'

'Then you'd better take the bike: she's got a head start on you.'

I reached down, and pulled him up.

'I don't think that's what she meant. I think maybe she meant that she was twenty-eight and that I was twenty.'

'Then she's saying no: you'll never catch up with her.'

'You never know: sometimes I already feel older than her. After we've done the tour I'll find her, and check that out.'

'There are so few who can grow old with good Grace,' he told me. 'I looked that up a couple of days ago. Some Englishman said it near here in 1700.'

'I like that. I'd like to grow old with good Grace.'

'I know you would, Charlie. Maybe she'll listen to you.'

'What about you?'

'I'll just settle for the growing old.'

We shaved at adjacent basins.

'If we're not on for it today, what say we parade old Pete in front of Brookie, and then take him out for a thrash to celebrate?' Grease suggested.

'I think we did that last night. Every part of me still hurts.'

'No; we only half did it. This time we'll get absolutely blinders: my speciality, remember?' Then his mind did its usual flip flop, and he changed the subject faster than a speeding bullet. 'When I told you to fuck off, sometime yesterday, you walked outside to talk to Samson's old lady. What did she say?'

'Nothing much . . .' I turned away, and made a production of drying my face and dabbing at the cuts.

I ran the conversation again, but in my head. It went something like this:

'How's the squadron leader?'

'All right, I think. They're keeping him in Ely, under observation. They've given me a small room in the grounds so I can be near him.'

I reached into the car and touched her face: she recoiled quickly.

'Don't, Charlie. Someone might see us.'

'What happened to him?'

'Something a bit strange. Gerry Brookman was down in the nose crouching behind the bomb aimer, so he says that he didn't

455

see what happened to Conny next. They were making a long approach to the target, Gerry told me. Apparently Conny put the aircraft on to autopilot and simply got up, walked to the rest station and lay down. When Gerry got back to the cockpit there was no one flying the aircraft. Just the engineer sitting there looking petrified.'

'I'm not surprised.' I offered her a Player's, and had one myself, leaning on the roof of their Hillman Heap with an elbow. What breeze was in the day swirled the smoke around me. 'Has the Boss said what the problem was?'

'He hasn't said anything to anyone: he hasn't *spoken* since then. He just sits in a chair smiling brightly at anyone who comes into the room. They want me to spend as much time with him as I can, just talking to him. They say that might bring him out of it.'

'I wonder what caused it?'

'Gerry says that no one knows. He says it was a pretty straightforward flight as far as these things go.'

What could she know about straightforward flights? She had a small spasm of coughing, and I realized that she was suppressing a laugh.

'What's the matter?'

'I've just realized what the nearest part of your body is, standing as you are.' She made it sound like we had been playing some child's game.

'You could reach out and touch me then.'

She clasped her hands together, and set them firmly in her lap. I loved her lap. She paused and sighed before replying in a very small voice, 'I'm sorry Charlie, but that bit's over. I'm going to have to think about nothing but Conny from now on. Perhaps it was a mistake in the first place.'

I said, 'OK.' What else *do* you say in those circumstances?

'You understand then?'

'Of course I do. It was fun.'

'Wasn't it just.'

'Maybe I'll see you around.'

'Maybe, Charlie: but probably not.' Something in my mind said that she meant *Not if I see you first*. I had the sudden feeling that there was more than one egg in her basket, and that maybe she wasn't ditching them all.

I bent down so that my face was close to hers. I wanted her to see that I wasn't upset. 'Bye, Jenny. Tell the Boss I might drop in and see him one day . . . just for a chat.'

I don't know why I said that. Maybe it was to see her flinch. In her world the peasants stayed discreetly out of sight, and went away for good when they were told. She put the car into gear and lurched away, crashing the gear change. She didn't say goodbye, but yards from me her gloved hand stabbed out of the window and waved briefly. She must have suddenly remembered her manners. Her gloves looked the same as Fiver's. I stuck my hands in my trouser pockets, and whistled as I sauntered back to the mess.

Grease and I paraded Piotr in front of Brookie.

'Who's *he*?' he asked us.

'Sergeant Paluchowski, sir. *Tuesday*'s rear gunner; the phantom Pole: you asked to see him,' I said.

'I don't recognize him.'

'With respect, Herr Oberleutnant.' Pete clicked his heels together, threw up his right hand for fingernail inspection, and said icily, and with an oddly emphatic European accent, '*I* don't recognize you either. The last time I was here we had a different squadron leader. A man with a great moustache and a red, spotted nose.'

'That one went mad, Pete,' Grease explained.

Brookie smiled to himself. 'Say something in Polish. Make me believe,' he said.

Pete said nothing at first. His eventual reply was in perfect standard English. 'You'll get all the booze and cigarettes from me that you'll ever need, Acting Squadron Leader, at half the NAAFI prices.'

'What are you calling yourself these days?'

'They call me Slippery Pete, sir.'

'He's a Pole all right,' Brookie told us. 'I suppose you're going to get him drunk now?'

There was a lady's stocking hanging over the back of Brookman's chair. It was the one he wrapped around his neck to keep himself warm, and ward off the gremlins when he flew. I recognized it by an unusual narrow zigzag seam. The last time I had seen one like that it was on Jenny Delve's short and shapely leg. I wondered if old Samson had seen it around Brookie's neck just before he went off his head. I could be a tricky little blighter too.

We were in the Eagle in Cambridge. Grease had wanted to add his name to those of the other Canadian crews scratched on the downstairs mirror in Betty's café in York, but we couldn't be bothered to drive there with him, and anyway he would have had to borrow a diamond engagement ring from a waitress to get the job done. This time he settled for burning a big black McKenzie on the ceiling of the small bar in the Eagle with a brass cigarette lighter he borrowed from Pete. We'd driven: Conners caught the bus and followed us. He said that he felt like reading some poetry, and the bus always worked well for him. I asked him what it was.

'Some of that *Irish airman foreseeing his own death* crap?'

'No. Too morbid. This is Rochester. The dirtiest poet that ever lived. He was a genius. This is his ode to a blowjob.' He read me 'His Mistress to Her Ancient Lover'. I was interested despite myself.

'I'd like to borrow that.'

'I'll give it to you. I'm always keen to promote literature.'

Conners gave us the good news: 'We're not flying today,' – and the bad news – 'because they're sticking a bloody great black blister of a thing under *Tuesday*'s arsehole. It looks like a bad touch of the piles, or a carbuncle on the face of a well-loved old lady.'

'I think that we'll hear that again,' Fergal said. 'Anyway, what's in *Tuesday*'s new blister then?'

'H2S. The radio navigation system that actually gives the nav and the bomb aimer a picture on a small screen of what we're flying over. It can see through clouds. They use it for blind bombing,' Grease said.

'I don't see the point,' said Marty. 'We're pretty good at blind bombing as it is. Just open the doors, and drop them bloody anywhere; that's blind enough for me.'

'Well, that's what Brookman told me,' said Grease. 'Every-one's getting them.'

Pete slipped over and lay on his side.

'Pete's drunk,' I said.

'He can't be; it's his round,' Fergal said. For some reason we all found that amazingly funny.

We air tested *Tuesday* the next morning and had the afternoon off. Brookman told Grease that the knack was to take off without scraping *Tuesday*'s new blister off on the runway as he got airborne. Grease didn't look too confident. He made a beautiful take-off: as he often did without bombs. He said that the aircraft was easier to handle empty, but the Toff said he thought it was something psychological. He said Grease's bad take-offs and landings were signs that Grease didn't really enjoy dropping bombs on people.

Marty looked genuinely puzzled about that. 'Why ever not?'

Conners showed me that he had a new head-up box in front of him, with a small round screen. Marty had another one, but whatever was supposed to be in the blister wasn't there yet, so they didn't work. Brookman, in Samson's old *Papa*, had joined the perimeter track behind us so Grease put us into a circuit at a couple of thou to wait for him. Brook-man's kite was called P-*Patron* now. I nearly popped a hernia trailing the aerial, and we had all the comms: intercom RT inside *Tuesday*, air-to-air voice comms with Brookie and flying control, and Morse if I wanted it. I always loved the Morse: I gave control a quick burst of it, feeling smug, and was let down when they came back even smarter. Whoever's finger was down there was faster and cleaner than mine. There were several like that on both sides: I remember we called them *the immaculate hands* just like they belonged to some exclusive club. There was one Fritz in particular who I used to pick up out of Venlo: I loved his Morse so much that I felt like replying to him – like a pen pal – but at the end of the day his people were trying to kill me, and mine him, so we probably had less in common than I thought.

Brookman set off across country very low, about one hundred feet.

'Wind her in, Charlie, we're going down,' Grease said.

So I had to kneel on the floor winding the aerial in like buggery, while Grease was diving to come up on *Patron*'s beam. I just made it. When I strapped myself into the small seat I was sweating inside my suit.

Grease clicked. 'Pilot to Sparks. You can come up here now, if you like, Charlie.'

I acknowledged, and began to move at the same time. Once I was behind Grease I looked around to get my bearings. Grease prodded a finger at some steeples we would have to dodge round. He dragged his mask down and shouted, 'Lincoln.'

I nodded, and looked to our left. I was surprised to see how close to Brookie we were flying, and how low, but he and Grease seemed to be enjoying themselves and know what they were doing. That was the good thing. The bad thing was that it went on for hours, or so it seemed, as we flew a huge low ragged circle around the heart of England. It got so that I flinched as soon as I saw a church tower or high tree on the horizon. They would fly straight at it, and at the last moment pull right and left around it, joining up together again on track as quickly as possible afterwards. Grease laughed a lot. Occasionally I heard someone scream: that would be Marty. As if to confound us Grease made his usual arse of a landing, flattening out and cutting back the power about twenty feet too high. The tail wheel dropped on to the hump with a colossal bang. And the main wheels followed it. *Tuesday* then gave a tremendous leap before flopping down again. Grease needed the emergency runway to get her stopped.

Piotr clicked, and just belched a long and rolling belch.

Marty clicked, and asked, 'Master, were you *taught* to land an aircraft like that, or is it something which comes with skill and experience?' but Grease didn't have time to reply because Brookman, who had followed us on, came through aircraft to aircraft.

'See you in my office after you've cleaned up, Mac. One or two things to clear up,' he said.

We immediately chorused. 'Bollocking! bollocking!' Well, he had it coming, didn't he?

We insisted on scrubbing Grease clean, and slotting him into his number ones before releasing him for his bollocking. They all piled into the Singer to deliver him, and stood around in the road outside to gloat.

I took the Red Indian and headed for Grace and Favour land. She couldn't just piss off like that.

Crifton glowed in the late sun, and the mixed woodland around it picked up the mood, with rich splashes of red and brown, orange and yellow. I noticed the horse chestnuts for the first time: thousands of them. I wondered if they let the village kids in for the conkers.

There was a woman in a white cocktail dress taking afternoon tea with two American fliers on the gravel in front of the house. She had long wavy mouse-coloured hair that fell to below her shoulders. They were all dwarfed by the length and the height of Crifton's golden stone. There was a battered jeep close by, and I parked alongside it.

'Hi, Charlie. Great afternoon. It's like this in New England in the fall,' July Johnson said.

'Old England, too,' said the woman, and held out her hand to me: for shaking or kissing – I wasn't too sure. 'I'm Adelaide Baker.'

She wore shaped sunglasses that hid her eyes on a heart-shaped face. I couldn't guess her age. Johnson told me.

July said, 'This is Herb, Herb Washow, my skipper. His family were Pollacks before they were Yanks.'

'Pollacks?'

'Europeans,' said Washow. 'Specifically Poles, although in my case they were Russian. In the States a certain class of man calls any white north European a Pollack. It's not a friendly term.' Washow had a quiet cultured voice and smoked a corn-cob pipe. There was almost no wind, and the sweet tobacco smell hung around us.

Johnson tried out the words, ' "A certain class of man," ' realized that he was being had over, and grinned.

Barnes appeared staggering under the weight of a cast iron garden chair to match those the others sat on and the round table between them.

Barnes said. 'Nice to see you back, Mr Charlie,' and breathed whisky fumes all over me. I could have lit the fire in the great hall with him.

Adelaide shrieked an improbable laugh I knew I'd heard over the telephone, and spluttered, 'Oh my God. This is the bun in Grace's oven, isn't it?'

'That was uncalled for Addy,' Washow said quickly.

Adelaide became serious, studied her brilliant carmine fingernails, and said, 'You're right. It was. Sorry. Can I have a drink, Barnesy?'

The butler made a production of consulting a fob watch from his waistcoat, then smiled with genuine affection at her. 'Yes Mrs Baker. You may. You're doing very well today.'

'Why, thank you, Barnsey. Make that a double.'

'Not *that* well, Mrs Baker.'

'Ah.' Then she told me, 'He minds me. He's very good at it.'

'And for Mr Charlie and the gentlemen?' Barnes asked.

'A Scotch please, if there's any left,' I said.

July got awkwardly to his feet. 'Count us out for a while. We got to go see the bomb men. We'll be back later.'

He jerked his head at Washow, who seemed reluctant to leave, but they both followed Barnes into the house. Washow had his hands in his pockets and seemed to watch his feet as he walked.

'Hello, I'm Charlie Bassett,' I said to Adelaide, 'I met one of those guys when I was here before. Who are the "bomb men" when they're at home?'

'Some bomb disposal people. They were working at an

airfield near here when friend Washow realized that not all the bombs on Tim's B-17 had gone off or been recovered. They just turned up, and have been here for a few days. It's jollied the place up a bit. I understand that there are still three or four bombs in the ground under the Long Ride. He says that they are 500-pounders. Is that very big?'

'Big enough. I wouldn't want them near my house.'

'What do they do with them?'

'Dig them out, cover them with sandbags and blow them up.'

As if on cue there was a flat and distant detonation, and a column of pale smoke curled up from the other side of the building. She said, 'Good old Crifton. It's been here for hundreds of years; I should hate anything to happen to it.' Then, 'The Americans call me Addy. I quite like that. You can too, if you please.'

Barnes spirited out with a huge Scotch for me, and what looked like a Martini for her.

'You must be Grace's stepmother,' I said.

She shook her head and smiled at me. 'No: I'm her *mother*; her real one. She has no stepmother. Did *she* tell you that?' I nodded. 'It figures. Wicked stepmother: that makes her Cinders, doesn't it?'

'I don't understand.'

'She lied. She has a natural mother, and a step*father*. You've met him, I take it?'

'If it's the big man I think he is, I repaired his radio. It's my trade in the RAF. I think that I heard you singing when I was up there working on it. I thought you were a ghost.'

'I never sing, so perhaps it was.'

'Why should she tell me you're her stepmother if you're not?'

'Good question Charlie-Barley.' She held up her drink and squinted at me through it. I noted that she was taking very small sips and savouring each one. 'It could be something to do with hating me.' When I didn't respond she added, 'Aren't you even going to ask why?'

'I thought that I'd leave that to you.'

She smiled. I liked her smile. She had a bags of character smile. There were sad things in it, and defiant things in it.

'Her stepfather dated her before he dated me. She was twenty and he was forty: so was I. You can work out the mathematics if you're that interested. He shagged the daughter first, and then the mother. Collected the complete set: you men are all little boys at heart. Then he confounded everyone by marrying the latter. He tells me that he hasn't had her since he met me, although she has tried often enough.'

'Do you believe him?'

'Yes; I do rather. It might explain the loathing she feels for me.'

'She also says that you are a lush.'

'She didn't lie about that. She doesn't lie about absolutely everything.'

'None of us do.'

'No.'

'Are you getting better?'

'Better at *what*, Charlie?' She suddenly had the voice of a sexy schoolgirl, and when I looked up quickly she laughed at me. 'I told you: Barnsey looks after me. If you want to know the story then I'll tell you.' I didn't, particularly, but that didn't stop her. 'I'm one of those lapsed Catholics who takes God half seriously, so when the booze buried a good friend of mine, and threatened to bury me, I went down to the chapel here with Mr and Mrs Barnes. We all knelt at the altar, and I promised God not to drink a drink here that they hadn't personally handed to me. Then I had them promise God never to give me a drink if they thought that it would be bad for me. It was a bit like marriage vows.'

'Did it work?'

'More or less. It meant giving Mrs B the run of the cellars, and that turned out to be a mistake. Her problem's almost as big as mine. Poor Barnsey!'

I tried again. 'Are you getting better?'

She sighed, and looked across at the sweep of the lawns, the narrow river and the distant trees. Her eyes were huge and brown and clear. Her chin was as narrow as her mouth was wide. I had been so used to the company of twenty-year-olds with million-year-old faces, that I was suddenly stunned by a middle-aged mother with a twenty-year-old face. There was half an inch of drink in her glass. She smiled, and suddenly inverted it onto the gravel. She looked at me and smiled again.

'Yes. Much better. What are you thinking?'

'I'm not going to tell you, Mrs Baker.'

I liked her laugh.

There was another deep thump from the Long Ride. I left the Indian there, and drifted slowly back in the Austin. Barnes told me he'd have one of the land girls deliver the bike.

Grace wasn't there; did I already tell you that? Neither was her father. I wondered if her mother and father were ever in the house at the same time.

There used to be an airfield at Great Gransden. It was the next nearest bomber command station to our own at Bawne. I had agreed to meet the chums there for the dance the Gransdenites were throwing. It was a mixed ranks affair, also open to civilians, in one of their great T sheds, and they had gone to town on the prep. They had commandeered small chairs and tables from all over the neighbourhood, and arranged them around a huge bare circle that formed a dance floor that could accommodate thousands – well, *hundreds*, anyway. They had decorated the hangar with red, white and blue streamers and fitted a long bar down each side. The band was a Brown Jobs band, but they were bloody good. They did Dorsey so you thought that it *was* Dorsey.

'Who *are* they?' I asked Grease.

'The RASC dance band. Service corps. They must all be bloody professionals. Bloody good, what?'

The 'what' threw me for a second, then Marty said, 'He didn't get a bollocking. Brookie told him that his landing was so piss poor that he *had* to become an officer, because he was embarrassing the sergeants.'

'What did you make?' I asked him.

Grease said, 'Pilot officer, but don't get excited. He then went all serious on me and said that the piss poor landing was so piss poor that even the officers wouldn't have me, so he was demoting me again immediately. I'm a flight sergeant at present, and things aren't looking good. I've got at least four landings to make before the end of the tour, and if I lose a rank each time I'll be an Erk before we finish.'

'My people would be right proud of me if I did that. Da hates the English. Ashamed of me being a sergeant in their air force,' Fergal said.

'What's with the "what" then?' I asked Grease.

Conners said, 'He's been speaking officerish ever since the interview. I've told him that it won't wash: he has to have the uniform to go with it.'

Grease had already had a few; he grinned cheerfully. 'Maybe that guy Braddock could get me one.'

I looked away and asked, 'Where's Pete?'

'Dancing with Harriet with his prick up her skirt,' the Toff told me. His toff accent always became more toffish with ale.

'He'd better be careful,' Grease said.

'Why?'

'I think that I might have given her something: I've been awfully itchy for the last couple of days.'

Within the limits of decorum Harriet was spreading herself around the team. She could see we were short of females. While she was dancing a smoochie slotted between Marty and Fergal, Pete topped up our beers from a flat bottle of bourbon, and asked, 'What did Grace say?'

'Nothing. Wasn't there. She only stayed overnight, and then picked up a Beau at Twinwood and flew it to Ringway; she's back in the business. She didn't tell them anything, but her mother knew.'

'What was the old lady like?' Pete asked.

'I'm not going to tell you. Not what I expected,' I said.

'Ah,' Pete said. It was a noise we were all learning.

Marty alarmed everyone by dancing a rumba with an empty 250-pounder bomb case, fins and all. He looked like a man very much in love.

'What about *Tuesday*?' I asked Grease.

He squinted at me through the smoke. Everyone had cigarettes except me. I was beginning to enjoy the pipe, and drank less when I had it stoked up. Tommo wandered over, gave me a half wave and wandered away again. I thought I saw Peter Wynn behind him, but when I shook my head the picture cleared. It was some fresh-faced lieutenant I'd never seen before. I tried again. 'What about *Tuesday*?'

'Oh. She's ready. They stuck the gadgets in, and fired them up. It all works apparently.'

'Who's going to show Conners how to work it?'

'No one. We're too close to the end of our tour. Not worth the bother Brookie says. He'll get it at his next OTU. We've got to fly her, and pretend they're not there. The next mob will be shown how to do the business with it.'

Brookman danced by with a huge Wren he'd magicked from somewhere. His leg was still troubling him so he flew a bit left wing low, and one of his legs would occasionally dart between hers: that was his excuse, anyway. It meant that they crabbed about the dance floor a bit. As he looped close to our table he slowed long enough to toss a bulky envelope in front of Grease and said, 'Get a uniform with a proper jacket, and get *these* up.'

When Grease shook out the contents in front of us it was the uniform ring, buttons, wings and cap badge of a pilot officer.

'Fuck it,' he said, 'I'm an officer again.'

'Don't be too pleased,' the Toff told him. 'So was Samson, and look what happened to him.'

'What *did* happen to him?' Pete asked us. He'd come back with a tray of beers. The Gransdenites served a decent pint at their parties.

'I think that Charlie arse-ended his missus, and then he went mad. I'm not sure about that; it may have been the other way round,' Conners said.

'Naughty, naughty,' Pete said, and waved a finger in front of my face.

It was a good party. I spoiled it by telling Pete, 'I think Brookie arse-ended Samson's missus as well. Probably still does. He wears one of her stockings around his neck.'

'Really? She's a matrosse then. That's what a German soldier would call her.'

'Tell me that again?'

'Three grades of Fräulein: matrosse, unter offizier matrosse, and uber offizier matrosse.'

'How do you know that?'

'Most of the Polish countesses I told you about. They been matrosses before they come here.'

'What about the ones who don't do it?'

'I'm Polish, Charlie. Do I believe in fairies?' he asked me, and leaned over to top up my beer with bourbon again. Hadn't I already said something like that about Brookie?

Some time after midnight the band was playing 'Stardust', and I found myself dancing with Fiver. She had come in uniform, and had managed to keep it on so far. I looked around for

Dougie and couldn't see him. As we danced I ran my tongue around the edge of her ear, not thinking about what I was doing, and whispered, 'Where's Doug?'

Although she had kept her uniform on she had undone the jacket. She moved closer as our feet shuffled to the tune. I felt as if I was in an earthquake.

'Tain.'

'Where's that?'

'Hundreds of miles away. North of Inverness: near Wick. In the Forbidden Zone. They're building huge new runways up there for the transatlantic flights. Doug got part of the contract: he'll be away for months.'

'Where's the Forbidden Zone?'

'North of the Neutral Zone: deepest Scotland. We'll be rich when he comes back.'

'Good for you.' Some of her hair got into my mouth. I gently displaced it with my tongue. 'Are you staying in the cottage or moving back to the Waafery?'

'In the cottage I think. I haven't told them at the station – my section officer would just move me back – I'm actually looking forward to it: I've never lived alone before.'

'Nor have I.' I slid my right hand down on to her breast as we moved: she put her left hand over it, but didn't pull it away. I asked, 'Can I stay with you tonight?'

Her voice was more a loud breath inside my ear than a voice. 'No . . . but you can fuck me if you like.'

OK Charlie boy: decision made. It was a bit like arriving at a destination I'd been travelling to for a while. What did I feel? I felt a deep sense of relief, and I'm told that that's not uncommon. Grease raised his glass to us as we danced past the table. When I heard him say to Conners and the Toff, 'They look all right together,' I felt childishly pleased. Fiver had heard him too, and smiled back at me. Somewhere in my head Grace vanished, like a genie at the pantomime. Back in her lamp with a puff of smoke. I could handle it.

I walked home from the cottage after 0530, still trying to whistle 'Stardust'. There was a sickle moon on its back about twenty degrees east of me. If you bisected the arc of the sickle and moved out to the west at about forty-five above it, there was a bright star hanging there. About four inches away: Jupiter, I think, or Venus. Together they were like a gleaming signpost into the sky. Wrens and robins dived in and out of the dawn chorus, and scolded me for trespassing.

When I took my head out of the bucket there was a low-slung red sports car close by: a beauty, with Brookman sitting in it gently blipping the throttle. He was dressed for flying, and Jenny's stocking was flapping prominently outside his jacket.

'Morning, Charlie,' he said.

'Morning, sir,' I said, at which he winced. My voice was probably too loud for his hangover. I relented: maybe one 'sir' per conversation would suffice. 'She's a beaut of a car. What is she?'

'A Beezer. BSA. The bint likes it, anyway. Where's your leader this morning?'

'Pounding the peri-track. He's fanatical about keeping fit. He was a sportsman before he joined up.'

'I know: ice hockey, wasn't it?'

'Do you want me to give him a message?'

'No, Charlie – I'll wait. I left some things out at Gransden last night, and thought I'd pop over in the old Annie and pick them up. Mac can second pilot for me.'

'Do you need a nav or the radio?' More for the form of it really.

'Charlie, I can almost *see* the Gransden windmill from here: even I can navigate to something I can see without getting lost!'

I grinned the daft laddy grin: damned if I wanted to fool around with them in that draughty old Anson at 0800 anyway.

In the Pit Marty groaned, and crawled out from beneath his bed, under which he had eventually slept cradling his bomb case. One of the fins had creased his face. I thought that he was seriously in love.

'What was all that about?' he asked me.

'Brookie's showing off his new car, and wants Grease to fly over to Gransden in the Annie with him to collect some gear he left last night. I think that pilots cure hangovers with the act of flight.'

Conners's voice came from beneath a heap of blankets on his bed. 'Landing practice.'

'What do you mean?'

'He's going to teach Grease how to land aeroplanes without bouncing them to buggery. He'll do it at Gransden, away from here, in order to save face for the chump. Grease is an officer now, don't forget.'

'Is that official?'

'Fuck knows,' said the Toff, 'but if he moves out, I bags his spot by the stove.'

For the second time since we had moved in I had forgotten to stoke it in the morning, and so it had died. I imposed on myself the penance of emptying and rekindling it: I needed the discipline, and it was like paying God back for the loan of a Fiver. The curtains were closed around number eight, and for a moment I thought one of the murmuring voices inside was Grace, but it was Pete and Harriet: they seemed to be grumbling about something.

At breakfast it was interesting how the rest of the squadron deferred to us. For instance, the crew at the window table we preferred scuttled away to the back of the room as soon as Pete's sharp nose and narrow moustache preceded us into the mess. It was an honour conferred on us by longevity alone: we were now the longest serving crew on the squadron, our predecessors having got chopped on the last raid. Statistically, if you looked at things from the pessimist's point of view we had already been dead a few weeks. If you took the optimist's point of view it was beginning to look as if we could make it. I stared around the breakfast tables and realized that I didn't know half the faces in the room, and my hands began to shake.

Berlin

Marty was last in, his face still creased from sleeping with a bomb. He said, 'Make the most of it: we're on for tonight,' as he tucked in to scrambled powder and sawdust sausages. He always seemed to know. I was already on the jam and wads. Oddly, as soon as he had said it, I lost the shakes. There was something in the tea again that morning; it had that irony taste.

We drove down to the briefing, clinging around the Singer like limpets. They let me drive because with my pipe in my mouth I had both hands free.

'Fucking Big City again, boys, but it'll be the last time,' Grease told us.

'How d'you know it's our last time?' Marty asked.

'Brookie promised me two or three milk runs after this, if I learned to land properly.'

'And did you?'

'First time. No worries.'

'Good on you, Skip!' the Toff said.

'Stop talking so bloody Australian: this is supposed to be an English squadron,' said Conners.

'Then what am *I* doing here?' Fergal asked.

'And me?' said Pete.

'You'll all get proper passports along with your gongs. Everyone knows that Johnny Foreigner can't get gongs!'

By then we were out of the car and joining the stream of bodies channelling into the corrugated iron shed where they told us where we were going die each trip. It was just the sort of nonsense we talked to get us there. The station commander was there again, and Brookie sat in Samson's old seat, looking for all the world like a keen gun dog off on a shoot.

The wing commander gave us the smoking light early, which was always a bad sign, and casually observed that he would be going out himself tonight, before sitting down and leaving the usual words to the usual ranks. Both the master gunner and master bomber were officers I hadn't seen before – or if I had I couldn't remember them – because we'd lost their forerunners the raid before.

I liked the gunnery officer immediately: when he stood up to the map of Krautland on the board he drew irregular shapes on it with a chinagraph pencil: then he hatched the shapes in with straight lines, and said, 'Regardless of what wing intelligence tells us, *these* are the shiteholes tonight, gentlemen. Flak, and fighter beacons. Shiteholes.' He got a murmur of laughter, then, 'Fly into them and you'll get flushed down the pan.' It was silent again: he had our attention. 'Solution: *don't* fly into them.' I could see Conners scribbling furiously from the corner of my eye: that was unusual during the gunnery part of the brief. 'If you do, you are going to need your gunners. Don't come crying to me afterwards; even if you are able to. Gunners, you are loaded up with 50 per cent tracer, and 50 per cent plain ball. I know that some of you don't like tracer because it tips the Hun off as to where you really are. My opinion is that the risk is offset by the hell of a scare you give him when he sees those coloured lights screaming towards him. Any questions?'

There was an apologetic cough from the back, and one of the new kids stammered something like, 'In that case, why can't we carry 100 per cent tracer bullets, sir?'

'One: because they tend to burn your barrels out, and two: even if they didn't, we couldn't afford them anyway.'

I was suddenly surprised to hear Pete speak up from alongside me. 'How many rounds will we be loading, sir?'

'Thank you, gunner: I've had a word with bombs and the squadron engineer, and the answer to that is as many as you damned well can, and *use* them if there's an opportunity. Nobody's going to get a bollocking from me for coming back empty! Ammunition conservation is a false economy where I come from!'

Some wag called out, 'And where's that, sir?'

Even the wing commander smiled at that. Guns grinned as he glowered at us with his fists on his hips.

'Nineteen hundred and bloody fifteen,' he roared at us, 'a bloody good year for Hun skinning.'

It was a bit of an anticlimax after that. I noticed Conners scribbling a lot again during the met briefing they topped it off with. I was pleased that Grease was wearing his sergeant's jacket: any change would have disturbed me at this stage.

Fiver and I didn't make a thing of it on the way out to *Tuesday*. I stayed in the back squashed between Fergal and the

Toff, whilst Conners rode up front with her the way we always used to. I think that Conners was keeping his hands to himself now though: *something* had changed.

Marty was already out on the hardstanding with *Tuesday*. He'd done whatever he'd planned before we got there, and was at the foot of the ladder sucking a fag with the Chief and Dobbo. He looked glum enough for seven.

'What's the matter with you then?' Grease asked.

'Nuffink, guv'nor.' He had borrowed an East End accent from somebody on the radio. 'You won't like the bomb load, though.'

'Why?'

'Two cookies and bags of kindling. *Tuesday* won't like the balance, will she?'

'She'll manage. So will I. I'm an ace pilot now: I can land as good as I can take off.'

'Aye, that's the problem,' said Conners.

'I got the cookies shackled as far forward as I could,' Marty said. 'It will put your c of g a few feet forward, and she'll be easier to trim – that's what the Chief says anyhow.'

The Chief added, 'Her tail will come off quicker, but she'll take an extra twenty feet or so to unstick. That's just me guessing.'

When Grease said, 'No probs,' Conners winced. Fergal stood at the foot of the ladder and blessed us as we filed up past him. Dobbo held up his wallet in his hand with the finger missing, and asked Fergal to bless that too. Of us all, Pete was the only one not to laugh. He crossed himself, and made a twitchy little movement that was part bow and part curtsey.

He was last in: I held back to help him secure the door – the way we did it was that one of us secured it, and the other checked that it was dogged home.

Pete touched my shoulder in the dark as I turned to go forward. 'Eggs for breakfast.'

'Sure thing, Pete. Lashings of them.'

As I was settling in I felt a tug at my right elbow. It was Conners trying to attract my attention. He gestured up at the office where Grease and Fergal were moving around. My presence was apparently needed.

'You got all your little lights on?' Grease asked.

'Yes, Skipper, but I'm nowhere near set up.'

'Do it later. Hold this up for me. Where I can read it.' He gave me a small book with a blue card cover.

'What's this?'

'Official Pilot's Notes for the Lanc. I never got one when they trained me. I nicked this from Quelch's room.' He had his goggles hanging around his throat and produced a pair of small rimless specs from inside his jacket.

'I didn't know you needed glasses to read, Skip.'

'Christ no, boy. I just need them to see! I nicked them from Quelch's room too: they must issue them with the pilot's notes because the print is so small.'

I held the book where he could read the small print without leaning forward.

'OK, now the new guy. Page twenty, paragraphs thirty-one and thirty-two, please Charlie.' This was a new pre-flight checklist. The authorized version. After we had completed that, Grease asked, 'What can we do now, Charlie?'

'You can taxi. The book says that that's the taxiing checklist.'

'Have we forgotten anything?'

'Fuck knows; *you're* the pilot. I'm just holding the book. How about taking the brakes off?'

'Good idea. You're officer material Charlie, same as me.'

'For Christ's sake, Skip; just watch where you're going.'

Tuesday felt ungainly: she was waddling around the peri-track about eighth in line.

'What's next?' Grease asked me.

I read out, *Checklist before take-off*. That took my mind off the lunacy around me. Grease grinned when we finished. 'To your places, gentlemen, I do believe dis bird will fly.'

'There they go,' Toff said from his seat in the gods. There were the two lights they always used at Bawne, arcing into the drizzle, and the first of the night's offerings to the fire god moved sedately along the runway. I didn't know who it was, but the Lanc about five in front of us didn't make beyond the end of the field. The flash and the shock wave immediately brought *Foxy* into my mind. Brookie held for about five minutes before launching the rest of us after the half squadron already in the air. During the wait Grease hissed that old tune he always did under stress: I tried to stop my hands from shaking.

Grease must have been counting the aircraft ahead of him in his head, because as we wallowed into the air above the scattered burning wreck, and our main wheels thumped back into their beds, he said. 'I do believe that that's a vacancy at wing commander level; that'll learn the bastard!'

'Nah.' That was Marty. 'I distinctly saw him in the field,

stark bollock naked with his tadger burnt off, gallantly directing the rescue effort.'

'Vain, of course,' added Fergal.

'He always was,' clicked Connors. 'It goes with the rank.' Then he said something that I've always remembered. 'That really was a very good take-off, Skipper. Thank you.' In the commotion none of the rest of us had noticed. We broke out of the drizzle some two thou before we were on ox somewhere over a city that Conners identified as Lincoln . . . or York. Another fine mess you got me into, Stanley.

'Doesn't that mean we're pointing in the wrong direction?' the Toff said.

'We could go north to bomb Glasgow; I never could stand the weegies: they're greedy little buggers who complain all the time, and never wash,' said Marty.

'My dad's in Glasgow,' I told him.

'Then we could level Edinburgh instead. It's got a fucking ugly black castle in the middle of it.'

'Don't do that,' the Toff came back into the round, 'don't they say that girls from Edinburgh never wear undies? That could be worth saving.'

Grease spoiled it. That was his job. 'OK: pipe down everyone. Conners, where the fuck are we going tonight?'

'Try 163 magnetic for starters, Skip.'

'Will that put us into the stream?'

'Negative, Skip. Can't you feel the drift? The stream is going to be all over the sky tonight. You'll have to keep your eyes open.'

'Thank you for that Navigator. You've cheered me up no

end. What are our chances of actually getting over the target at zero.'

'None at all, Skip, but no worries.' It was catching.

I set up for the listening watch, but all I could hear was the usual Kraut jabber and my sixteenth sense told me that it was nothing to do with us. Dobbo had regreased the trailing aerial and its internal crank handle: it went out sweetly, but I still ended up sweating so I clambered back up to the office. Grease and Fergal seemed intent on doing the business and ignored me, so I stepped back down to Conners's department just behind and beneath the skip.

I clicked and asked him, 'When you say "Enemy coast ahead" you mean Holland, don't you? That's not strictly true. Don't we have an army somewhere in Holland these days?'

'Whoever they are they still fire their flak at us don't they? That's good enough for me.'

Grease pulled us back with, 'Shut up you two. Charlie, go back to your radios, and listen to the Kraut. It's what you're paid for.'

About ten minutes after that I heard Conners click. 'Navigator, Skip. Enemy coast ahead.'

He was right. Whoever they were they fired anti-aircraft shells at us. The bastards.

For once Conners's pessimism wasn't exactly justified, because his skill compensated for the wind drifts that were scattering the raid all over the shop. The problem was different wind directions and speeds, at different heights. What Conners did was go back to the notes he had made at briefing of wind speed and direction at different strata, and dead reckon our course changes from that. He wasn't far off either, with the result that although we bombed the Big City at more or less the predicted time, the stream had thinned out around us and we were among the first hundred over the target, instead of in the last couple of dozen as planned. Tough titty for some poor sod of a planner, but not us: we did our job. With the final wind drift pushing us to the south, that was the direction from which Conners crabbed us in to the target. From thirty miles out you could see the fires burning from the American daylight raid that had preceded us.

After Conners's final vector, the Toff asked Marty what our aiming point was. 'What are we bombing tonight Marty? A girl guides' camp or Adolf's VD clinic?'

'*Shut up*, Toff. Watch for fighters,' Grease said.

Marty ignored him. He clicked, 'There's no such thing as Girl Guides in Germany: they have the Bund of German Crumpet, Madchen to us, where they are all taught to fuck for Greater Germany. I love Berlin, you know; I love it so much that after tonight it won't have a zoo any more.'

'They sent us to bomb the *zoo*?' Conners said, incredulous. 'What's the matter with the *zoo*?'

'Even the elephants are Nazis.'

'. . . and two fucking great flak towers that clobber people like us,' Grease said. 'Now, for fuck's sake, *shut up* and do your jobs!'

'OK Skipper, keep your hair on, four minutes to run,' said Marty.

Flak bracketed us twice. A shell would burst behind and just over you, then below and just in front of you, and you waited for the third to turn you into brawn. I think that I physically shrank inside my flying suit waiting for the number threes. Showers of shrapnel from the exploding shells pattered over *Tuesday*'s skin like hail driven by the wind. The bomb run and the *Tuesday* vespers went on for hours. Marty was doing the chat, while Grease's straining hands and feet provided the responses.

'Up a bit, Skipper . . . up a bit more . . . right a bit, right a bit. Steady. I see it . . . I see it. Down a bit. Again . . . and steady,' and then that great leap as *Tuesday* shook herself free of her bombs, and the dreadful pause for the photograph.

'Bombs gone. Bomb doors closed. Let's fuck off,' Marty said, but Grease had anticipated him, and rolled us over to starboard to dive away.

As he straightened up for the first time, Pete's guns chattered astern, Grease jinked her left and right, and called, 'Fighter?'

Pete clicked and breathed. 'No, Skipper. One of us: a Halifax. He got too close: I scared him good.'

You scared me good, too, Pete, I thought.

We saw maybe three or four aircraft over Berlin that night; all Brits. I don't know what happened to the night fighters: probably as fucked up by the winds as we were. I saw one flamer about ten miles distant north of the city. It could have been one of ours or one of theirs. Hell knows what it was doing out there. Seeing as we came in from the south, Grease perversely took us out that way as well. At the bottom of the long dive away from the target he did the stomachs-to-the-heels-of-your-boots thing as usual, and pointed *Tuesday*'s unlovely bulbous nose up into the night sky. That was the dangerous part where we had been caught before, so we hopped about a bit scanning the black for fighters. They can't have thought we were worth coming after. Grease flew us into clear, clean air with miles of vis. Conners slotted us between the flak belts of Magdeburg and Schonebeck, and north around the high ground between Nordhausen and Halberstadt. He said that there was something funny going on at Nordhausen because they'd defended it with a huge flak ring. It might have been a very nice mountain in its own right, but flinging 10 per cent of your available anti-aircraft defences around it was surely a bit excessive. Grease told him to mention it to the intelligence wallahs because that wouldn't have occurred to them.

Being sweat-wet inside my flying clothes wasn't so unusual now: I clambered between a listening watch on my radios and a genuine eyeball job from the astrodome. As each mile of Germany fled beneath *Tuesday*'s tail the relief inexorably began to grip, and conversation picked up. Grease chipped in with reminders to watch the bloody skies and kill the chit-chat.

'What about the Berlin *zoo*, then?' Toff asked.

'There isn't one. Just toasted tiger, and holes in the ground,' said Marty.

'What about the flak towers?'

'Oh, Christ no. *They're* still there: it'll take more than a few cookies to knock them down.'

Pete came on and said, 'I see a dark mass on the ground, and some lights and maybe some flak. Yes, flak.'

'Where, Pete?' asked Grease.

'Port, maybe seven or eight miles away.'

'Hoxter,' Conners said, 'we're on track, Skipper.'

'One aircraft going down,' Pete reported. That shut us all up for a while.

Half an hour later Conners said, 'Navigator, Skip. I think that that's us over Belgium now.'

'Thanks Nav. Name a famous Belgium.'

'General Bernard Montgomery.'

'Don't be fucking daft.' That was the Toff. You could hear him snort.

Conners said, 'That's where his army is. The uniforms we're flying over are khaki jobs now, not grey.'

The Pole came back on with a click, and said, 'Should have saved some focking bombs, then.'

God must have heard him. Two things happened.

The first was a lightning strike somewhere over a large river running south west to north east, and near a large town. Later Conners told me it was named Roeselare. I didn't hear the concussion. There was a bright flash in front of me that lit up my little space. It seemed to jump from the crank handle of the trailing aerial to the radio array, which simply exploded in its cases. I saw it physically shaking like a rat being shaken by an Airedale, one of the blue-coloured knobs burst into flame, and then extinguished itself as quickly . . . and I was shaking as hard as the radio cases myself, with my hands glued splayed to the table. There was a savage burst of pain between my ears, and I suddenly recalled Tommy Hanley moaning 'My brain hurts' in an ITMA show, and us all laughing at him. I probably grinned despite the fact that I was dying. I could feel electricity crackling in my teeth. *Tuesday* lurched, and I was flung clear, my stolen straps holding me sloppily in my seat.

When I opened my eyes again I hadn't a mask, and Conners was mopping my chin because I had been sick. He must have seen the panic in my eyes because he shouted, 'It's OK, Charlie. OK. We're under the oxygen line. We must have lost five thou.'

'What happened?'

'Lightning. The compasses are fucked as well. Are you OK?'

'I can't stop shaking.'

'Neither can I,' he actually laughed, 'but with me it's funk!'

It's a fact that something as simple as losing their compasses has killed more aircrew than bullets have. Conners had a secret weapon in his map bag. He unwrapped it in front of me. It was a rubber ball the size of a cricket ball. The rubber was an old rolled-up bicycle inner tube. After he stripped that off, there was a package of bandage and greased paper. Under that was a cheap, metal dry compass from Woolworths about two inches across. Later he told me that it was a tip he had from one of his trainers, who had pioneered the aerial routes across Africa. They used to call that the Dark Continent, until the Kraut invented Fortress Europe.

The second thing that happened killed Pete. We flew over Ostend quite low, with many of *Tuesday*'s systems not coming out to play: in fact almost anything that had electricity running through it was buggering about like nobody's business. I had stopped shaking, but ached everywhere, and was just testing my abilities to move about when the flak bracketed us again. Brown

Jobs flak, it must have been, our own. I was too tired and ill even to brace myself for the third shell, and was as surprised as anyone when the bastard almost turned us over.

When I opened my eyes for the second time that trip, after a short period of time out of it, I was huddled up against the main spar. Again it was Conners's face bent over me. 'Are you still OK?'

'Yeah. Think so.' My arms and legs seemed to be working again.

'Can you move?'

'Think so. What's the Skip doing?'

'Swearing a lot. Fergal's crying, and Marty's trying to straighten them out. Can you get down the back and see what's happened? The old cow is flying OK but we took a hit in the fuselage, and your radios have had it: Grease needs to know the score.'

I nodded. I felt desperately tired and wondered why Conners couldn't go. Then he said, 'I've got to see to the Toff,' and, looking back, I could see that his legs were dangling loose and floppy from the turret. It was definitely a case of stop fucking about and get on with it, Charlie boy. I nodded again, and hauled myself over the spar on my belly.

There was a hell of a lot of noise inside *Tuesday* that shouldn't have been there. There was also a smell of aviation spirit, and overturned Elsan. Shit, piss and petrol are not alluring companions. There were high-pitched shrieking whistles made by the airflow through a number of holes punched in her skin by the shrapnel shower over Berlin, and this new world of noise and sharp smells was lit by crackling blue flashes of electrical circuits shorting out or protesting: hell had entered *Tuesday*. The door I had secured with Pete several hours earlier had gone. So had the rear turret. So had Pete.

I braced my arms and feet on either side of the fuselage where the turret door should have been, and looked out. The drag from the slipstream tugged at me. Between my legs the air-stream sucked out some of the mess slopping around on the floor, and from my eyes it claimed a few tears, while beneath me I could see the North Sea slipping away. I don't know how long I hung there until I got scared; then I struggled uphill – Grease was trying to put a few feet on the old lady again – to tell them what I'd found. Or what I hadn't found. I passed the Toff on the way: he was strapped on to the stretcher and his eyes were closed. I stopped long enough to ensure that he was breathing. It was odd having all of us crowded up in the office with Grease and Fergal, and by the time I got there they seemed to have everything under control anyway. It was odd that the office, which was usually one of the noisier parts of *Tuesday*, had become one of the more bearable ones.

Conners turned and told me, 'Toff's banged his head. I think he might be OK – I can't feel any depression on his skull, and he has a pretty thick one, anyway.' He was standing between Grease and Fergal with his cheap little compass in his hand. He held it so Grease could see it without turning his head. Grease had a frown of concentration: it made him look older.

'How's Pete?' he asked.

'He's gone. The turret's gone: the shell must have taken it clean off. He wouldn't have felt a thing.' I was just saying it, of course. Then I told Fergal that the rear fuselage stank of aviation spirit, and that there was electrical arcing. 'You'll have to isolate the circuits or do something. We could burn.'

He nodded slowly; too slowly, so I took his elbow and tugged him back with me, saying, 'I'll help, if you like.'

He nodded again. Once his fingers got busy on the sprung wires and melted connections his brain seemed to get back up to speed as well. It took him less time to fix things than it took us to get down the fuselage to the tail. One of the circuits he had to isolate was one that had supplied the tail turret: there were bare wires buffeting in the slipstream. I held on to him as he worked, to stop him being sucked out. Against the hollow bulkhead alongside us, Pete's parachute pack still nestled snugly in its slot. Instinctively, when we turned to go forward again I pushed my trailing mike jack into a remote to tell Grease, and got another electrical shock for my stupidity.

Fergal jerked it clear and shouted at me, 'Leave the electricity alone: it doesn't like us!' I hope that I managed a weak grin. What I do know is that the shakes I had by the time we got back to Grease's office were more from the cold than from fear.

What are the lives of six young men worth? Easy. They're worth a penny each. A tanner was what Conners had paid for the Woolworths compass which he used to put us back into Cambridgeshire. We would have been pleased if he had found us England, let alone Cambridgeshire, but he actually found us Bawne, and after I twinkled up the caravan we were the first of its birds to roost.

We must have caught everyone by surprise because we had to mooch around the dispersal until Fiver drove up in a hurry.

The Chief and about half of the ground team were on the pan waiting for us – they had a sixth sense which always saw them there before us: or maybe they never went away, I never asked them. The Toff was with us, looking a bit dazed and not walking straight, but definitely *with* us. The Chief hauled himself up into *Tuesday*, and we heard him moving around: he poked his head through the space where Pete's turret was supposed to be. When he climbed down again he had Pete's flat parachute pack in his hand: he looked reproachfully at us and then suddenly threw it down on the concrete with enough violence to split it so that some of the white silk edged out. Then he stumped away with his eyes glistening.

Fiver could count to six and could count to seven, and she knew the difference. She gave me a good long hug, and then hugged each of the others in turn. She made us feel as if she needed us to comfort her, and as a result, of course, it was she who comforted us. Just as she knew it would. She didn't get to drive me to the intelligence debrief. I missed that, and I missed Harriet's face when they told her.

Just as we were getting organized to mount up the crew bus, a jeep fussed up. The Doc prised himself out of the front passenger seat, and Alex slid from behind the wheel. We suddenly realized that we had lost the Toff, who had wandered off across the grass into the infield. Alex saw him a hundred yards away, and fetched him back: he must have had better night vision than a cat. I was rubbing my hands together, and when the MO reached out to take one I found that both were shaking. They shanghaied us both back to the slaughterhouse.

There was a pretty but firm-faced nursing auxiliary, with

short blonde hair and broad shoulders. I hadn't seen her before. She helped me to undress, and washed me down under the hottest shower I'd ever had. After that there was a bed with starched white sheets. After that there was the Doc with a big needle. After that there was that big sleep. Whilst I was showering I heard the Toff laughing with someone in the next cubicle: maybe his nurse was less severe than mine.

Toff was sitting on the edge of my bed when I awoke, and said, 'Wotcha, Charlie,' in his outrageous toffy tone. 'Sleep well?'

'Great. What about you?'

'Great: a needle job. I was just feeling up the nurse who was turning back the sheets when I got the jab in my arse. Bloody spoilsports!'

'Dashed unfair!'

'Knew you'd agree, Charlie. I could have dreamed it though.'

'I witnessed it.'

'No you didn't, you little turd; you were already spark out. They ambushed you first.'

My arms were above the sheets, and when I raised my hands they were bandaged again. For some reason that struck us as funny, and we laughed.

The nurse from the night before came in and hushed us. 'There's a poor smashed-up boy from the CO's plane up there. Give him a bit of peace.'

'Sorry.'

'Sorry, nurse.'

She had a good smile that said she understood that we were

cretinous children who would never mature: but that she liked us anyway. She went away to tidy up the heap of bandages and blankets on a bed at the furthest end of the small ward. She took her time to make everything straight, and said as she walked back past us, 'It's OK. Carry on. He can't hear you any more.' I thought that her voice was a little tighter than before.

They collected us an hour later. Grease horsed around a bit until he noticed the smell. 'What's that niff? Smells like pork and aquaflavine.'

'Close enough.'

'Oh Christ, yes! They got one of the gunners out of the crack-up yesterday didn't they? The lucky sod made it.'

'Only for a matter of hours, I think,' I told him. 'I think that they're only waiting to get us out of the way until they move the body.'

'Shit, Charlie: you move in the *best* of circles, don't you?'

The little blonde came in to see us off the premises. I was still in a dressing gown and explained that, with my hands injured again, I would need help to dress. She had a cheeky London voice to go with her bounce, and said, 'Then it's good that all your pals have come round, isn't it?' She pouted and stood with her fists on her hips the way Samson used to.

They often gave you a couple of days after a really shaky do, but you can't do much with a couple of days. We mooched. I found that if I smoked the pipe for too long it made me feel muggy and queasy, although I definitely preferred it to the cigarettes. Every time I put a match to it I thought about Grace . . . that made me uneasy too, so I didn't start smoking until the evening if I could help it. *Tuesday* was in the hangar. I drove up there with Grease on the Indian: he seemed to have got the hang of starting it. There were bright new riveted patches on her hull covering the spaces that the shrapnel had made: nothing could hide the gap where Pete's turret should have been. Chief Bryan was there with a ruler and pencil, measuring her up for a replacement I suppose. He looked up and grinned when he saw us; ready to talk.

'She'll be as good as new in four days. Did you know that we had to rewire her?'

'I guessed,' I told him, and held up my hands. The thin bandages were away and you could see the weals on the pads of my fingers, and palms.

'What was it? A lucky hit?'

'No. God did it. He threw lightning at us for the sin of hubris.'

'Don't *say* that, boy. He might hear you.'

'He did. I *want* him to. He heard Pete, and killed him for it. I want him to hear me too, and to know that I'm not afraid of him, and that I think he's a cowardly, rotten old bastard.' I hadn't realized it, but my voice had been rising, and by the time I had finished I was shouting at the cavernous roof of the hangar. Everyone had stopped working, and my voice echoed like the rolling thunder of an Old Testament prophet. In the silence that followed I whispered, 'Sorry.' Even that was magnified by the iron building.

There was a funny looking turret standing on a dolly under the port wing. It was slightly bulbous and had odd perspex panes. The Chief said, 'I got you a new FN turret. It has twin five-calibre Brownings – carries a good punch. It will be a bit of

495

a pisser for us, loading two different calibres – that's .303 for the nose and upper guns, and .5 for these – but it will be worth it.'

'You're the boss,' Grease said.

'I heard they made you an officer?'

'I heard that too, but I don't know if it's true. Brookie gave me the badges and told me to put them up, and made me sign for the pay increase, but I'm still not sure it's not a wind-up. Can they do that sort of thing: just create an officer by saying that to a man?'

'That's how they knight people, isn't it? Then someone puts it in the *Gazette*, and Bob's your uncle.'

'Then I'll wait for the *Gazette*,' Grease said.

Grease and I sat outside on a couple of oil drums. I wished that it was time to fire up my pipe. I wondered what Grace was doing. Grease looked at the grey sky, and then at his shoes. He said, 'I did history at college. No one believes me when I tell them that. They always assume I had a sports ticket.'

'I'll believe you.'

'The Chief's "Bob's your uncle" reminded me. It's one of the stories I remember.'

'What was it?'

'Years ago your prime minister Robert Cecil kept on appointing his nephew to well-paid jobs. When the dope turned round and asked someone why he got all the best jobs, they told him, "Bob's your uncle". People always get it wrong. They think it means a cert; something all right: it really means something crooked.'

'Nothing fucking changes, does it?'

'As the actress said to the bishop.'

'No: she would have put it the other way round.'

We both sniggered. I drove the Indian back: Grease sat in the sidecar facing backwards and whooping like a redskin. There was a raid the next night, and we weren't put on the board for it. That actually felt a bit odd. *Tuesday* wasn't ready, but there was an old hack we could have had, or they could have rested another crew . . . and they would have had to find us another rear gunner.

I couldn't help myself: I thought of Grace again. Which is how I wound up in Fiver's bed again. And again. There was a raid the next night after that. We weren't on the board for that one either . . . and the following morning Brookman put us on parade.

There were too many of us for his flight office, so his clerk took us to the small briefing hut. They'd laid out a long table with one chair on one side, and six on the other. Brookie sat in the single chair. His clerk had a chair at one end, and Alex stood behind him, wearing a funny Brown Job's uniform without flashes or rank badges. It looked like a bloody court martial, except that Brookie stood up and grinned when we were marched in, and off-capped.

'Morning, gentlemen. Morning, Mac. Still a sergeant?' he said.

'I haven't had time to get a new uniform, sir, and to be honest the promotion seemed a bit unofficial.'

'It isn't now. For Christ's sake sit down everyone.' He tossed a file of papers over to Grease. 'You'll find they're all in order: Squadron Leader Delve had them all signed off before he left; all I did was forward them.'

'How is he?' Grease asked.

'Mad as a hatter! Doesn't talk much: when he does he's ordering around a squadron of dead men.'

'How's Mrs Delve taking it, sir?' I asked.

He gave me the look. And then the pointed finger. 'I've told you before, Sergeant Bassett: leave it out!' It was obviously his first setback of the day. 'Anyway. I've brought you in here to tell you I'm taking *Tuesday* off your hands once she's been repaired; and Chiefy Bryan and his crew as well. I'm flying her myself from now on: she's a good kite, and they're the best ground crew.'

He said all that with a slightly defiant note in his voice, which I could understand, because Grease was surely going to belt him one now. Maybe that's why Alex was there. What I *couldn't* understand was the fact that he was still grinning; or smiling, rather. I had expected something like this as soon as we got the parade order, but what was there for him to be so goddamned cheerful about?

If you open up my heart after my body is dead, and find words engraved inside it, they will be what he said next, because it came without warning.

'I'm expiring you, lads. You've done your bit; well done.'

There was a silence.

'What . . .?' Grease began.

The clerk corporal at the end of the table coughed, and said, 'Congratulations.'

Alex said, 'Yes. Congratulations. I'm really pleased for you.'

The corporal had a pile of files in front of him; he handed them round, keeping one back. Brookie said, 'They're your personal service files. I thought you'd like to see what the RAF really thinks of you.'

Mine was pretty slender, like the others, but there was something the matter with my eyes because I couldn't read it anyway. 'Perhaps I could see it later, sir?' I said.

'Of course. You're all up for something.'

Grease got his head back into gear faster than the rest of us. 'We thought we had another couple to do; that's all, sir. This is good, I think, but I didn't expect it. There's nothing wrong with us, is there?'

Brookie leaned forward in his chair. His voice was low.

'Mac: the plane you brought back from Germany is a bit of a fucking wreck. It'll take a week to put back together again. Your rear gunner is dead.' He was quite clever when he wanted to be, Brookie: he paused there, and let his words sink in 'Your sparks has been wounded twice, and has bad hands. The gunner you have left has been wounded twice, and has concussion. Your nav has more stitches in his arse than my Aunt Maud's sampler. Your bomb aimer is as mad as a monkey, and *you*'ve got the twitch. You've done twenty-eight trips, and twenty-eight is enough for you. You're expired. Screened. Finis. Kaput.'

Anyway; it was in black and white already, wasn't it? The next thing my brain wanted to know was what Alex was doing there.

'He's going to be moving on in a few days, as well. Wanted to say goodbye.'

'Goodbye, Alex,' I said. 'Why are you wearing a funny uniform?'

'It *is* my uniform. I just borrowed the other one.'

'Just borrowed it.'

'That's right, Sergeant.' If I had been sharper I would have realized that he was never quite dumb enough to be proper RAF NCO material. Someone had to be watching Pete, I suppose.

Nobody seemed to know what to do next. Then Brookie said, 'Don't get maudlin, get pissed. That's the best way,' and then in my memory we are on the road outside, looking at each other.

Conners said, 'I think we just fell through the looking glass.'

Marty suddenly bent double with laughter, and pointed a shaky finger at me. He wheezed, 'For you zee vor iz over!' and fell over.

He was still in the foetal position, laughing hysterically, when we carried him into the bar. The friendly sergeant from the mess was in charge: they hadn't sent him a replacement officer yet. It was outside their permitted times but he dressed a round table for us, and kept serving as long as we drank. It was a strange, almost reflective, session. I didn't know what to say for some of the time. It was almost as if I didn't know the others at all. I'd never bothered to find out too much about their lives before *Tuesday*, because that might have meant learning about their hopes for the future as well: despite what everyone told me, I had never quite believed that we had one.

Now we had. I know now that some crews became intimately bound up in each other's lives: they learned everything there was to know, and then kept up with each other for the rest of their lives. That didn't happen to us. We were as close as a family: closer, maybe. But it was a family which had no history before the day it mustered, and none after it stopped flying together. Anyway, I was a late addition: I've told you that already. Now I had to start with them all over again; frankly, it was easier to get pissed.

'What the hell happens now?' I asked Grease.

'We hang around for a few days until our postings go up. Have a big thrash – squadron do in all likelihood – then go off on fourteen days' leave until we join our next squadrons. Training jobs or desk jobs. Bound to be.'

'I thought I'd pop off for a couple of days. Find Grace. It was a sort of promise.'

'You told me. That's a good idea, Charlie. Get things settled.'

'That's what I thought. You won't have our party without me?'

Conners gave a rasping laugh, and said, 'Course not. The boy's talking crap again.'

'I'm going to take the Singer. I may have a fair distance to travel.' There was already another plan in my mind, but I wasn't telling them that.

Pete said, 'Sure.'

'Thanks, Pete.'

And then everyone looked at me, because it hadn't been

Pete talking to me, but Marty. Pete was dead. I had to keep reminding myself that Pete was dead.

I began at Crifton Hall, in a huge, long, empty room with twenty-foot windows running down the whole of one side. It was chilly. Mrs Baker, dressed in flappy silk French knickers, a tight running singlet and plimsolls, pounded around its periphery. Barnes brought me an upright chair and an upright whisky: I sat in the middle of the room while she orbited me at a quarter revs; my visit was not going to cut short her exercise regime.

'She's been here. Once for tea, and once to stay over. She had a nice young American with her.'

'How is she?'

'Still pregnant. It's beginning to show if you have the eye.'

'And you *have*, Mrs Baker?'

'It's what mothers are for.'

'What's she going to do about it?'

'Don't know.'

'Will she tell you?'

'Don't know.'

I swallowed the whisky. It was rough and fiery; I put the glass down carefully on the polished pine boards, and stood up. She stopped running alongside another chair, which had a towel hung over it. She draped the towel around her neck, and looked out of the windows.

'For God's sake Charlie. Don't sulk. It isn't manly,' she said.

'Pete told me that. He's our rear gunner. He died. What *is* manly? I thought that I knew once; now I'm not so sure.'

I had been about to walk out, but walked over to join her

instead. We were looking away from the back of the house to the dip and the climb of the Long Ride. It had several more scars.

'What was this room? A ballroom?' I asked her.

'No; an orangery. Before the last war it would have been full of plants, and a full-time gardener would have worked here.'

'I'm glad you still use it. You could fit a U-boat in here.'

There was a small airy sitting room alongside. Barnes had laid a tea tray with a high swan-necked teapot, glasses instead of cups and a tiny clear jug of milk on a low table. Grace's mother and I faced each other across it on small sofas.

'The tea's Earl Grey. That's slightly scented,' she said.

'I know it. My mother liked it when she was alive . . . so, what *do* you think of me?'

'Too good for my daughter. Excessively middle class.'

'Is there a cure for that?'

'Of course there is: but it would alter you. We may not like what you become. Then, of course, you wouldn't be good *enough* for my daughter. Heads we win: tails you lose.'

'What happened to Grace's real father?'

'Peter killed Jack. Maybe eight years ago.'

'Some sort of accident?'

'No. He killed him in a duel. In Germany. The Germans still allowed it then. Perfectly legal. I think that they were drunk when it cropped up, and too proud to back down. The Germans would have loved that. Peter hasn't drunk so much since then.'

'Was it over you?'

'No. It was about business, I think. They were both in the firm. Grace and I came after that.'

'How?'

'Peter and Jack had made a legal agreement that the business went to the survivor; nothing for me except a piddling little pension. I think that sort of thing is called a tontine arrangement. Don't know why. Grace went to confront Peter in London when he got back. She was going to kill him. That was about a month after the funeral. I understand from Peter that she was in his bed that night – she did *so* like to shock us all when she was a child. She's better than that now.'

'I'm glad. When did you become involved?'

'A few months later: Grace brought him down here to shag him under her dead father's roof, and he met me. I was drunk: had been for weeks. I can't have been hard to roll on my back that night; if it *was* on my back. Initially I think he did it for the mother and daughter thing: you know, a matched pair. Later he said that I was a better fuck than my daughter, and would do for him. Privately I think he'd fallen in love with the house, rather than me: thank God he did; his money saved it.'

'It was *your* house then?'

'After a fashion – but we'd only been here a few months, and I couldn't afford to keep it.'

'What's Grace doing?'

'Based at Ringway again. She's ferried several old Beaufighters from Twinwood I understand.'

I drank the tea sharp: without milk. I loved its tartness on the back my tongue. I told her that my war was over: temporarily. She said, 'I'm pleased for you,' then asked me, 'What are you going to do now?'

'Find her. Talk to her. Make sure she's all right. I suppose that that's excessively middle class of me?'

She paused before replying. A hit; a palpable hit. And then she spoke quietly, studying the floor. 'I would probably say *endearingly* middle class, I think. I wish I was again.'

'I think that I'd better be going.' I stood. The room suddenly seemed small; like a woman's room. It wasn't her face I looked at as I left. OK: I had a last minute glance at it – she was smiling again.

Twinwood seemed to be a much more professional set-up than Bawne. The RAF police guy at the gatehouse kept his white helmet on all the time; ever ready to repel the wily Hun. He didn't like the look of me, or my paybook, and kept me kicking my heels for half an hour while he made calls and checks. Then I made for the watch office. A bored, middle-aged lieutenant, who was sharing the place with an equally bored AC2 telegraphist, offered me a mug of tea. Unlike at Bawne, most of their aircraft were stored under cover in single-aircraft-sized Blister hangars. They hadn't bothered with camouflage, but painted them with heavy matt black tar paint, and had allowed trees to grow close to them. The aircraft I saw – Beaufighters and Mosquitoes – looked purposeful, deadly, and ill-used, with patches and dents: they had rockets and bombs hung all over them. I counted three empty Blisters; somebody was out.

The officer perked up at the mention of Grace. They had a sweepstake out on her, but no one had claimed it yet. There was a young American with her sometimes, but everyone agreed she just seemed to mother him.

'I've just come from her family's house.'

'That big place up at Crifton?'

'That's right. I was with her mother: there's some family business which needs to get settled up, and I needed to speak with her.' It wasn't exactly untrue.

That brought a third voice into the conversation. A tall, slim, bespectacled American Major unwound himself from a chair in the telephone switchboard behind the watch office: he must have been dozing there. He said, 'You looking for a lift to Ringway then, son?' He had a quiet speaking voice: I strained to hear him. I gave him my sloppy salute, at which he smiled.

'Yes, sir. That was the idea. If she wasn't here I needed to get wherever she was; if you see what I mean.'

'I do indeed.'

'If that's not on, I'll drive. I have transport, but it'll take that much longer.'

'Indeed it will. May I make a suggestion?'

'Please do, sir.' He was one of those men you would have called sir with or without his major's badges.

'Let me offer you a lift. I'm away from here in an hour, an' I don't like flying, an' I would appreciate your company. Flying makes me nervous.'

What I wanted to say, was *Then why the fuck are you in the air force?* but instead I said, 'Thanks. This means a lot.'

'You ever been to Manchester, son?'

'No sir.'

'Then don't thank me until after you have.'

'OK, Major.'

'Wake me when we're set up, Shorty.' I had a new name.

The aircraft was an American Norseman; the American pilot, John Morgan, was a sociable, very professional type who seemed to have heard all of his passengers' grumbles already. They had an easy relationship. I thought that the major was probably an admin wallah. Morgan assured the major that the little aircraft had a better than average passenger kill rate. He grinned at that, and the major winced and popped a tab. I think that they had both been through the routine before. The major slept all of the way to Manchester. The pilot told a lot of jokes, and laughed at them all. He didn't laugh at any of mine. Behind us, the major snored.

Don't believe everything they say about Manchester. It only rains half the time. I must have just missed it. The runways were wet, and the sun was shining. The wind was cold, as it often is on large airfields where there's nothing to get in its way. The ATA had its own set-up at Ringway. The man in charge wore an old, food-stained Imperial Airways uniform with about a thousand rings on his sleeve, and pince-nez spectacles. He was working alone in a brick office, writing up a ledger of some sort. He didn't even look up when I asked how I could find out where a particular ATA pilot named Grace Baker was.

'You can't. Now bugger off, there's a good fellow,' he said.

'No,' I said.

He sighed, decided that I was just a figment of his imagination, and that if he ignored me I would disappear; like a cartoon character in *Fantasia*. He carried on writing. I kicked his desk. It was a good solid desk. I gave it a good solid kick. His pen nib jumped on the page, and about a quarter of an inch of navy blue ink pooled in a place his signature was poised for.

'Balls!' he said, and looked at me for the first time. He hadn't an unkind face: just a very old, ugly one. Most of his hair had migrated to his nose, and curled out of it like tusks. 'Look what you made me do.'

'I didn't come here to do that. I came here to meet Grace, because she asked me to.'

'Not in so many words, if I know our Grace. Do you want to sit down?'

'Don't mind if I do, sir, but it won't change my mind.'

I had had my pipe in my hand since leaving the aircraft. Turning it this way and that; putting off the hour.

'What do you put in it?' he asked me.

'Tobacco.'

'Clever little sod. What kind?'

I just relaxed; I don't know why. 'Navy Cut. I've only just started; I find it a bit heavy.'

'Here. Have a go at this. It's called Sweet Chestnut. You can get it if you search about a bit.' He threw a smallish leather tobacco pouch on the desk. Didn't Red Indians do that sort of thing instead of punching each other's lights out? He was right. It was a nice light tobacco. The smoke was sweet, and very blue.

'Forget the fillies: stick to the pipe – it won't let you down the way they will,' he told me.

'Are you *going* to tell me where I have to go to speak to Grace Baker, sir?'

He sighed. His pipe had gone out. He fiddled with it, and sighed. 'Just how many sergeants, lieutenants and jumped-up whatnots with stars and oak leaves do you think sit in that chair every day, and ask for one of my girls?'

'Loads, probably, but I'm different.'

'And how many of them tell me that?'

I grinned despite myself. 'Loads probably.'

'And how are you different from them?'

'Her mum sent me.'

'Not bad, but not different enough.'

'Grace told me to find her when I could.'

'Still not different enough. She's probably told dozens that in order to get rid of them.'

'I fly in a Lancaster that's named after her: *Tuesday's Child*. All of us in the crew are indebted to her, one way or the other. Mostly the other.'

He still shook his head.

'She's pregnant.'

Damn. He managed to light his pipe from an old brass Great War petrol lighter. 'She's staying in a pub with the others out on the Altrincham road; her little American chum is probably there too: so watch out for yourself, you'll hardly be welcome.'

'She'll kill me for telling you, anyway.'

'And she'll kill *me* for telling you where to find her.'

'Then we'd better un-have this conversation, and find a better way of doing it.'

The room was thick with smoke, like a Wild West saloon after a gunfight. He barked a quick loud laugh. 'Pragmatism: and you so young! It's most likely why you're still alive. Come and see me after the war: you'll do all right in the merchant service.'

'And in the meantime?'

'Come back tomorrow ack emma. Say 0930. She's taking an Oxford down south at 1100.'

'Twinwood?'

'Can't say, old boy. Ears have walls. But if it were, it would be because we were taking all their old Beaus away, and giving them brand new aeroplanes to play with. Their CO is up for a new station hack though; hence the Oxford.'

'Don't you mean walls have ears?'

'Do I? You work it out, old son; toodle pip.'

That was it. He looked down at his book again, made sure the ink blot was dry with an overused piece of blotting paper, and set to signing his name laboriously underneath. That's when I noticed that he had lost all of the fingers of his right hand down to their first joints. They swung their own propellers in the early days I remembered. The chair scraped as I stood up. He didn't look up.

Their provos were friendlier than our southern breed: bigger, too. Perhaps that was something to do with it. One of them gave me the name of a small hotel close to the main gate with which they had an arrangement.

Mrs Madigan, the landlady, was a slightly overfilled goodtime girl of about fifty, with a flowery scarf around her hair. She had an accent I loved immediately. It was as wet as a suet pudding. She said she only had a double room left, but that I could have it if I could pay. Her part of the bargain was throwing in a breakfast, she boasted, the like of which I wouldn't have seen since before the war. She invited me to go to a local WVS hop with her, and hinted that the evening needn't end there. I pleaded battle fatigue and weariness, and said I'd drink a glass with her if I was still up when she came home.

I ate hot, peppery faggots, and bread and cheese at the pub next door, and took back three bottles of beer, which I drank lying on the bed listening to tinny dance music from a small wooden box radio receiver on the bedside table. Lou Praeger and 'Coming Home' stuck in my head. Later I fetched a large bowl of piping hot water from the shared bathroom, and gave myself the luxuries of a proper stand-up wash in it, and then an evening shave. I hadn't done that for months.

I heard Mrs Madigan come in about midnight, but I didn't go down. Lying back warm and clean, in a double bed, slightly squiffy, and not having to fight the Kraut tomorrow or for the next few months: life didn't get much better than that.

I dreamed of flying over Germany.

A persistent tapping at the door woke me out of it. When it opened I saw the silhouette of Mrs Madigan. It looked as if she was unsuccessfully buttoned into a pair of men's heavy-duty pyjamas; she had a glass in each hand, and gently punted the door shut behind her with a foot. The weak light from the doorway had destroyed my night vision, and it took thirty seconds or so to readjust to the darkness in the room. I realized that I was sweating. My face was wet.

'Do you want the light on?' Mrs Madigan said. The bed dipped heavily as she sat on it.

'No. I'm OK.'

'Here; get this down you. You were shouting so loud I was scared you'd wake the other guests.'

'Sorry. I was dreaming.' I sipped the drink she put in my hand. It was warm port and lemon. There was something else in it.

'Port and lemon and . . .?'

'Tansy. It's a herb I grow in the garden. It'll help you to sleep.'

'Thanks.'

'You fly in the RAF then?'

'Yes. I'm a radio operator. Bombers. I've finished for a while: done my trips.' I was glad that she couldn't see me because tears were rolling down my cheeks.

I turned up the next morning as early as a nervous bridegroom: which I certainly wasn't. The ATA-in-Chief put me on one of several hard chairs in the corridor outside their flight office with a huge mug of char in my hand, and directions to a galley where I could refill it on demand. They seemed a nice relaxed bunch, and their lack of bull could even teach the Aussies a thing or two. I quickly noticed that the women all seemed older than those in the so-called fighting services, and had about double the IQ.

There was one in her mid thirties who introduced herself to me as Sheila: she was taller than me, had long blonde hair and was zipped into an olive American flying overall that clung to her like a second skin. She would have completely knocked me over if I hadn't been there for another reason. As it was I settled for letting her tongue-tie me, which seemed to amuse her.

'You're sitting in the taxi seats,' she said.

I shook my head, and eventually spat out, 'Sorry: I don't understand.' Which was almost as good as keeping my trap shut

'The chairs Arthur sits people in if they're looking for a lift. We just come along and pick the ones we fancy. I'm taking a Messenger up to Glasgow and then Grangemouth; back again tomorrow with a Halifax. Any good?'

I think I blushed. Ninety per cent of me was screaming to say *Yes, I'll go anywhere with you*.

'I'd love to, but I'm heading south. Anywhere in Cambridgeshire or Bedfordshire would do.'

'Pity.'

'Yes.'

'Let me know if you change your mind. I'm off at 1015.'

A smart sergeant with a flashy haircut, and an old observers wing on his uniform, came and sat near me. His service cap was buttoned under his epaulette. He seemed to know most of the pilots who passed him by name, but wasn't having any luck.

Grace arrived with about four others, three men and another woman. She was in her baggy old brown lifesaver Sidcot suit. Her voice was the quietest of the lot, but I picked it out before I saw her, amongst the banter and laughs.

'Excuse me,' she said as she pushed past, and then turned back to say, 'Charlie.'

The group stopped for her, but she waved them away with,

'Go on: I'll catch you up.' Then she said to me, 'What are you doing here?'

She would have looked more pleased to have found a snake in her sleeeping bag.

'Looking for a lift?'

She smiled at that. It was a tight little smile with anxiety behind it somewhere. 'Not looking for me?'

'That too.'

'That's what I thought as soon as I saw you. My heart gave a great lurch. You shouldn't have come here. It's not fair: I want time away from you lot. To think.'

'I didn't have much choice, you'll get all the time you want soon. I've been screened off ops. By the time you've finished thinking I'll be somewhere else, and we won't know where each other is. What happens to "find me after the war, and I'll marry you" then?'

'You haven't forgotten that yet?'

'Am I supposed to?'

She looked down at her scuffed flying boots like a guilty schoolgirl. After one of the long pauses she was expert at, she let out her breath with a long sigh, and said, 'No. I suppose I meant it. I didn't know if you did.'

She sat on the chair alongside me facing slightly away. We must have looked a strange pair. The sergeant observer coughed, stood up and walked to the end of the corridor to light a cigarette.

'You shouldn't chase after me. I hate men doing that; it makes me feel crowded: hemmed in. I get panicky, and behave badly,' she said.

'OK,' I said, 'tell me what you *do* want of me.'

'I want to know where you are. So I can find you in my own time when I want to. That's your best chance.'

'OK. I'll leave forwarding addresses for the rest of my life with Barnsey, and your mother and stepfather. I won't chase you. You won't have to worry that I'll walk around every next corner you come to.'

My hands were on my knees. She put one of hers over one of mine. 'Thank you, Charlie.'

'But I won't stop loving you either.'

'I know that too.'

'Why did you tell me she was your stepmother?'

'I didn't want you to think I might grow up to be like her. She and I have too much in common.'

'Who are you with these days?'

What she said next she almost growled under her breath, and I understood for the first time how much of the anger she often radiated was directed at herself.

She said, 'Charlie, I'll sleep with any man who asks me persistently enough. Haven't you learned that yet?'

I hope that my grin hid the turmoil I felt. I said, 'Are you still pregnant?'

'Yes; I think so.'

'You'll have it then?'

'I suppose so. I haven't made up my mind.'

'You'll have to: quite quickly. I don't know much about these things, but . . .'

'I do, Charlie; no matter how late, it's a problem that responds to the usual solution.'

'Which is?'

'Money. Where there's a wallet there's a way.'

I don't know why it surprised me, and made me laugh.

'Did I say something funny?' Grace asked.

'No. I was remembering your mother's description of me. She said I was excessively middle class.'

'If she tried to hurt your feelings then she must like you. It's what we do in our family.'

'What about my lift?'

'I'm taking an Oxford to Twinwood. We won't be alone though.'

'With you, I'm not sure that matters.'

At least the smiles we were firing at each other were genuine now.

The other passenger was a small American pilot. I thought his face was familiar, but couldn't place him. Grace had me sitting beside her, and he sat at the nav's table behind us. What goes around, comes around; he was the kid Lee Miller had reduced to tears with kisses. He stonewalled all of my attempts at conversation, and whenever I turned to look at him he was glaring at me.

At last Grace told us, 'You two are going to have to talk to each other eventually.'

'*Why*, Grace?' the Yank asked.

'Because you'll need Charlie to smuggle you off Twinwood. I'm just stopping for lunch and a quick turnaround.'

'I'd wanted to stay with you.' He sounded about seven years old, and in need of a thick ear.

'You can't. I've told you.'

'I love you, Grace,' he said.

'Everyone loves me. It doesn't make any difference. You can't stay with me.'

'Why not?'

'Because I don't want you.'

He lapsed into a sullen silence. Then he said, 'I just needed to hear you say it.'

'Well. Now I have. Now, say hi to Charlie.'

He gave me a rueful grin, which reinforced the impression of his youth. 'Hi, Charlie. You with Grace?'

'Sometimes; when she lets me.'

'She never lets me.'

'Well, there's a first time for everything,' I said. At which Grace yelped, and laughed and punched me. This entailed letting go of the aeroplane, which promptly fell off to port, and pointed its nose at the Beacons below us. Grace lost 1,000 in collecting it again. She and I were laughing, but the American looked scared.

'What's your name?' I asked him.

'Louis. Louis Max Maxwell the Third.'

'Why do I have to smuggle you off Twinwood?'

Grace answered for him. I think she thought he wouldn't tell me the truth. 'Louis is a runaway. He's AWOL.'

'Where from?'

'Bassingbourne,' Louis said.

'It's the war. He can't take it,' Grace said.

'Why should I?' said Louis, 'I'm only just sixteen.'

I thought I'd better double-check. 'Grace, is that true?'

'Yes, unfortunately. It's a bit of a mess.'

'You can say that again.'

'It's a bit of a mess,' the kid said helpfully. I wasn't sure that he was quite all there.

'Don't worry Louis. It will be all right now that Charlie's here. He always knows what to do,' Grace added.

Thanks, Grace.

Louis, Grace explained, came from an old family with more oil than sense, which had let him learn to fly by the time he was thirteen. Fancying himself as a hotshot pursuit pilot he over-declared his age by three years the year before, to slide into the USAAF through the side door. Only they put him into aircrew training for bombers, as a co-pilot, and after three trips he'd had it. 'Scared cow stupid' was the phrase he used. He'd hitched a lift to Twinwood, with Glenn Miller's executive officer, he said, and smuggled himself into the back of an old Beau which Grace had piloted. He'd followed her around like a pet ever since. I didn't believe the Glenn Miller bit, but Grace confirmed the rest. I was tempted to tell her, *Not my problem*.

'If I did this for you I might have certain expectations,' I told her.

'Not this trip you don't, but I'll get a two-day stopover in Crifton soon. You can stay if you like, but I warn you, I just may not be in the mood. You'd be surprised if I told you the name of the last man I was with.'

'*Don't.*'

Grace shrugged. 'OK.'

It was the way she said it. I'd missed something.

*

Grace kissed me when we parted. Somehow I hadn't expected that. Her lips seemed fuller and darker than I remembered and her mouth had a foxy, earthy flavour. It wasn't like kissing a mouth at all.

As she pulled away I hung on to her for a minute and said, 'Pete's dead. He bought it on his first trip back.'

'What?'

'Pete's gone. I meant to tell you at the beginning, but things got in the way.'

'You're just saying it: I don't believe you,' she said.

'It doesn't matter if you do or don't.' I think that was the first time I had ever walked away from her. The look she gave me scalded me: I felt the skin over my cheekbones crisping and curling back. After that, getting little Louis off the station was a doddle. The thing on the gate even saluted him as we drove away.

He had me drop him off on the Goldington road leading out of Bedford.

'What are you going to do?' I asked.

'I'll make out; but thanks.'

'Yes Louis, I'm sure you will, but what are you going to do? I have some contacts in the Eighth: maybe they could help.'

'They black marketeers, pen-pushers or flyers?'

'Some of each.'

'OK. Thanks but no thanks.'

'So?'

'I'm maybe going back to the station to tell them I won't fly for them again. Then when they threaten to throw me in the pokey for thirty years I'll tell them my real age, an' sit back an' watch the panic. I'll be back in college in a week. That's my guess.'

'You're not so dumb, are you?' I said.

'*You* are, Charlie, if you let that woman get away from you.'

So that's what I was down to: taking advice from a schoolboy.

I dropped in at Crifton. Barnes was ruling the roost. I told him two things: that I had seen Miss Grace, and that she was fine.

'I'm pleased to hear that, Mr Charles,' he said, and I couldn't work out if he meant both or either. I asked after Grace's mother – 'She's with an American gentleman, I believe, sir' – and her stepfather – 'Missing the young lady, I'm sure, sir.' I'll bet. Barnsey was no one's fool, either. 'Shall I tell him you called?' No. Fuck the lot of them.

Everyone was in the Pit, except Pete of course. But the feeling wasn't there. It was unnaturally quiet. It had no purpose.

Conners looked up from a book of poetry and said, 'Some new coppers came and cleaned out Pete's gear. There was a non-issue pistol, some bullets, and a bundle of foreign money in the locker; we said we knew nothing about them.'

'Anything else?'

'No. They were just looking for what they could filch. They were satisfied with his clothes, a carton of Luckies and a bottle of rum.'

'Yo ho ho.'

'That's about it. Fucking pirates the lot of them. Worse than Brown Job medical orderlies.'

Grease was cleaning his shoes: his running clobber hung drying on the line strung across the stove.

'Are our postings on the board yet?' I asked him.

'Uh-huh.'

'Training squadrons?'

'Mostly.' He seemed subdued or evasive. Something wasn't right.

The Toff was lying on his bed with his eyes closed and ankles crossed. He opened his eyes to say, 'Grease is going home to be an officer. He's pissed off about it, but won't say so.'

'Why not?'

'Because he's a prat.'

'Canada.' I said to Grease. He gave me a wan smile. 'You'll be a war hero: I can already hear the knicker elastic snapping every time you walk across a room.'

'You think?'

'Cert.'

The Toff dropped one of his superfarts: it was a restrained one, as if it had been routed through a flame suppressor.

'I'll *miss* that,' Marty said.

'I'll miss you *all*,' Fergal said. That sort of thing was often left to Fergal to say.

'Fergal's been let off homework. He's going home to Ireland and a priest's school. No more war,' Marty told me.

I went over to sit alongside the Ulsterman on his bed. 'That true, Fergal?'

'Yeah. Me mam's chuffed.'

'I'll bet. When did you apply for that?'

'Before the tour actually. They'll give me the quick course

in godliness and spin me back into uniform as an officer and a chaplain. The job carries rank.'

'Don't worry; you'll be good at it.'

'I'll live.'

'That too.'

There was a definite something in the air. Two somethings, as it turned out.

'Well, what about *me*? Tell me someone,' I asked.

Grease said, 'You're going to a squadron. At Tempsford. I complained to Brookie and he assured me it was just a training job, but it doesn't say that. It just says *Special Duties* Tempsford, and 138.'

'Balls: Tempsford's operational. I'll have that out with Brookie myself.'

'No you won't,' said Marty, and I knew that this was it.

Conners finished it for him. '*Tuesday* didn't like Brookman. She flew him into those electrical cables at Staploe yesterday, and burned like a bitch.'

A silence you could swim in. I was aware that they were all looking to me for my reaction.

'Anyone get out?'

'Ready for the laugh?' Conners asked me. 'Just the bloody rear gunner.'

'*Tuesday* owed us a gunner,' I told them. 'Party tonight, then?'

Someone said, 'Indubitably.' It sounded like Pete, and I looked round, but I couldn't make out who had spoken.

Party.

I got so plastered that I couldn't feel my legs: that had never happened to me before. It seemed to take a long time and a lot of beer to get that far. Everyone was there. I danced with Fiver. Pete was there: I saw him with Harriet. Then I blinked and saw it was Grease. He had hoisted up her dress and danced with his big hands on her bum, under her pink knickers. She wore pale stockings and her legs rubbed against his old uniform number ones as they moved. Bawne Billy was leaning against a door-jamb: he raised a glass of beer to me: I kept looking for Grace. Conners and Marty danced, sandwiching the small girl from the mess between them, whilst Fergal wound up the gramophone, changed the records, and conducted the pianist. Peter Wynn was in a flying argument with Quelch: his hand movements describing flight were short stabbing motions; Quelch's were fluid, like a ballet dancer's. I leaned over and told Fergal.

'Quelch has bought it. He won't come back this time.'

'How did you know?'

'I just *do*. I just saw him with Peter Wynn.'

'We heard this morning. The Swiss said they shot him at the border when he tried to escape. We forgot to tell you.'

'I know. I told you. I just saw him.'

'You're pissed, Charlie.'

'I know that too.'

I have other memories of that night: leaving eight bum prints on the ceiling, the six of us and Harriet and Fiver; the Doc pissing in a fire bucket in the corner; Chiefy Bryan sitting in the other corner with a couple of other ground crew chiefs, periodically bringing a piece of oily rag out of his pocket, and wiping his hands on it, as if they were dirty. Jennifer Delve was around somewhere: I'm sure that I saw her, but we never did get to dance with everyone looking. I didn't really pull that night. Could have done. Willing girls came on like medals, it seemed to me, after you got through your trips. I think that most of the others pulled.

I was in the Pit on my own, eventually, anyway. Fiver said that when she found me I was curled up in a ball in a corner, and the stove was glowing cherry red from the roaring I had given it. Pete's praying candle was lit in its jar on his bedside cabinet, but I can't remember lighting it. She said that I told her that the Pink Pole, Peter Wynn and his Redskin, Brookman, Black Francie and all the others were there with us as well. Later I felt hot tears on my shoulder, and her hair brushing them away. Come to think of it the women were mostly good to me. The Indian, in his flying duds, danced chanting in a small circle, the big rattler spitting and wriggling, held at arm's length: they grinned at each other. Piotr smiled critically and watched Fiver; I'm sure he was scoring her performance. Peter Wynn leaned over and blessed us. With one of my hands I tried to hold on to one of his, whilst with the other I caressed Fiver's head and hair. What happened is what always happens at the end of all things: sacrament and absolution. You can't avoid them.

In the morning I awoke without the hangover I deserved, and with Fiver's head snuggled into my armpit, which I didn't deserve.

'You asked me to marry you last night, and I said no. Was that all right?' she said.

'Good job you did. I think I may have promised someone else.'

'I'm glad. Dougie's going to be a very rich man. Probably make it on to the town council: maybe even mayor – I shouldn't like to miss that.'

'You can still slip out to see me for a knee trembler if I'm around.'

'No. Not after the war. We'll all pretend that shagging is what other people did, not us. We'll just tell war stories like our mums and dads.'

'Do you really think so?' I asked her. 'Can we really go back to how it was?'

'We have to, I heard it on the radio. It was on *Gert and Daisy* yesterday.'

She gasped as she fitted herself over me, but it wasn't for a flattering reason. 'It's not you: I adore feeling a man sliding into me. It's the best feeling in the world: better than sex.'

'I thought this *was* sex.'

'You still have a lot to learn about women,' she said, and started to move. She pinned my shoulders to the bed as if I was a wrestler. Her hips rolled as if she had an offset cam at the base of her spine. The stove was out. One of the windows was partly open. Far away on the hardstands I heard a Lancaster's Merlin engines cough and fire up one by one, and knew that *Tuesday* was gone. Which is how it should have ended, really, with a decent bang and a bit of a whimper; if you'll forgive me misquoting an unfashionable poet.

Fiver and I had the last of the decent coffee together: I roared the stove up again. We didn't say much, because I was only moving just down the road anyway. She was standing up, straightening her clothes and getting ready to leave as the rest bumbled in looking past their best.

Marty gave her a leery, beery smile, pushed his hand into her shirt and asked me, 'Can I have her now, if you've finished?'

Fiver slapped him. It was a grade A welterweight slap that you could have heard in St Neots. Then she began to cry and ran outside. Marty was still too boozed to have felt it. He asked, 'Was it something I said? Was it?'

'You can have Charlie instead,' Conners said.

I told Conners, 'You spent too much time around Quelchy and his team.'

He grinned: I think that, like me, he had escaped without much of a hangover. Mornings like that must be in God's gift.

'Maybe. You heard he bought it in Switzerland?'

'Yeah. Fergal told me last night.'

'Funny that. I always thought that the Swissies were a peace-loving folk.'

'Quelch always brought out the worst in people.'

It took the rest of the day to sort ourselves out. We found a few bottles of beer and finished them. Marty took the Red Indian motorbike, and Fergal the Austin Seven. I got the Singer because everyone thought I had been given a tough deal. Grease gave everyone an embarrassing hug – he had movement orders for a train to Liverpool, and then an old trooper to Halifax NS. He should have been excited to be going home, and out of the way of the bullets forever, but it doesn't work like that. Marty was funny: it turned out that he'd stolen a pocket bible from a hotel and he'd carried it with him on every trip. He got us all to sign our names on the flyleaf. Then he gave it to Fergal. Grease got us to sign the slim pilot's notes booklet he had filched from Quelch. We signed under where Quelch had neatly printed his own name in brown ink. Nobody said anything about Pete: his name wasn't even mentioned. We made plans for that meeting at Betty's in York, where we promised Grease we'd scratch his name on the mirror downstairs with the other Canadians. Nobody believed it would happen.

The goodbyes were drawn out, as we left the Pit in ones and twos. I was the last. I went round all the beds, and left the sheets and blankets folded to regulation squares at their feet. I banked the stove up, drew the curtains around number eight, and left it all without a glance back. I didn't dare. I locked its unique little storm porch – the clothes hooks were empty apart from Pete's greatcoat, and I couldn't bear to move that – and handed in the key at the guardhouse where they checked my movement orders. They had been signed by someone I had never met. There was a new Bluto there: he shook my hand and wished me luck. I had two weeks' leave before joining my new squadron, and actually made the decision as I drove out through the gate: I turned north for Glasgow and the old man, with the sun somewhere behind me. I suddenly remembered that it was Wednesday: we had had our party on Tuesday. Goodbye, *Tuesday*.

Epilogue

I'm writing these last few words sitting in the garden. It's early autumn: I always dream about Germany in the autumn. I have an aluminium folding table to write on, and an aluminium and nylon folding chair. In 1944 nylon was something which covered a girl's legs, and which your hand ran over on its way to getting lucky. At these northern latitudes the sun is often hard and bright and hot in the autumn, after it has burned the dew from the grass. The long grey house is behind me, and fields and rough pasture in front of me run down to the Scotsburn road. I can clearly see the remains of the Tain airfield where Dougie built the huge runways on the way to his first million. What goes around, comes around. Beyond that I can see the sunlight bouncing off the sea in the Dornoch Firth.

The old lady brought me my morning whisky just now, and said, 'Look. You have company again.'

Glancing to my right I see a man leaning against the Wellingtonia, which is the nearest of the great trees to the buildings. It is at the edge of the tunnel of rhodies that leads to the wilderness of trees and ruined Victorian garden that dwarfs the house. I have seen him many times before. He wears a long leather flying jacket and riding trousers; an old soft leather flying helmet and goggles hang from one hand. We get older, but he doesn't, and he seems to stand closer to me these days.

Falling in Love with Emily, and a Little History

Anyone with an Ordnance Survey map of the Cambridgeshire–Bedfordshire border, and half a brain, can identify the villages at the centre of Charlie's story, their airfields, churches and pubs . . . and anyone with access to a car can visit the places he describes in a day.

The airfield at Twinwood Farm north of Bedford has lost its runway, but its watch office, sheds, offices, accommodation and Blister hangars are said to comprise the most complete World War Two airfield left in the UK: some of it is listed. The watch office has recently been refurbished, and can be visited. Thurleigh was taken back by the Brits after the war, and became a flight-testing establishment with a huge new runway . . . but you can pick up the contours of the 1944 USAAF base from the map, and around its periphery you can find many forties buildings, including the Snake Pit on the Backnoe road. You can lunch at the Jackal, and from it walk the footpath north along the fringes of the fields and stream until you reach the airfield. The site of the ARC Officer's Club in Bedford is now a car park at the junction of Kimbolton and Goldington roads, although the box-like building you can see at its eastern edge was once its boiler room. In the Eagle in Cambridge you can still read the names burned on to the ceiling. Grease is up there some-where.

There *is* a maze in the church at Bourn, and it's not that difficult to find, neither are the houses which used to be the pubs. They still fly from Bourn airfield, but it is a fraction of its former size: you need to walk the surrounding fields to find the mouldering station buildings. Most of the main runway, including the 'hump' is there, and recently the Dutch air force returned the pieces of a Lancaster which set out from Bourn in January 1944 but got no further than Amsterdam: home at last. It *was* also the airfield which lost a squadron to the fog.

In Everton you will find a perfect English village churchyard, overlooking what is left of Tempsford airfield. There is a short row of RAF graves, and another which may make you smile. The Thornton Arms at Everton serves the best beer south of Edinburgh, and you can walk from it down the sunken track the RAF crews used, to the airfield on the plain below. Many of the RAF buildings, one still disguised as a wooden barn, remain there, as does a section of the short east/west runway and the perimeter track. If you want to see the main runway it shows as an immense mark in the crops twice a year.

Glenn Miller didn't make it. He and his pilot, John R. S. Morgan, famously disappeared on a flight from Twinwood Farm to Orly in mid-December 1944 in that Norseman Glenn so disliked. Stories of his reappearance surface from time to time – like Elvis pumping gas at a way station in Alaska – but none of them ever seem to come to much. The most recently accepted theory is that the aircraft was flying low over an area of the English Channel cleared for the ditching of unused bombs, when it met a Lancaster flight coming the other way for exactly that purpose, and that the bombs dropped from the Lancasters overwhelmed the small aircraft.

Charlie was as wrong about Lee Miller as he was about most of the women he met in his twenties. Undoubtedly one of the most beautiful women in the world in the 1920s – you can see the nude studies made by her father, and Man Ray – she walked away from the war and much of her photography at the same time, having run through to the Axis surrender and beyond. Her powerful photographs of the liberation of the concentration camps are often the ones you see in the history books these days. In 1946, exhausted, she took a conscious decision to rebuild her relationship with her husband, the English surrealist Roland Penrose, and rarely – apart from taking images of visiting artists, family and friends – picked up a camera again. The Penroses' English farm became a haven for a new generation of European artists, and was a springboard for the renaissance of modern art in the UK in the fifties: it is always likely that the wonderful gouts of colour you see in galleries around you today began there. Then she wrote a cookery book that redefined the standard for cookery books thereafter. Forget Delia and Nigella; Charlie would say, 'What goes around, comes around' – there's nothing new under the sun. My favourite Lee Miller story tells that she was in the van of the allied troops descending on Paris in August 1944, and while the other war correspondents fussed around de Gaulle and the other high-ranking military officers, she sloped off to find her pre-war artist friends. In the thirties she had sat for Picasso, and when she made it back to his studio in her army uniform, Pablo hugged her and said, 'This is the first Allied soldier I've seen, and it's *you*!' I wish that I had been there. There was only one limited exhibition of her photographs in her lifetime, and that was before the war. It wasn't until after her death that a major touring exhibition of her work in 2001 really woke us up to the fact that a goddess with a camera had walked among us for a while.

I saw Lee's friend Dave Scherman interviewed in a documentary about her a couple of years ago. His once black hair was wavy and iron grey, and his eyes twinkled with humour. He looks like a half-scale retired lumberjack, still a ladykiller, and is full of good stories: I hope that he is still around.

Braddock won his VC, and flew his way into the hearts of generations of schoolboys in the fifties and sixties through the pages of the *Wizard* and the *Hotspur*.

At Madingley, near Cambridge, there is an American Forces cemetery. I think that there are about 4,500 folk lying there: the ones who never went home. I first wandered in by accident late one autumn afternoon, and the words my mother had so often used to describe the Americans to me sprang into my mind: *overpaid, oversexed and over here*! I wished immediately that she had still been alive, and that I could show her the monstrous hill of white crosses, and say, *Yes; and some of them are still here*. War costs: they paid. You should make a visit, if you haven't already; it's the perfect antidote to a war museum. On the wall dedicated to the memory of the unburied dead you will find the names of Alton Glenn Miller, and his pilot John Morgan.

And you can find Emily there. Charlie was wrong about Emily Rea too: not only did she know Glenn Miller, but was close enough to him to be chosen to present his major's oak leaves when he was promoted from captain. In return he gave her his captain's bars as a keepsake. All they could find of Emily to bury was her hipbone: that and her purse, in which they found Glenn Miller's captain's bars. They all went down into the grave together.

Emily Harper Rea was born in Madison, Indiana, on 25 October 1911, and educated at Madison High School and Hanover College, Hanover, Indiana. There are traces of her still in the school yearbooks of the period. Her first job was in a bank, but she went on to become the PA to two state governors in turn. She joined the American Red Cross as a staff assistant in January 1943, and worked in the ARC Officers' Club in Bedford as a senior staff assistant in 1944. She got a posting to Paris, where she was programme director at the ARC Grand Central Club in Paris from late 1944 through to 1945. I might have misplaced her in the Bedford club in September and October of 1944; who knows, perhaps she was revisiting old haunts? Unmarried at thirty-three – a little unusual in the forties – she seems to have made an immediate positive impact on all who met her. One old USAAF man from Thurleigh remembers her as 'mother, kid sister and girlfriend' all rolled into one, and 'one of the very best'.

She was killed as a passenger on *Combined Operations*, a B-17 that crashed on the Isle of Man on 14 April 1945 in thick weather, just nineteen days before the end of the war in Europe. The war-weary but serviceable bomber was on a flight between

Thurleigh and Langford Lodge in Ireland. Langford Lodge was an R&R destination for the US forces, and it is probable that most of the five crew and six passengers were on the flight for a few days' escape from the war. The reason for Emily's presence on the flight is less clear: two theories have been put to me, but neither has been easily verifiable. The least plausible makes the best story. Emily left Paris on leave a few days before the announcement of the death of President Roosevelt. She spent a few days in London with friends, before moving up to Bedford and Thurleigh to be among the folk she knew best. A story goes that she was on the flight to Langford Lodge to catch an onward transatlantic connection to Washington for a memorial service to the dead president; one of the few Americans brought home from Europe for it because of her acquaintanceship with the president from her days as PA to politicians. Several of the dead from *Combined Operations* were buried at Madingley, and moving contemporary photographs show hundreds of distressed service and civilian mourners, most of whom were there for Emily: her coffin is a small mountain of flowers. Among the personal letters of condolence received by Emily's parents was one from one Mrs Michael Bowes-Lyons, an aunt of the present queen. The written and oral memoirs of those servicemen who met her are shot through with affection: it is almost as if it was impossible for someone to know her, and not fall a little in love with her.

Sleep well, Emily. Hang on tight to the captain's bars; you earned them.